# TEMPTED BY THE WRONG TWIN

BY
RACHEL BAILEY

MILLS & BOON

First Published in Great Britain 2017
By Mills & Boon, an imprint of HarperCollins*Publishers*
1 London Bridge Street, London, SE1 9GF

© 2017 Harlequin Books S.A.

Special thanks and acknowledgement are given to Rachel Bailey
for her contribution to the Texas Cattleman's Club: Blackmail series.

ISBN: 978-0-263-92831-0

51-0817

Our policy is to use papers that are natural, renewable and recyclable products and made from wood grown in sustainable forests. The logging and manufacturing processes conform to the legal environmental regulations of the country of origin.

Printed and bound in Spain
by CPI, Barcelona

**Rachel Bailey** developed a serious book addiction at a young age (via Peter Rabbit and Jemima Puddle-Duck) and has never recovered. Just how she likes it. She went on to earn degrees in psychology and social work but is now living her dream—writing romance for a living.

She lives with her hero and four dogs in a piece of paradise on Australia's Sunshine Coast, where she loves to sit with a dog or two, overlooking the trees and reading books from her ever-growing to-be-read pile.

Rachel would love to hear from you and can be contacted through her website, www.rachelbailey.com.

This book is for Amanda Ashby,
who is most excellent at brainstorming,
can both cheer and cajole (often simultaneously!),
has good taste in TV shows, makes a
mean bliss ball and writes amazing books.

Bunches and bunches of thank-you's to
the awesome Charles Griemsman for, you know,
pretty much everything. Also, thank-you hugs for
Barbara DeLeo and Sharon Archer, who read early
drafts of this book and had fabulous suggestions.
And to my fellow TCC authors—it's been fun!

# One

When his twin brother's name flashed on his cell phone screen, Nick Tate accepted the call—it was pretty much the only number he didn't let go through to voice mail these days.

Before he could even offer a greeting, Malcolm's voice thundered, "Goddammit, Nick. You slept with our lawyer, didn't you?"

The blood in his veins froze. There was only one woman he'd slept with since he'd returned from his last tour of duty, and they hadn't stopped to share life histories. They hadn't even stopped to exchange names. And now it seemed as though that had been a mistake.

"She's our lawyer?" he asked. Maybe he'd misheard.

"Harper Lake has been Tate Armor's company attorney for just over two years."

Nick winced. That was the problem with being a silent partner in their business—he missed out on all the details. And it turned out that their lawyer was one hell of an amazing detail. It had been three months since their night together and he still hadn't stopped thinking about her, but he'd had no way to track her down. Until now.

"And," Malcolm continued, "it seems you didn't tell her who you were. She thinks she slept with me."

Nick swore under his breath. Most people couldn't tell them apart at the best of times, but add a half-face mask—since it had been a masked ball—and his pretending to be Malcolm, and the task would have been virtually impossible. They hadn't switched identities since they were kids, but when Nick had heard that a disgruntled customer had threatened his twin and would be stalking him at the ball, he didn't hesitate to step in and make things right. It had been going on for several weeks, and enough was enough. He might not be good for much anymore, but this was something he could fix for his brother. Even if it had meant dragging his sorry ass out of seclusion.

So, yeah, since Harper knew Malcolm, she must have mixed Nick up with him that night. He just hadn't realized it at the time. Their connection had been instant and explosive, and there hadn't really been time to explain. Or even make it to the bed.

Despite the annoyance emanating from his brother on the other end of the phone, Nick smiled at the memory. He'd never met anyone remotely like Harper Lake.

But now wasn't the time for reminiscing. He pulled himself together and addressed the problem at hand. A rare night of letting go had created consequences for his brother, the twin who'd always had enough finesse and charm for them both.

"I'll handle this, don't worry." Now that he knew her name and where she worked, he'd be able to talk to her.

Maybe he could wait for her after work tomorrow. Or perhaps he could drop in at lunch and offer—

"This isn't some simple glitch that you can ride in on your white horse and sort out, Nick."

Something in Malcolm's voice had Nick's SEAL training kicking in, and his entire body went on alert. "What do you mean?"

"Harper's pregnant."

The power of the word hit him square in the chest. *Pregnant?* Only his training kept him on his feet as the world tilted around him.

Harper was pregnant with his baby.

And then a second wave hit him with even more force than the first. *Ellie.* His three-year-old daughter—the only reason his heart still beat after the horrors of war had pummeled it—could suffer the fallout of his behavior. His ex-wife's lawyers would use this to further their case that he was an irresponsible and unfit father. Especially if they knew the circumstances of how he'd swapped identities with his brother. His temples throbbed, and he rubbed them with his free hand.

Dammed if he was going to let them take Ellie from him. He'd fix this. Fix it for all of them.

He jerked his wrist over to check his watch. It was almost seven. "Are you at work? Is Harper still there?"

"She just left," Malcolm said. "She waited until everyone else had gone for the day and came into my office. She said she wanted me to know and offered to do a paternity test if I wanted."

He could see the scene playing out in his mind, and he hated it. Hated that he'd put his brother in that awkward position, but mostly hated what he'd done to Harper. What must she be feeling? Cursing him—or the Malcolm version of him—at the very least. She was probably overwhelmed.

He had to swallow hard to get his voice to work. "Did you tell her you weren't at the masked ball? That it was me?"

"I said I had to go, apologized and promised we'd talk about it in the morning. She seemed taken aback, but I figured it was your job to tell her."

"You figured right." This situation was complex enough without her getting the details from his brother.

"You know how dangerous this is, don't you?" Malcolm said, his voice a note lower than it had been. "You're an owner of the business, and sexual harassment cases are no laughing matter."

"Yeah, I get it." Nick had always been responsible, even when he was a kid, so he'd never thought he'd be the guy his brother would have to give this talk to, and it sat uncomfortably.

"Plus, with this Maverick guy going around town spilling everyone's secrets, don't count on this situation being private for long. He might already know."

Nick frowned. He might have been out of the loop, but even he had heard about the blackmailer causing headaches and heartaches for people all over Royal. Still, it was a little premature to be thinking about interference here.

"How could he possibly know when I only just found out?"

"How did he know that Wes Jackson had a kid with Isabelle Grayson? How did he know about Cecilia Morgan's background? He's obviously got some serious hacking and investigative skills."

"True," Nick said on a sigh. Local businessman and manufacturer Wesley Jackson was a friend of Malcolm's and Nick had met him a few times. Wes and Isabelle were decent people who hadn't deserved what Maverick had put them through.

"Also, all Maverick's targets seem to be in the TCC, and since you and I are both members, we can't discount the risk."

"Hell." Malcolm had a point. And the new proposals he'd been working on for the supply of body armor were all for security agencies. Given the nature of their business, handing Maverick ammunition to use on them in the form of a scandal like this would make them look like amateurs.

He blew out a breath. "Our clients need to know that any information they give us about their organizations is secure and not susceptible to a hacker."

"Yeah," Malcolm said, sounding weary. "Now is the time to have everything aboveboard. No secrets that could make us vulnerable."

"I'm on it." Nick grabbed his Kevlar riding jacket and slid his arms in, one at a time, switching the cell to his other hand as he went. "I'm going to need her home address."

"It's in Pine Valley. I'll text it to you."

"Thanks. And Malcolm?" he said, glancing up at the ceiling.

"Yeah?"

Nick drew in a long breath and held it for a moment before replying. "I will handle this. I'll make everything right." There was no other option. He'd make things right for Ellie, for Harper, for Harper's baby, for Tate Armor—for everyone.

"Good luck."

Nick disconnected the call, grabbed his wallet and keys

and headed out the door. Hell would freeze over before he'd ever let down someone he was responsible for again.

But by the time he'd reached Harper's place—a "country cottage" that was far too impressive to deserve such a description—he was having doubts. How was he even going to convince her that he, not Malcolm, was the father of her baby?

*Hi. You might be interested to learn that Malcolm has an identical twin brother.*

Nope.

*Hey, Harper. Remember that night you thought you were with Malcolm and conceived his baby? Well, it was me. Surprise!*

Not even close.

*Harper, I have something to say and you might want to sit down. My name is Nick, and I was impersonating my twin brother when we met. I should have told you before things got out of hand, and I apologize.*

He'd need to find much better words in the next thirty seconds or risk having the door slammed in his face.

He knocked on her front door, still having no idea how he could possibly explain everything. Then the door swung inward and she was there and he had no air left to form words anyway. Her almond-shaped brown eyes widened at the sight of him, and he knew he had to say something. Anything. But her haunting beauty overwhelmed him. He'd barely been able to stop thinking about her since that night, and now here she was in real life. Filling his vision. Smelling like heaven.

"Malcolm?" she said, her voice breathy, and instead of explaining, he found himself mute, reaching out to feel the silky-soft skin of her cheek. His palm cupped the side of her jaw, his fingers feathering over her cheekbone, and he was lost.

Her eyes widened in surprise and she took a small step back, out of his touch, but her gaze didn't falter. He waited a beat, waited in agony, waited until she swayed back toward him, and then he reached for her again. Her lips parted as she tilted her head into his palm. The world around them faded, and he took an infinitesimal step closer, being drawn by the magnetic force that had been there since he'd first laid eyes on her three months ago.

He was supposed to say something, tell her something, but there were no words in his mind, only Harper and the way her eyes had darkened as she looked at him. Breathing ragged, he lowered his head and speared his fingers through her long, glossy hair. This was wrong, so wrong, yet the *rightness* of it overwhelmed him, crushing all other thoughts.

She lifted herself on tiptoes and met him halfway, her mouth finding his, her lips soft, welcoming, wanting, her arms wrapping around his shoulders and gripping tight. With a groan of surrender, he slid his tongue along hers and hauled her flush against him.

*This.*

This was what had driven him crazy the night they'd met. This was what had kept her in his waking dreams since. This was what was making him dizzy now.

Of course, a little voice at the back of his mind whispered, this was also what had led him into trouble in the first place.

He had to stop kissing her. To find the strength to pull away and explain everything. Oh, but her mouth and what it was doing to his was divine…

Reluctantly, he eased back a little, then brushed his lips over hers one last time before straightening. She dropped her hands—all contact was broken—and he blinked hard to make his mind work. She gazed up at him, her eyes unfocused and her lips rosy from their kiss, and previous thought deserted him. In that moment, all that mattered was that Harper Lake knew she'd kissed *him*. Knew she'd made love with him. Nick Tate.

So, with his voice as rough as gravel, all he heard himself say was, "I'm not Malcolm."

Harper gripped the edge of the door for balance but didn't take her eyes from him as she said, "I know."

If there was one thing for sure in the world, it was that the man in front of her was not the man she'd spoken to less than an hour ago. He might look like her boss, but there was an intensity in every part of him—from his gaze to the way he held himself—that easygoing Malcolm had never had.

And now that she was paying more attention, his hair was shorter, and there was a tiny scar in one eyebrow. But how was that possible? Then she remembered a little-discussed feature of Tate Armor Limited—it was jointly owned by Malcolm and his brother, Nick. A brother none of the staff had met and many of whom wouldn't know existed.

"Twins," she whispered, and he nodded.

All the pieces finally fit into place—her world made sense again. She'd been confused about why she'd never been drawn to her boss before the night of the masked ball, and why he hadn't stirred a reaction in her since. But she'd made love with *Nick* that night. Things between them had happened so fast that even though she'd thought she'd sensed something different about him, she hadn't had time to stop and question it. He'd kissed her and she'd melted and all coherent thought had stopped.

And it was also why Malcolm had been able to act like they hadn't shared a night of passion when she saw him the next morning at work. At the time she'd been surprised—and relieved—that Malcolm had been able to carry on working with her as if they had an unspoken agreement to never mention their night together again. The first day had been awkward, but he hadn't batted an eye when she'd walked into his office with contracts for him to sign.

As if nothing had happened.

Because nothing *had* happened with him.

Nick, on the other hand…well, he'd rocked her world.

She drew in a long breath and gripped the door a little tighter.

Nick was watching her warily, waiting to see what her reaction would be. Or perhaps he'd been as disoriented by their kiss as she had. Either way, they needed to talk, and standing on her porch was not the place to do it.

"You'd better come in," she said as she opened the door wider and stepped back into the hall to let him pass.

Once they were in her kitchen, she made him a coffee and herself a peppermint tea—something that seemed to be keeping the morning sickness steady.

Nick accepted the steaming mug, set it on the counter beside him and blew out a long breath. "Look, about the ball—"

"No need," she said, cutting him off. It wasn't something she wanted to revisit in the cold light of day. "We're beyond that now."

He shook his head sharply. "I have to say it. I should have been up front. Told you who I was."

Looking at him now, dominating her kitchen with no effort at all, she wondered how she could have confused the brothers, but hindsight was twenty-twenty.

"If I'd known Malcolm's brother was his identical twin, I might have put two and two together on the night. I've worked with Malcolm. He's attractive, sure, but he never made my knees go weak."

"And I do?" Nick said, a cocky grin forming on his lips.

"I think we've proven that. Twice now. But that's not what you're here to talk about."

The grin widened, then faded again. "I just wanted you to know that I wasn't deliberately deceiving you."

She arched an eyebrow. "You were there on Malcolm's ticket. That's pretty deliberate."

"That's a fair point," he said, wincing. "There was something I needed to do for Malcolm."

"Deal with his stalker?"

Nick's head jerked up and he met her gaze, surprise clear in his eyes. "You saw that?"

The whole staff at Tate Armor knew about the guy— an ex-customer—who'd been so angry at Malcolm personally that he'd begun to make threats. Malcolm, nice as ever, had been trying to use diplomacy to defuse the situation. No one else had believed that had a chance of working. And the fact that the entire town was on edge thanks to the blackmailer Maverick only made things worse. There were whispers in the office that the guy might be working for Maverick, but Harper had always thought it was unrelated—Maverick's modus operandi was completely different. Which had left them with a run-of-the-mill jerk who wasn't responding to Malcolm's way of dealing with the situation.

Then, at the masked ball, Harper had been fascinated when the man she thought was Malcolm had calmly but firmly laid down the law for the man. He hadn't even had to say much. It had been in his slightly menacing stance. In his lethal tone of voice. The troublemaker hadn't been happy, but he'd clearly known he was up against a brick wall and had let it go.

"Yes, I saw you. You were…formidable." He hadn't had to do anything sinister, but it had been obvious to both Malcolm's stalker and to her that Nick was almost entirely composed of tightly coiled energy only just held under control. It had scared one of them off. Harper, however, had pulled him out onto the dance floor and made love with him soon after. "But you still could have told me."

"I wasn't sure if you knew Malcolm. You never called me by his name, so I thought you were meeting me just as me. Besides," he said, his cocky grin back in place, "neither of us seemed to be in the mood for chitchat."

She sipped her peppermint tea and hoped he'd attribute the heat in her cheeks to the steam curling up from the drink and not from blushing at the memory.

"And I would have told you afterward, but you left in a hurry." He let the statement hang in the air—not quite an accusation, but clearly waiting for an explanation.

For a moment, she was back in the suite Nick had rented in the hotel where the ball was being held, straightening her clothes, mumbling an inadequate "I have to go" and trying not to break into a sprint, hoping Malcolm—Nick—didn't get his trousers on and catch up to her before she made it out to her car.

She didn't even meet his eyes as she said, "I suddenly realized I'd slept with my boss. There may have been some freaking out happening."

He considered that for a moment and waited until she looked at him before replying. "I get that. Although, at the time, not knowing the background, you could say I was somewhat surprised."

"It might have been different if I'd known you weren't my—" She didn't complete the sentence as the logic tripped her up. "Actually, you're still my boss. Just the silent partner at the company."

"True, but let's leave that aside for the moment." He took a mouthful of coffee, then put his mug on the counter and dug his hands in his pockets before meeting her gaze. "No excuses. I should have told you, and I apologize."

"Accepted," she said and blew out a breath, glad to leave the topic behind.

Nick picked up his coffee mug again and downed another mouthful. The silence was heavy with all that still sat unresolved between them, but she wasn't sure how to start now.

Finally, he said, "We'd better talk about what we're going to do."

She pushed off the counter she'd been leaning on and headed for the living room. "Come in and sit down." This conversation could go well or could be a disaster, and the only thing she had to help smooth the process was comfortable seating, which wasn't particularly reassuring.

"So, we're having a baby," he said without preamble once they were settled on the sofa.

She nodded, glad he'd brought the subject up. He'd obviously known she was pregnant—the timing of his appearance was too coincidental to mean anything else—but she was relieved not to have to announce the news for the second time in one night. "We are."

"I assume since you sought me—well, Malcolm—out, when you didn't have to, that you're planning on keeping it?"

"Yes." She'd turned in her seat so her back was against the armrest. She wanted to be able to see his reactions more easily and also create a little distance. Clearly she needed all the help with that she could get. "Are you on board with that?"

"Absolutely," he said without hesitation. "Don't doubt for a second that I want our baby."

Unease prickled across her skin. His gaze was deadly serious, and she didn't know him well enough to read him. Did he just mean that he didn't want her to end the pregnancy, or was there a more ominous message? Was Nick Tate the sort of man who might try to claim sole custody? This man was a stranger, and to a certain extent she was at sea in knowing how to handle him.

Her lawyer's sense of justice kicked in, pointing out that, by the same token, he had to be equally at sea with her. He was likely trying to read between the lines to discover all that she wasn't saying, so for now she should give him the benefit of the doubt.

She drew in a breath and said, "Two babies, actually."

His eyes widened. "Twins?"

"Yes."

He sat back with a thud. "Okay, we're having *two* babies." A smile tugged at the corners of his mouth and he seemed lost in thought for a moment before returning his focus to her. "How are you? Any morning sickness?"

Instinctively, she laid a hand over her stomach. "Only a little. I'm a bit queasy in the face of milk and greasy things, but not too bad."

"Does the doctor say everything is okay?" His gaze flicked from where her hand rested on her belly and back again.

"She said everything is perfectly normal." She tapped her fingers against her thigh, unsure of what else to say, then remembered that she had something she could show him. "I have a picture from the sonogram. Would you like to see it?"

He grinned. "You bet."

She pulled the printout from inside the pages of a large

hardcover book on the coffee table and handed it to him. Since her appointment, she'd spent so much time staring at this picture in wonder. It was almost surreal—they were *her babies*, growing inside her right this minute. Despite knowing so little about them, her love for these tiny beings was so strong, it enveloped her, vibrating with power, practically a living thing itself.

Speaking past the emotion that filled her throat, she pointed out the same things the doctor had highlighted to her, then waited, fingers laced, while Nick had a moment to absorb the first image of their children.

When he handed it back, his eyes had misted over. "Thank you. That's…incredible."

She blinked back tears before they could fully form. "It is, isn't it?"

"If it's okay with you," he said, eyebrows drawn together, "I'd like to be at your future appointments."

The sense of unease returned. They were his babies, too—he had a right to know how they were doing. And of course she'd dreamed of having someone there to share the excitement and the fears, someone who understood what she was feeling, someone who would be a priceless support.

Still…she was the one who was pregnant, and having him attend her appointments, where she would be prodded and scanned and intimate details of her body would be discussed? Even contemplating that happening with a stranger in the room—albeit a stranger she'd slept with once… A shudder ran down her spine. It was too much, too soon.

"Nick, I want you to know that I won't keep the babies from you."

He nodded, as if she'd confirmed something for him. "Good, we're on the same page, because I plan to be involved."

It was just what she'd been hoping to hear from the father of her unborn children, and yet, it made it so much harder to deliver the news she had to tell him. She bit down on her lip, trying to find the perfect words.

"At some point during my pregnancy, I'll be moving home to Connecticut. I'm going to need my mother's support with the twins, but you'll be more than welcome to visit any time you want." Her mother had been the first person Harper had called when the stick had turned pink. And thank God she had—her mother had put everything into perspective for her, taking her from being overwhelmed to getting her head around her impending motherhood and believing she could do it. A big part of that had been her mother's offer to help her raise the twins. It was just what she'd needed to hear while she was panicking.

"Leaving?" he said, his tone a little sharper than it had been moments before. "You can't leave."

She laid a hand on his strong forearm, hating that she was doing this to him, but having no option. "I'm really sorry, Nick, but I honestly don't think I can do this without my mom's help."

He reached over and closed his hand over hers, holding it to his arm, infusing her hand with the warmth of his skin, sending her pulse into an erratic rhythm. "I already have a daughter. Ellie. I can't put into words how much I love her—she's the most perfect thing in my life."

Harper felt her mouth open, but she quickly caught the expression of surprise before it fully manifested. She wasn't sure why she was surprised he had a daughter— she knew so little about him that there could be much larger secrets and she'd have no idea.

"Ellie's a pretty name. She's lucky to have you."

"Well, that opinion's in the minority. Her mother—

my ex-wife—is trying to keep her from me. That is not happening again. I want to be a hands-on dad with our babies."

Harper withdrew her hand from his grip and wrapped it around the nape of her neck. It was one thing for him to say he wanted to be hands-on, but they weren't a couple, and at the end of the day it would likely still be her on her own with newborns. She couldn't make this situation right for everyone. It was impossible.

Nick stood up in front of her, feet shoulder-width apart, hands on his hips. "Look, we've just met each other again, I've found out I'm going to be a father to twins and you've realized it was me and not Malcolm that night. This has been a big night for both of us."

"That's putting it mildly."

"How about we take some time to let this all sink in before we discuss the future? I'll come by tomorrow night and take you to dinner. We can talk more then."

Harper hesitated. If she had to make a guess, she'd say Nick wanted to take her out to soften her up so he could change her mind about moving away. Agreeing to dinner felt like going out under false pretenses when she knew she couldn't stay in Royal. But it was getting late, and he was right that it had been a big night. She'd been crashing into bed earlier now that she was growing two babies, and right now she was exhausted. All she wanted was to reheat some dinner and climb into her bed. So maybe putting the conversation on hold wasn't a bad idea.

She stood as well. "Sure, that sounds good."

"Great." He headed for the front door and paused with his palm resting on the handle. The memory of the way he'd greeted her when he'd arrived flooded her mind, and she wondered if he was thinking the same thing. If he'd kiss her again as he left.

But he simply said, "Is seven o'clock okay?"

Seven? Then her brain clicked back into gear. To pick her up. "Seven is good."

He gave her a guarded smile and opened the door. "See you then."

As she reached the door to close it behind him, he disappeared down the path and was gone. Barely an hour had passed since Nick Tate had exploded back into her life, and now everything was different.

And she was still unsure whether that was a good or a bad thing.

# Two

The next night, Nick left for Harper's place with a bit of time to spare. He wanted to get her something, a token to show he was acting in good faith while they tried to work things through. Besides, she was in a tough place—pregnant with twins and thinking she had to leave Texas to get the support she needed. At least he could show her she was wrong about the last part.

He wanted a small gift, just to show he was here, ready to play his part. He'd heard some men bought their wives or partners jewelry when they became pregnant, but from the way Harper had reacted during their talk last night, he guessed a gift that expensive would overwhelm her. He just needed something to make her smile. Maybe he could start with flowers?

He ducked into the local grocery store and was confronted with rows and rows of buckets overflowing with blooms. And he hit the snag in his plan. In his experience, most women had a favorite flower, but he knew so little about Harper that he had no chance guessing. Sure, he knew more than he had twenty-four hours ago, but there were certain things that a man should know about the woman who was carrying his babies. Starting with her favorite flower…

"Daddeee!" The sweet, familiar voice rang out and his heart melted into a puddle. He turned in time to catch his three-year-old in the air as she launched herself at him.

"Hey, beautiful girl," he said, squeezing her tight against his chest.

She leaned in to whisper in his ear. "Can you have dinner wiv us tonight?"

When she leaned back to see his face, her eyes were huge with entreaty, and it killed him to have to say no. Her mother, Melissa, and Melissa's fiancé wouldn't welcome him into their house, so even if he hadn't had plans with Harper, he would have to decline.

He glanced around, and sure enough, Melissa and Guy stood about ten feet away, both holding various grocery items, and neither smiling.

"Aw, baby, that's probably not a good idea. But I'll see you this weekend. How about we go to the park this time?"

Immediately distracted, Ellie nodded. "The big one wiv the swings?"

He grinned. "That's the one."

"I love you, Daddy," she whispered, gripping his neck tight.

"I love you, too, Ellie."

"Flowers. Are you going on a date, Nick?" Melissa was closer now. "You know I don't want girlfriends around Ellie. It's too disruptive for her. And my lawyer agrees."

Nick stifled the retort that sat on his tongue. He was

perfectly capable of working out what was and wasn't good for his daughter. But getting into an argument in front of Ellie was definitely something that wouldn't be good for her.

"Nice to see you, Melissa." He tipped his chin at the other man. "Guy."

"I mean it, Nick," Melissa said, undeterred.

"You know what?" her smarmy fiancé said. "How about you go ahead and do it, and we'll have a much stronger custody case. Ellie tells us everything anyway."

Despite the pressure building in his head, Nick refused to rise to the bait. He gave Ellie another squeeze and put her down. "I'd love to stay and chat some more, but I have to go." He grabbed the closest bunch of flowers, said, "See you soon, baby," to his daughter, gave the adults a tight smile and headed for the checkout.

A few minutes later, he slid into the driver's seat of his car and paused before starting the engine. His lawyer had given him similar advice about women—if he was trying to prove that he was a stable influence in Ellie's life, then a parade of girlfriends would work against him. That had been such a nonissue at the time, he'd barely paid attention. But now…

…now a woman he barely knew was carrying his twins.

He didn't have to run it by his lawyer to know that this would make him look irresponsible. And, as Malcolm had said, there were no secrets in Royal with Maverick on the loose, so Melissa could find out any day. Added to the PTSD he'd struggled with since his last deployment, it might be enough for the judge to award full custody of Ellie to her mother instead of the shared custody he was asking for. He couldn't go on with only a day every two weeks with his daughter. His lungs squeezed tight.

He had to do something.

Something to make him look more stable.

He ran through scenario after scenario, but, really, there was only one solution.

If he and Harper were married, not only would he avoid any appearance of irresponsibility, but, in the judge's eyes, he'd have a stable family unit to offer Ellie. Turning a negative into a positive.

The more he thought about it, marriage would not only help him with the custody case, it would also keep Harper here in Royal so he could be involved in the babies' lives. It was a win-win.

But could he do it? Marry a woman who was practically a stranger? Could he convince her to do it?

Movement at the front of the store caught his attention. Ellie danced around Melissa's legs as they made their way out the door and toward their car. His heart thumped hard. He'd do anything for that little girl. And he already felt the same about being a part of the twins' lives, too. For all three children, he'd do anything. Even marry someone he didn't love.

Decision made, he started the engine. Now he just had to convince Harper.

Glad he'd allowed extra time, he drove by the Texas Cattleman's Club, where he'd made the reservation for dinner tonight. A few extra touches would help when he proposed. At this stage all he had going for him was that he and Harper had enough chemistry to light the city, so he wanted to do anything extra he could to sway the odds in his favor. It wasn't much, but he'd been on missions with less auspicious beginnings. He'd make it work.

On the way in, he heard his name and turned to see the tall, solid form of Gabe Walsh stepping out of his car. Gabe was a former special agent with the FBI who now ran the Walsh Group, his family's private security firm. Before Gabe had taken over, the Walsh Group had bought their body armor from Tate Armor, and Nick was loath to lose their business. One of the proposals he was working on now was the first one for TWG with Gabe at the helm.

"Walsh," Nick said, waiting until the other man reached him, and then shaking his hand.

"Not often we see you out and about, Tate. Is this a special occasion?"

For a long moment, Nick considered telling him about Harper and the babies, trying to make it sound like casual chat, but really letting him know early in case Maverick released the information. At least that way it wouldn't look like a security breach; instead, it would just be old news.

But, in reality, there was no way to announce such large personal news to a work acquaintance in a parking lot and make it sound natural. And Gabe had been in law enforcement—dropping something like that with no context would make him suspicious.

So, instead, he worked the other angle. "Just checking on a reservation. Hey, have you been looking into Maverick?"

Gabe's head cocked to the side. "You know something?"

"Actually, I was hoping you would."

Gabe winced. "Nothing. But I sure would love to know who it is."

"You and everyone in town." They reached the front doors, and both men stopped. Nick thrust his hand out, and Gabe shook it. "Good to see you. I'll have that proposal to you in the next few days."

"Looking forward to it." Gabe went through the doors, and Nick let out a breath.

If there was about to be a breakthrough on the case, Gabe Walsh would know about it—he had connections everywhere. Which meant the situation with Harper was ripe for Maverick to milk or try to blackmail him over. The only way forward was to neutralize the potential threat before Maverick acted on it.

And that brought Nick back to the one way to resolve the situation on all fronts.

He had to marry Harper Lake.

Harper glanced across at Nick as he sat on the other side of their relatively secluded table at the restaurant in the Texas Cattleman's Club. The table had the same crisp white tablecloth, sparking crystal glassware and thick, luxurious napkins as the others, but theirs definitely had something extra. To start with, there was the cascading arrangement of tiny white roses, and gold cutlery instead of silver on the other tables. And Nick had arrived to pick her up with a bouquet of pink lilies, which she'd put in a vase before they'd left. It all gave her a sinking feeling that Nick was pulling out all the stops. And she was going to tell him she was leaving anyway…

She'd been thinking about tonight almost constantly since he'd walked out her door twenty-four hours ago, and knew Nick would try to use their dinner to convince her to stay, so she'd decided to share one of her deepest fears with him, to be completely up front about why she had to go. Maybe then he'd understand—even if he didn't like it—and wouldn't make it more difficult than it already was.

At the very least, she owed him an explanation of why she wouldn't risk staying and failing. Afterward, they could work out visitation arrangements and do their best to ensure the babies had a relationship with their father.

But she had a feeling Nick wasn't going to make it easy to leave him.

She glanced at him now, the strong column of his throat emerging from the collar of his charcoal dress shirt, his mouth that she knew from experience could take her to heaven, dark eyes that were smoldering as they watched her... She tore her gaze away and looked down at her place setting. Leaving this man would never be easy.

In the car, as if by unspoken consent, they'd tabled the discussion about their situation and instead talked about the town and people they both knew. But now they were at the restaurant, and Harper didn't want to put it off any longer. She needed to let him know where she stood before he started his pitch.

"Nick," she began then paused to find some air for her lungs. "This is not how I pictured having my first baby."

"It's not how I pictured having my second and third, but we can make it work." He seemed so sure, so confident he could make things right, and that broke her heart.

A waiter brought the two glasses of sparkling water they'd ordered, and Harper took a sip, both to help her dry mouth and to wait until they were alone again to resume the conversation.

"I need to explain something." She tucked her hair behind her ear and met his gaze. "I grew up in a broken home. My mother did a great job, but some experiences will leave a mark. I made a vow that I'd never subject a child to the same pain, confusion and self-blame that I felt growing up."

He cocked his head to the side, surveying her. "You don't come across as someone who's riddled with doubts."

"How do I come across?" she asked, despite herself. She didn't want to be sidetracked, but she was suddenly very interested in his opinion of her.

"When Malcolm talked about our attorney, he always said you were a go-getter. Someone who doesn't back down for anyone or anything. Of course, I didn't connect you to the person he was talking about until last night, but I'd have to say my initial assessment of you is the same."

That was the image she'd tried to project. More than that, it was the person she'd worked hard to become. But life was always more complicated than that.

She shrugged one shoulder. "Appearances can be deceiving. The tough persona is an invisible armor I developed against being abandoned and rejected." She hesitated, unsure how far to expose herself. But it was fair that he knew, that he understood. Despite her body wanting to fold itself up into a ball, she straightened her spine and went on. "It started back when my father left. The night he went, he was angry, maybe it was defensive, I don't know, but he took it out on me as well as my mother. My last memories of him are him yelling at me in our living room then walking out the door."

And despite the yelling, she'd followed him and thrown herself on the lawn outside, sobbing as his car drove away. She closed her eyes for long moments, trying to contain the emotions the memory always stirred up. The only sound was the clink of dishes from other tables and a low hum of distant conversation. She was almost scared to open her eyes in case she'd said too much. Given too much information too soon.

But she did open them and found Nick's understanding gaze resting on her.

He drew in a deep breath. "God, Harper."

She shook her head. "Believe me, I'm not telling you this for sympathy. In fact I haven't told a soul that story before."

"Then why are you telling me?" he asked.

"The thing is, that night triggered something for me. I don't handle abandonment well, and I've never been able to move past it." In fact, she'd been repeating the pattern through poor choices in men, dating guys who turned out to be commitment-shy to say the least. And so the cycle had continued. Being aware of what she was doing hadn't helped her stop it. "Knowing how debilitating fears like that can be and how instability when you're young can have lifelong effects, I've always wanted my children to only know the love and security of an intact family unit. That's not an option now, but I still need to do the best I can to make the household they grow up in secure."

"You don't have to leave to get that. We can do that right here."

"I'll never keep them from you, Nick. I know how tough it can be to be separated from family members. But these babies are going to need a stable unit around them. You and I can try to work something out, but let's be realistic. We've just met."

"Sure, we just met," he said, gaze not faltering. "But we're not your garden variety of strangers. We're expecting babies together, Harper. Unusual circumstances call for unusual measures."

His reasoning was compelling, but still…

She lifted the spoon in her place setting and turned it in her fingers as she composed her thoughts, then lined it up neatly with the other cutlery again. "I wasn't ready for one baby, let alone two, and I know I'll have trouble coping with two babies with absolutely no experience. My mother will be there for us. Full-time. I'm really sorry, but the right thing for these babies is for me to move back to Connecticut."

The waiter came by and, after telling them the specials, took their order. Once he left, Nick picked up the conversational thread again.

"I appreciate you telling me that. It couldn't have been easy." He squared his shoulders. "And I'll be as honest with you in return. You need to know that I have post-traumatic stress disorder from my time in the Middle East, and I've pretty much been living as a hermit since I got back. But I'm changing things." Frown lines appeared across his forehead. "I need to change things. My ex-wife is getting remarried, and she wants me to sign over my parental rights to our three-year-old daughter."

"That's crazy," Harper said, her lawyer's sense of justice kicking in. "Why would she want to keep a father and child from seeing each other?"

He speared his fingers through his hair. "She's claiming my PTSD is making me an unfit father."

"Is it?" she asked and tried not to hold her breath as she waited for the answer.

"No." His voice was clear and sure. "I might be screwing up a heap of things in my life, but Ellie isn't one of them. I'd do anything for her. Plus, she needs her father. She needs me. But—" he winced "—having two babies on the way with someone I'm not in a relationship with will probably damage my case."

"Oh, Nick." She hadn't thought the situation could be any more complex. She'd been wrong.

"There's something else we need to consider. With Maverick active and causing people real grief, this is a secret that may be released at an inopportune time."

Maverick. She hadn't even considered herself a possible target before—there had been nothing juicy enough in her life to interest him—but now she was just the sort of target he seemed to like. "If he announces that I'm pregnant by the boss, it would reflect badly on Tate Armor.

It has the whiff of a workplace tinged by sexual harassment."

"Worse than that. The breach of privacy itself would make the company look like we don't know what we're doing in the security field."

"Of course," she said, running through the ramifications. "So we need to tell people ourselves soon so we're controlling the information."

"Ideally, yes. And if we ensure that everything looks unquestionably aboveboard, all the better."

"How can we do that?"

"The way I see it, we have a few problems that have arisen from this pregnancy. You're feeling overwhelmed and in need of backup. You also want an intact family unit for the babies. And I have to consider that I'll look irresponsible when my custody case is heard. And finally, Tate Armor's reputation is at risk."

She winced. "That does sound like a lot when you list everything out."

"I've thought about this, and I see one solution that addresses all of these problems."

"That must be a pretty powerful solution."

"It is." He rolled his shoulders back. "We should get married."

She coughed out a laugh. "Are you serious?"

"Very much. Think about it—you'd have my commitment that I'll be in this with you one hundred percent. You'll have all the backup you need without having to leave town. A hands-on father is the only way I know how to do it, anyway. The babies get two parents. Our relationship would look like a positive in my court case. And Tate Armor would be safe from Maverick. Everybody wins."

*Everybody wins?*

"Nick, we don't even know each other." It seemed like

a point too obvious to say, but apparently it did need to be said aloud. Maybe this was the one detail he hadn't factored into his solution?

He tilted his head, conceding the point. "And if this was a first date, that would be a reasonable objection. But you're having my babies." His entire body stilled, but his eyes blazed with focus. "Marry me."

She leaned back in her the chair, heart racing double time. Marriage? It was too much. He was watching her closely, expression expectant, obviously thinking there was a chance she'd say yes. "Still, it's a really big step, Nick." Her gut was churning just thinking about it. "*Really* big."

"Also," he said, and the corners of his mouth tugged into a half smile as if he knew he was starting to bring her around, "my mother raised twins. She's here in town, and she'll be over the moon about our babies. She'll help out as much as we want. And if you want your mother around, too? No problem—we'll fly her down."

Harper sucked her bottom lip into her mouth and bit down on it. Marrying without love hadn't been in her life plan, but neither was being pregnant with twins. Nick was clearly committed to being a father to their children… Oh, God, was she seriously considering it? Her pulse felt erratic under her skin. It was completely ridiculous. Wasn't it?

"I've had a pregnant wife before, and even though I wasn't home through all of her pregnancy, I know there are things I can do to help."

"What sort of things?" she asked, curious. She'd spent the first three months of this pregnancy alone, and her thoughts had often strayed to how the experience would be different if she were part of a couple.

He shrugged. "Going to the store for olives at two in

the morning. Massaging feet. Help with the heavier chores and picking things up from the ground. Just the regular things a pregnant woman might want."

Massaging feet? Ducking out for whatever she wanted to eat? She smiled. "That does sound useful." But her smile faded as she thought about the reality of their situation. "Nick—"

"I know we can do it," he said. "I love babies and kids. When Ellie was a baby, I was between tours, and her mother and I shared all her care. We can do this."

Try as she might, she couldn't see it working, but her legal training wouldn't let her ignore the fact that it was the only solution on the table that addressed each issue they faced, so she owed it to herself and the babies to at least give the idea due consideration.

She smoothed her skirt over her lap. "Did you see us living together?"

"Absolutely," he said, seemingly unfazed by her zeroing on the specifics.

"Are you thinking we'd live at your place or mine?"

"Mine. There's more room."

She almost smiled at the irony that they worked for the same company, yet she would commute to the company's office each morning and he would stay in the house she also lived in.

Then she realized she hadn't even seen his place. It could be a cabin in the woods with no running water. "Hang on. What's your place like?"

"Big. Just outside town." He rubbed a hand over his jaw as he thought. "Modern. Everything inside was done by a decorator, and she used words like *minimalist* and *sleek*. You can make any changes you want. I'm not fussy about that sort of thing."

"Can I ask you something?" Did she imagine the wariness flickering briefly in his eyes before he answered?

He sat back and picked up his glass of water. "Sure."

She laced her fingers together and, for a moment, wished her lawyer's heart could just *go with the flow* instead of insisting she gather all the facts to file neatly in their slots.

"If we went ahead with this plan, do you see us as a couple?"

He chuckled. "We would be married. That's pretty much the definition of a couple."

But it was an important issue—just *how* married did he want to be? "That's the legal arrangement. And we've discussed physical arrangements for me to move in. But what about us as two people?"

He raised an eyebrow. "You mean lovemaking?"

"I do," she said. "It's a reasonable consideration since we're not strangers on that front."

"No, we're not." A small muscle twitched in his jaw. "I'm open to the idea of a consummated marriage."

Her skin heated. She swallowed. Hearing him say the words brought memories racing to the fore. Memories of their bodies sliding against each other, of sensitized skin, of the sounds he made as he found his release.

The waiter reappeared with their meals, and Harper was thankful for the timing so she could regain her poise. There was no doubt he made her melt inside. And they already knew they had explosive chemistry. But things were different now—so much more entwined and complex. Would that dampen some of the chemistry between them? Or would his touch always affect her?

She needed to move on, to stop thinking of his touch…

She cleared her throat. "What about length of time? Are you suggesting a lifetime commitment?"

"No, that would be unreasonable. Ideally it would last until our children were grown, but if we both made a commitment of, say, five years, we'd address all of our issues."

"Except the one about the intact family unit."

Nick reached out and covered her hand, his gaze softening. "It would never be the way it was with your father, Harper. Since we'd be going in with a businesslike arrangement, we'd be able to dissolve the union with little mess and drama. We'd prioritize the children and both have major roles in their lives. There would be no words in anger. Neither parent would just disappear."

He gave her hand a reassuring squeeze then released it and picked up his utensils to twirl a forkful of pasta.

Her skin immediately felt the absence of his touch, which seemed to highlight the inherent problem of having to deal with *his* absence at the end of their marriage. What if they came to the end of five years and she'd fallen in love with him? Would she be setting herself up for another abandonment?

The weight of everything they were discussing came crashing down on her shoulders, and she could barely keep herself upright. She couldn't do it. There had to be another way. There had to be.

She put her fork down, her dinner barely touched. "I'm sorry, Nick, but I don't think marriage is the right way forward for us."

He stilled, eyes focused on her. "Do you have another solution?"

"Not yet," she said. She'd figure something out, though. She always did. "Give me a few days."

He shook his head. "With Maverick on the loose, we might not have the luxury of a few days."

She blew out a long breath, considering the factors. "Okay, give me twenty-four hours."

"Sure. I can do that," he said and signaled the waiter.

The short moment of relief that his agreement granted her soon faded as she realized that she had one day to achieve the near impossible.

Pushing that thought aside, she picked up her handbag and squared her shoulders, ready to meet the challenge head on.

# Three

By the next afternoon, after looking at the situation from every angle, Harper had to concede that Nick's plan was the only option that addressed all of their issues. If she moved to Connecticut, her mother would give her the support she wanted, and they'd form a little family unit—the twins, their mom and their grandma. But it would make Nick look bad in his case for shared custody of Ellie. She couldn't make a decision that solely benefited her babies and threw their half sister and father under the bus. It would also risk the reputation of Tate Armor, and not just for Nick's sake—she'd worked there for years and had a lot of loyalty to the company, to Malcolm and to the staff.

She'd brainstormed, even tried to match various smaller plans together to achieve the outcomes, but it seemed only Nick's plan would deliver on all fronts.

Her heart had been heavy since the realization had dawned. Marrying a man she didn't love, a virtual stranger, simply wasn't the path she'd dreamed her life would take, even if he did make her pulse race every time she saw him. Or thought of him.

As she listened to the ringtone, waiting for Nick to answer, her brain was still frantically trying to come up with an alternative.

"Harper." His smooth, deep voice sent a wave of heat over her skin. "Have you made a decision?"

As no alternative had presented itself in the last thirty seconds, she closed her eyes and faced her fate. "I think you're right. Getting married is the best option we have."

He blew out a breath. "Thank you. And I'll do my best to ensure you don't regret this."

She appreciated the sentiment, but she had a feeling she'd just stepped into something that was bigger than both of them.

"I have a few contacts at city hall," she said, "so I'll see what I can do about fast-tracking our license just in case Maverick is on the scent."

"Good idea. Hang on." In the background she heard a door opening and closing before Nick spoke again. "Have you given any thought to when you'd like to move in?"

She needed some time to steel herself, but since part of the reason they were doing this was for appearances, she couldn't move in with him any later than their wedding day. "I'll need to take a day of vacation leave for the wedding, so we could do it then."

"Sure," he said. "That suits me."

They'd touched on the length of their marriage last night, and although it was a discussion she'd rather have face-to-face, she was unlikely to see him before the wedding—especially if she managed to speed up their license—and she'd rather they agreed before vows were exchanged.

"I was thinking, too," she said, "about how long we should commit to being married."

"And what did you come up with?"

"The five years you suggested is reasonable. I can't imagine I'll have any energy to date with two tiny humans at home, anyway." And it was hard to imagine any man affecting her the way Nick did with only a look. In fact, he might have ruined her for other men for life.

"Good to know I won't be cramping your style," he said, heavy on the sarcasm, along with a note of something else she couldn't quite put her finger on.

"That gives the babies a solid five years with us together, so they'll have a strong relationship with both of us."

"And," he added, his voice confident, "as long as we handle the divorce well, it shouldn't impact them too much."

She looked up at the ceiling. Nick was probably being overly optimistic, but she'd definitely do her best to make the transition seamless.

She paced from her kitchen through to her dining room. There was one other issue they hadn't agreed on—their love life. Nick had said at dinner that he was open to the idea of a consummated marriage, and then their meals had arrived, so she'd been saved from having to give her view. She'd thought about it since, but she still didn't know what she wanted. Correction. She knew she *wanted* him, but she wasn't sure an active love life in a relationship they were trying to keep practical was wise. She waited a beat, wondering if he'd raise the topic, but either he thought it was decided, or he was waiting for her.

And instead of facing how they'd handle one of the most important aspects of marriage head-on—and despite Nick's view of her as someone who didn't back down from anyone or anything—she let it go. They'd already agreed to marry, so it wouldn't change things now. After the wedding? They could play it by ear.

So she simply said, "I'll let you know when I have any information about the license."

"Till then," he said and disconnected the call.

Harper kept the cell in her hand an extra minute, wondering why she'd flaked from discussing their potential love life.

And, more importantly, what she would decide to do once she was finally confronted with the option of having Nick Tate in her bed.

Friday morning Nick arrived at his own wedding at city hall, hoping like all hell that his bride would turn up. She'd agreed to the plan, but reluctantly, so he wouldn't have been completely surprised if she'd changed her mind.

Harper had managed to fast-track their civil ceremony and had phoned earlier in the week to share details, but it had been a short call. Just the details.

His gut had been in knots all morning thinking about whether she'd changed her mind. He'd shot off a text saying, Everything okay for today? and she'd replied Yes, which was somewhat reassuring, but he wouldn't relax until the vows were said and his ring was on her finger.

Squaring his shoulders, he walked into the small, carpeted waiting room and found her there, looking elegant, and his entire body practically sighed in relief. She wore a knee-length dove-gray skirt with a white silk blouse, her hair fell in dark, glossy waves down her back and her lips were painted a soft pink. He'd never seen anyone more beautiful.

"Late to your own wedding?" said a familiar voice beside him. Nick scowled at the interruption and turned to his brother, who was making a mock-concerned face. "Gee, I don't know, Harper. I think you could probably do better. Find someone who prioritizes you and your wedding enough to arrive on time."

"I'm not late. In fact, we're all early." Nick saw his mother beside Malcolm and stepped past his twin to embrace her. "Thanks for coming on short notice."

When he'd called with the news, she'd been staying with her sister in Dallas and had to come home a day early. He'd put a lot of thought into how to tell his mother and decided that the truth would break her heart—she and his father had enjoyed a strong, loving marriage, and the last thing she'd want for her one of her boys was a loveless union. So he'd stretched the truth a little and told her that he'd been seeing Harper for months and left out any reference to the fact they were embarking on a marriage of convenience. Even though his mother had admitted to some surprise, she'd clearly interpreted the story as a whirlwind romance and was thrilled about both the wedding and the babies.

She patted his tie. "Of course I came. I had to meet the woman crazy enough to marry you."

"Jesus, Mom," Nick said and shot a glance at Harper. His mother and brother's humor didn't always translate well to strangers, but thankfully Harper was chuckling. He shook his head. "So much for family support."

"It's okay, honey," his mother said. "Harper and I have had a few moments to chat. I like her. And your father, bless his soul, would have liked her, too."

Nick lifted a fist to his heart to push against the pressure that always came with the mention of his father. It had been nine years since he'd died, and they all still missed him like crazy. But today the grief was complicated by something else as well—by his mother giving a blessing on behalf of his dad. It was bad enough lying to one parent, but he felt like he was deceiving both of them now.

He managed to hold back the flinch and hoped any reaction she saw would be attributed to simply missing his father on his wedding day. He found a smile and said, "Thanks, Mom."

"Now," she said, reverting to her teasing tone, "are those for me?" She pointed to the bouquet in his hand that he'd forgotten he was carrying.

Not bothering to reply to more ribbing, he handed them to Harper. "I wasn't sure if you were getting one, so I figured I'd pick this up just in case."

"Thank you. That was very sweet," she said and gently touched the petals of the cream and pale pink flowers. "They're beautiful."

She snapped off one cream rose and threaded the stem into the top buttonhole of his suit jacket. As she adjusted it, her tongue peeked out, the tip coming to rest against her top lip. His skin heated. If they weren't surrounded by people—including his mother and brother—he'd pull her close and kiss that lip. She glanced up when she finished and must have seen the thought in his eyes, because her breath hitched. He held back a groan—her reaction certainly wasn't going to help rein in his own response.

Straightening his spine, with his gaze on hers so she understood, he stepped back.

"You know," Malcolm whispered as Harper turned away to talk to their mother, "this act for Mom is so good even I'm starting to buy it."

"Don't get carried away by the sight of a bouquet and a celebrant."

"Don't get carried away? Hang on—you know this is a real, legally binding ceremony, right?"

"Harper and I have talked it through. We have no illusions about romance. We're doing what's right."

Malcolm raised an eyebrow. "Do the two things have to be mutually exclusive?"

"Just tell me you have the rings."

Malcolm grinned. "I have the rings. The rings that symbolize your commitment—mind, body and soul—to this woman."

Nick prayed for the strength not to murder his brother on his own wedding day and turned to talk to his mother and Harper.

Ten minutes later, they were shown into another room, where a waiting city official greeted them and checked that they had two witnesses, rings and the paperwork.

Nick glanced around. This simple, practical ceremony was nothing like his first wedding to his high school sweetheart. That had been a big, white wedding—more of a spectacle than anything. He'd been uncomfortable being the center of attention, but he would have done anything for Melissa back when he'd thought in terms of forevers and true loves.

And yet, despite its lack of trappings—or maybe because of it—there was something so very real about this ceremony. He gave himself a shake. He couldn't lose sight of the facts—this arrangement was strictly practical. A way to solve all the issues that had arisen from Harper's pregnancy and his custody case, nothing more.

The formalities were surprisingly short, which suited him because he didn't want to linger, and since neither of them had written their own vows, the rite was even more streamlined.

Then, when they exchanged rings, something shifted inside him. The slow, ritualized movement of their hands carried meaning, carried weight that he hadn't suspected.

It was as if the air around them was thick, insulating them, holding them, drawing them closer. He'd told his brother that he wouldn't get carried away, and yet he was in danger of doing exactly that.

And, curiously, from the flicker of emotion in Harper's eyes, she wasn't unaffected by the act of placing her ring on his left hand and having his slide down her finger, either.

But the time passed quickly, and soon they were being congratulated—his mother hugging them both, Malcolm slapping him on the back and shaking his hand. Through it all Nick was torn between accepting the congratulations in the spirit they were offered and feeling bad about deceiving his mother. He settled on allowing himself to feel satisfied that the plan had come together.

"So," Malcolm said and checked his watch, "it's almost noon. How about we get some lunch to celebrate?"

"Great idea." His mother looped her elbow through Harper's as they all headed for the exit.

"Maybe another time. We're spending this afternoon moving Harper's things to my place."

"Need some help?" Malcolm asked.

The rest of the day with his twin in an obnoxiously cheery mood, taking potshots at him? Not appealing. Besides, Nick wanted some time alone with Harper to start working out what their marriage would look like.

They stepped out onto the sidewalk in front of city hall, and Nick took Harper's hand. "We'll be fine."

Malcolm tuned to their mother. "I think the lovebirds want to be alone."

She nodded sagely. "They only have a weekend for the honeymoon, so it makes sense not to waste today with us."

Despite the grain of truth in the teasing, Nick didn't

rise to the bait. "Thanks again for coming along. It means a lot."

"It really does," Harper echoed.

"Our pleasure," his mother said, and kissed each of them on the cheek. "But we can take a hint, can't we, Malcolm?"

"Oh, I understood the hint. I was just planning on ignoring it," Malcolm said cheerfully.

"Don't worry," their mother said, "we're going now." She grabbed a protesting Malcolm's arm and marched him toward the parking lot the way she had when the twins were ten.

Harper laughed. "I like your mother."

"I'm glad," Nick said. He dug his free hand in his pocket and let out a long breath. "So, we're married."

The look in her beautiful brown eyes seemed uncertain. "It appears we are."

A light breeze picked up a few strands of her hair and blew them across her face, so he tucked them behind her ear. "Ready for the move?"

Her stomach rumbled, and she smiled ruefully. "As long as we can grab some food on the way."

"Deal," he said, glad for at least one task that didn't involve lying and where he could make everyone happy.

# Four

When he pulled up in front of Harper's house, Nick switched off the engine and grabbed the Mexican take-out they'd bought on the way. Everything was happening so fast, from discovering he was going to be the father of twins, to the wedding today and now moving her things to his place. The adrenaline from the changes was leaving him restless, but hopefully once she moved in, things would slow down some and they could find their feet. They got along well and had chemistry to burn, so he was feeling optimistic this whole plan would work.

He followed Harper up the small pathway, and after she'd unlocked the front door, he put the food just inside, then scooped her up and carried her through.

She gasped, but gave a rueful laugh. "I think you're only supposed to carry the bride over the threshold of the marital home. We won't be living here, so there's no need."

"I don't want to tempt fate," he said, trying not to dwell on how good her weight felt in his arms. "This isn't a normal marriage—there's no point pretending otherwise. Yet we both have things riding on it, so I'm planning on doubling up on tradition and doing it at both places."

Her amusement slowly faded as the pulse at the base of her neck began to flutter, and he gave himself a moment to fully appreciate that he was holding her curves against his chest. He could feel the heat of her skin through her thin blouse, hear her breath catch in her throat.

"Nick…" she said, her voice unsteady. "We need to talk about…this. About…intimacy in our marriage."

He wanted to lift her a little higher in his arms, bring those pink lips up to meet his, to take his time and kiss her thoroughly, to learn how she liked to be kissed. And he could see from the heat in her eyes that she'd be right on board with that, despite her words. But if they did, they wouldn't stop. He knew that from experience. From the insistent beat in his blood. And he had a feeling from her tone that she wanted that discussion about intimacy first.

He put the brakes on every instinct he had and lowered her feet to the ground. The slide of her body lit his every nerve ending, and he had to close his eyes and grit his teeth until she stepped away.

When he opened his eyes again, she was adjusting her blouse and shaking her head as she looked down at the floor. "And maybe we should talk about it sooner rather than later."

"That sounds like a good idea," he admitted and tried to ignore his body still protesting at the distance between them.

"Just give me a minute to change. These aren't moving clothes," she said, waving a hand at the outfit she'd worn for their wedding. "If you want to get a start on lunch, there are plates in the cupboard above the counter."

He wasn't fooled as he watched her leave. Sure, she needed to change, but the timing was to give her a moment to compose herself. And, if he were honest, he could use the time, too. So, he imagined himself in a cold shower until he had his body back under his control.

She emerged a few minutes later, having changed into a soft lavender summer dress that set off her tan skin and swirled around her legs, and within moments he was right back needing a cold shower again.

He cleared his throat and held up the plates, cutlery and food. "I had a look around. The deck out back looks like a good spot for lunch."

She smiled, but it didn't reach her eyes. "That sounds lovely."

Once they were settled at her outdoor table with lunch on their plates, he leaned back in his seat. She didn't start eating; instead she pushed the food around her plate, clearly uncomfortable. So he gave her a hand and said, "You wanted to talk about where we stand on intimacy."

"Yes." She straightened her spine. "You said you were okay with consummating our marriage, but I'm not so sure."

It was what he'd expected she'd say, but still, he couldn't see why it would be a problem. "What are you worried will happen?"

She lifted one shoulder and let it drop. "We've talked about this being a practical arrangement, and that we'll be able to walk away after five years if we want. So, wouldn't the best thing be to keep those boundaries clear?"

That sounded sensible on the surface, but he had a feeling there was a deeper reason. "You think we'll fall in love if we sleep together again."

"Not necessarily fall in love," she said, her brows drawn together, "but maybe things would be...messier."

In general, he agreed—making love was a big step, and once you'd taken it, there was no going back. And yet... "We've already crossed that line. Is holding back now really going to help?"

She circled her throat with her delicate hand. "It's different now."

"Yeah, I know." He reached over and unwrapped her hand from her throat, then held it between his. "We've done this thing completely backward. Getting pregnant, then getting married, then getting to know each other."

"And I think adding intimacy in the middle of that is almost like throwing a grenade in. It's volatile and unpredictable."

"Point taken." He wondered if she'd deliberately used military imagery to help him see her meaning. Either way, it had worked. "How about we focus on getting to know each other and then revisit the topic in the future."

"I'm happy to revisit it, but I can't see anything that will make me change my mind. If we want that clean break at the end, it might be safer to not cross the line again."

He wasn't sure if she was suggesting they both have lovers outside the marriage, or that they both be celibate for the five years—neither of which was a palatable option—but now wasn't the time to push it. The day they wed and moved in together already had enough intensity for any twenty-four-hour period.

"Noted," he said. "We'll revisit once we're more settled."

They chatted about simpler subjects as they ate, but there was one topic that was important and couldn't wait for another day.

He put his plate down and brushed off his hands. "Do you have plans for tomorrow?"

"I was going in to the office for a few hours." She picked up a stray chili and popped it in her mouth.

"Tomorrow is Saturday," he clarified in case she'd lost count of the days amid the wedding preparations. "Do you often go in on the weekends?"

She finished chewing and found another chili while she spoke. "Sometimes. Depends what I have on my plate. But I was planning on heading in tomorrow because I took time off today for the wedding."

His brows drew together. "Does Malcolm expect you to make that time up?"

"He hasn't said anything." She shrugged.

"I'm guessing not, since he was there, too."

"Ah, but he's the boss. Things are always different for those in power—they follow a different set of rules entirely. I can't afford to let things slide just because of a wedding ring."

"I think you're forgetting something." He gave her a cocky grin. "I own half the company, too."

"You're pulling the boss card?" she asked, her tone halfway between surprised and amused.

"Sure, why not?"

She shook her head. "That's not a free pass for me, Nick. If anything, it means I have to be more careful. Once they know, the rest of the staff will be watching, waiting for signs of favoritism. Everything will need to be business as usual at work—I wouldn't risk my reputation."

"Tell me this. Do you have time off saved up?"

"Some."

"Why do I get the feeling it's more than *some*?" he asked mildly.

"There's always more work to be done and never really

a good time to take the hours off. Besides, I take pride in my job and like to see that the work gets done. That's more important than the number of hours in my contract."

"Is there anything on your desk that can't wait until Monday?"

She finished the last of her lunch and laid down her cutlery.

"Not technically."

He had a feeling that the real answer was not at all. That she'd made sure that anything urgent was already taken care of, just in case.

"Then I have an alternative plan." He paused and smiled. "I have Ellie tomorrow, and I want you to come with us."

Harper bit down on her bottom lip.

"Are you okay?" he asked, watching her closely.

"I know that one of the reasons we got married was to present the picture of a stable family unit to the outside world. And the only way to do that is for me to meet Ellie, and to let people—especially your ex-wife—see the family we're creating. I guess I just didn't expect it to be this soon. I thought I'd have time to prepare."

There was tension in her expression that she was trying to cover, so he took her hand again. "You don't need to prepare. Just be yourself and Ellie will love you."

Harper thought about it for a moment, then drew in a breath and gave him a tentative smile. "I'd love to spend the day with you and Ellie."

He nodded, feeling more satisfied that she was going to meet his daughter than he would have expected. And it felt like it was about more than just the plan, the groundwork for his claim to be able to provide a stable family environment for his custody case. A sense of unease began to creep over him, prodding him to consider the level of their entanglement already, but he pushed it away. This was simply his strategy to achieve all their goals. And it was going according to plan. Everything would be fine.

Harper stepped through the internal door from the staircase that connected the garage beneath Nick's home to the living room and looked around. He'd been right in his description—it was sleek and modern with lots of white. She'd expected that would mean cold and impersonal, yet the warm caramels and chocolate browns, polished wood floor and highlights in lush greens somehow made it feel more like a crisp, natural setting. And with all the trees visible through the windows, the room blended in with its surroundings. She smiled and a little of the tension left her shoulders. This was a place she could be comfortable.

"A quick tour?" Nick said from beside her. "Or do you need something from your suitcases right away?"

She hadn't brought much in the suitcases—work clothes, casual clothes, laptop, bathroom items and a few extras. Her place wasn't that far to go back and grab things as she needed them. And keeping the connection to her house meant she still had a place that was all hers if things went wrong with Nick. She winced, uneasily aware that it could look as though she wasn't one hundred percent committed to the marriage by leaving herself an escape route, but, as Nick had pointed out, this was a practical arrangement. She was just being practical about the possibility it wouldn't work.

She draped the clothes she'd brought on hangers over the back of the huge plush sofa and straightened. "I'll take the tour, thanks."

"Good choice," he said. "Then you can start settling in. I'll bring your bags to your room when we're done."

She hitched her handbag a little higher on her shoulder as she followed him through an archway.

"Kitchen," he said as they moved into a room of gleaming silver appliances and stone counters, then headed into a hallway.

He pointed to a room to her right, said, "Main bathroom," and kept going. Farther down the hall, he waved his arm from one side to the other. "Two of the guest bedrooms."

She looked down a staircase beside the one that went to the garage. "Where do those stairs lead?"

"Home gym. You're welcome to use it anytime. And next to that is my Tate Armor office. Most of the place is on one level except for those rooms and the garage." He continued on, and she had a glimpse of a darkened room, equipped with lots of technology. "Media room," he said, but they passed too quickly for her to peek.

They reached the end of the hall, where it branched off to the left and right. "That goes to my rooms," he said, nodding to the right. "Down here, though," he said, guiding her along the left hallway, "is the guest wing, which is now yours."

A few steps down the hall was a large bedroom, decorated in pale green and cream, with a king-size bed taking center stage. Windows filled the wall on two sides, and through another door, she spied an en-suite bath and shower. Nick crossed the room to built-in cupboards that lined one wall and opened one to reveal drawers, shoe racks and space to hang garments. "If there's anything else you need in here, let me know."

The room was beautiful, but it didn't have the feel of her bedroom at her own house, where she'd lovingly chosen every element to create her own sanctuary. Perhaps this would come to feel that way with time...

"I can't think of anything," she said. "It all seems lovely. Thank you."

"There's another room through here," he said, striding over to a door on the far wall. "I thought we could use this as the nursery."

She followed him in and found a room painted in the same pale green and cream color scheme, empty but for two armchairs.

"It was a sitting room for the guest wing," he said. "I took the rest of the furniture out to make way for nursery furniture."

At his words, tears pressed at the backs of her eyes, and she laid a hand over her stomach. Her babies would share this room. Sleep here. Smile and laugh here. She'd read them stories in this room. "It's perfect," she said.

After a moment of heavy silence, Nick cleared his throat. "We'll need to go shopping for baby furniture and equipment."

She dug into her handbag for her cell and brought up a screen before handing it to him. "I made a list."

He raised an eyebrow as he took the phone. "Already?"

"I like to be prepared."

As she waited, she watched him scroll through the list. He had no expression while he was reading—he wasn't giving anything away. She fidgeted with her fingernails. Past boyfriends, and even friends, had chided her for being too obsessive with planning and lists. One had called her regimental. She hadn't taken it personally—mostly—because being organized had been a huge advantage in her career. But suddenly she was gripped with an unfamiliar bout of nerves. It seemed that it mattered what Nick thought. A lot.

"What do you think?" she asked brightly when she couldn't wait another second. "You're the experienced one."

He looked up with wide eyes and a lopsided grin. "This is amazing. We weren't this organized for Ellie. We should start getting the stuff on this list soon."

She let out a long breath that she hadn't realized she'd been holding. He hadn't been put off by her detailed list. In fact, he seemed to see it as a positive. She smiled. "That would be great."

He handed the cell back. "Any thoughts about names?"

"I looked at a few websites, but I was overwhelmed." Most of the time, she was still having trouble imagining herself with two children, let alone what their names would be.

"That's okay," he said, digging a hand into his pocket. "There's plenty of time."

"What about you?"

"I've always liked old-fashioned names—Eloise was my contribution to the name list—but we can decide together when you've had a chance to think about it."

She wandered over to the armchairs and trailed her fingers along the soft fabric.

"What about work?" Nick asked. "Do you see yourself working through the pregnancy?"

She turned back to him and wrapped her hand around the nape of her neck. "Good question. I haven't had a lot of time to think about it, because my original plan had been leaving Tate Armor and heading home to Connecticut. I thought I'd look for some consulting work there that I could do from home."

"And now that you're staying?" he said, leaning back against the wall and digging his hands into his pockets.

"I guess I'd like to keep working while I can. I'm not sure how I'll feel during the pregnancy, so it's hard to know." There were so many unknowns at the moment that could overwhelm her if she let them. She was definitely in favor of not letting them.

"One thing Tate Armor has given me is a very healthy bank balance. So if you decide you want to take a year off, or whatever, we have the financial freedom to do that."

Without warning, her throat constricted with emotion, and she couldn't speak. It wasn't about the money—though that was nice. It was him talking about them as a team. *We have the financial freedom.* It had been so long since someone other than her mother had said they had her back, or was willing to make contingency plans around her needs. It felt so very *nice.*

Nick must have noticed her expression change, because he pushed off the wall and crossed to take her hand. "Are you all right?"

"I'm good." She smiled at him. "I just like the idea of us being a team and facing the world together."

"I like that, too," he said and rubbed his thumb against her palm.

She opened her mouth to say more, but hesitated. There was a danger here. They'd made this plan and committed to it, but she couldn't allow herself the luxury of coming to depend on him. Real partnerships were the ones that were built on a foundation of trust and knowing each other. Those had the potential to stand the test of time. Her relationship with Nick was too new to know anything for sure.

And she couldn't risk being lulled into a false sense of security.

# Five

Nick switched off the engine, and they sat in his exwife's driveway for a moment in silence.

"Do you want me to wait here?" Harper asked.

Given that Melissa always seemed to be on the offensive, having Harper wait in the car would be the path of least resistance. But that wouldn't achieve the effect he wanted. He needed the appearance of a family unit. It was the first step in his new campaign for shared custody of Ellie.

He reached over and squeezed Harper's hand. "We'll start as we mean to go on."

They walked along the pathway hand in hand, but before he could knock, the door swung open and he was confronted with the woman he'd once thought was the love of his life. And she wasn't happy.

Gripping the door handle tightly in one hand, and pointing at Harper with the other, Melissa wore an expression of pure accusation. Without bothering with a greeting, she said, "No girlfriends. We've talked about this. It creates an unstable environment for Ellie when they change."

Melissa's scumbag fiancé, Guy Hansen, appeared behind her, his half smile all affability, but it was a thin veil covering the menace in his eyes. "I'm afraid that's a non-negotiable. No girlfriends around Ellie. I know we're all worried about Ellie's best interests."

Nick felt his blood pressure rise. Who was this man to lecture him about his own daughter's best interests? He drew in a steadying breath and smiled even more broadly than the other man.

"No need to worry. Harper isn't my girlfriend. She's my wife." He held up their joined hands to show Harper's wedding ring, then his other hand to display his.

Melissa gasped. "You're *married*?"

The sleazy fiancé put an arm around Melissa's shoulders and gave him a stern look. "Now, Nick, this joke is in poor taste. You know how seriously Melissa takes things when it comes to Ellie."

Nick gritted his teeth and ignored the unspoken accusation of the statement—that he didn't take his daughter seriously enough—and instead pulled his eyebrows together in mock confusion. "Legally binding marriage vows are no laughing matter, Guy."

Melissa's expression morphed from disbelief to suspicion. "You weren't even seeing anyone."

"It's been a while since we knew each other's movements, Melissa," he drawled with a hint of a smile. "We're divorced, remember?"

Guy bristled and drew Melissa even closer against his side. "You're just doing this for the custody case."

He felt Harper stir beside him, ready to come to his defense, but he squeezed her hand, silently letting her know that he was fine. "Now, why would I need any help with the custody case?"

Guy opened his mouth, but Melissa cut him off. "How did you two meet?"

Easy. "Harper is an attorney for Tate Armor."

Melissa's eyes narrowed. "Are you trying to tell me that you're hands-on with the business now?"

"Actually, I'm not trying to tell you anything. As I pointed out, we're divorced. Now, I'd like to see my daughter."

Melissa met his gaze and held it, clearly deciding whether it was worth trying to satisfy her curiosity further or not…and gauging the likelihood of him telling her more. He didn't blink.

Then she called over her shoulder, "Ellie. Sweetheart, your father is here."

Seconds later, his daughter came tumbling from the living room in a red-and-white polka-dot dress, arms outstretched, calling, "Daddeee!" He scooped her up, gave her a loud, smacking kiss on the cheek and held her tight. As he breathed in her sweet scent, the world was suddenly a better place.

Harper listened to Nick and Ellie chat in the car for the entire trip to the park. She was impressed by Nick's patience as the little girl jumped from topic to topic. From what Ellie had for breakfast—pancakes. To science questions—how do birds fly? To sightings of her favorite color car—yellow.

Given how reluctant Nick had been to make small talk with his mother and brother, Harper was pleasantly surprised at how easily he seemed to engage in chatty and convoluted conversations with Ellie. Of course, Ellie was adorable and clearly idolized him, which would make her a much more charming partner in discussion than a brother who seemed to delight in trying to get a rise out of him.

When they pulled up and Nick unbuckled Ellie from her child restraint, Harper decided it was time to join in. Developing a relationship with Ellie was an important part of being able to make a good impression on the judge, but more than that, Ellie would be the big sister to the babies. That sibling bond would be priceless, and Harper wanted to start building bridges between them now. Which meant she needed to forge a relationship with Ellie herself.

They wandered over the crisp green grass, the angelically beautiful Ellie holding Nick's hand, and Harper casting around for something to say. Then she saw a group of older kids at the other end of the park flying brightly colored kites.

"Ellie," she began in a chirpy voice, "would you like to go and see those kites?"

Ellie glanced up at the sky, her long, ice-blond hair dancing in the breeze, one hand shading her eyes. "No, thank you," she said politely, then went back to chatting with her father.

Nick threw Harper a rueful smile, then said, "How about we head for the swings?"

Ellie leaped a step and flashed her enchanting smile. "Yes!"

"I love swings," Harper said. In fact, swings made a whole heap of sense—they were more interactive and fun than watching other kids playing, which was all that would have happened with the kites. She mentally filed the information away for future reference.

Once they reached the swing set, Nick lifted Ellie into a swing and Harper tried again.

"Would you like me to push you?" she asked.

Ellie twisted around to see her, her gray-green eyes earnest. "Can Daddy do it?"

It was a totally reasonable request from a little girl who loved her father, so despite a small pang of disappointment, Harper couldn't begrudge her wanting Nick.

"Of course," she said and stepped back.

Once Nick had a squealing Ellie swinging in rhythm, he glanced over at Harper. "You okay?"

"Sure." She focused on Ellie's utter delight in soaring through the air, her hair flying behind her. "I guess I didn't think it would be this hard."

"It's only because she doesn't see me often enough," he said, as if that was all there was to it. And maybe it was, but deep down, Harper suspected it was more.

"It's just that if I can't get a three-year-old to let me push her on a swing, it doesn't bode well for parenting two babies." Her stomach dipped as she said the words aloud. This was why her first plan once she'd known she was pregnant had been to move home and get help from someone experienced with children.

He pushed the swing and turned to her. "You'll be a great mother, Harper. Are you having doubts?"

"About that, and pretty much everything," she conceded.

He arched an eyebrow. "About us?"

"Actually, this has shown me that you're the person I need to help with the babies." If he could inspire love and devotion in a child he didn't get to see often enough, then he'd be a beautiful father for their twins.

"*We'll* be great," he said, his focus intense. "Together."

It meant a lot that she had his support, especially when she was doubting herself. She smiled at him. "Thanks."

"Right," he said more loudly. "Who's ready for the best snack in the state of Texas?"

"Me!" Ellie said from high in the air.

It was a fairly quick trip to the Royal Diner, a journey once again filled with father-daughter chatter. The diner, with its '50s style decor and informal atmosphere, was popular, but they managed to squeeze in and were soon settled in a red faux-leather booth with menus.

A tall man in uniform stopped by and greeted Nick. Harper recognized him as Sheriff Nathan Battle. They might not have met before, but she'd seen him on TV. After shaking the man's hand, Nick introduced Harper to him as his wife. The sheriff never missed a beat, but his eyes widened.

"Good to meet you," he said and stuck out his hand.

She took his hand and shook it. "You, too, Sheriff Battle."

He turned back to Nick. "Don't suppose you've heard any whispers about anyone being targeted by Maverick?"

Nick shot her a look, and Harper was relieved all over again that they'd managed to marry before Maverick had gotten wind of their situation and caused trouble.

"Not a word," Nick said. "Wouldn't you be the first to hear?"

Sheriff Battle shook his head. "Some of the information Maverick has been digging up has been…of a sensitive nature, so if he has a new victim, there's no guarantee the victim will want law enforcement involved."

"I'll keep an ear out and let you know if I hear anything."

"I'd appreciate that," the sheriff said and turned to go. "By the way, you should try the curly fries. I might be biased, but Amanda Battle makes the best curly fries in the state."

Nick laughed. "Will do, Sheriff."

After the other man left, Nick glanced across the table, his daughter by his side and his eyes full of mischief. "I know what Ellie wants."

It was clearly a game and he was including her, and Harper felt a rush of gratitude. "What does Ellie want?" she said, playing along.

"Ellie wants…a tall glass of pineapple juice."

The words were barely out of his mouth before Ellie said, "No!" and giggled.

Harper grinned. "You know, Nick, I'm not sure she wants pineapple juice."

He held up an index finger, as though he'd remembered something. "Then I know what she *does* want."

"Oh, yeah?" Harper made an exaggerated serious face. "What's that?"

Nick threw his hands out as if making a big announcement. "Iced tea. With lots of ice cubes."

"No, Daddy," Ellie responded, giggling louder. "I want—"

But Nick cut her off. "No, no, don't tell me. Because I know she really wants a nice, big, cold glass of tomato juice."

"No!" Ellie practically squealed in between laughs.

Nick looked down at his daughter, confused, then over to Harper. "That's strange, because I thought they were her favorite things."

"Milk shake," Ellie said, in between gasps of laughter.

"Oh, right. A milk shake. Now I remember. But," he said conspiratorially to Harper, "she doesn't like them thick. The runnier the better for our Ellie."

Ellie fell into fits of giggles again. "No!"

"No? Not runny?" When his daughter shook her head

in wide sweeps, he shrugged. "Okay, when the waitress comes, I'll order a double-thick milk shake for you."

"Triple!"

"Triple?" he said, running a hand over his chin. "I'm not sure you can handle a triple-thick milk shake."

"I can, Daddy!" She grabbed at his hand, as if that would reinforce her point. "I can!"

He picked up a menu and scanned it as he spoke, his tone suggesting it was the end of the matter. "All right. A triple-thick watermelon-flavored milk shake."

"Banana!"

Finally, Nick burst into laughter. "Okay," he said, looping an arm around Ellie's shoulders and pulling her into his side. "Banana. And a bowl of curly fries. When the sheriff of the town tells us to try his wife's curly fries, we'd best take heed."

"Yay! I love you, Daddy." She reached her little arms up, pulled his head down and planted a kiss on his cheek. For a fleeting moment, there was an expression of pure, unadulterated happiness on Nick's face.

If there had ever been any doubt that his daughter meant the world to him, that look proved it without a shadow of a doubt.

The waitress came and took their orders—Ellie ordered her own milk shake, just to be safe—and Harper glanced over the menu. Her morning sickness hadn't been too bad, but she wasn't going to be able to stomach a triple-thick milk shake and greasy fries, so she ordered some plain toast and tea.

"Feeling okay?" Nick asked when the waitress left.

She nodded. "I'm fine. I just couldn't handle all that rich food."

Nick clearly didn't want to ask about morning sickness in front of his daughter. He gave Harper a reassuring smile and started chatting with Ellie again. Which was the exact strategy Harper wanted to take as well—leave the grown-up stuff until later, and have another go at bonding with Nick's little girl.

But what did three-year-olds talk about? She couldn't ask Ellie what her career plans were, or if she'd tried the new restaurant in town. And all she knew about the little girl was that she loved her dad, swings and triple thick-milk shakes, none of which provided a new topic of conversation.

She glanced over at Nick's daughter, looking for clues. She wore a bright red dress with white polka dots. Perhaps she'd chosen it this morning and especially liked the colors or pattern? It was worth a try.

When there was a break in conversation on the other side of the table, Harper said, "Ellie, that's a lovely dress you're wearing."

The little girl smiled. "Thank you, ma'am."

*Ma'am?* Harper cringed inside. God, she was going backward.

Nick dropped a quick kiss on the top of his daughter's head. "You can call her Harper."

"Okay," Ellie said, but she didn't repeat the name.

Once again Harper cast around for something to talk about and then noticed a little fluffy toy wedged on the bench seat between Ellie and her dad. It seemed to be an animal.

"Who's that?" she asked, pointing at the toy.

Ellie pulled it out and tucked it up under her chin. "Annabel."

Now that Harper could see it better, she made out that it was a stuffed dog. Harper practically sighed in relief—finally a topic she knew something about.

"I love dogs," she said brightly.

Clearly having experience with insincere adults, Ellie looked skeptical, so Harper explained more. "I always had a dog growing up. There was Marshall the Great Dane, and Darcy the Labrador. Do you know what type of dog Annabel is?"

"A beagle," Ellie said, her expression a little less suspicious now.

"Oh, I love beagles, but I've never met one before. Will you introduce me to Annabel?"

Ellie looked down at her little dog then whispered in its ear. She waited, as if listening, then looked back up at Harper.

"Annabel, this is Daddy's friend Harper. Harper, this is my Annabel." She held the toy across the table, but her grip said she wasn't letting go.

Harper reached out and shook one of the little paws. "Lovely to meet you, Annabel. I hope we can become friends, too."

Ellie put the dog up to her ear and nodded during the imaginary conversation, then turned back to Harper. "Annabel says okay. You can be friends."

Harper's heart lifted. It might only have been a small step—one with a stuffed toy, at that—but it was a step, and she'd take all she could get.

"Thank you, Annabel. I'd like that a lot."

The waitress returned, bringing their food, and the conversation returned to center on the banter between father and daughter, but Harper didn't mind. That small step of Ellie letting her toy dog be friends with her was enough to make her day.

As Nick bit into a bunch of fries, he met Harper's gaze and grinned broadly. The shared moment of triumph was almost like a window into the future—where they might end up as they jointly parented the twins, and further, as their babies grew into children.

And it felt good.

That night, they grabbed some Chinese takeout on the way home and ate it while watching a movie. Nick was feeling pretty good about life. He'd spent the day with his little girl, and now he was on the sofa with Harper.

She'd tried so hard today to form a relationship with Ellie—and it had been more than just for appearances' sake, he felt that deep in his bones. She'd *wanted* to create a bond with his daughter. His heart had swelled as he'd watched them talking at the diner. But he was feeling something completely different now when he looked at Harper...

The TV was on, playing a show he normally watched, but he couldn't follow the storyline. Not with Harper's body mere inches away. The occasional brush of her leg against his as she leaned forward to pick up her drink from the coffee table set every nerve on edge; the smell of her floral shampoo curled through his senses.

But she'd made it clear she didn't want the complications that would arise from taking their intimacy any further, so he really needed to distract himself.

"Do you want dessert?"

"I'm not normally a big dessert eater, but maybe I could tonight." She placed a hand on her stomach. "These babies must be hungry."

"I'm not surprised they're hungry. We Tates have big appetites."

She laughed. "Go on, then. What options do you have?"

"There's fruit in the bowl on the counter."

"Nope," she said. "That won't satisfy these two. What else?"

He ran through the options in his mind. "I'm pretty sure there's ice cream in the freezer."

"Now that's more promising. What flavor?"

"To be honest, I don't remember."

"Are you serious? You have ice cream in the house and you haven't paid enough attention to it to know what type it is?"

"It doesn't matter that much, does it? It's all ice cream."

She pressed a hand to her chest, as if aghast, but her eyes were twinkling. "The flavor is *everything*."

He burst out laughing. She was laying it on thick, but she clearly cared about ice cream a hell of a lot more than he did. "Should we go and check?"

"I think we should."

He stood and held out a hand. She put her smooth palm on his, and he wrapped his fingers around it and pulled her to her feet. For several heartbeats, he didn't move, just held her hand, standing a little too close. His body heated, and her eyes widened a fraction, but before he could do something stupid like kiss her, he remembered that the purpose of offering dessert was to distract himself from wanting her.

He released her hand and stepped back. "I can guarantee one thing," he said, trying for and luckily finding a light tone. "It's not mint ice cream."

"You don't like mint?" she asked, clearly trying to match his tone.

"Sure I do. In toothpaste. Why would I want toothpaste-flavored ice cream?"

She shrugged. "Point taken."

They reached the freezer, and he pulled out an unopened tub and read the label. "Peanut butter with caramel swirl."

She frowned, so he held up the container for her to see.

"You're a man of surprises, Nick Tate."

"What were you expecting?" he practically drawled.

"I'm not sure. Maybe coffee, maybe dark chocolate. But not—" she looked down at the label "—peanut butter with a caramel swirl."

He kept a poker face, but he liked this playful version of Harper. "Don't knock something until you've tried it." He pulled open the cutlery drawer and grabbed a spoon. "You're going to be singing my praises in a few minutes."

"Is that so?" She grinned, her brown eyes dancing.

After removing the lid, he scooped out a small spoonful and held it out to her. Harper leaned in. Her lips closed over the ice cream and pressed firmly together. His pulse spiked, and he realized the flaw in his plan. Dessert was meant to distract him from his wanting, not increase it.

He clenched his jaw and tried to suppress every scrap of desire that hummed through his blood.

Then she moaned, and her eyes drifted shut. "That. Is. Sinful," she murmured.

Her eyes opened again, and he focused on the spoon in his hand. On autopilot, he dug out another bite-size scoop and fed it to her. This time, she leaned forward to meet him partway, and as she opened her mouth in readiness, he glimpsed her pink tongue and damn near groaned himself.

Her eyes closed again, and the look of bliss that stole over her face almost did him in.

"Harper," he rasped.

Her eyes flew open, and the want, the need in her gaze were as strong as ever, but she was looking at him instead of the ice cream.

He was a goner.

Harper watched Nick and tried to keep her breathing under control. Being so close to him on the sofa as she'd

pretended to watch TV had set every single nerve ending she had on edge. And then he'd fed her ice cream…
Her skin yearned for his touch, but if she gave in now, all would be lost—she might not be able to pull back.

Then she noticed the strong, insistent beat of his pulse at the base of his neck. The tension in his muscles as he held himself in check. The way his gaze smoldered.

And she forgot what they were fighting against.

"Nick?" she asked, her voice breathless.

"Yeah?"

"What would happen if we gave in?"

His gaze flicked to her mouth then back to her eyes. "Gave in to what?"

"To this." She motioned back and forth with a finger. "To what's burning between us."

He swallowed hard. "You really want to know?"

"Yeah, I do," she whispered.

He looked down at her in the dim light of the kitchen, then lowered his head until his lips brushed over hers, just once. "This."

A sigh built within her and escaped her throat as she leaned into him. "Oh. This is a good plan."

She lifted herself on tiptoes and found his mouth, warm and dark and inviting. He wrapped one arm around her waist, hauling her flush against him, and sank into the kiss she offered. The sizzling impact of his tongue, the decadence of it, had her whispering his name against his lips.

He pivoted and pushed her against the wall, pinning her with his weight as he kissed her like he hungered for her. Like she was the only thing necessary for life.

Panting, she wrenched her mouth from his. "I vote we stop fighting it for tonight," she said, then paused to catch her breath. "Just give ourselves this one night."

He leaned his forehead against hers, his breathing labored, too. "You have my vote."

"Okay, then. Well, if we're agreed—" she stepped away, leaving their laced fingers as their only connection "—this time we should aim for a bed."

One corner of his mouth hitched, and he headed off down the hall. She followed as he led her to his room. She hadn't been this way before, but she only barely noticed her surroundings—all her attention was on the man beside her.

He stepped into an open doorway and hit a switch with his fist. Soft light diffused through a large room dominated by a king-size bed. There were closed blinds on three sides, though small windows up high allowed fresh air in, and through another door, she spied an ensuite bath and shower that looked similar to hers. But now was not the time to explore. Now was the time for Nick.

"One more thing," he said and disappeared into the attached bathroom, returning seconds later with a little packet of protection.

She grinned. "I'm already pregnant."

"I'm clean, but I want you to know for sure."

"I'm clean, too, but thank you." She stepped closer. "So, I guess dessert is out of the question?"

"There's no more ice cream." He kissed her softly before saying against her mouth, "But I've been dreaming of tasting every square inch of you."

Spearing fingers into her hair, he cradled her head as he kissed her—taking exquisite care with ravishing her mouth. It wasn't enough. Would never be enough. With hands flat on his chest, she gently pushed, needing the room to explore his body, and he took the hint. Clothes were in the way, but still, she took advantage of the opportunity and roamed her hands across his broad shoulders, down his arms, across his chest, acclimatizing herself to him again. And he stood still, allowing her the freedom to do what she wished.

"My turn," he said, his gaze burning. She wasn't nearly finished, but it was fair, so she dropped her hands and waited to see what he'd do.

Button by excruciating button, he unfastened the front of her summer dress and pushed the sides open, exposing her skin to the cool night air. Her pulse fluttered madly. In simple movements, he unhooked her bra and let it drop to the floor, and she felt her breasts tighten in the light breeze from the high windows—and under his all-consuming gaze.

"Harper," he said and swallowed hard. "You're so damned beautiful."

She didn't answer. Couldn't. So instead she reached for him again and focused on touching him, on feeling him touch her.

His hands sliding down her sides, across her stomach, felt like fire licking at her skin. In idle moments she'd wondered if their electric connection that first night had been because of its illicit nature, and whether making love with him now that he was her husband would have less of an edge. Less intensity. Now she had her answer. He…they…*this* was so much more than anything she'd experienced before. More than she'd imagined.

She pulled at his shirt where it was tucked into his trousers. Then, not bothering with the buttons, she tugged it over his head. His skin was beautiful, so beautiful, and the scars and marks that showed his history of putting his body on the line for others only made it more beautiful. The muscle definition on his abs was crazy—he'd obviously kept up whatever training the SEALs had him doing—and the crisp hair scattered across his chest called to her fingers. As she walked her fingertips over the dark hair, he shivered, and she smiled, glad she wasn't the only one affected this badly.

He captured her mouth. Not breaking the searing kiss, he took a step backward, taking her with him, then another, until they reached the edge of the bed. He finally released her mouth, grinned wickedly and fell backward onto the mattress, bringing her down on top of him.

The sensuous slide of their bodies set every nerve ending she had alight, but it wasn't enough. She reached for his belt, wanting all the fabric separating them gone, but he stayed her hand.

"Not yet," he said, his voice unsteady.

She could feel the blood pump through her body, strong and insistent. "I want more, now."

"No can do," he said as his thumb grazed the curve of her breast.

A delicious shiver raced over her skin, and she had to wait a moment for it to pass before she could speak again. "Why the holdup?"

"I want this to take all night." He hooked his fingers in the scraps of fabric around her hips and dragged them down over her legs before letting her underwear follow her bra over the side of the bed to the floor. "We have a lot to make up for."

"What do you mean?" she asked, starting to lose her train of thought.

"The night of the ball, our first time, it was rushed." He kissed a trail down the inside of her arm to her wrist, his hair tickling her ribs as he went.

She gasped, then found her breath again to reply. "I thought it was excellent."

Grinning, he caressed a pattern on her stomach. "Phenomenal."

"Then what's the problem?" She slid her leg up his thigh and hooked it around him, locking his hips against hers. What a shame he was being reluctant about removing his trousers…

"Now that we have more time," he said, rocking against her in defiance of his words, "I want to take it slow. To do all the things we didn't get around to."

He kissed her again, and while his mouth was busy, she unzipped his trousers and pushed them—and his boxers—as far down his legs as she could reach. Then she broke the kiss to remove them all the way before smiling back up at him. "See, it's all about your perspective."

He dipped his hand down until it slid between her legs, moving in patterns and with a rhythm that was going to drive her crazy. The way one corner of his mouth hooked up as he spoke told her he knew the effect he was having. "What other way is there to look at it?"

Her eyes drifted closed, but even if she couldn't see him, she could feel him everywhere. "You want this to be different from last time."

"I do," he said, his voice husky as his hand still moved to the melody of silent music.

"See, I'm thinking that's too prescriptive—" she paused to moisten her lips so her mouth could form the words "—for making love."

His hand stilled, and she opened her eyes to see him. His gaze was squarely on her, his brow creased as if he was trying to discern where she was going with this. "What do you have in mind?"

"That we stop thinking and just let it happen." There was something about his skin that she couldn't get enough of. Its texture, its scent. She dipped her tongue to sample the skin just above his collarbone, and dug her fingernails into his back. Dug them in and dragged them lightly across his shoulder blades. She could touch this man forever.

"I like your idea...really like it—" he drew in a quick breath and swallowed hard "—but I still want to take it slow."

Deciding the time for talking—for negotiating—was over, she found the foil packet on the bedside table and quickly sheathed him before pushing at his shoulder until he rolled onto his back. She rose up over him and hesitated. The sight of him lain out on the bed, for her, the perfection of him, was overwhelming. He reached out, found her hand and linked their fingers palm to palm. It was exactly what she needed, securing her in the moment, grounding her. Then she sank down onto him, and, as their bodies connected, he let out a guttural groan.

She moved, drunk with desire, and he matched her rhythm, so they danced together as one. She was flying, free—the only things that mattered were Nick and the pleasure that was engulfing her.

He hooked his hands behind her knees and held them, anchoring her, changing the angle, and wave after wave of blinding heat consumed her as she imploded. While aftershocks still assailed her body, Nick called her name and a fierce shudder ripped through him.

Breathing ragged, she slid down to lie beside him, a possessive hand across his stomach, and he looped an arm around her shoulders. Cocooned with him, by him, her world slowly returned to normal, and she drifted off to sleep.

# Six

Harper woke with a jolt, her heart in her mouth. The first thing she was aware of was shouting. The room was dark except for glimmers of moonlight through the blinds, which was enough to show unfamiliar surroundings, and the man beside her.

Nick.

His shouting eased to incoherent mumbling. Despite still being deeply asleep, his head moved with jerky rhythms and his hands seemed to punctuate his words.

Should she wake him? This was no happy dream—he was far too agitated for that to be possible—but wasn't there a rule about not waking someone from a nightmare? Or was that sleepwalking? She bit down on her bottom lip, wishing she'd paid more attention to wherever she'd heard the advice.

"No," he barked, eyes still closed as his hand sliced through the air. His wedding ring glinted in the moonlight, and it struck her anew that the man in her bed was her husband.

*Husband.*

They were married, and she knew less about him than about many of her coworkers. A wave of panic washed over her. She didn't really know this man, and she certainly didn't know how to help him now.

He shouted again, louder this time, then he screamed. It was a raw, guttural sound, full of pain and anguish, like nothing she'd ever heard before, and it sent cold prickles racing across her skin. She had to act.

Not wanting to wake him suddenly, she began to talk softly, soothingly, gradually raising her volume. The way his face contorted into expressions of utter despair broke her heart. In that moment, she wanted nothing more than to wrap him in her arms and take his pain away, but all she could do was keep up the litany of soothing words. Slowly, steadily, she talked him around. His screams died to tearless sobs, and she raised her voice again, to just above normal speaking volume. He drew in a deep, shaky breath, and as he released it, his eyes opened.

For a millisecond, the pain she'd witnessed was reflected in their depths until his eyes focused on her. She saw the moment he realized what had happened—just before the shutters came down. Hard.

He jumped out of bed and stood on the rug, skin covered in a sheen of perspiration, muscles clenched, his pose rigid, every inch of him proclaiming his military past. Despite being naked now, he'd been more exposed when he'd been asleep and covered by the sheet.

"Harper, I'm sorry," he said, his voice rough yet controlled.

"It was a nightmare." Smiling, she shook her head,

wanting him to know everything was okay. "You have nothing—"

Expression flat, he cut her off. "You shouldn't have had to experience that."

Her heart broke a little for him then. He shouldn't have had to experience that, either. "It's okay, Nick, really—"

"I'll take a guest room." Without making eye contact, he reached for his phone and wristwatch from the bedside table, turned and walked through the door.

Stunned, she watched him go.

He was *leaving* her.

As he disappeared into the dark hallway, she had trouble filling her lungs. He might be virtually a stranger, but he was her husband, the man she'd made love with only hours ago. And now he was leaving the bed where they'd shared that passion.

A small, hard knot of panic sitting in the middle of her chest grew, enveloped her and bestowed the familiar taste of abandonment.

She tried logic, always her first line of defense—he'd left because he was still upset about the nightmare, not because of her. But it didn't ease the sour taste at the back of her mouth. She'd offered to be there for him while he dealt with the nightmare, so, yeah, he'd walked out on her.

Logic rarely worked when she was dealing with the slap of rejection, and she usually moved right on to the second line of defense—comfort eating. But she wasn't in her own home, and having to riffle through his kitchen cupboards for carbs and sugar would probably cancel out any comfort effects. Besides, she was trying to eat healthy for the babies.

So that left her with two options—curl up in a ball and let the emotion overwhelm her, or...

Or find Nick and get him to talk his nightmare through,

both for his sake and so she could let go of the image of him walking out the door the way so many people in her life had done before him.

She stood and rubbed her hands over her face. This night had shown her one thing—she'd been right to think that sleeping together would make their relationship messy. They already had so many challenges in making their arrangement work, making love had been foolhardy. They'd risked their tentative cohesion merely for physical desires.

They couldn't afford to take the risk again.

But she couldn't dwell on that right now. First, she needed to deal with the fallout of this time and make sure Nick was okay.

Nick flicked the light on in the guest bedroom's bathroom and headed for the shower, trying to forget the look of horror on Harper's face. A look that had the power to haunt him forever.

That wasn't the expression he'd planned to leave on his new bride's face the first time he'd taken her to his bed…

He stepped under the hot spray of water and rested his palms on the wall behind the faucet, dipping his head to bear the full force of the spray.

*Hell.*

He should have known. Should have expected he couldn't just walk into a marriage the way a normal man could. Especially a marriage of convenience like this, where they were plunged into it with barely any emotional preparation. He'd been shot at and felt shells detonate close enough to make his teeth rattle too many times to count. He was partially deaf due to an explosion that had blown to bits some of the fiercest warriors he'd ever had the privilege to fight alongside. He'd been captured and held prisoner by a faction of rebels notorious for their treatment of prisoners. After all he'd been through, after all the damage to his soul, what made him think he could have special things in his life?

Like a marriage.

Like Harper.

He elbowed the tap and the water abruptly ceased, but he didn't immediately reach for the towel, letting the water drip from his body instead.

He'd have to find a way to apologize to her, to try to make this up to her—if that were even possible. But not tonight, not while he was raw from both the nightmare and waking to see the trauma in her eyes.

He grabbed a towel and roughly rubbed it over his skin until it was dry, and if he was a little overzealous and left red marks, then all the better. Soft and gentle weren't things he deserved. Not when he'd come out alive and better men had come home in body bags.

Wrapping the towel around his hips, he headed through the door that connected the bathroom to the guest bedroom and stopped short when he saw Harper sitting on the edge of the bed in a fluffy blue robe tied firmly around her middle.

In the gentle light of the bedside lamp, she was so beautiful. Her back was straight, her chin jutting at a proud angle. She looked strong. Sure of her place in the world. Things he couldn't claim to be anymore. He glanced away.

"Harper, this is not the time."

She crossed her arms tightly under her breasts, clearly having no intention of going anywhere. "I think this is exactly the time. I have a feeling that if we leave this until morning, it will be even harder to discuss."

True enough, but he shook his head. "I'm not sure I

can discuss it. It is what it is." Lord knew he'd tried hard enough to pretend otherwise.

"That may be, but we do need to talk," she said, her gaze on him unwavering. "Because this is not how I see our marriage working."

He planted his hands low on his hips. "It was just a nightmare, not our entire marriage."

"We entered into a marriage of convenience. There are already enough obstacles in our way without secrets. I think the only way we're going to make this whole thing work is if we have honesty and openness between us," she said, her voice steady, but her eyes asking—hoping for—so much of him.

"We're doing fine." The statement was so far from the truth that he was surprised she didn't laugh in his face.

But she didn't. Not his Harper. Instead she looked at him with eyes as deep as oceans, as raw and vulnerable as he'd ever seen in another person, and said, "I have to be honest. This feels an awful lot like being rejected on the same night we made love for the first time as a married couple."

That stung, deep in his chest. She'd told him about her past and her fear of abandonment, and he'd just played right into that fear and made it worse for her. Hell, someone needed to smack him upside the head.

"It's not you," he said, knowing the words were clichéd and inadequate. "It's me."

"Okay." She sat up straighter. "Then tell me about you."

He knew what she meant—tell her about the events that had led to the nightmares. And she was right—as his wife, she deserved to know—but he simply didn't know if he could say the words aloud. He rubbed his fingers across his forehead, then dug them into his temples.

"Nick, we have a difficult road ahead of us parenting two babies together, and we're both flying blind because we don't know much about each other." She reached for his hand, and he let her take it. "Tell me about this. Help me to understand."

He flinched. Flying blind—that's exactly what they were doing, and she deserved more. He sank down onto the bed beside her, his shoulders slightly hunched as he prepared to face the worst. For her.

"Nine—" Everything inside him clenched tight. He cleared his throat and started again. "Nine months ago, I came home from the Middle East. As far as everyone is concerned, I'm a decorated war hero."

"But you don't feel like one, do you?" she asked gently.

Yeah, understatement of the century. "The military might have given me a medal, but I've always known I didn't deserve it."

Her smile was kind. "I don't think they give those medals out for no reason."

"Men died while under my command," he said fiercely. A wave of nausea washed through him, and he pressed a closed fist to his gut to try to stem its progress. Those fine men were gone forever. Their families had lost sons. Children had lost parents. Wives had lost their husbands.

He stood and paced to the other side of the room, as if that could give him the distance he needed, even though he knew it wouldn't. Couldn't. He felt every one of those losses deeply. He saw their faces in his mind. He apologized to them every day, but it made no difference. It wouldn't bring them back.

Too damn little, too damn late.

"Oh, Nick."

He shook his head rapidly, trying to dispel the emotion from the story. He didn't want Harper's sympathy. He wasn't the one who deserved it.

He straightened his spine, squared his shoulders and told her the truth. "They gave me a medal because I was able to save most of my team, but it wasn't enough. That wasn't near enough. It was my responsibility to save them all."

"I'm sure you weren't solely responsible for those men's lives."

He squeezed his eyes closed tight against the memories. "I let them down."

There was silence for long moments until he opened his eyes again and found her watching him.

"It's torn you up inside, hasn't it?" she asked, her voice soft.

He met her gaze and almost smiled. Almost. "You could say I'm kind of a mess."

"Tell me," she said, and there was something in her tone that made him want to do just that. Wanted to share this with someone, and wanted that someone to be Harper, even though it might change her opinion of him forever.

"The doctors gave me painkillers for my wounds—" he paused to find the strength to admit the rest "—and I became addicted to them." To his eternal shame.

Her brows drew together. "I haven't seen you take anything."

She wouldn't have. Not now. He breathed in a lungful of air. At least this was one thing he could feel okay to admit. "I didn't want to be dependent on a chemical, so I did some treatment and learned to deal with the addiction."

"You're clean now?" she asked, her gaze steely.

"One hundred percent." He wouldn't have contemplated being part of Ellie's or the babies' lives if he wasn't. They were too precious.

Her gaze softened. "That takes a lot of strength."

"Oh, yeah?" He coughed out a laugh. "Did you notice the screaming nightmares?"

"I did," she said, with no judgment in her tone. "Tell me about them."

He leaned on the wall a few feet from her and slid to the carpet, wrists resting on his bent knees. "They started when I was in hospital, but they'd eased off a bit." He shrugged. "I didn't realize I was still having them."

Her head tilted to the side. "You don't remember them in the morning?"

Oh, he remembered them. Lord above, did he remember them. "I didn't realize I was yelling anymore." The thing was, he hadn't shared anyone's bed since the nightmares had started. Sure, he'd yelled during nightmares when he'd been recovering in the hospital after the last mission, but he'd assumed that phase was long over. It just went to show, he should never assume anything about his condition. "I swear, Harper, if I'd known that you'd be woken by them, that they'd affect you, I wouldn't have suggested we get married. I wouldn't have tied you to… this."

She dismissed that with a wave of her hand. "So, what do you want to do now?"

"What do you want?" he asked warily.

"I want us to make this marriage work for our children. We owe them that." Her eyes were intense. Certain.

"I'm as committed as ever to our vows—we're doing the right thing for the babies. I haven't been this sure about something in a long time."

"We're in agreement, then," she said and stood.

He gave one slow nod. "Next time we make love, it

would be better for everyone if I left right after." The last thing any woman—especially a pregnant woman—needed was to be woken by someone in her bed screaming, and he simply wouldn't do that to her.

She crossed her arms under her breasts. "I don't think that's the right way forward for us."

He hauled himself to his feet and scrubbed his hands through his hair, wishing he had all the answers. "Harper, I saw you back there in that room. I won't be responsible for putting that expression of horror on your face again."

"I think we need to go back to our original plan. Bringing sexual intimacy into our relationship was a mistake."

He stepped closer and cradled the side of her face in his palm. "We can make it work, I promise. I just won't stay the night."

"Please don't make this harder than it is." She'd told him that her trigger was people walking away from her, and at the first test of their relationship, he'd done exactly that. He needed to take a step back, respect her boundaries and give her a chance to feel settled again.

"Are you sure that's what you want?"

"There's already so much pressure on this relationship. It can't be sexual as well." When he didn't reply, she added, "Nick?"

"Okay," he said reluctantly. He might not agree, but if she didn't want to, then there was no way forward for their physical relationship.

He took her hand and walked her back down the hall to her bedroom. In the doorway, he stopped. He wanted nothing more than to sink into that bed and pull Harper against him, but he couldn't. He laid a soft kiss on her lips, hoping she understood all that was still unsaid, and turned to go.

"Nick," she said.

He couldn't turn back. If he let his guard down for a single second, he'd join her in that bed. So, instead, he turned his head and spoke over his shoulder. "Yes?"

"Thank you."

She was *thanking* him? "For what?"

"For trusting me enough to share your past with me. I know that must have been hard, and I just want you to know I appreciate it."

Not sure of his voice, he nodded once and walked down the dark hall to his empty bed.

Harper opened her eyes the next morning to see Nick coming through the bedroom door holding a tray. She yawned and stretched, giving herself cover for a few moments to study him. The man before her was different from the one she'd sat with last night as he'd poured out his pain. This man had his mask firmly back in place. As someone who wore an invisible suit of armor to protect herself, she had no trouble recognizing his.

A stab of disappointment struck, as if she'd been given a gift that had been taken away again. But at the same time, part of her had to admire the skill and self-discipline it took to hide his pain from the world so well. It hadn't just been his words last night that had told her about the pain consuming him, it had been the soul-deep anguish in his eyes. Sharing that with her had been a huge act of trust. She wondered if he'd shared that with anyone before. Did Malcolm even know the depths of his torment?

"Morning," he said, giving her a smile that didn't reach his eyes.

She wriggled up in the bed so that she was sitting against the headboard, and he unfolded the legs on the tray and set it over her lap.

"Good morning," she said. The tray held a plate with

two eggs on toast, a glass of juice and a small vase with a purple flower that looked to be from the bush beside the driveway that she'd seen last night. There might have only been a few items on the tray, but they were laid out in a neat and ordered way. She was still getting to know her husband, but this seemed to sum up his personality perfectly—he'd cared enough to cook her food, but kept it basic. He'd been sweet enough to cut a flower for her, then laid it all out with military precision. He was a study in opposites.

As he straightened, he rested his hands low on his hips. "Look, I'm sorry about last night."

"It wasn't all bad," she said, then took a sip of the juice.

He looked at her skeptically. "Yes, it was."

For him, it would have been beyond awful to talk to her. She got that. And it had been wrenching to see him in so much pain. But the thing was, they *had* been able to talk about it, and that gave her hope for the future. Now she just needed him to understand how important that process was for them going forward.

"I appreciate that you opened up to me. I'm sure it was hard, but you did it."

He blew out a breath. "That's part of what I'm apologizing for. I shouldn't have dumped all that crap on you. It wasn't fair. It's mine to deal with, not yours."

She reached out and took his hand, and he let her. "We're in this together, Nick. We can share things that are important."

Deep grooves appeared in his forehead. "Okay, sure. Why don't we do something together today? Get to know each other."

She'd already made plans with friends, but she suddenly realized that she wasn't single anymore, and that had broader ramifications than she'd expected. Another person had a stake in simple things like her plans for the weekend. As someone who'd always fiercely protected her independence, it felt a little strange.

"I was going to meet up with some friends for lunch today, but if you think we need—"

"You should go," he said and sat on the end of the bed.

"I'm sorry. I made the plans a couple of weeks ago—back when I was single—and, to be honest, with everything going on, I just forgot to mention it."

"Harper, I want you to go. Our marriage was meant to give you extra support, not get in the way of existing supports."

"Okay, I will." Some time with other people would probably be good to give her some perspective. "What will you do?"

"I need to go for a run. In fact," he said and stood, "I might go now."

"Okay, I'll see you tonight."

He gave her a smile and headed out her bedroom door. It wasn't the same as watching him leave last night—he was going for a run because she already had plans without him—but there was still something vaguely unsettling about watching him go. Perhaps because they didn't have the core bond to their marriage that most newlyweds had, where they knew they could depend on the other.

She looked back down at her tray and picked up the purple flower he'd added. Nick Tate was a good man. Maybe she needed to relax and let things happen naturally. They'd known going in that this wouldn't be easy, so now she just had to trust the process.

# Seven

A few hours later, Harper arrived at the Texas Cattleman's Club for lunch with her friend Sophie Prescott and two of Sophie's friends, Natalie Valentine and Emily Knox.

Sophie was already at a table, looking elegant as usual in a mint-green summer dress, her long red hair pinned up in a topknot. Harper had met her about six months ago at a charity fund-raiser, and she'd clicked with her from the start. But ever since Sophie had found love with her boss Clay Everett recently, there was even more sparkle in her eyes, and Harper couldn't have been more thrilled for her friend.

Natalie sat across from Sophie, and they were chatting about something that was making them smile. Harper had only met Natalie a few times, but she liked her, and she really admired the way she was building up her wedding dress design business while still running the Cimarron Rose B&B.

"Harper," Sophie said as she neared the table, and stood to envelop her in a hug. "So good to see you!"

Harper hugged her back, then leaned in to kiss Natalie's cheek. "So good to see you both, too."

Natalie flicked her hair over her shoulders. "I've been looking forward to this. I've been so busy, it's going to be great to unwind with my girls."

"Absolutely, I was—" Sophie said, then froze. "Harper, is there a ring on your finger?"

Harper looked at the gleaming gold band and bit down on a smile. She'd been wondering how to bring the topic up, but it looked like she didn't have to. "Yes, actually, there is."

"As in a *wedding ring*," Sophie said, her expression incredulous. "That has appeared since I saw you just over a week ago…?"

Even though she tried to hold it back, Harper felt her grin sneak out. "There's a story."

Sophie laughed. "I'll just bet there is. Maybe we should wait until Emily arrives so you don't have to repeat it."

Natalie pointed to the main door. "There's Emily now."

"Thank God," Sophie said. "I'm not sure how long I could have waited to find out what happened."

While Emily made her way over, her tall, athletic body graceful as she moved past the other tables, Harper tried to find a way to explain the last week to these women. So much had happened, and she'd stepped way outside her comfort zone. Would they tell her she was crazy? That she'd gone too far? Perhaps a reality check was just what she needed. Especially from Sophie, who was expecting a baby with the love of her life, and so would have a good perspective on the situation. Her opinion was the one Harper wanted the most.

Sophie stood again and hugged Emily. Then, after the

greetings were done, she said, "You're just in time, Emily. Harper was about to explain how come she's married now when she wasn't seeing anyone when we last spoke. A. Week. Ago."

Emily's eyes widened. "Oh, that is juicy. Glad I made it in time."

Harper still wasn't sure how much to tell, or how to explain, so she just started talking and figured she'd work it out as she went along. "Do you all know my boss, Malcolm Tate?"

Natalie gasped. "You married Malcolm Tate? He's divine."

"Not Malcolm," Harper said. "He has an identical twin brother. Nick."

"How have I never heard that he had a twin?" Natalie asked. "You'd think I'd remember a detail like that."

"Actually," Emily said, "I think I do remember something about him. Didn't he join the military?"

Sophie nodded as she picked up her glass of iced tea. "Oh, that's right. He married Andrea Miller's sister Melissa. I never could warm to her."

"Have you been dating Nick long?" Emily asked.

Dating? Harper tucked her hair behind her ears. Dating wasn't something she and Nick had indulged in at all.

"We met at Simone Parker's masked ball." She didn't mention that she'd thought he was Malcolm that night...

"That was a great party," Natalie said. "Still, that's fairly quick to a wedding."

Sophie sighed happily. "It must be true love if you knew so quickly. But why didn't you mention you were seeing him?"

"Well," Harper began, looking around at the women's faces. Her gut said she could trust these women with the truth, but it wasn't only her life that would be affected if she was wrong. When Nick's custody case for Ellie was heard, if something leaked out that their marriage wasn't real and his ex-wife's lawyers used that against him, Nick and Ellie would be the losers. So she settled on a half-truth. "It was a bit of a whirlwind, and it sped up when I realized I was pregnant."

Sophie squealed. "You're pregnant, too? How fabulous!"

The others joined in the congratulations and asked questions about how far along she was and details of the pregnancy.

"There's more," Harper said.

"How much more can there be?" Natalie said with an expectant grin.

"I'm carrying twins."

"Oh, my Lord," Sophie said, putting a hand over her chest. "This is the best story I've heard in ages."

The relief and gratitude at her friend's simple acceptance was overwhelming, and Harper had to blink away the moisture seeping into her eyes. Now she regretted that she hadn't shared the news with Sophie as it happened. "I'm sorry I didn't let you know. It just all happened so fast that I haven't had a chance to stop and think."

"Are you happy?" Sophie asked, her gaze serious.

Harper smiled. "I am." It was partly true. When she wasn't worried about the details of how they'd make it work, or the fallout if they failed, she was filled with happiness about the babies. And getting to spend time with Nick was just a bonus.

"Then, that's all that matters. Truly. Hang on," Sophie said and waved a waiter over. "We need something to celebrate with. A bottle of your best nonalcoholic champagne, please."

The waiter nodded, headed for the bar and quickly returned with a bottle and four sparkling glasses.

Once they were filled, Sophie lifted her glass into the air, and the other three women raised theirs to match. "To Harper," she said. "And to Nick, and their marriage. And to their babies. I can't wait to meet them!"

The other two women said, "To Harper," and Harper had to pretend to sip because she knew she wouldn't be able to drink anything with the ball of emotion lodged in her throat.

"Thank you," she said. "That means a lot."

"Actually," Emily said, her eyes dancing as she ran her fingers over the condensation on the side of her glass, "since we're celebrating, I have something, too."

"Really?" Sophie said and sucked in a breath, waiting.

Emily leaned in, practically vibrating with excitement. "I'm pregnant."

"Oh, Emily," Sophie said and jumped up to hug her friend. "I'm so happy for you and Tom."

Harper remembered Sophie telling her about Tom and Emily's tragedy when they lost their child—it had almost destroyed their marriage. They'd only recently found their way back to each other, so the news they were expecting again was like a blessing from heaven, and Harper couldn't have been happier for her.

Emily dabbed at the corner of her eye with her napkin. "Thank you. We're very lucky, and we know it."

"Do you know any details yet?" Natalie asked.

"We know it's a little boy," Emily said, laying a hand over her stomach, "and we've already decided to call him Jeremy Ryan Knox."

Sophie lifted her glass again, and the others immediately followed. "To Emily and Tom, and to little Jeremy Ryan Knox."

"Hear, hear," Harper and Natalie said, and they all clinked glasses.

"Well, y'all know that Clay and I are expecting, so that's three of us." Sophie turned to Natalie. "So now it's your turn. Can we toast a pregnancy for you, too? Make it four for four?"

Natalie coughed out a laugh. "Not a chance of that, I'm afraid. Colby and Lexie are keeping my hands far too full to contemplate another baby. Though there *is* something, and I'm really excited about it."

"Okay, spill," Emily said, still visibly glowing from her own news.

"Brandee Lawless asked me to design her wedding gown and the bridesmaids' dresses. I've had a sneak peek at some of the details of Brandee and Shane's wedding plans, and it's going to be amazing. I'm so thrilled to be a part of it."

"That's fabulous news," Sophie said, raising her glass for the third time. "To Natalie's amazing designs!"

The others joined in, and then they fell into discussing the details of all three announcements over their lunch and another bottle of nonalcoholic champagne.

As Harper finished her last bite of salad, she pushed her plate aside and sat back to listen to these amazing women talk. She'd never had a wide social circle, and making new friends hadn't felt like a priority since she'd moved to Royal a couple of years ago, but she could see that might have been an oversight. And now—when the structure of her life was changing in so many ways— would be a good time to address that, so she made herself a promise to stay in touch.

Once their plates were cleared, Emily said, "Has anyone heard anything about Maverick? He doesn't seem to have attacked anyone lately."

"That's a good point," Natalie said. "He was really active for months and months, but I haven't heard anything since he targeted Clay."

Harper ran her hand through her hair, wishing she could be optimistic. But harassment campaigns like this were never that simple. "I don't know anything about Maverick, but, working as a lawyer back home, I saw a couple of similar cases and how things shaped up once the perpetrator was caught. Sometimes the pattern of the attacks is uneven because of factors outside the blackmailer's control. Or they're building up for a bigger attack. I hope I'm wrong, but I don't think we should let our guard down just yet."

Sophie scowled. "Someone needs to stop that man."

Only last month, the anonymous blackmailer who had been targeting residents of Royal had planted a series of fake news stories online about Everest, Clay's business. Even before Sophie and Clay had been an item, Sophie had worked at Everest as Clay's secretary, so she'd taken Maverick's actions personally. And a few months before that he'd sent Emily some photos to make her believe her estranged husband had another secret family. Luckily they'd worked their way through it and were stronger than ever, but there was no love lost for Maverick at their table. Or anywhere in Royal, for that matter.

"I was talking to Sheriff Battle yesterday, and he said there are some good people working on discovering Maverick's identity," Emily said. "As soon as they know who he is, they can arrest him."

Sophie blew out a tightly controlled breath. "Either way, let's hope he's out of our lives before he can hurt anyone else."

"I'll drink to that," Emily said and took another sip from her glass.

Natalie pushed her chair back and put her handbag on her lap. "Hey, sorry to eat and run, but I have to get going."

"No problem," Sophie said. "You have so much on your plate right now."

They all said their goodbyes, and once the three remaining women had settled back in their seats, Sophie reached over and laid a hand on Harper's arm. "Honey, I'm so pleased about all your news. But—how do I say this?"

Harper gave her a reassuring smile. She'd been expecting an extra question or two after the news settled in. "Just say it. I won't be offended."

"For a newlywed who's carrying her husband's babies, you look a little...subdued. Is everything okay?"

Sophie's eyes were kind, and Harper knew her heart was in the right place. Should she confide in her? She didn't have anyone outside the situation to talk it through with—even her mother had been concerned on the phone about whether she'd made the right choice, so she hadn't wanted to worry her more. Perhaps telling Sophie—heck, even saying it out loud—would help her sort through her thoughts.

Since you never knew who was listening at the clubhouse, she lowered her voice. "I'm a little worried about Nick."

Sophie leaned in, her voice a little above a whisper. "He didn't want to get married?"

"It was his idea. He's totally committed to the marriage." She took a sip of her drink, and the other two women waited. "He developed PTSD after his time in the military, and while he's wrestling with that, he's involved in a custody case over his little girl, Ellie, and now to have two new babies on the way and a new marriage…I just wonder if it's all too much." She thought of the look on his face when he'd woken from the nightmare and realized she was there. "And I have no idea how to help him."

Emily opened her mouth as if to speak, then shut it again, her brows drawing together, and then she sucked in a breath as she leaned forward. "I hope you won't mind me butting in since I don't know you that well and I know nothing about PTSD, but I do know something about emotional pain and how it affects a marriage."

Emily hesitated, waiting for encouragement, so Harper said, "You're not butting in at all. I'd appreciate your thoughts."

"After our little boy died, grief tore my marriage to Tom apart. And we let it. If I could have that time over, I'd do something to not let sleeping dogs lie. As I said, I don't know much about your situation, but I'm now a big advocate for trying something. Anything."

The hairs on the back of Harper's neck stood up. *Try something.* The idea was so simple, and so complex, and so right. It was as if she'd turned the headlights on at night—she could see a little of the way. And a little was enough for now. All she had to do was figure out what to try first, and she was good at that—research, weighing options and making decisions. She could do this. Help Nick.

"Thank you," Harper said, gripping Emily's hand in hers. "I think that's exactly what I needed to hear."

"And in the meantime," Sophie said brightly, "we should order another bottle of bubbles. Between the three of us, we have four babies on the way!"

Harper laughed. "You're right. We'll be Royal's own baby boom."

"To us!" Emily said.

\* \* \*

When Harper's car pulled into his driveway after work on Monday, Nick was ready. Living as something of a hermit, he'd fallen into a few bad habits, and he realized now that he had a wife, he'd have to raise his game. After an afternoon session in his home gym, he'd usually shower, throw on the first pair of shorts his hand fell on and then order some takeout.

Today, though, he'd found an ironed pair of cargoes and a T-shirt and even managed to use a comb on his hair instead of simply running his fingers through it. And to really ensure he was turning over a new leaf, he'd made a start on chopping vegetables for a stir-fry.

All in all, he was feeling pretty pleased with himself. Perhaps he could pull off this husband thing.

Well, except for the nightmares and not being able to share a bed. And the constant, all-pervading fear that he was going to let Harper down the way he'd let down Ellie and the men who'd died under his command. And the blackness that surrounded him more often than not, and the constant fight not to let it seep into his relationship with Harper…

Gut churning and hands trembling, he swore and dropped the paring knife onto the board.

When he felt the blackness descending, all he could think was that he'd done the wrong thing by dragging Harper into his world. He should have let her go back to Connecticut, where she'd have her mother and be unsullied by his issues. The idea had been haunting him badly today, which was why he'd made a special effort to be the model husband when she arrived home.

The internal door that led from the garage opened and Harper appeared, her hair swinging around her shoulders as she turned to close the door behind her. He took in her long legs in her knee-length charcoal skirt and how her eyes softened when she saw him, and his heart surged. He knew he couldn't give her up. There was a radiance about her, soul-deep, and he couldn't look away. Now that she was his wife, he'd work as hard as he could, do whatever it took, to keep her in his life.

"Welcome home," he said as he reached for her briefcase.

As she handed the case over, she smiled. "If this is marriage, I think I could get used to it."

"It gets better—I've made a start on dinner," he said, depositing her bag on the coffee table and heading back to the kitchen. "Can I get you a drink?"

"Actually, there's something I want to do, but I'm not sure how you're going to react."

He shrugged and dug his hands in his pockets. "We're still getting to know each other's routines, so it's probably best at this stage that we're up front."

"Okay, but this isn't about routines." With a rare display of nervous energy, she picked up an apple from a bowl on the counter and rolled it from hand to hand, then dropped it back in the bowl. "In fact, it's pretty random."

Surprises weren't something he normally liked, but he was already enjoying this one—or more precisely, he was enjoying watching Harper deliver it. He rocked back on his heels. "Now you have me intrigued. Tell me."

"I heard about this dog today," she said in a rush. "His name is Frank, and he's in a pretty desperate situation." She took Nick's hand and laced their fingers together. "I think we need to rescue him."

His brows shot up of their own accord. A dog? That had been the last thing he'd expected his wife to say. And despite the childhood dogs she'd mentioned to Ellie, she'd struck him more as a cat person. He, on the other hand, was a dog person through and through, and if a dog was in trouble, he was ready to help.

"What sort of rescue?" he said, thinking through the logistics. "Will we need bolt cutters and grappling hooks?"

She chuckled. "You know, you can take the man out of the SEALs, but… It's nothing that drastic. Can we do it?"

"Tell me a bit more about the dog and its situation."

She started for the steps and said over her shoulder, "How about I tell you in the car?"

Ah, there was his Harper. She might not be a dog person, but she was a good negotiator. In fact, she seemed to have just undercut the negotiations.

He planted his feet shoulder-width apart and crossed his arms over his chest, waiting. She wasn't the only one with negotiating experience.

After a few beats, she retraced her steps and stopped in front of him. "Nick?"

He dropped his hands and grinned. "Sure, let's go take a look."

She leaned into him and threw her arms around his neck. "Thank you."

Unable to resist with her pressed against him, he hugged her tight, just for a few moments, before dragging himself back. The feel of her curves against him was dangerous. It had the power to make him forget they'd agreed to no lovemaking, at least until his nightmares were under control.

As he tried to catch his breath—and his train of thought—he said, "You need to get changed first?"

She glanced down at her silk blouse and knee-length skirt, so he added, "I'm not sure where we're heading, but if a dog needs to be rescued you'll probably want to wear clothes that you can get dirty."

Her forehead creased for a millisecond then cleared. "Good point."

She disappeared down the hall, and he took the couple of minutes before she reappeared in a T-shirt and loose pants to put the vegetables back in the fridge. "Ready," she said.

He looked at the way the pants fell, accentuating her long lines and curves, and was sorry they were leaving the house. But this appeared important to her, so he shook it off, grabbed his wallet and keys, and they set off.

Once they were in the car, he backed out and swung the wheel around to head down the street. "Where am I driving?"

"The Royal Safe Haven Animal Shelter."

An animal shelter? He'd been thinking he might need to do the rescue part and take the dog to a shelter. If they were *starting* at a shelter...

"Harper," he asked mildly, "are we adopting a dog?"

"I don't know." She tapped her fingers on her thighs. "Maybe?"

"We're headed for a shelter. What other option is there?"

"We could foster him until we find him a home. Or maybe we could sponsor him. Or we'll find some other way to save him. It's just that I heard about Frank today and knew we had to do something."

Frank. Good, solid name for a dog. "What did you hear?"

"I don't know much, so it might be better to wait until the shelter manager explains his story." Her voice was confident, upbeat and probably would have convinced a jury.

"Hang on," he said, flicking his wrist over to check his watch without losing his grip on the wheel. "Is the shelter even open now?"

"The manager said she'd still be out back doing paperwork, so she'd let us see Frank."

He had a feeling that more was going on here than she was saying, but he had no idea what. He could press Harper and try to work it out, or he could stop worrying and simply roll with the punches. He chose the latter approach.

When they arrived at the shelter, Harper called a number, and a woman with bright red hair, green eyes and a sprinkle of freckles across her nose came out and unlocked the front door. She wore a friendly smile and a shirt with Royal Safe Haven across the pocket. "Are you Harper?"

"Yes," Harper said brightly. "And you must be Megan. Thanks for letting us in after closing time."

"No problem," the woman said as she closed the door behind them again. "I have a soft spot for Frank."

Harper glanced up at Nick, as if judging his reaction, then turned back to Megan. "Can we see him?"

"Sure. Follow me." The shelter manager led the way past an office to a small room that had a couple of chairs and a dog bed on the floor. Over by the wall, a skinny chocolate Labrador lay with his head on his paws. "This is our meet-and-greet room. I thought I'd bring Frank down here in case you turned up."

"You thought we wouldn't come?" Harper asked.

"Let's say that Frank hasn't been too popular." She turned to the dog. "Have you, sweetheart?"

At hearing his name, the dog moved his eyes to check without lifting his head. He clearly had little interest in what was going on around him, which seemed unusual for a Labrador, especially one who had new people to meet.

Nick crouched down, held out a hand and said, "Hey, Frank. How are you doing?"

Frank glanced over suspiciously, then went right on ignoring them. Something was very wrong.

"What's his story?" Nick asked, still focused on the dog.

Megan leaned back against the painted brick wall. "His owner was in the military and left Frank with family while he was on deployment. Unfortunately, he never came home from his tour, so Frank ended up here."

Nick felt it like a punch to the gut. He could barely draw breath. Since he'd returned home, he'd been tormented by thinking about the people in his unit who hadn't gotten to go home themselves, and here was a dog who was suffering for the exact same reason.

Harper crouched beside him, but said to Megan, "Is he sick?"

"Nope, he's depressed. He's been like this since he arrived. The staff has tried all sorts of strategies to get him to engage, but no dice. We even have trouble getting him to eat. It's like he's given up hope."

Trying not to look big and menacing, Nick got down on his stomach and wriggled over to the dog. He held out his hand, and Frank lifted his head, sniffed in the hand's general direction and dropped his head to his front legs again. Every protective instinct Nick had reared up.

"What's the plan for Frank?" he asked, speaking softly so as not to spook the dog now that he was closer.

"Best-case scenario," Megan said, "he's adopted by someone who understands his situation and emotional state, and they're patient and loving while he recovers."

"Worst-case scenario?" he asked, not taking his eyes off Frank.

"He stays here longer and gives up a little more each day."

Nick held back a shudder. That wasn't going to happen. "Other options?"

"We find him a foster home, so he's out of the shelter while he heals, then he gets adopted."

He looked over at this sad dog who'd lost his human due to the same war that haunted Nick. Frank clearly couldn't stay in the shelter, and what he needed wasn't a temporary foster home. This dog needed someone to commit to him. Someone who'd stay and have his back. Someone who'd never let him down.

Nick drew in a deep breath. He might not have been able to save every man in his unit, but he could save Frank.

He glanced over at Harper, one questioning eyebrow raised, and Harper nodded.

Nick threw Megan a look over his shoulder. "What paperwork do I have to fill out to adopt this dog?"

Harper leaned to look in the backseat of Nick's car at the sad dog who hadn't yet realized his fortunes had turned. All in all, she was pretty pleased with her night's work.

Nick started the engine and said, "We don't have any of the things at home Frank will need."

"Hang on." She picked up her cell to check online for the nearest pet supplies store. "There's a place not too far away that's still open." She gave him the directions, and he turned the car.

When they reached the store, she stayed in the car with Frank while Nick ducked in to grab what they needed.

"So, Frank," she said once they were alone, "you'll like Nick. We're both pretty lucky he picked us."

Though luck might have had a bit of a nudge in Frank's case. Since Emily had urged her at their lunch yesterday to "do something," Harper's mind had been whirring. She'd researched and found two pieces of interesting information. First, programs that matched former military personnel suffering from PTSD with trained service dogs who could intervene and head off some of the symptoms were seeing some amazing outcomes. Getting Nick a trained service dog would have been the ideal solution, but there was a waiting list. She'd made a mental note to do something about fund-raising for the group that was training the dogs to help them help more veterans.

In the meantime, she'd found another piece of useful information—one recommendation for PTSD sufferers was to do something to help someone else. Nick was so concerned about letting someone down again, she wasn't sure he was ready to do that yet. But then she'd wondered, what if the someone who needed help wasn't a person…?

One call to the Royal Safe Haven Animal Shelter and she'd found the perfect dog. The fact that Frank had lost as much to war as Nick had meant they were perfect for each other. Megan had said Frank would need someone dedicated to help him get through his depression, and the look on Nick's face when he'd asked for the paperwork to adopt the dog had told her all she needed to know about that.

Helping Frank would help Nick. And, hopefully, they might even be able to get Frank some training to help Nick even more after that. Win-win.

Nick emerged with his arms full and loaded the bags in the trunk. When he slid into the driver's seat again, she said, "All for Frank?"

"Just a few things to get us started—food, a bed, collar and leash, treats and toys."

"Just to get us started?" His arms had been so full that Harper would have needed two trips to bring all the purchases out.

He arched an eyebrow. "Didn't you tell Ellie you had dogs before?"

"A Great Dane and a Labrador."

"Marshall and Darcy."

He'd listened to her and remembered the names of her childhood dogs. The thought warmed her heart. "That's right. But I don't remember having so much paraphernalia for them. Maybe things were simpler back then."

He grinned at her. "Or maybe your parents handled that side of dog ownership."

"True." She smiled back. "So have you had a dog?"

"Most of my life." He threw Frank a quick greeting before starting the car again. "Dogs make life better."

She waited while he pulled out into traffic, thinking his words through. There was a gaping hole. "Why didn't you have one already, then?"

He shrugged like it was no big deal. "I was coming and going on deployment, and Melissa said she wasn't interested in looking after a dog while I was gone."

"But you've been divorced for almost two years, and, more to the point, you're not in the military anymore." She turned in her seat a little to see his profile better. "You're not coming and going."

"I hadn't thought about it," he said as he smoothly changed lanes to overtake a slower car.

She didn't believe that for a second. Even if he hadn't considered it, which was unlikely given his reaction to Frank and his comment about dogs making life better, the conversation in the diner with Ellie would have prompted thoughts about a pet dog. There was something else.

"Truth?" she said softly.

He blew out a long breath and rolled his shoulders back. "I guess I didn't think I was in a fit state to take on any big responsibilities."

"But you have," she said, laying a hand over her stomach. "You've taken responsibility for these babies. You didn't have to—you had several chances to bow out. But you stepped up."

He was quiet for a few minutes, until they stopped at a red light. Then he turned to her, brows drawn together. "Before that day Malcolm called and told me you were pregnant, I was basically a hermit." His voice was like gravel, his gaze serious. "The babies and our situation have forced me out of hiding. Prodded me back into the world."

"Are you glad?" she asked, thinking about the discussion she'd had with Sophie and Emily the day before. "Not about the babies, I mean, but are you glad that you've been pushed back into the world?"

He speared the fingers of one hand through his hair. "I think so, but truthfully, I don't know." The light changed to green. His attention returned to the road, and he eased down on the accelerator. "All I know for sure is that I'm pleased you and the babies are in my life, and you three are all tied up in the package of me being out in the world."

She slid her hand over and let it rest on his thigh, offering wordless support.

He seemed to give himself an internal shake, then when he spoke again, his voice was brighter. "Hey, you know who's going to be the most excited about Frank?"

"Ellie," she said, unable to stop the smile as she imagined the little girl's face. "She'll be thrilled."

He laid a hand over Harper's on his thigh. "Seriously, though," he said, and his Adam's apple bobbed down, then up. "I am glad."

She knew he was talking about her and the babies again, and her heart clenched tight. She turned her hand over so they were palm to palm. "Me too," she whispered.

Less than an hour later they were home, Nick's stir-fry

was sizzling on the stove and Frank had settled on his new bed, his belly full. He'd sniffed around the yard a little, peed on a plant, then explored a few rooms in the house before curling up in his bed with a sigh. He obviously didn't have high expectations of this place, but then, he wouldn't think of it as his own home yet—he was probably still waiting on his original owner to come back for him.

But he was keeping his gaze on Nick in the kitchen. It could have been because of the food, but Harper was hopeful it was more than that. That they were bonding already.

She wandered over to the stove. "This smells great. Anything I can do to help?"

"Not really," Nick said. "I'm not sure what sort of food you like, so I just grabbed some things from the grocery store today."

She looked into the sizzling pan. "This is exactly my kind of food. But you're right. We should go shopping together when we get a chance so we can see what we both like."

He considered her for a moment, his expression serious. "We've been trying to cover big-picture stuff, but I guess there's still a lot of day-to-day stuff to learn about each other."

She laid a hand over her stomach and glanced from Frank to Nick. "I think we're doing pretty well. We just need to keep moving forward and not let the big stuff overwhelm us."

He smiled at her. "You know what? I think you're right."

# Eight

It had been ten days since Nick had married Harper and she'd moved into his place, and a week since he'd adopted Frank, and already he couldn't imagine his life without them. He spent his days with Frank—there was a deluxe dog bed in the downstairs office for Frank's naps while Nick worked on Tate Armor business, then when they needed to work out the kinks, they'd go for a walk together. He hoped to build that up to a run as Frank's fitness increased.

The evenings were for Harper. They'd been taking turns cooking, then sometimes they'd watch a movie. Other times they'd talk about the smaller details of their lives—getting to know each other. But they'd avoided ice cream, and they'd especially avoided all unnecessary touching.

And that part was slowly driving him insane.

Each day he wanted her more. Each hour. Each minute.

He wanted her with a ferocity that surprised even him. And it wasn't just about making love—he wanted the casual intimacy that lovers had. Stealing a kiss when they crossed paths in the hall. Gathering her close when she arrived home from work. Simply touching her, being near her. He wanted it all.

So that night when they stood on his back lawn in the moonlight waiting for Frank to have his final toilet stop before bed, Nick decided he needed to broach the subject.

"I've been thinking about something," he said, gaze on Frank. "You know that if we'd just met tonight, I'd want to date you."

She shrugged. "But we didn't just meet. Our situation is far too complex already."

He turned to face her and dug his hands in his pockets. "What if we kept it simple? And agreed that whatever happens, we wouldn't let it affect our parenting of the babies."

She turned to face him as well, the moonlight catching on her dark hair, making it shine. "What exactly are you suggesting?"

"That we start dating," he said simply.

She arched an eyebrow. "You want to date your wife?"

"More than you can imagine." So much that he'd been having difficulty concentrating on anything else but her.

"I don't know, Nick." Harper folded her arms tightly under her breasts. "There's so much risk, especially for the babies and Ellie."

"But there's also so much potential to have more," he said. "More for us, the babies and Ellie."

For one hopeful moment, her eyes sparkled, then she winced and shook her head. "I think our window of opportunity is gone. Maybe if I hadn't gotten pregnant and we'd met again in a supermarket or socially…"

Her voice trailed off, and she wandered farther into the yard, pausing to rest her hand on top of a dense shrub. Part of him wanted to leave the topic there, but the bigger part of him couldn't let it go, so he followed.

"It's crazy that the one woman I want to date is off-limits because we're already married."

"We had good reasons for putting that intimacy rule into place," she said, her voice sounding strained.

That was true, but there was something undeniable between them. Something that wasn't fading away by ignoring it. "My last tour taught me is that life is short and unpredictable. And I don't want to live with regrets."

"But that's my thinking, too." She ran her fingers through her hair, pulling it tightly back from her face as she spoke. "I don't want to move our relationship into new territory and come to regret that."

"Harper, we're never going to be a couple who only react to each other like friends." He reached for her hand and laced their fingers together, relishing the sizzle as her skin slid along his. "We have chemistry. If we continue like we are, the tension will eventually explode. The best way forward is to manage that tension as much as we can."

There was silence for three beats, four.

"Okay, if—and I'm only saying if—we tried to manage this, how would you see it working?"

"We'd date. We'd treat it as a totally separate thing from our marriage. The marriage is the legal agreement that we entered for the sake of the babies, and Ellie, and Tate Armor, and to ensure you had support." He took an infinitesimal step closer. "Dating would be just for us."

Frank came ambling over, finished with his nightly business. Nick gave him a short pat, and, obviously realizing the humans might take a while, Frank lay down at their feet.

"*How* would we date, though?" Harper asked. "We've just watched a movie together on the sofa. Our life together has moved past dating scenarios."

"Just because we live in the same house doesn't mean we can't go out on dates. Maybe we fool around if the mood strikes, the way a dating couple would."

Her brows drew together. "Sex is a line in the sand for me in this relationship."

"It doesn't have to be sex." He took another small step closer. "Holding hands. Making out. Just like if we were any other dating couple. And we see how it goes. If it's making things messier, we haul it back again."

She pulled her bottom lip into her mouth as she considered and he watched, mesmerized. He'd kissed that plump lip. What he wouldn't give to be able to kiss it again right now. To pull it into his mouth and gently bite down...

She released her lip and blew out a breath. "If we keep crossing that line and then retreating, the line is going to get completely blurred."

"It comes down to one question." He took her other hand as well and brought them together—all four of their hands in one grip. "Harper, do you want to do this?"

She closed her eyes tight, as if in pain, before opening them and meeting his gaze head-on. "Of course I *want* to. That was never in question."

"Then let's give it a try. We're both well aware of the potential pitfalls, which means we'll be on our guard for them. Let's just give it a try."

She opened her mouth to say something, hesitated, swallowed hard, then nodded. "Sure. Okay. But it needs to be a trial, just to see how it goes."

He wanted to haul her against him and hold her, but

he knew the only way forward was cautiously, so instead he just said, "Deal."

But inside he was smiling.

The next day, Harper was unwrapping a sandwich at her desk so she could work through her lunch break when she thought she heard Nick's voice float through her open door. She glanced through the plate-glass walls of her office to the open-plan area outside. Sure enough, Nick was wending his way through the desks, heading for her. Her heart stuttered to a stop at the sight of him, and when it kicked back in, it beat faster than before. Oh, the way that man moved—prowled—was a sight to behold, and the movement of each step pulled his clothes against his body, hinting at a physique toned by his daily workouts. She only just managed to restrain a sigh of appreciation.

A few people greeted him as Malcolm, and, not bothering to correct them, he said a casual "Hey" and kept moving.

She shook her head. The idea of mixing the two men up was ludicrous. They might look the same, but Malcolm was a warm, sunny day to Nick's dark, brooding night. Of course if she hadn't recognized that he wasn't Malcolm on the night of the masked ball, she couldn't expect that people who were only seeing him pass by to realize it. Besides, Nick was the silent partner—there were probably a few people working here who didn't even realize Malcolm had a twin who owned half the company. Still…

He reached the desk just outside her office, and her assistant, Tom, glanced up to check if she was available then waved through the man he obviously thought was Malcolm. Nick barely seemed to notice that he was being given permission—his gaze was firmly locked on her. A delicious shiver of anticipation raced down her spine at the sparking intensity in his eyes.

Tom must have noticed something was a little off—perhaps since Nick hadn't slowed to greet him the way Malcolm normally would have—so he turned and watched as Nick entered her office.

He gave her a lopsided grin and said, "Hey."

"Hey, yourself." She stood and rounded her desk. "This is a surprise."

"Since we started dating, I thought I'd drop by and take you to lunch. You know. On a date."

"I was expecting we'd do things at night or on the weekends." And, to be honest, she hadn't expected anything quite so soon.

He took her hand and linked their fingers. "It wouldn't have been much of a surprise that way."

She coughed out a laugh. "I guess not."

Over his shoulder, she noticed there was something of a scene unfolding on the other side of the plate-glass walls. Several people had dropped by Tom's desk—some had taken the time to grab some paperwork so they could at least pretend they had a legitimate reason to be watching the events unfold, but others weren't bothering with trying to be subtle. Of course, office life at Tate Armor was normally fairly routine and boring, so an event like the man they thought was the CEO walking into the company attorney's office and holding her hand would be an interesting diversion, and word spread fast.

Normally she was a private person and would cringe at being the center of a scene. But with Nick smiling at her, she couldn't bring herself to care. Instead, she looked back to him and murmured, "We have an audience."

She looked down at their linked fingers and wanted to just focus on this new feeling of being courted by her husband, but she couldn't completely ignore her coworkers, so finally she glanced up at Nick again.

"I haven't told anyone here yet."

He tucked a strand of hair behind her ear. "About the babies, about the wedding or about me?"

"Any of it," she admitted, trying not to wince but probably failing. A couple of times she'd almost told Tom but had changed her mind each time. She'd never shared much personal information before, so she hadn't known how to start.

Nick raised an eyebrow. "No one noticed the wedding band?"

She shrugged. "I don't tend to hang out at the water cooler."

"I seem to have let part of your secret out," he said, clearly pleased with himself.

"It seems you have."

With a finger under her chin, he tipped her face up to look into her eyes. "Are you sorry?"

"Not really," she said, and realized it was true. "I wasn't deliberately keeping it a secret, I just haven't told anyone. I'm normally fairly self-contained."

He smiled knowingly. "Seems I'm not the only one with hermit tendencies."

"I suppose that's true." She'd never thought of herself as a hermit or considered cutting herself off from people the way Nick had since he'd returned home, but she had always been a bit of a loner. "You've been physically isolating yourself, and it's probably fair to say I emotionally isolate myself."

"Well, maybe you *used to* emotionally isolate yourself," he said. "Now you're married with two babies on the way and stepmother to a three-year-old."

"And I'm adjusting," she said, attempting a reassuring smile before adding, "slowly."

"How about we help it along a little?" His voice was deep and smooth and laced with mischief, daring her to put a foot out of line.

"How?" she asked, equal parts curious and wary.

Raising an eyebrow and keeping her gaze, he lifted her left hand up to shoulder height and pointed to her wedding ring, then his own. The murmurings floating through her door increased to a buzz.

She laughed and rested her forehead against his chest. "Not into subtlety?"

"Not really my forte." He stepped back, smiled generously at the crowd then placed a hand on Harper's stomach. The assembled group—which, by now, was almost the entire staff of the company—gave up any pretense of being there for any other reason but gawking. They clearly thought they were at the unveiling of a secret office romance between the CEO and the company attorney—the most delicious piece of gossip all year. Most people were grinning, a couple had their mouths open in a wide O, and Tom gave her a double thumbs-up.

Harper blew out a breath and caved in—she gave her coworkers a little wave and then put her hand over Nick's on her stomach.

"You know," she said, "it's going to be impossible to get any work done for the rest of the day."

"Worse things have happened."

"You should care about this, as a co-owner of the company."

"As a co-owner of the company, I find this scenario more amusing and satisfying than a few extra hours of completed work."

The elevator pinged, and the doors slid open, revealing Malcolm. The murmuring stopped as the actual CEO walked through, glancing around, clearly wondering why the people he paid to work at these desks weren't actually doing that.

Then he caught sight of his brother, and understanding dawned on his face. He headed over to them. The silence dissolved, and the gathered people realized that they hadn't just witnessed a scene between Harper and Malcolm—which was juicy enough—but this was, in fact, a rare sighting of the fabled identical twin. The buzz began again, people not even bothering to whisper anymore as they shared tidbits of information they had about the other partner in Tate Armor.

"So," Malcolm said as he reached Harper's office door, "the newlyweds can stop traffic. That's as good an omen as any for a marriage. Though I'd be careful with these displays of unprofessional behavior in the office, Nick. One of the company owners is ex-military, and I hear he takes the professionalism of his staff very seriously."

Nick rested an arm around Harper's shoulders. "Our marriage doesn't need good omens—it's doing fine on its own. In fact, I'm here to take my wife out to lunch."

Malcolm checked his watch, his face deadpan. "Is it that time already? I haven't had lunch, either. I might join you."

Harper was enjoying the banter between the brothers, but Nick clearly wasn't in the mood. "This is a private lunch date," he said and tugged on Harper's hand.

She grabbed her bag and let him lead her to the elevator. Nick hit the down button, the doors whooshed open and they stepped in. As she turned, she saw all her coworkers and boss gathered together, having been thoroughly entertained by her and Nick, and instead of finding it intrusive or a nuisance, as she would have a few weeks ago, she felt stirrings of mischievousness. Like she was playing hooky by going out to lunch…and enjoying it. Just before the doors closed, she bit down on a grin and gave another little wave to the crowd.

When they reached the security desk just inside the building's front doors, Nick stopped to thank Steve, the guard, and pick up Frank, who'd been sleeping behind the desk.

The dog even looked a little pleased to see him. When Nick had left him there on his way to get Harper, Frank had seemed to accept it as if he was being handed to yet another owner. The fact that he seemed to be moderately pleased to be back with Nick was an improvement.

Harper gave Frank a hello pat and waved to Steve. Once they were outside, she said, "I've never seen any of the guards here provide dog-sitting before."

"We knew each other in high school. Besides, he's a navy vet, and when I told him Frank's story, he offered to help out with him if we needed it."

He didn't need help for Frank, but he'd been thinking about organizing some fund-raising for a charity he'd read about that looked after the dogs of military personnel while they were on deployment. Maybe he'd come back another day and see if Steve was interested in getting involved as well.

"So," Harper said when they reached his car, "I'm guessing with Frank tagging along, we're not going to a fancy restaurant?"

He opened the back door, and Frank jumped in, turned a couple of times and lay down.

"If it's okay with you—" Nick closed Frank's door and turned to Harper "—I had the kitchen at the TCC clubhouse put together a gourmet picnic basket."

Her eyes lit up. "That sounds perfect."

Feeling pretty happy that he'd planned something for their first date that put that look in her eyes, he held her door as she slid into her seat, then rounded the car and settled in on the driver's side. Before he started the ignition, he reached for her hand again.

"I want to show you a special place. We might not make it back in the hour that Malcolm allots for lunch, but we shouldn't be too late."

"As you pointed out," she said, grinning, "I have quite a bit of vacation saved up, so a little late will be fine."

Nick drove them to a spot just outside town that not many people knew about. It was pretty much still in its natural state, with a small waterfall—nothing too spectacular, but the rhythmic sound of the water was one of the few things that helped center him. And he wanted to share that with her.

He parked, let Frank out and grabbed the picnic basket and a blanket from the trunk while Harper took in the setting.

"This place is amazing," she said, resting her hands on her hips, watching the waterfall. "I've never been here. How did you know about it?"

His lungs cramped tight. He'd known the question was coming—anyone would have asked in this situation—yet it still managed to blindside him. He carefully took a breath, then another. Harper turned curious eyes to him.

He cleared his throat and gave half an answer. "I've been coming here for years. Sometimes there are other people, especially on weekends, but often it's deserted."

"Well, I love it." She smiled, seemingly satisfied with only half an answer, and his lungs released their tension, allowing him to draw in blissful gulps of fresh air.

Frank trotted over, sniffed around a little and relieved

himself on a tree trunk, then came back to where Nick was setting up the blanket and curled up on a corner. Watching the simple, practical movements of his dog helped Nick regain his equilibrium.

Harper slipped off her heels, knelt on the blanket and helped unpack the basket. She held up a small container of mixed olives. "This all looks fabulous. Did you choose the food?"

"I left that to the clubhouse kitchen." He reached in and came out with a sealed plastic bag that contained a silver bowl, a small bottle of spring water, some dog treats and a ball. He chuckled. He'd asked for a picnic basket, and when they'd asked how many were going, he'd said just him and his wife. He'd added, "And my dog," as an afterthought, simply because he liked saying he had a dog, not thinking they'd include anything for Frank. It was nice of them. He appreciated attention to detail in customer service—he'd have to send them another tip later.

He poured the water into the silver bowl and offered it to Frank, along with one of the treats. The Labrador sniffed the treat then carefully took it from him and chewed. It tore at his heart that Frank still felt the need to be so careful about everything.

Gaze on his dog, Nick casually said, "I've been wondering something."

As Harper pulled the last contents from the basket—china plates and thick, luxurious napkins—and laid them out, she threw him a look over her shoulder. "It just so happens that plying me with delicious food is a good way to get me to answer just about anything."

He grinned. "I'll file that away for future reference."

She settled back on the blanket, stretched her long legs out in front of her and leaned back, resting her weight on her hands. "What do you want to know?"

"The other day you said you'd heard about a dog and we had to rescue him."

"Mmm-hmm," she said, her tone noncommittal.

He reached over and rubbed Frank's soft ears. "How, exactly, did you hear about him?"

"Ah." She busied herself serving food onto their plates. He wasn't sure if it was a strategy to avoid eye contact or not, so he waited until she sat back and met his gaze. "Well, to be honest—"

"Always the best policy," he interjected, amused.

"—I called the Royal Safe Haven Animal Shelter and asked Megan to tell me about their special needs dogs. She ran through a few, then when she mentioned Frank's history, I asked her to hold him for us."

"Right." He'd started to suspect as much. Something in her story had always been a little suspicious. "So, why make the call to the shelter in the first place?"

"Because the wait was too long for a trained service dog."

He opened his mouth to reply, then shut it again. She'd lost him in that last leap of logic. "You know, this might be easier if you just start from the beginning."

She handed him a plate piled high with food, then took hers and put it down on the blanket. But she didn't start eating. She stared at her food for long moments, then lifted her gaze to him. Totally open—no avoidance, no games.

"I wanted to do something to help you with what you're going through. So I did some research into PTSD."

He stilled. The last thing he wanted was Harper thinking he was a charity case or pitying him. "Learn anything interesting?" he asked, trying for a casual tone and unsure if he'd achieved it.

She nodded, clearly warming to her subject. "I saw

some really good outcomes for veterans with a trained service dog. The dogs could head off anxiety attacks and wake their person from a nightmare."

He'd heard similar things. "A friend mentioned once that he knew a couple of guys who had them."

"But there was a waiting list, so I kept researching." Her eyes were shining with enthusiasm, so he bit into a roll and lost himself in her light as she talked. "Another piece of advice I found was to do something for someone else. To help someone. But I knew you were worried about letting someone down again, and you already felt your plate was full with me, Ellie and the babies, so that wasn't a great plan. It could make things worse rather than better."

He winced. That was a harsh but fair assessment. Still, he didn't want her feeling like she was a burden to him. "Harper, I don't think of you as—"

But she interrupted him. "It's okay, Nick. I know what you mean. And anyway, then I had an idea—what if the someone you helped wasn't a person? What if it was a dog who needed you as much as you needed them?"

Her plan finally made sense. "So you called Megan and asked about special needs dogs."

"And you met Frank and fell for him at first sight. Now that I think about it," she said, her mischievous smile peeking out again, "you seem to have a habit of committing to people and dogs before getting to know them."

"Since it worked so well with you, I thought it was worth a shot with Frank." He glanced at the dog, who carried the weight of hope and expectation on his furry shoulders. It was a lot for a boy dealing with his own issues. "Harper, what if he doesn't help me?"

Her gaze didn't falter. "Then we'll have a gorgeous family pet for Ellie, the babies and us."

"Sounds like a perfect plan," he said.

She popped a juicy olive in her mouth and chewed, watching him carefully, and when she'd swallowed, asked, "Are you mad at me?"

She'd lied by omission and had been poking around, researching something he found intensely personal. He should be annoyed. Strangely, he wasn't.

"I'm grateful. That you researched it and came up with a strategy, and for Frank himself." Frank looked up at his name, probably hoping for some cheese, and Nick ruffled the top of his head. "I think he's already helping."

She'd been right—it had been good to have someone else who needed him during the day when Harper was at work and Ellie was with her mother. He'd even taken to talking to him on their daily walk. Frank was a good listener.

They sat in companionable silence as they ate their picnic lunch and listened to the waterfall. When they were done, Harper lay back on the blanket, her hands behind her head, and Nick stretched out beside her, feeling surprisingly content.

"So now I'm wondering something," she said, looking up at the clouds.

"It just so happens that delicious food and good company make me feel like sharing, too."

"This place." She waved an arm around to encompass their surroundings. "Tell me how you found it."

Ah. He shouldn't have been surprised she'd circled back around to the topic. After all, she was a lawyer. He braced himself and exposed a guarded part of his heart. "My dad brought me here. He said it was our place."

She rolled to her side, her cheek resting on a palm. "Not Malcolm, too?"

"Our parents were always careful to let us do things

together when we wanted, but to let us have our own experiences, too."

"That's a good tip for a mother-to-be of twins," she said. "Why did he choose this spot for you and not Malcolm?"

Good question. In some ways it was such an obvious thing, but how to explain it?

"Malcolm was always more…social than me. He and our mother are two of a kind. Dad and I, on the other hand—" he glanced around at this place that had always been theirs "—well, we always craved a bit of space. Quiet space."

She was silent for long moments, and when she spoke, her voice was gentle. "How long ago did he pass away?"

"Nine years." Though it didn't feel that long at all—occasionally Nick even forgot he was gone. "It was his heart. He'd had problems before, and he was on a transplant waiting list, but it gave out before they found one."

"Oh, Nick." She scooted closer and leaned into him. "I'm so sorry."

He wrapped an arm around her shoulders and allowed himself the luxury of absorbing the nearness of her and her unquestioning support when he needed it. "In some ways we were lucky. He knew there was a chance he wouldn't make it, so he had time to say his goodbyes. Not everyone gets that."

There had been lots of family chatting, teasing and laughing—just as his father had wanted. And there had also been time for his father to have deep, one-on-one talks with each of them.

One time when they'd been alone, Nick's dad had gripped his hand and told him—not for the first time—that he was the strong one, and he'd have to look after his mother and Malcolm. It had made a deep impression on his soul, and he'd done his best ever since. When things were hard, he often thought of his father's face as he'd said those words and it was enough to keep him going, keep him moving forward.

One thing he was glad about was that his father had seen him in uniform before he died. Swiping away tears, his father had told him how proud he was, and it had been one of the best days of Nick's entire life. He'd tried to be the man his father had expected him to be, which was one of the reasons he'd found struggling with his PTSD so hard. A strong man—the man his father had wanted him to be—would have handled it, right?

He glanced over at Harper—an intelligent, brave woman, who had barely blinked when he'd told her about his PTSD, and had even gone out of her way to research strategies to help. Just the thought of what she'd done for him made his chest ache in a way it never had before. An ache just for her. He reached for her hand, gripping it tight, and, as she smiled at him, a sliver of optimism shone through the dark parts of his mind. If she didn't think he was a lost cause, then maybe, just maybe, there was hope for him still.

# Nine

It was just past midnight, and Nick was sitting out by the pool, watching the moon, Frank snoring by his feet.

He hadn't been able to sleep, so earlier he'd sat up in bed with Frank across his lap and begun, hesitantly, to tell his dog some of the less painful stories from his time in the military. It had been strange at first, but he'd read some articles online about talking through upsetting memories with a dog. As Frank had lain attentively, with no judgment in his gaze, it had slowly become easier. He'd talked for maybe an hour, and his shoulders felt a fraction lighter at the end. Sleep had still evaded him, though, so he'd come out here to watch the shimmering water in the pool and breathe the cool air. Frank—with his job done—had decided to catch a nap.

Movement at the sliding glass doors caught his eye, and he turned to find Harper in a long nightdress coming over to him. Bathed in the pale blue moonlight, she seemed ethereal, and the gentle night breeze draped the fabric against her body, revealing the growing roundness of her belly. The sheer perfection of her stole his breath. She was a goddess—so much more than he would ever deserve.

"Did I wake you?" he asked when she reached him. Uncertain if she was a light sleeper or not, he'd tried to be quiet when he'd been near her room.

She shook her head and grimaced. "Leg cramps. I was hoping walking might ease them."

He was instantly more alert. Cramps were no laughing matter—experience from both training and missions had taught him that. "Has the walking helped?"

"Not so much." She rocked from her heels to her toes and back again.

He cast an assessing glance over her. "Is it just your legs?"

"Well," she said, drawing out the word as if not really wanting to admit more, "my back is aching."

He pushed to his feet. In some respects he might have been a poor choice as a husband, but this was one thing he could do something about.

He slipped an arm around her waist. "Come on, I have a couple of ideas."

As they started walking, she leaned in to him and whispered, "Thank you."

"I haven't done anything yet."

"You have," she said and looked up at him, her sweet brown eyes filled with emotion. "You're here and you're willing to help. You have my back. They're things I really appreciate."

"You're welcome," he said around a lump in his throat. To have a woman as strong as Harper Lake say that to him…it meant a lot.

They reached her bedroom door, and he released her. "You go curl up in bed. I'll be back in a minute."

Once in the kitchen, he quickly made up a hot water bottle. When he returned, he found her already in the bed. He tucked the hot water bottle against her back, then sat on the side of the bed, feet on the floor. "Here, give me the leg that's worst."

She lifted her right leg to lie across his lap, and he went to work, gently at first, looking for any knots and tightness, then easing it with rhythmic hand movements.

"The pregnancy books said I might get cramps, so I shouldn't be surprised." She offered a half smile that made him wish he could scoop her up, hold her tight and protect her against anything that might hurt her.

Instead, he kept massaging her leg and said, "What else do the books say we should be looking out for?"

"So many things," she said, watching his hand sliding along her calves. "Those books are quite scary, to be honest."

He'd been home between tours when Ellie was a baby, but he'd been away for a big chunk of Melissa's pregnancy. He was only realizing now what he'd missed and was determined not to let any details pass by this time. "Okay, so we'll ignore the books for the moment. Tell me what it's like for you."

As he rubbed the muscle, up and down, gently digging his knuckles in, she opened up about the little things she hadn't shared before now. At one time he might have thought he was tough as nails, that war had hardened him, but listening to Harper describe the miracle of pregnancy, the ways her body was changing as it grew his babies, he could practically feel his heart melt into a puddle.

They changed positions so he could do her other leg,

and he asked more questions, drawing out her own feelings of wonder about the experience.

"You can probably stop now," she said with a soft smile.

Her eyes were drooping, so he ran his hands one last time over her calf, as much for himself as for her, then pulled the sheet up over her shoulders.

"Sleep well," he said and reverently kissed her forehead. Reluctantly, he steeled himself to walk away and leave her until morning.

"Nick?"

He didn't dare look back at her, knowing his willpower was already stretched thin. "Yeah?"

"Stay with me." She lifted the sheet as invitation. "Just for tonight, stay and hold me."

His stomach rolled and sank. He'd been the one to propose marriage, and he'd been the one to suggest their new dating arrangement. No question, he'd been the one pushing their relationship forward. And now Harper was finally asking for something, wanting more…and it was something he couldn't give.

"Harper, I'd do it if I could, but you know I can't."

She sucked her bottom lip into her mouth and bit down, her gaze watchful, uncertain. "Is this just about your nightmares?"

She thought that he didn't want to be in her bed? That he didn't dream of waking wrapped around her warm body? "I promise, nothing else could keep me away from you."

"I don't care about them." She wriggled up to a sitting position against the headboard.

God, the temptation of the idea. *Of her.*

"Sleep is essential when you're pregnant." He said it like it was a mantra.

"It's just for tonight." She glanced at her bedside clock. "Or what's left of it. I'll sleep better if you hold me."

In asking for this, he knew she was going out on a limb. She'd been so cautious about taking their relationship too far or too fast up until now. And *this* was the thing she chose to ask of him. The one thing he couldn't grant her.

His chest ached from having to deny her, but he had no choice. "Harper, I can't. You know I can't."

He'd have given anything in that moment to climb into that bed and lie with her all night. If he ever healed from this damn illness and was able to spend his nights wrapped around her, he'd never take it for granted. Not even once.

"Harper, I'm so damn sorry."

"It's okay," she said, but there was hurt in her eyes. Hurt he'd put there with what was, in effect, another little abandonment, and that pierced something deep in his chest. He squeezed his eyes against its power, brushed a kiss over her forehead and walked away before he could change his mind.

Nick sat on the end of Harper's bed, looking at the paint swatches she'd taped to her wall. They'd spent the evening measuring the nursery for furniture, and thinking about colors and decor.

"I'm not sure I can look at another yellow swatch. I might have reached my limit of yellow."

"Not a problem," she said, her voice holding a note of teasing. "This one isn't yellow. It's lemon sorbet."

He groaned, then chuckled and fell backward to lie across the width of her bed. "Just come and sit for a few minutes and give me a break."

"Would you rather look at the seven swatches of various whites for the trims?" she said, but she came over anyway and lay down beside him.

As he stared up at the ceiling, he felt her hand sneak into his, and he squeezed it tight. And though he never would have predicted it a few months ago, there was nowhere he'd rather be than lying side by side with this woman, talking about setting up the nursery and holding hands. It was scary how much he simply wanted to be near her.

"How do you think us dating is working out?" he asked mildly.

Two days ago he'd thought he might have blown it by not staying the night when she'd invited him. Thankfully, she'd been fine the next morning, acting as if nothing had happened, and he'd been beyond relieved. They'd gone out to a movie and dinner last night and talked the whole way home about the movie's plot, so he hoped they were back on solid ground again. But Harper was sometimes hard to read, and he knew he had to check in with her.

"I think we're doing fine," she said.

He rolled his head to the side so he could see her. "You seriously mean that?"

"So much." She leaned in to him and brushed her lips over his. His eyes drifted closed to savor the feeling. Harper had been so adamant about not adding intimacy into their arrangement that he wouldn't push. But then her lips brushed past his again, and he kissed her back.

He still couldn't believe he'd come so close to not having this woman in his life. If he'd gone in to the Tate Armor office at any time in the past two years that Harper had worked there, he would have met her. Instead, they'd met at a masked ball where he hadn't known who she was and she'd thought he was his twin brother.

That very first time he'd laid eyes on her, every thought

in his mind had fled. All he could see, all he could register, was her. She'd worn a gold mask that she held in front of her face by a long stick that served as a handle. She'd lowered it for maybe a minute while she ate a canapé. No one else was watching, but Nick was. She wasn't just beautiful; there had been something else that called to him. Something he couldn't name but that was soul-deep and unable to be denied.

And she'd been watching him. The realization at the time had damn near stalled his heart.

"Do you remember when we met?" he asked, running a lazy hand up and down her arm.

She snuggled closer into him. "I'll never forget that moment."

He wanted to believe it but refused to let fantasy get tangled up with their real story—not when their real story was already enough—so he had to call her on it. "You thought I was Malcolm."

"My mind thought you were Malcolm. But the rest of me thought you were…"

"Yes?" he whispered in her ear, then sucked the lobe into his mouth.

"Mine," she said on a sigh.

She reached up to cup the side of his face, the motion making her top ride up. His fingers found the exposed stretch of skin along her side, across her stomach.

His eyes drifted closed again. He was lost in the feel of her under his hands now and the memory of her then. "You were wearing a glittering gold mask at first."

"And you had a black mask that covered half your face," she said, her breath coming a little faster and her hands slipping under his shirt.

He had a brief thought about their agreement not to bring lovemaking into their marriage, but surely they were past that by now? And Harper didn't seem to be slowing down. They'd agreed that their dating would be a trial, so he decided to give in and let what had been building between them play out this once.

Needing more, always needing more, he pulled her top higher, then, as she raised her arms, lifted it over her head before quickly dispensing with his own shirt. He settled back, satisfied his hands now had a wider range of skin to explore.

"I love it when you do that," she said, turning over to face him, then kissing him lightly, her lips brushing over his, teasing, luring.

"I aim to please," he murmured. He stretched out on the bed and adjusted her so she was lying along his body, gravity ensuring their skin-to-skin contact was firm, just the way he liked it. "You wore a dress the color of autumn leaves."

She arched an eyebrow. "A dress you had off me in less than an hour from first sight."

"Which was no disrespect to the dress," he said as he unhooked her bra and threw it over the edge of the bed. "I dreamed about that dress every night until I found you again."

And that would have been a whole lot sooner if she hadn't run before he could get her number. The day he'd discovered she was pregnant and they'd reconnected, she'd admitted that she'd freaked out that first night, thinking she'd just slept with her boss. It was understandable, but still a shame that they'd lost those months.

A smile slowly spread across her face, even as she pushed his trousers and boxers down his legs. "You dreamed about me?"

"Oh, yeah." They had been most excellent dreams—almost enough to make him not hate falling asleep at night.

He stroked his hands down her bare back, still marveling that he didn't need those dreams anymore. She was here with him. Touching him with as much urgency as he touched her. "And you weren't just in my dreams," he continued. "Thoughts of you filled most of my waking moments as well." He unsnapped the clip at the back of her skirt and tugged it, then her underpants, away, leaving all her glorious skin available to his roaming hands.

"Tell me," she said as she kissed a trail along his collarbone.

When her tongue flicked out and joined her lips on their mission, he had to pause and find his breath before he could reply. "When I was jogging, I could hear the sounds you made." She lightly bit his shoulder, and his breath became jagged.

"Tell me more," she said, moving down his chest.

"Whenever I closed my eyes, I could see your eyes, and the way they burned with wanting." He speared his fingers through her hair as she kissed his abdomen. "When I stood under the shower spray, I could feel the smoothness of your skin."

"Keep going," she said, but then her teeth grazed across his abdomen and he stopped being able to talk at all.

Deciding to even things up a little, he rolled so she lay beneath him. She gasped, and he grinned. Surprising Harper was one of his favorite things to do. Then, supporting himself on one arm, he snaked a hand down to the juncture of her thighs, moving in rhythm until she whimpered—another of his favorite things to do.

"Now you tell me," he practically growled. "Did you think about me?"

Finding his gaze, she nodded. The emotion in her warm brown eyes melted something inside him, and he slowed his hand.

"I was confused," she said, "because I'd see Malcolm at work and not feel anything, but when I was home, in those moments between sleeping and waking, where my mind wasn't in control…it was you." He saw her throat work as she swallowed. "Everything was you."

Beyond words now, he leaned in and kissed her, less gently this time, and she matched him move for move. Her skin was awash with heat, almost singeing his fingers, and he couldn't get enough. He was addicted to her.

"Hold that thought," he said, reluctantly summoning the willpower to tear himself away, and took off at a run for his own room, returning seconds later with a foil packet. Once he lay back beside her, she took the condom from him and sheathed him with efficient movements. His heart kicked into a higher gear.

He entered her in one fluid motion, finding himself home again, unable to stop the groan of pleasure that came from deep within him. She whispered his name, then again, and it was like a vow, a promise, and he whispered her name back, sealing the vow between them. As he moved inside her, he gave himself over to her. Surrendered himself. To Harper. She enveloped him, besieged him, possessed him.

She gripped his shoulders, and the bite of her nails in his flesh made everything more real. It was too much, not enough, too much, then her release took him further, wanting, reaching, then imploding into electric light, floating, happy. With her.

Snuggled together on the bed minutes—or hours—later, she stirred, and he found the energy to rearrange their bodies so she was tucked into his side.

"Nick," she whispered against his skin. Then she lifted herself onto an elbow and met his gaze. "Stay with me tonight."

"Don't ask me that," he said, his voice gruff.

"Please?" she added softly.

His heart tore in two. Denying her two nights ago had been hard. After what they'd just shared, denying her was close to impossible.

The memory of the horror on her face when she'd witnessed his nightmare still haunted him, and it rose again now, chilling the blood in his veins. What kind of monster would subject anyone, let alone the woman pregnant with his babies, to that kind of torture? He leaned away and prayed for strength. Spending the night in her bed was out of the question. He wouldn't let her go through that experience again.

The problem was, if he couldn't stay, and he couldn't walk away—what other option was there?

"Please, Nick," she whispered and laid her hand flat over his heart. "Stay with me tonight."

Maybe it was because it wasn't the first time she'd asked, or maybe it was the way she'd said "please," like all she wanted in the world was him, but he couldn't hold out against her another second. He nodded, and twenty minutes later when they were finally ready for bed, he grabbed the edge of the sheet and slid down beside her, his legs rubbing against hers as he got comfortable.

She sighed as he wrapped an arm around her waist and snuggled her back into his chest a little more. Carefully, he dropped a kiss in the place where her neck sloped into her shoulder, the scent of her warm skin filling his head, wrapping around him, luring him into never letting her go.

But she was pregnant and needed solid sleep, and she wouldn't get that if he slept, too.

Only one of them could sleep. And no way in hell would he let her be the one to miss out.

Her breathing changed into a soft, steady rhythm, and despite his own sleepiness, he called on all his SEAL training, every ounce of self-discipline he had, and refused to give in to the pull of slumber.

And, as the dark of night eventually gave way to the early morning light, he realized something: holding her all night while she slept might be difficult, but it was also a blessing. He was damn lucky to have an angel like Harper in his life, no matter the complications, and he'd never let himself forget that.

Harper checked on the tray of cupcakes in the oven and began a batch of pink icing. Nick would be back soon with Ellie for their day together, and she wanted freshly baked treats to greet her. This time she'd be ready, unlike when they'd first met two weeks ago. Sure, it was practically bribery to make the little girl like her, but Harper didn't mind—if a judge asked Ellie if she liked spending time at her father's house, she wanted Ellie to have no hesitation.

Since Nick had started sharing Harper's bed at night, they'd become closer. And their lovemaking had only gotten better, too—her hormones were going crazy, and carrying twins, she had double the amount swimming through her bloodstream.

Even Frank seemed to be improving with Nick's love. He was more interested in food and had begun to relax when they gave him affection. He still hadn't made the step of approaching them for attention, but he was making progress, and that's what counted.

The sound of the garage door opening floated through the house just as she pulled the cupcakes from the oven, and a few minutes later Nick emerged from the internal stairs with Ellie on his hip, one hand over her eyes.

He threw Harper a smile before saying to his daughter, "Are you ready for your surprise?"

"Yes!" she yelled, pumping her little arms in the air.

Staying a safe distance from Frank, who was lying on his soft bed, but still keeping the dog in his line of vision, Nick took his hands away from Ellie's face. She blinked, looked around, then her gaze landed on Frank. She stilled, not moving a muscle, then burst into tears and threw her arms around Nick's neck, holding him in a death grip with her face buried in the crook of his shoulder.

Alarmed, Harper moved closer. Was Ellie scared of real life dogs? Should she do something?

"Do you want me to take Frank outside?" she whispered.

Nick looked up from soothing his daughter, but his face was smiling. "Come closer," he said. Harper did, and he added, "Listen."

Ellie was sobbing, but on each exhale were the words, "Thank you, Daddy, thank you."

"She's happy?" Harper asked, confused.

He kissed his daughter's forehead and held her a little tighter. "This is a very happy girl. Just a bit overwhelmed." He smoothed back Ellie's hair and crooned soft words to her.

Harper's eyes misted over—partly in reaction to Ellie's joy and partly from watching a father's love in action. She couldn't take her eyes off her husband—the scene was too beautiful.

It was a good five minutes before Ellie had calmed enough to actually meet the dog. Nick explained to her that Frank had been sad, so she had to be quiet and gentle with him, and Ellie took that advice to heart, practically becoming Frank's nursemaid. Nick supervised, and

Harper retreated to the kitchen to ice the cupcakes and watch the father-daughter bonding time.

The morning was going even better than she'd hoped. Fingers crossed, the rest of her plan for the day would be as much of a hit.

After a while, Nick brought Ellie into the kitchen.

"Do you like Frank?" he asked.

Her face was earnest. "I love him, Daddy."

"Do you want to know whose idea it was to bring Frank into the family?"

Ellie nodded her head solemnly.

"Harper's." Ellie turned wide eyes on Harper, and Nick continued. "She called the Royal Safe Haven Animal Shelter and asked about all the dogs, and when she heard about Frank, she thought he'd be perfect for us. So she came home to get me and we went to meet him. We both loved him right away, so we brought him home."

Ellie grabbed Harper's hand. "Thank you, Harper. Frank is the best dog in the *world*."

Emotion thickened her throat, and she had to swallow hard before she could reply. "I'm glad you like him."

Then Ellie's eyes landed on the iced pink cupcakes on the counter and widened more. "Who are they for?"

"They're for all of us," Harper said. "I was thinking we might want to have a tea party today. What do you say?"

"Yes! Can Frank have one, too?"

"Dogs shouldn't eat pink cupcakes, but we have some other treats here that Frank will like even better."

"I will give it to him," Ellie said as if that settled the matter, and Harper smiled at Nick.

"Absolutely, you can," Nick said.

Once they were set for their tea party—all sitting cross-legged on a picnic blanket on the living room floor, Frank sprawled between Nick and Ellie, a cupcake on each plate—Harper brought out a bag she'd left on the coffee table.

"We bought you something," she said as she handed the bag to Ellie.

Ellie drew in a quick breath. "A present?"

More of a way of explaining the news to her through a picture book, but it probably counted as a present, too, so she nodded and said, "Yes, it is."

The little girl pulled the book from the bag, ran a hand over the shiny cover and passed it to Nick. "Can you read it to me?"

"Sure." He held out his arms, and Ellie scrambled into his lap. As she snuggled into his embrace, Nick began to read the story of a little girl who gets a baby brother. Ellie watched the illustrations on each page, enthralled. When he finished, Nick said, "We have some news for you."

Ellie looked up expectantly into her father's face. "Am I getting a baby brother?"

Nick chuckled. "Actually, you're getting *two* baby brothers or sisters. We just don't know if they're boys or girls yet."

"Really and truly?" Ellie asked, seeming close to tears again.

"Really and truly," Nick said solemnly.

She threw her arms around his neck. "Thank you, Daddy!"

Harper sighed happily as she watched them. Ellie was having a pretty good day, between the babies, Frank and the pink cupcakes, and there was something so very satisfying about being part of the team that made a little girl so happy.

When Ellie released her father, she looked over at Harper and said, "Can I keep it?"

"Of course you can, honey, it's yours." Harper settled back against the sofa and laced her fingers over her stomach. Maybe she was starting to get the hang of this stepparenting thing.

Ellie picked up the book from Nick's lap and put it on her own outstretched legs, stroking her hands over the shiny cover. "I love new books."

"I do, too," Nick said. "Harper bought me a new book, too."

Still playing with the cover, she turned curious eyes to him. "What's yours about?"

"It's about a policeman who looks for clues," Nick said.

Ellie nodded as if that was just the right plot for one of her daddy's books. "Does the policeman get a new baby at the end, too?"

"No, at the end of mine, the policeman solves the case then gets a new job."

Harper's breath caught. *He knew the ending?* She'd bought both books yesterday, and Nick had only started his when they went to bed last night. The book wasn't short. If he'd finished the entire thing, he must not have slept a wink…

Nausea that had nothing to do with the pregnancy rolled through her stomach. He'd agreed to sleep with her at night, but it appeared no actual sleeping was happening for him. She thought back—she was always the first to fall asleep, and he was already awake when she woke in the mornings.

He'd been lying to her.

They were in the middle of a crazy situation, a marriage of convenience to achieve several goals—but at the core, she'd thought at least they could depend on each other. That they were open and honest with each other.

Their marriage might be a practical arrangement, but

that only made it worse—you don't go into business with someone you know you can't trust.

"Daddy?" Ellie said as she jumped up. "Can I give Frank my teddy?"

"I'm sure he'd like that, sweetheart. Which one will you give him?"

"Can Harper help me choose?"

Harper glanced over. This overture from Ellie was exactly what she'd been hoping for—Nick's daughter had accepted her enough to want her help with something special. And yet, she couldn't feel the joy the way she'd hoped. Not when she was starting to question everything.

Ignoring the confusion buzzing through her brain, she found a smile for the little girl. All she could do was compartmentalize the thoughts about her marriage, focus on Ellie and talk to Nick once they were alone.

So she helped Ellie choose a teddy for Frank from the collection in the room she had at Nick's house—"A brown one like him, so he will know it is his"—and then walked back out to the living room with the little girl.

Nick had cleared away the plates and assorted clutter from the tea party and was back on the blanket, sitting beside his dog.

Ellie carefully sat beside Frank and placed the teddy on his front paws. "This is for you," she said.

Frank sniffed it over, nudged it a little with his snout, then laid his head on it. Harper suspected he wanted to lay his head on his paws anyway and the teddy just happened to be there, but, either way, Ellie was thrilled.

"He likes it!" she said. "Good boy, Frank."

For the rest of the day, as they played with Ellie and had a barbecue lunch, Harper felt like she was simply going through the motions. Nick had said he'd sleep in her bed, but he'd been staying awake all night. He'd purposefully hidden what he was doing, lied about it. It was vital that she understand the reality of Nick's condition, partly because she could be called on to make a statement to the court in Ellie's custody hearing. She was a lawyer and would already be lying to a court of law—that was bad enough. To be caught in that lie because her partner in crime had withheld information from her? That would be bad for all of them.

More importantly, she was bringing two precious babies into the world with this man—she had to be certain she knew how he was handling his condition, and that he'd tell her of any changes, so she could mitigate any issues for the babies and for Ellie. Sure, she knew he would plan around any sleepovers Ellie might have in the future so she wasn't affected by his nightmares, but Harper would be irresponsible not to wonder if there was anything else he wasn't telling her…

How could their arrangement survive if she couldn't be sure what was truth and what was lie?

# Ten

Nick arrived back from dropping Ellie at Melissa's house feeling like crap. It was getting harder and harder to let his daughter go—one day with her every two weeks wasn't nearly enough time. The only thing that made it close to bearable was knowing Harper was waiting at home.

But when he walked into the living room, emotionally wiped out, he found her sitting on the edge of the sofa, strangely alert. And she wasn't happy—there was an air of tension radiating from her.

"Everything okay?" he asked warily as he dropped his keys and wallet on a side table.

"We need to talk." Her voice was clipped and precise.

Nick winced. It was worse than he'd thought. He headed for the sofa and sat across from her, needing the angle to see her expressions—he hadn't seen Harper angry before, so he didn't want to be flying any more blind than he already was.

He paused to take a breath, then plunged headlong into whatever was waiting for him. "Have I done something you're not happy about?"

She crossed her legs, and the foot hanging in the air bobbed to a silent beat. "You could say that."

*Hell.* He squared his shoulders. "Tell me."

"The question is whether you were going to tell me," she said, her cheeks flushed pink.

Pulse racing now, he scanned through everything that had happened since breakfast. They'd definitely been happy together then—Harper had kissed him as he left and made all sorts of promises about tonight. He'd ducked out to pick up Ellie, introduced her to Frank, and Ellie had thanked Harper for getting the dog. Harper had seemed really affected by the moment, so things were still good then. After that they'd had a picnic on the blanket, told Ellie about the babies, then had a barbecue. In fact, they'd both been with Ellie all day—there hadn't been much chance to do or say anything controversial, so he was at a loss.

"You'll have to give me a hint," he admitted.

She reached behind her to a long table that ran along the back of the sofa that had photos and other paraphernalia on it. She grabbed the murder mystery he'd been reading—and which he'd left beside the bed—and held it up. "When did you read this?"

His stomach dropped as it all clicked into place. "Last night."

"The entire book?" she asked calmly, but her eyes were steady in their focus. "In one night?"

"Yeah," he said and blew out a breath.

She tossed the book onto the cushions beside her. "Have you slept at all since you started sharing my bed?"

He shook his head and admitted the truth. "I normally

catch a nap in the morning before I start work. I don't need a lot of sleep."

She crossed her arms under her breasts. "You've been lying to me."

The accusation was like a slap to the face, even though it was true. He *had* been lying to her—lying by omission—and it had felt wrong every time he hadn't told her. But he'd chosen the lesser of two evils, and he still thought it had been the right call for them. Convincing Harper of that would be another matter, though.

"I'm sorry I haven't been honest about when I sleep, but you have to see that it's the best option for us."

"How?" she asked. "Explain that to me."

"Harper," he said gently, "I saw your face when you witnessed me having a nightmare. It's burned into my memory banks—there's no way you can pretend it didn't scare you."

"Yes, it did scare me. Of course it did—I had to try to make sense of your anguish and agitation while I was half-asleep. I had no warning, so it was a shock. Now that I know, I'll be prepared if it happens again."

"You need your sleep while you're pregnant and working full-time. Being woken each night because of my nightmares is not good." He scrubbed his hands through his hair. "Look, I can see why you're upset—I'm just not the man I used to be. I can't do all the things I used to."

"No," she said, her voice low. "I'm upset about the lie. We're in the middle of this intense situation together—we married to protect your custody of your daughter from your ex-wife and her fiancé. To protect our babies' relationship with both their parents. To protect Tate Armor from Maverick. All while you're dealing with the aftereffects of fighting a war on the other side of the world. Plus we can't tell anyone about our marriage arrangement except Malcolm, just in case Melissa finds out. In the midst of this, all we have is each other."

"You're right," he said. "We do have each other."

"The thing is, we never had a bond of love to hold us together. This was always a partnership between two people who have mutual goals, and any feelings and intimacy that developed were a bonus."

He cocked his head to the side. "We're in agreement about all of this."

"All right, then. Here's my point. What we have is a shared situation, as well as respect and trust. And if you take out the trust, you undermine the agreement that everything else was built on."

It suddenly all clicked into place. "Okay, I get it." Being completely open with the mess that was in his head wasn't second nature to him, and it wasn't an appealing thought, either. But he'd committed to this marriage, and he had a lot to lose, starting with relationships with his three children. He needed to step up his game. "I'll keep you in the loop with what's going on for me. And if I slip up, just ask. I promise I'll do my best to explain."

"Thank you." The word was whispered so softly, he barely heard it. "And I promise not to pressure you to give more than you feel you can. If you want to go back to sleeping in your own room, that's okay with me. And the alternative is okay, too—staying the night with me, risking that you'll have a nightmare and trusting that I'll be able to handle it."

The fear rose up and threatened to overwhelm him, but he wanted to do this. Wanted to try. Could he? Dare he?

He moved over to her sofa and sat beside her. Then he stepped over the edge of the cliff. "If you really mean it, I'm willing to try actually sleeping with you."

She wrapped her arms around his waist and leaned her head on his shoulder. "I really mean it."

He pulled her tighter and hoped like hell that he hadn't just made the biggest mistake of his life.

It was a few hours later, when they'd had dinner and were ready for bed, that Nick found himself in Harper's room, wanting desperately to climb under the covers with her but still not sure if he could risk it.

Causing Harper pain or distress went against everything he believed in, and yet, he'd already agreed to stay the night with her. And actually sleep. Breaking his word also went against everything he believed in...

She stroked a hand over the sheet and smiled at him. "Come on in, the water's fine."

At war with itself, he took a step, then another until he reached her. "Are you sure?"

"Nick," she said, her gaze steady, "you need to trust me. And trust in my capacity to cope."

Still torn, he sat on the edge of the bed. "It's not that I don't trust you."

Her expression changed, and he saw glimmers of the courtroom lawyer. "When you were in the military, you were part of a team. Everyone had a job to do, and you had to trust one another to do your jobs, right?"

"Right," he said, warily.

"This is the same. You need to let me play my part." She pulled his shoulder until he lay down beside her. "Promise you'll trust me and you'll go to sleep?"

He knew, without a shadow of a doubt, that this was a turning point in their relationship—tonight could bring them closer or push them apart.

He let out a long, controlled breath. Whatever the outcome, he'd made the decision earlier when he'd agreed to sleep with her, so it was time to step up to the plate and put his words into action.

He wrapped an arm around her waist. "I promise."

"Thank you," she whispered and snuggled her back into his chest.

He pulled her closer, adjusted the pillow under his head and let his eyes drift shut. After a few minutes of listening to Harper breathe and trying to relax himself to sleep, the world began to fade.

*A flash of light amid the dirty dark of night... Ground shaking, walls shaking... Diving for cover... Screaming from all directions... Another flash... Noise filling the air leaving no room for anything else, not even oxygen... Screams of the dying... Trying to shout orders but smoke stealing his voice... His men. Where were his men? Searching... The stench of vomit and blood... a pile of clothes—no, a man. Gregson. Lifeless... No! Oh, God, no... So sorry... Flames... Shouting... An arm. Moving rubble. Adams. Alive... Dragging to safety, going back in... Flashes and noise... More dead... Screaming... Sorry, so sorry...*

A soft voice floated through the darkness, soothing, telling him he was safe. It was a beautiful voice, one that stirred his soul and drew him away from the horrors still clinging to him. But the darkness wouldn't release its grip that easily, and the place between sleep and wakefulness was the worst...

In dreams, there was still a small hope that he'd find more of his unit alive this time. That he'd save them. He would have thrown himself between his team and danger to protect them, no question. But each time present-day reality intruded, he'd remember all over again that he hadn't saved them. And there was nothing he could do to fix it now. Adrenaline pumped through his system, urging him to act. To do something.

The voice was still there, anchoring him. Harper's voice. And another sound. Soft whining from his other side.

Heart thudding against his ribs, he pried his eyes open to see Harper filling his vision, her achingly beautiful face surrounded by a soft halo of light.

"Hey," she said gently.

He couldn't yet form words, and he didn't know what he'd say anyway, but he did know she was the only person he wanted to see right now. The only one who could make the darkness inside seem a little more bearable. Though, even as his arms wanted to reach for her, he locked his muscles tight to stop them. Dragging her further into his darkness would be selfish.

More than that, he didn't deserve the comfort. The nightmares were a fair penalty—reliving the horrors was the least he deserved. After all, some very fine people hadn't made it through to be *able* to remember it.

This was his penance.

His father had told him to stay strong. Good advice. No matter what was in his memory banks, he should be able to handle it. He drew another shuddering breath and clenched his hands to stop them shaking. He had to be honest with himself—he was clearly *not* handling it. Worse, Harper could see his failure. She was bearing witness to his shame.

Something wriggled on his other side, and he became aware again of the soft whining in the background. He turned to find Frank on the bed, stretched out alongside him, burying his face in Nick's side.

"I didn't invite him," Harper said. "When I woke up

and realized you were having a nightmare, Frank was already here, leaning in to you, making those noises."

Nick put an arm around Frank, and his dog settled against him, feeling solid and reassuring. The presence gave more comfort than he would have expected. There were treats in that dog's immediate future. Just as soon as Nick mastered basic things like breathing and moving again.

He began to silently count his breaths, a technique he used to calm his body and slow his pulse, relying on the steady strength of both Harper and Frank to help. Three breaths in, Harper lay down and wrapped her arms around him, holding him. It was more than he deserved. She was always more than he deserved, more than he should accept, but, God help him, he couldn't bring himself to push her away. Pathetic as he was, he wrapped his arms around her and took the comfort she offered, grateful she at least hadn't been horrified this time.

As Harper watched her husband beside her, she was determined not to let the tears pressing at the back of her eyes form. He wouldn't want them. Instead, she lay quietly, letting him deal with whatever was in his mind at his own pace, trying to be a calm presence.

Calm was a big ask when she was torn between despair at seeing him in pain and hope because he hadn't shut her out this time. She rubbed his tense shoulders and settled for calmish.

After long minutes, he pulled himself up, but still he didn't push her away—he sat on the edge of the bed, his elbows resting on his knees, his head hanging low, as if he was still trying to regain his breath. She swung her legs around to sit beside him, laying a hand gently on his back so he knew he wasn't alone.

Without looking at her, he reached out and snagged her other hand, bringing it to rest on his thigh, their fingers tightly entwined. Her heart stopped dead at the meaning in the simple gesture, then roared back to life, flooding her body with emotion. By reaching for her instead of pushing her away, Nick had let her though a major barrier.

"Thank you for trusting me," she whispered. "For sharing the parts of you that I know you'd rather keep hidden."

He didn't look at her, barely moved beyond his chest rising and falling more roughly than it should. "I'm still not feeling great about dragging you into this mess."

He might not feel great about it, but she was happy to be dragged anywhere with him. It was being left behind that hurt.

She stood and drew him to his feet. "Together, we can face this."

"I'm starting to believe we can face anything together."

"I think you're right."

Pulling gently on his hand, she led him into the attached bathroom, and once they stepped past the door, she lifted onto her toes and kissed him. He returned the kiss—not one of passion, but sweetness, trust, bearing witness to the depth of their relationship. Tears stung at the backs of her eyes, but she didn't realize one had fallen until he wiped it from her cheek with his thumb.

Wordlessly, she stepped back and turned the shower on, testing it with her hand as the water warmed to the perfect temperature. Then, their fingers again entwined, she stepped in, tugging his hand to bring him in after her. One corner of his mouth lifted in a shadow of a smile, and he followed. Her pulse kicked up a notch. She released his hand and placed her palms on his chest, gently pushing him under the spray.

As she soaped him up, she allowed herself the luxury

of admiring his body, loving the ridges and hollows, the scars as well as the smooth perfection. And he allowed her—turning when she nudged him, letting her take the lead.

"No need to think," she said. "Just feel."

His shoulders relaxed a fraction more as he gave himself over to her. His body followed her movements as if they were in a dance, his breaths becoming fast and shallow, matching hers.

She wanted to give him this—the mindlessness of his body's reaction, all traces of the images that had haunted him banished under the weight of desire. So she touched him the way she'd learned he liked to be touched, lightly feathering her fingertips over his abdomen, kissing along his collarbone, scraping her nails over his back.

"Harper," he rasped against her throat. Her skin felt too tight for her body, and his hands roaming only made her restless for more.

With a hand under one of her knees, he picked her leg up and brought it around his waist, then gripped her hips and lifted her. She leaned her weight against the cool tiles at her back and wrapped her other leg around him.

As the shower spray fell against her skin, Nick thrust forward, filling her, moving in a rhythm that quickly took her to the brink, then higher, building, higher, past the point she could contain it anymore, until she was bursting, flying free, and even before she could land, she felt him follow her, shouting her name. And in that moment, she felt more connected to him than she had to any other person, and she could believe that nothing would ever tear them apart.

Once she regained her breath, she lowered one leg to find the shower floor again—even slumped against her, he'd still been holding her weight. He released her, placed a tender kiss on her lips, then ducked his head under the water. This time he soaped up his hands and washed her, then when they were done, he dried her off and wrapped her in a thick towel.

"Thank you," he said, his gaze holding hers. She didn't pretend to misunderstand. He wasn't thanking her for what she'd done with her body—it was more than that. He was thanking her for looking after him. For caring. For accepting him.

"We're in this together," she said. "We're a team."

He swallowed hard and nodded before gathering her against him and holding tight.

# Eleven

Harper arrived at Natalie Valentine's bridal store at the Courtyard Shops five minutes late for their lunch date with Sophie Prescott.

Natalie met her at the door, her shoulder-length red hair swept up in a messy ponytail, and handed her a glass of champagne.

"Sorry I'm a little late," Harper said as she slipped inside.

"Don't worry." Natalie smiled. "I'm running even more behind than that. The champagne is to make up for it. It's nonalcoholic for you and Sophie."

Harper tasted the cool drink. "Random glasses of champagne make up for just about anything."

"Come on, Sophie's already over here. I'm doing a fitting for Chelsea Hunt's bridesmaid's dress, and she said she doesn't mind if you two are here while I finish up."

Natalie showed her over to a set of sofas where Sophie—her own glass of champagne in hand—was already sitting with a gorgeous woman with glossy honey-brown hair around her shoulders. Harper had never spoken to Chelsea before, but she'd heard nice things from other people, so she was pleased to have the chance to meet her.

"Harper, this is Chelsea. She's Brandee Lawless's maid of honor, and I just need to make a couple of quick alterations to her dress before we can go." She turned to the other woman. "Chelsea, this is Harper Lake. She's an attorney over at Tate Armor."

"Nice to meet you, Harper," Chelsea said, holding out her hand. "Tate Armor. Isn't that Malcolm Tate's company? That man is seriously gorgeous."

Caught off guard, Harper felt heat creep up her neck to her cheeks as she shook the other woman's hand. Though it wasn't Malcolm she was thinking about.

"Oh, I'm sorry," Chelsea said, her gaze roaming over Harper's face. "Did I put my foot in my mouth? Is there something between you and Malcolm?"

"Not Malcolm," Sophie said. "His identical twin brother, Nick. Who one assumes must be just as seriously gorgeous."

*Just as seriously gorgeous.* Harper almost laughed. How did she explain that the two men were identical, yet looked nothing alike? One was easy on the eyes. The other made her burn with want and fire and need and *love*…

She stilled. As soon as the word formed in her mind, she knew it was true. Hard to believe she'd fallen in love so quickly, but there was no other way to describe the intensity of her feelings for him. The way her heart skipped a beat whenever she saw Nick or heard his voice. Or even thought about him.

The other women were still looking at her, waiting for

her to confirm that Nick was as gorgeous as Malcolm. She gave a quick nod and slipped into a seat on the sofa.

Natalie took a step back. "Can you just excuse me a minute? I need to check a couple of things on the dress."

Sophie raised an eyebrow. "We don't get to see it?"

"Not until the wedding, along with everyone else," Natalie said with a smile, then disappeared into another room.

"So, the last time we were together, there was lots of juicy gossip," Sophie said good-naturedly. "I'm hoping for at least as much today."

Chelsea glanced up. "Juicy gossip? You can't say something like that then not explain."

"Well," Sophie said, grinning, "the juiciest of all was that Harper here got married since we'd last seen her less than a couple of weeks before."

Chelsea's eyes widened. "To Nick Tate?"

"Yes," Sophie confided. "And they're expecting twins."

"Okay, that *is* juicy." She turned to Harper. "I'm impressed—you make good gossip."

Chuckling, Harper raised her glass to her, said, "Thanks," and sipped the amber liquid, hoping the conversation would flow in another direction. She was in no state to chat coherently. After all, she'd only just realized she was in love with her husband.

"Now, Chelsea," Sophie said, "your turn. What have you got that will go well with this glass of bubbles?"

"Okay, there is something." She took a mouthful of her champagne, then grinned.

Harper grinned back, feeling a little light-headed. The drink was nonalcoholic, so it had to be from her realization about Nick, but she liked Chelsea already, so she was happy to share her good mood. "Anything you say won't go any further," she said and touched a finger to her lips. "Our lips are sealed."

"Well—" Chelsea glanced around, clearly trying not to smile "—I've been seeing a fair bit of Gabe Walsh since we've been doing the best man–maid of honor duties for the wedding."

"Gabe is another man who's seriously gorgeous," Natalie said, poking her head around the door from the other room.

Chelsea bit down on her lip and seemed to lose herself for a moment before continuing. "We were out at Brandee's Hope Springs Ranch the other day, doing a few things for the wedding, and there was…how about we say there was a little extracurricular activity."

"Did you kiss him?" Sophie asked, her eyebrows raised in happy surprise.

"I will say this," Chelsea said with a dreamy look in her eyes. "That man has a mouth made for kissing."

There were several happy sighs around the group seeing the expression on Chelsea's face, then conversation moved on for a few minutes until Natalie refilled their glasses and said, "So, any news of Maverick? I haven't heard anything lately."

"Still seems to be quiet," Sophie said with a shrug.

Chelsea glanced around. "Actually, I have something to confess on that front."

"You figured out who he is?" Sophie asked, her eyes wide.

Chelsea shook her head. "The next best thing. I called an old friend, Max St. Cloud, to come help with the investigation."

"What could this Max do that the town's not already doing?" Natalie asked as she came out and took a measurement of Chelsea's shoulders before disappearing again.

"I used to do a bit of hacking when I was younger,

and so did Max, which is how we met. Honestly, he's a genius." Chelsea's smile held a small flicker of pride in her friend.

"Actually," Harper said, thinking the case through, "he could really help. Since Maverick has been stalking and threatening people through email and on social media and he's obviously stolen files to use as blackmail, an ex-hacker on the team is a great idea."

"Any new tactics are worth a shot," Sophie said. "Maverick has already caused too much damage."

"Hear, hear," Natalie said coming back out to the main room. "And on that note, I'm done. Chelsea, you're free to go."

"Thank, Natalie," Chelsea said, reaching for her bag. "I can't wait to see the finished dress."

Sophie stood. "Chelsea, you're more than welcome to join us for lunch if you'd like."

"That's so sweet of you, but I have a couple of other maid of honor duties to take care of, so I'll take a rain check. See you all later!"

As Chelsea swept through the door, Harper turned to look at her friends and had a moment of blissful satisfaction. Everything in her life was going so well. She had a wider circle of friends than she'd ever had, her pregnancy was progressing nicely, things with Ellie were going great and her marriage with Nick had never been better. In fact, she was in love with him. Which was more than she'd dreamed possible for their fledgling relationship. It was as if the pieces of her life were all falling into their slots, and a sense of bone-deep contentment and happiness settled over her.

The only thing that could make her life even better was to share her feelings with Nick. Now she just needed to find the perfect way to tell him.

* * *

Nick stood as his ex-wife joined him at a corner booth in the Royal Diner. Now that things were going so well with Harper and he could see them making a family with the babies, he'd decided it was time to do something about Ellie's custody situation, too. He'd asked Melissa to meet him—just the two parents, on their own, looking out for their kid's best interests. He'd mentioned the idea to Harper for a lawyer's take, and she'd said it made a lot of sense. What surprised him was that Melissa had agreed to it.

Not knowing how to greet her, he stuck his hand out. This was new territory for them. In the past, they'd dated and been newlyweds, expectant parents, spouses in a crumbling marriage, then exes at war. What were they to each other now? Only time would tell.

Melissa looked at his outstretched hand, then reluctantly took it for a few seconds before dropping it.

"Thanks for coming," he said as they took their seats.

She gave him a steely glare that carried a note of warning. "I almost didn't."

He understood that, and she'd never been one to hold back, so her honesty was a good sign. "What changed your mind?"

She shrugged. "First and foremost, I want what's best for Ellie. It's what I've always wanted."

"I appreciate you giving this a shot." A trace of optimism started to stir in his chest. Maybe they could work out some sort of agreement and he'd be able to be a proper father to all three of his children.

A waitress came, and they ordered drinks. When she'd left, Melissa speared him with a glance and said, "Okay, let's cut to the chase. What do you want?"

"More time with Ellie. To be a bigger part of her life."

She dismissed that with a flick of her wrist. "That's what the lawyers are for—to work out those arrangements."

"Come on, Melissa," he said. "We're the two people who care most about her. We're her parents. We should be able to work it out between ourselves."

"And you honestly think that would be best for Ellie, given your…"

"PTSD," he supplied. "I've made some solid progress with that." Thanks mainly to Harper and her limitless patience and support.

Their drinks arrived, and Melissa fiddled with the straw in hers for a few moments before excusing herself to go to the bathroom. Nick sat back in the seat. Getting her here had been step one. Step two was telling her what he wanted. Now all that was left was to get her to agree. When she came back, he'd push more and they'd avoid a legal battle.

As soon as she was out of sight, her fiancé strolled over and stood at the table.

"Guy," Nick said, narrowing his eyes. "I didn't know you were coming."

He gave a smarmy, insincere smile. "Look, Melissa is too nice to say it, but we both know what kind of man you are."

"And what kind is that?" he drawled.

"A screwup."

From someone whose opinion mattered, that might be insulting. From this pathetic excuse of a man? Borderline amusing. "And how do you figure that?"

"You're not quite right in the head anymore, are you, Nick?"

He barely held back a sigh. "I have PTSD, if that's what you mean."

"And that's not all."

"I think it's time you left," he said, trying to keep his tone even despite his growing annoyance.

Guy reached into his jacket pocket and withdrew a handful of tablets and laid them on the table in front of him. Nick recognized them immediately—over-the-counter and prescription pills. All painkillers. For several seconds he couldn't breathe. All he could see was the pills. He hadn't seen that many together since he'd beaten his addiction to painkillers after his last mission. And here they were, inches from his hand, their siren's song calling him.

Then Guy whipped out his phone camera. "I think our friend Maverick could do some real damage with this photo—"

There was movement to his left followed by Melissa's voice. "Guy, I didn't know you were back." Then she noticed the pills. "What the hell, Nick?"

"They're not mine," he said, his voice gravel as he forced his lungs to work. "Guy dumped them here."

"Guy?" she said.

"I'm sorry, baby," her fiancé said, his voice dripping with slime. "We know he's going to relapse at some point and put Ellie at risk. I just thought if we speed it along so it happens before the custody case instead of after, then it would be better for all of us."

"You did this?" Melissa looked appalled. "Guy, this has to stop."

"You know I only want what's best for you and Ellie. And, seriously, Maverick would love something juicy like this. We post it online and he'll find it—he's really good at sniffing a story out."

Nick could hear the argument between his ex and her

fiancé going on, but his gaze was stuck on the pills, and he felt his skin breaking out in a fine sheen of sweat.

"This," she said with a sweep of her arm, "is crossing a line. You'd better leave."

Surprised, Nick looked up at that, to see Guy blink and cast a furtive glance around before focusing back on Melissa. "But, baby, I'm doing this for you."

"Someone who crossed the line for one person will cross it again, and I can't have that around Ellie."

Guy frowned. "Hang on, what are you saying?"

"This is the last straw. It's over, Guy." She took off the sparkly ring on her left hand and held it out to him.

"Over *him*?" Guy asked incredulously.

"No, over you," she said, hands on hips. "Because now that I've seen you pull this stunt, I'll never trust you again."

"Baby girl," he said, but she cut him off.

"You can sleep at a hotel tonight and we'll work out the rest tomorrow."

Clearly stunned, Guy simply stared at her, then visibly regrouped. "Okay, sure. We'll talk about this more tomorrow when everyone is calm again."

Guy kissed her on the cheek and sauntered out. Melissa watched him go then turned back to Nick. "I'm sorry. You and I don't see eye to eye on a lot of things, but you didn't deserve that."

He gave a tight nod, looking at her but keeping the pills in his peripheral vision.

"And you know what?" She blew out a breath. "You're probably right that it's time the two of us sat down and did discuss Ellie's arrangements. Let me deal with Guy first and I'll give you a call in a few days. We'll work something out."

"Sure." Nick kept his poker face in place despite knowing his voice was strained. "That would be good."

Melissa turned and headed out the door, which left Nick alone at the table. With the pills. His hands were trembling with the need to take one. Just one. His heart raced. One couldn't hurt, could it? Just one. He swallowed hard.

Logically, he knew it would never be just one. And that was the problem—he knew that and he still wanted one anyway.

He checked, and no one was watching. The angle of the booths meant that it was hard for others to see unless they were standing right in front of him. Very carefully, he slid the pills closer and filled his trouser pockets with them. Then he pushed to his feet, threw some cash on the table to cover the drinks and a tip, and left.

He made it to his car, and all he could think about was which pill he'd have first.

And where he'd go to take it.

What he'd drink to wash it down.

And how many he could manage in one day.


Harper arrived home with her heart overflowing. The realization that she loved Nick had her practically floating all the way to his house. They'd married for the babies—to fall in love as well was more than she'd dreamed possible. A fairy tale come to life.

When she walked inside, she found Nick sitting on a stool at the kitchen counter, his gaze bleak. Her stomach clenched tight.

"What's happened?" As she neared him, she reached out, but he turned away from her, so she stilled. "Nick?"

He opened his mouth to speak, then closed it again. His Adam's apple bobbed in his throat. Unease prickled across her skin. Something was very wrong. She glanced around, and her gaze landed on a thin stack of papers on the kitchen counter. It was too far away to make out the wording, but she'd seen countless legal documents in her career. Enough to recognize this as one.

She took another step and reached for the papers. Nick held up a hand to block her, then dropped it.

"Harper," he said, his voice raw. "This is not—"

But she'd seen the first lines. These were divorce papers. And their names were typed in black print. The room began a slow spin around her.

"You're divorcing me?" she asked, not quite believing it was possible. Waiting for him to explain how this was part of a grand plan...

"Yes."

The word was plain and stark, and all the air rushed from her lungs. *He was leaving her.* Visions from when she was six years old began to flood her mind—the devastation as the front door closed behind her father, the tears, the desperate heartache—but she pushed it aside. This was different.

This was *Nick*.

It made no sense. They'd been so happy. They'd moved past their biggest hurdle and were now sleeping together through the night. What could possibly have changed for him? He'd kissed her this morning when he'd left to meet... *Melissa*.

Could his ex-wife have sabotaged their marriage?

She swallowed against the lump forming in her throat before she could get her voice to work. "What did Melissa say to you?"

"She was surprisingly reasonable," he said. "Things only went bad when Guy showed up."

Everything inside Harper wanted to demand answers, to push hard against the threat to her marriage, but the small part of her brain that was listening to rational thought knew that wasn't a good idea. She called on all her self-control and calmly said, "What did he say?"

"His usual bluster and crap." To a casual observer, Nick's face would appear expressionless, but she was no casual observer. There was a slight tightening around his jaw; the edge of his lips was pale. "And then he tried to set me up by dumping painkillers on the table in front of me. He wanted to send a photo to Maverick."

Her skin went cold. Blackmail was bad enough, but her first priority was Nick's health. "Where are the pills now?"

"I threw them out," he said, not meeting her eyes. "And Melissa caught Guy in the act, so it failed. It was a clumsy attempt."

"So everything's fine now? The blackmail attempt failed, and you didn't take the pills." Though she was clearly missing a piece of the puzzle, because there were divorce papers on the counter.

"But that's not the point," he said far too calmly for the conversation they were having. "I wanted to take them. Real bad."

She rubbed her fingertips over her temple. "But you didn't."

"You don't understand." He cleared his throat. "It made me face something. This is part of who I am, and it's not healthy to have this hanging over you and the babies. I won't let it affect you."

"Nick, I don't care," she said, finally giving up on trying to stay calm and allowing the desperation to leach into her voice. "Divorce isn't the answer."

"You said that as a SEAL I had to rely on everyone to do their jobs, and that's true, but sometimes as a leader I had to make the hard calls." His spine straightened, and his chin lifted a fraction. "And that's what I'm doing now. Stepping up. Making the hard call to keep everyone safe."

Angry now, she planted her hands on her hips. "Who made you the leader of our marriage? I thought we had a partnership. You don't get to make some sort of a noble sacrifice all on your own."

He didn't flinch from her anger. Didn't move a muscle. "You didn't see me when I was in the throes of the addiction. You and the babies are precious. I won't risk any possibility of that touching you and them."

Nothing seemed real—more like a bad dream or something happening to someone else. Or a practical joke in poor taste. He wasn't making this up—his body language showed no signs of deception. He honestly believed she'd be better off without him, despite this being so much bigger than the two of them.

"What about the babies? They need their father. What are you going to do?"

His eyes squeezed shut for long seconds before he met her gaze again. "They don't need a father like me around. If you need to go back to Connecticut, I understand. We can talk about visitation after they're born."

He pushed to his feet, and for the first time she noticed a bulging duffel bag on his other side. The air in the room seemed thicker as her lungs struggled to draw enough in.

She looked pointedly from the duffel bag back to him. "So you're leaving all three of us?"

"I'm a mess, Harper. You know that." He ran a hand down his face, then dug it into his pocket. "I need some space to decide how best to be a good father to all three kids. I want to get it right, as best I can."

This was all so very wrong. Yet how could she convince him how wrong it was when he'd already convinced himself otherwise?

At Nick's movements, Frank ambled over, probably hoping for a trip in the car.

"What about Frank?" she asked.

He leaned down to rub Frank's ears, and Frank grinned up at him. "He'll be better off here, with you. And the babies will love him."

He picked up the bag and hooked it over his shoulder. Waves of panic washed over her, making her cold.

"You're really going to walk out on me, Nick?" she asked, hardly believing she was saying those words aloud. "This can't be what you want."

"I'm fixing things. I might not like how I'm fixing it, but I can and I will." He crossed to her side, placed a lingering, chaste kiss on her forehead, then stepped back. "I'm freeing you."

Freeing her? She pinched the bridge of her nose. How was this even happening?

He took a step to the door, and she threw up a hand. "Hang on. This is your house. Why are you walking out? If you really want to separate, I'll go back to my place."

"No, stay as long as you need," he said simply. "I can't sit still right now anyway."

This was beyond crazy. "Where will you go?"

"I don't know." His forehead scrunched up, and he rubbed it with his free hand. "I'll stay at Natalie's B&B tonight, and when I decide what I'll do after that, I'll let you know."

He took another step toward the door, and a sob crept up her throat. She only just managed to hold it back. "Nick, don't leave me."

"I'm sorry, Harper. Really sorry." And the look in his eyes said that was true. "I think this is the best thing to do."

He turned and walked through the door. Her husband, the man she loved, the father of her unborn babies, had just left her. Abandoned her. She covered her face with her hands as the sob in her throat finally broke free.

Heart still racing double time, he kicked the sheet off.

"What the hell have I done?" he said to the empty room.

He'd left the best thing that had ever happened to him. Someone who made his life better just by being in it. Someone he wanted so badly he ached with it.

But leaving had never been about what he wanted. What he needed.

Leaving had been about what was best for Harper and the babies. He had to protect her, no matter the cost. And the cost was him.

He'd freed her to find someone who could meet her needs. Someone who wasn't messed up. Someone who wasn't him. A red-hot poker slammed into his chest at the thought.

His father's words came back to him. *"You're the strong one. You have to look after your mother and Malcolm."* If his father had met Harper, he would have included her in that group. And even if he hadn't, *Nick* included her in the group of people he was responsible for.

When you were the responsible one, sometimes you had to make sacrifices for them.

In the dark of an unfamiliar bedroom, snatches of memories and old dreams assailed him, of losing men in his unit. He'd been responsible for them, too, and he'd had to make hard calls for their sake. The familiar weight of grief and failure landed on him, smothering him. But this time, something was different. On the movie screen in his mind where the past had been stuck on a relentless loop, the scenes seemed to reorganize themselves. He'd replayed his options that day over and over in his mind and had never come up with a scenario where all his team survived. He'd always considered his lack of solution even in hindsight another failure. But now it hit him—if he hadn't made the hard call with his unit, more would have died. He'd made the best decision with the information, resources and options he had. Everyone had told him that, but it finally made sense. He finally believed it.

He didn't feel better—members of his unit had still died—but his heart was somehow a little less chaotic.

He said a silent prayer for those who'd been lost that day, and this time, he made a start at letting them go. Not to forget, never that, but to stop tormenting himself. He'd made the only decision possible that day. The price had been unspeakably high, but it was the best he could have done.

Now he needed to do the same with his marriage—hold fast now that he'd made the hard call to minimize casualties. A shudder ripped through him—his body revolting at what his mind knew was right.

If he could be granted one wish in this moment, he'd use it to have their family together. Harper, the babies, Ellie and him. But that would be selfish.

This sacrifice was his price to pay for their happiness, and for their sakes, he'd pay it a thousand times over.

All he had to do was learn how to keep breathing while he paid it.

Harper sat on the sofa in Nick's living room, watching the sun peep over the horizon and gradually reveal its full self. Despite the gorgeous view, her mind was still numb, and even her body felt only half there.

She'd spent the night in this one spot, unable to face the bed she'd shared with Nick now that she was alone, and equally unable to face leaving his home and severing that link to him. She'd checked her cell regularly in case he was trying to contact her, then while she had the cell in her hand, she'd searched the web for the effects of stress on unborn babies. It was another thing to worry about, but at least she was past the first three months, when the effects were worst. She rubbed her belly and tried some of the breathing exercises Nick had told her he used after his nightmares.

Frank had stayed with her and was now lying at the door, his head on his paws, staring forlornly, waiting for Nick to come home.

In the short time since they'd adopted Frank, he'd become devoted to Nick. It shouldn't have been surprising—while Harper had been at work, Nick and Frank had spent their days together. But it was more than that. They'd been helping each other heal.

"Frank," she said, but her voice was hoarse from crying and the word was practically unrecognizable, so she tried again. "Frank."

This time he dragged his furry head up to look at her.

"Come over here, boy." She patted the sofa cushion beside her.

For long moments, his dark eyes simply contemplated her, then he stood, shook his body, ambled over and climbed up on the sofa. Harper lifted her arm so he could rest his head in her lap.

"I know," she said softly. "I miss him, too. But we'll be okay together." She laid a hand over the small mound of her stomach and rubbed Frank's ear with the other. "You, me and the babies. We'll be fine," she said, unsure if that was a lie or not.

Frank snuffled then let out a sigh. She sat with him, sharing comfort, until her tummy rumbled. She didn't feel like eating, but she needed to have something nutritious for her babies. With a final stroke of Frank's soft ear, she pushed to her feet and headed for the kitchen.

Fifteen minutes later, she'd made and drunk a smoothie and Frank had eaten a bowl of kibble.

She'd need to get ready for work soon, but she couldn't find the energy. A sleepless night and a bleak heart combined to steal all of her motivation, so she slumped onto the sofa again.

Frank glanced her way, then turned and trotted off down the hall, only to reappear a minute later, one of Nick's T-shirts in his mouth.

The sight brought tears to her eyes again. "Oh, Frank, come over here."

He and dropped the shirt at her feet. She wrapped her arms around his neck, letting her tears spill onto his fur. "I want him back, too."

The thing about being the one left behind was that as well as the grief about the ending, there was an overwhelming feeling of helplessness. That feeling had lurked inside her after her father had walked out on her and her mother, and it left her feeling paralyzed now.

Frank pulled his head from her grip and curled up on Nick's shirt at her feet. Her heart broke for him—his helplessness in the situation was as bad as hers.

She stilled. *As bad as hers?*

Something about that didn't seem right. *Frank* was powerless in the situation. She wasn't.

Yes, she'd been powerless as a child when her father abandoned her, but she'd worked hard over the years to become a confident person who was in charge of her own life. She drew in a long, shaky breath. She was still in charge of her own life.

Nick had ended their marriage because he'd made a decision about what was best. He was wrong. And she wasn't helpless, having to sit here and accept his view of how things should be.

She wasn't powerless.

It was time to take matters into her own hands and shape her own destiny.

After a quick shower, Harper was ready for action. She called Nick's cell, but it went to voice mail. The next few minutes of waiting to redial were spent trying to ignore the butterflies in her belly, but she got the recorded message again when she tried.

Not to be deterred now that she was taking charge of her own destiny, she called Natalie Valentine. Her friend picked up on the second ring.

"Cimarron Rose B&B, how can I help?"

"Natalie, it's Harper." She tried to sound casual despite her erratic pulse. "Is Nick there?"

"Hi, Harper," Natalie said. "Actually, no. He was here last night, but he left early."

She chewed her bottom lip. "I don't suppose he mentioned where he'd be today?"

"Not a word. He said last night he wouldn't want breakfast this morning then left early, before I was up. To be honest—" she paused, as if not sure how deliver bad news "—I'm not sure if he's coming back. He paid up front for one night."

Harper's heart missed a beat, but she sucked in a breath and steadied herself. He'd said he'd stay at the B&B until he made a plan, so maybe he'd spoken to Malcolm or his mother and decided to stay with them for a while. She straightened her shoulders. It might take a little longer than she'd hoped, but she'd find him. "Okay, thanks."

"Sorry I couldn't be more helpful," Natalie said, and Harper could imagine her friend's brows pinching together in concern.

"No, that's useful." She was already narrowing down the places he could be.

"And, Harper," Natalie said, her voice lowering, "I'm not sure what's going on between you two, but whatever it is, I'm really sorry."

Harper wrapped a hand around her throat. "I appreciate that."

The next call was to Nick's brother. She dialed Malcolm's cell since he wouldn't be at work yet. He picked up on the first ring.

"Harper, how are—"

Before he could finish the greeting, she interrupted him. "Do you know where Nick is?"

"What's happened?" he asked, his voice suddenly serious.

Something about Nick's twin brother being worried sent a fresh wave of panic through her system. "I just have to find him."

"Harper," he said, sounding every inch the man who ran a large, successful company, "you need to tell me what happened."

"He left me," she said, trying to ignore the quaver in her voice.

"Oh, hell."

"So I guess he didn't come to you." It wasn't a question, but she needed to say it aloud, because now her best lead was gone.

"No." Malcolm swore under his breath. "And he's always had an uncanny knack for disappearing without a trace. Even when we were kids." There was rustling in the background, as if he was picking things up as he spoke. "I'll head out and check a few places. I'll call Mom on the way, too. Let me know if you find him."

"Thank you," she whispered, almost overwhelmed by his support.

"Harper, no matter what idiotic idea he's got in his head, you're good for each other. Remember that."

She managed to smile. "I will. Also, I won't be in to work today."

"Of course not. Just let me know when you find him."

"Sure," she said.

After disconnecting, she felt her shoulders slump. The only other place that was worth trying was the waterfall, so she grabbed her things, bundled Frank into the car and headed off. The journey seemed to take forever. The time had gone so quickly when Nick had first driven her out here, but now, desperate to reach her destination and her stomach churning with anxiety about how he'd be and what he'd think when he saw her, it was more like a journey of a thousand hours.

As she pulled into the parking lot, she glanced around, but Nick's car wasn't there.

"He's not here," she said to Frank, who stood up to look out the windshield the way he did whenever the car slowed down, hoping they'd arrived somewhere interesting.

She couldn't go back to the house. So what else could she do? She clipped Frank's leash on and walked over to the spot where they'd had their picnic. She let Frank sniff around for a while, then sank down on the grass and watched the waterfall.

She had no idea how long she'd been sitting there when her cell rang. She answered quickly, hoping it was Malcolm with a lead, but it was Nick's number that flashed on her screen.

"Nick?"

"Where are you?" he asked, and she closed her eyes, savoring his deep, smooth voice.

"At the waterfall." She opened her eyes again to glance around at his favorite spot. "Where are you?"

"Home, looking for you." His voice gave nothing away. "Wait where you are. I'm coming to you."

After the call disconnected, she quickly called Malcolm to let him know he could stop searching, and then paced around the grassy area, letting Frank sniff all the smells he could find, trying to keep herself occupied so she didn't implode. He could be coming to discuss a divorce and access to the babies. Maybe he wanted to get back together. Or maybe there was even worse news that he couldn't deliver over the phone.

She was sitting on the grass, Frank resting beside her, when she first caught a glimpse of Nick rounding the corner and heading her way. Frank took off, his leash trailing behind him, and leaped on his human, resting his paws on Nick's chest. Nick took a minute to properly greet his dog, talking to him and rubbing his ears, then looked up. His gaze snagged hers, and goose bumps raced across her skin.

He walked toward her, his expression still giving nothing away. But his steps were sure. Her heart beat unevenly and roughly against her ribs, and she had no idea what to say or do. She stood, brushing off the grass from her pants, and offered him half a smile. She wanted to crawl into his embrace and hold on as tight as she could, but they didn't have that relationship anymore, so instead she simply waited until he reached her.

He stopped just beyond touching distance and cleared his throat. "Hi."

"Hi." She looked down at Frank, who was still bounding around, happy to have them all in the one place again, then back to him.

"Are you okay?" he asked.

"Fine," she said, lying. "You?"

"Fine." He gave her half a smile, clearly lying as well. "Harper, I need to ask. Do you hate me?"

Hate him? Not even close. "No."

"I walked out on you, even though you told me on the day we got engaged that it was a trigger for you."

She nodded slowly. "Yeah, you did that."

"I'm more sorry than I can say about that." His gaze was fathomless. "You should hate me for it."

She'd always known she'd made bad choices in past relationships, practically setting herself up to be left behind. Nick was different.

She lifted one shoulder and let it drop. "And yet, I don't."

"Then I have another question," he said, everything about him solemn. "Do you love me?"

She'd been so excited to tell him yesterday that she'd realized she loved him—it would have been a joyous moment. This wasn't the way she'd pictured it going at all, but she couldn't lie. "Yes," she said. "I love you."

He nodded as if he'd been expecting that. "And I love you so much it's tearing me up inside."

Those were words she'd been desperate to hear, and yet they didn't make her heart sing, because she still had no idea where he was going with this. "Why did you want to see me, Nick?"

"Were you serious when you said my addiction doesn't matter to you?"

"Absolutely," she said without hesitation.

His brows drew together, and he looked over at the waterfall for endless seconds before clearing his throat. "I realized something today."

She was almost too scared to ask but couldn't help herself. "What's that?"

"Growing up, we weren't close to my aunts and uncles, so the only marriage I saw close up was my parents'."

"Which sounds like it was perfect." It wasn't just the way he'd spoken of his parents, but it had shone brightly in his mother's eyes when she'd mentioned her husband at their wedding.

"I wouldn't say it was perfect, but it was certainly a good one." A faraway smile flitted across his face. "They were devoted to each other."

She sighed, glad there were people in the world who were able to live out the fairy tale. "They were lucky."

He tilted his head in acknowledgment. "And your parents' marriage was—"

"A disaster," she supplied so he didn't have to say it. "Even before my father left."

"So, what I realized is that since you and I said our vows, I've been trying to live up to my father's example of being a perfect husband and you've been worried that we'll turn out like your parents and I'll leave you."

She stilled, absorbing that, and realized it was completely true. She pulled her hair back from her face, then let it drop. "That's a fair amount of baggage. Maybe we were always going to fail."

He cupped the side of her face. "We just needed a clean slate and different vows."

"What do you mean?"

"I've been trying to make everything perfect. Fix things for everyone. For you. But it didn't need to be perfect, to be *right*. It just needed to be *us*." He took her hands in his. "The thing is, even though I'll do my best never to give in to painkillers again, I'm never going to be a perfect husband. And I don't want a perfect marriage. That's like wanting a fantasy, not a real relationship."

He reached into his pocket and withdrew a small box,

then opened it to reveal two gold bands. He took one out and laid it on the flat of his palm.

"Here are my new vows," he said, meeting her gaze squarely. "I choose you, Harper Lake, to be my wife. Not because you're carrying my babies, and not because I'm expecting you to be a perfect wife. I choose you because instead of being scared of my darkness, you were patient and persistent and you got me a dog."

She hiccupped a laugh, and he reached for her hand with his free one and intertwined their fingers.

"I love that you overcame your preference for privacy at work and held my hand in front of all of your colleagues. I love that you tried so hard to bond with Ellie. And I especially love that you stood by me each time the darkness tried to carry me away."

Tears welled in her eyes, and she brushed at them before they could fall. The rest of the world faded away, and all she could see was Nick. He was magnificent, and she couldn't imagine ever loving anyone the way she loved him.

"If you choose me today, I vow that I'll always try to make you happy. And even when my demons whisper to me, I vow that I'll never give up on you. On us."

He offered her the gold ring on his palm, and she nodded once, so he slipped it on her ring finger next to the first gold band he'd given her. Beyond words, she reached up and found his mouth, found his kiss. She melted into him, wanting the kiss, the moment, to never end.

Eventually, he pulled back. "Harper," he rasped.

When she'd regained her breath, she picked out the other gold ring from the box in his hand and held it on her upturned palm. Then she looked into his eyes and finally gave her love free rein.

"I choose you, Nick Tate, to be my husband. Not because you're the father of our babies, and not because I'm expecting you to be a perfect husband. I choose you because I love your noble heart. I love the way you love Ellie. I love that you jumped on board with my plan to rescue Frank before you even knew the details. I love that the people under your command still matter so much to you. I love that even though we disagree on things, you always have my best interests at heart."

He lifted her hand and brushed his lips across the tops of her fingers.

"If you choose me today, I vow that even though I'll always want you to be as happy as you can, I'll accept you as you are, with all your glorious imperfections. And I know there will be bumps along the road for us, but I vow to never give up on you."

She slipped the ring on his finger, and the sight of it there with all the extra meaning of these vows made the tears that had been welling in her eyes finally burst free. He pulled her to him, cradling her against his chest, and whispered, "I promise you, Harper. I'll never give up on us."

"Neither will I," she said.

Frank appeared and tried to stick his snout between them to work out what the noise was, but gave up and flopped down at their feet.

With a finger, Nick tipped Harper's face up so he could see her eyes. "By the power invested in me by—" he glanced around "—Frank the Labrador, I now pronounce us husband and wife. For real this time."

"For real this time," she echoed and smiled.

And then he kissed his bride.

\* \* \* \* \*

*Don't miss a single installment of the*
TEXAS CATTLEMAN'S CLUB: BLACKMAIL
*No secret—or heart—is safe in Royal, Texas...*

*THE TYCOON'S SECRET CHILD*
by USA TODAY bestselling author Maureen Child

*TWO-WEEK TEXAS SEDUCTION*
by Cat Schield

*REUNITED WITH THE RANCHER*
by USA TODAY bestselling author Sara Orwig

*EXPECTING THE BILLIONAIRE'S BABY*
by Andrea Laurence

*TRIPLETS FOR THE TEXAN*
by USA TODAY bestselling author Janice Maynard

*A TEXAS-SIZED SECRET*
by USA TODAY bestselling author Maureen Child

*LONE STAR BABY SCANDAL*
by Golden Heart winner Lauren Canan

*TEMPTED BY THE WRONG TWIN*
by USA TODAY bestselling author Rachel Bailey

*and*

*September 2017: TAKING HOME THE TYCOON*
*by* USA TODAY *bestselling author*
*Catherine Mann*

*October 2017: BILLIONAIRE'S BABY BIND*
*by* USA TODAY *bestselling author*
*Katherine Garbera*

*November 2017: THE TEXAN TAKES A WIFE*
*by* USA TODAY *bestselling author*
*Charlene Sands*

*December 2017: BEST MAN UNDER*
*THE MISTLETOE*
*by Jules Bennett*

# "There's more, Lara… I haven't reached the part that includes you," Marc said.

Startled and curious, Lara stared at him.

"I've only told you part of my grandfather's demands. There's another part. I'm to marry this month and stay married for one year."

He reached across the table to take her hand, which was an action so unlike him that she nearly gasped. For a few seconds, she couldn't speak. She could only continue staring at him.

"Don't say anything until I'm through. You're surprised, just as I was when my grandfather told me."

While she heard his words, she was still focused on his hand wrapped around hers. It was warm, his grip light, yet the instant they touched, she tingled from head to toe.

Somehow, the touch of his hand had changed their relationship. She was certainly more aware of him as a man. And that awareness made it impossible to find words for a response.

He continued, "I want to see if I can make a deal with you…and make you my wife."

\* \* \*

**The Texan's Baby Proposal**
is part of the Callahan's Clan series—
A wealthy Texas family finds
love under the Western skies!

# THE TEXAN'S
# BABY PROPOSAL

BY
SARA ORWIG

MILLS
BOON

First Published in Great Britain 2017
By Mills & Boon, an imprint of HarperCollins*Publishers*
1 London Bridge Street, London, SE1 9GF

ISBN: 978-0-263-92831-0

51-0817

**Sara Orwig**, from Oklahoma, loves family, friends, dogs, books, long walks, sunny beaches and palm trees. She is married to and in love with the guy she met in college. They have three children and six grandchildren. Sara's one-hundredth published novel was a July 2016 release. With a master's degree in English, Sara has written historical romance, mainstream fiction and contemporary romance. Sara welcomes readers on Facebook or at www.saraorwig.com.

# One

Facing a problem he never thought he would have, Marc Medina sat in his spacious Dallas office on a Tuesday evening and, through his open door, watched Lara Seymour, his executive secretary. It was almost an hour after closing time, but she had a six-o'clock appointment to talk to him. He knew she would appear promptly at six, not a minute early, not a minute late. He wondered what problem she had and hoped she wasn't planning to quit because she was the best secretary ever.

And the best looking.

He stifled that line of thought. CEO and President, Marc had built this company, Medina Energy. He had a policy of never dating a coworker, never getting emotionally involved with one, never flirting with one. Instead, he maintained a professional relationship at all times. Nothing would make him deviate from that policy, especially now that he was widowed.

Of all the women he had worked with, Lara was the biggest temptation. She was the only one he was keenly aware of as a woman. Still, their relationship had never gone beyond business friendly.

His thoughts returned to his ailing grandfather and his ultimatum to Marc—marry within this month and live on his grandfather's ranch for one year. If he did so, Marc and his mother stood to gain a large inheritance of mineral rights and producing wells, and he stood to gain the ranch. Marc wanted that inheritance and he wanted his mother to get hers, as well.

Knowing his grandfather, Marc was sure the old man figured that, since Marc dated some very beautiful ladies, he'd have no trouble getting a wife right away and then settling on the ranch. Marc knew what his grandfather ultimately wanted. Rico Ruiz's doctors had given him a limited time to live and he was no doubt making arrangements for his two greatest loves—his wife and his ranch. With Marc running the ranch, Rico would be reassured that his wife, Marc's grandmother, could live there in the house she was accustomed to for the rest of her days and Marc would care for her.

His grandfather had always thought Marc should live on the ranch. He thought Marc loved that life more than the corporate world, but as much as Marc did, he wasn't quite ready yet to be a rancher. He was sure his grandfather thought he knew what was best for his grandson. Marc loved the old man and he wanted to make his last days happy, so he'd try to do what his grandfather wished, but…

Where in blazes would he get a wife in a month? One he could tell goodbye later and dissolve the marriage.

That was the big catch. He didn't think any of the women he dated would want to marry and then split. He couldn't think of one woman friend he'd want to live with, even at the ranch where they had lots of space. He glanced at a short list of names on his desk. Each one already had a line drawn through it.

His attention was diverted as Lara passed the open door again. There went someone he could have around for one year. As a secretary, she was a huge help and yet she stayed in the background, usually barely noticeable, but always there when he needed her. Pity he couldn't ask her. He looked at his list of names again and wrote down another one, crossing it out as soon as he finished writing.

Searching his memory for anyone else, he glanced at Lara, who was seated at her desk putting something in a drawer. He suspected she was coming to see him to turn in her resignation. At her interview a year ago she'd mentioned she was saving her money to go to medical school someday. At the time he'd dismissed her statement as wishful thinking, but after working with her, he now believed what she said. When Lara set her mind to something, she got it done—fast and efficiently.

She reminded him of someone else he knew. Marc glanced at Kathy's picture on his desk and pulled it closer. "I miss you and need you," he whispered, thinking about his pregnant wife who'd died in a plane crash fourteen months earlier. It still hurt like hell to be without her. In that crash he lost his wife and his baby. Kathy had been two months pregnant.

He shifted his thoughts back to his ailing grandfather—another big, painful loss that was coming in his life. That made him think of his grandfather's ultimatum—or bargain, actually. Marc had two giant reasons for wanting to meet his grandfather's criteria. The first reason was that he wanted the ranch and the inheritance that would benefit not only him but his mother.

The other big reason was that he loved the old man. His grandfather had been the father figure in Marc's life since he was twelve years old and his dad died. Marc loved his grandpa and he wanted the man's last days to be happy ones. He wanted that with all his heart—he just hadn't known that would mean that he'd have to marry within a month.

"Damn," he said aloud, shaking his head and wondering what he was going to do. The stakes were too high and he loved his grandfather too much to say no to his proposition. But where was he going to find the perfect "wife"?

A knock on the door called a halt to his rambling thoughts. He looked at the clock. Six on the dot. As usual, Lara was right on time.

"Come in."

In a white cotton blouse with a tan tie at her throat and a matching tan skirt, she looked professional, tailored and so conservative she could easily fade into the background. In fact, there had been times she had to bring him papers during meetings and she had been barely noticeable, slipping in and out, a quiet, shadowy figure while so efficient at her job. Once again he hoped she wasn't going to quit. He knew she'd had a recent broken engagement, but he had never talked to her about it other than to say he was sorry. She had thanked him and only said she and her fiancé had had differences of opinions on some major issues.

Lara closed the door and turned back to him. "What I have to say is private and very personal."

He hid his surprise as he pointed at a chair in front of his desk. "Have a seat and tell me what's on your mind."

She had a graceful walk. Actually, she was damn attractive, with big blue eyes with amazingly thick, long lashes. She kept her dark brown hair in an upsweep; in fact, he'd never seen her with it down, falling free, but he imagined it was long and thick and luxuriant.

He gave her his full attention, curious about what was personal and important enough to warrant this meeting. She crossed her long legs, her tan skirt falling over her knees. She didn't need prompting but immediately began to speak.

"I have a situation that eventually I'll have to let everyone know about, but for now, it's private. I'll need to take some time off later."

"Sure, Lara. Whatever you need. We can fill in until you return," he said, relieved she wasn't quitting her job.

Her cheeks became flushed, adding to her looks. She wrung her hands and looked at the floor. The reaction surprised him because he had never seen her lose her poise or appear upset. She hadn't even appeared bothered by her broken engagement.

"I'm dealing with things I never had to deal with before and never expected to have happen in my life," she said, looking away as if lost in thought. "This is something I just never expected to have to discuss with my employer."

"Short of quitting your job, I doubt there's anything

you really need to tell me. Unless you need help of some kind."

She gave him a fleeting smile that was gone in an instant as she shook her head. "Oh, no. I don't need your help. Maybe just a little patience and understanding," she said with a tiny twist of her lips that she may have meant to be a smile.

"Lara, just say what it is. I'm not going to get angry. You're a great secretary."

With a deep breath she turned back to face him. "This is so hard, but I feel you should know."

"Go ahead and tell me if you think I should know," he said gently, wishing he could ease her discomfort.

She tightened her entwined fingers until her knuckles went white. "Oh, my," she said, looking away from him. When she turned back, her blue eyes gazed directly at him in a wide-eyed stare as she said bluntly, "I'm pregnant."

She drew in a deep breath and surged forward. "We didn't expect this to happen and Leonard Crane—my fiancé—really did not like it, so that's why we're no longer engaged." She paused a millisecond and went on.

"You see, my ex-fiancé didn't want children for a long time yet. He wanted me to get an abortion and I—well, I can't do that. I want my baby," she said with a note of fierce determination in her voice that startled him.

Marc understood now why she was so upset. No matter how much she wanted her baby, an unexpected pregnancy had to push her life off course. Lara was in such perfect control of every facet of her job and helped him keep control of his. She was efficient, intelligent, orderly, capable, dependable, driven. In fact, he was surprised that anything unplanned had occurred to her, especially a pregnancy.

He resisted the temptation to let his gaze drift over her figure, but he knew from the past few days of seeing her move around the office, she didn't show her condition at all. She was tall, probably five feet ten, and she was still slender.

"Is there anything I can do to help you?" he asked. He wondered if Lara needed money or a different place to live. He wondered if she had family to rely on. They had worked closely together and he thought a lot of her. He'd do whatever he could to help her and her baby.

She merely shook her head and gave him a small, forced smile to reassure him she was okay. Instead, it only made him aware of her good looks again.

And that's when the thought hit him. Lara had a dilemma…and he had a dilemma. She was pregnant, working to support herself and to save for her education. He needed a temporary wife to win his inheritance. Perhaps he had a solution to help them both out…

Would she be a candidate for a marriage of convenience?

He had no doubt Lara would be willing to dissolve the marriage later. That was the best thing of all. She had her own agenda, plus the drive, the willpower and the stamina to stick with it. In a temporary marriage of convenience, she wouldn't make demands on him or expect him to fall in love. He couldn't. His heart was still with his wife. He hadn't gotten over her loss and he wasn't ready for another relationship.

He'd been able to work closely with Lara for a year without ever crossing that line and getting personal. He knew he'd be able to keep their relationship the same as it had been.

In the meantime, he could give her the financial support that would take away a lot of her worries about her baby.

Yes, the more he thought about it, the more appealing the idea became.

He wasn't aware she was even speaking until she shifted in her seat and drew his attention.

"If I continue to feel good, I'll work until it's time for my baby, if that's all right with you."

"It'll certainly be fine with me. You take the time you need for leave," he hoped he said. His thoughts were still on the prospect that she actually might be a good candidate for a short-term marriage. Again, he thought about that awareness he had of her as an attractive woman. Would that make it more difficult to keep his distance in a marriage of convenience than it had in the office? He didn't think it would.

The more he mulled over the thought, the more he knew. Lara Seymour was the answer to his dilemma.

He tried to pay attention as she talked about her plans, but his thoughts could not be corralled. He was so sure of his plan that he wanted to pose the offer right away. But he couldn't do that here in the office. No, he'd rather get his offer lined up in his own thoughts and ask her to dinner to tell her. Somewhere private where they would not be interrupted.

"I'm only in my second month, actually not far into my second month, so this is very early. I'd prefer not to announce this to the office, which is why I wanted to see you after hours."

"Of course. I won't mention it. I appreciate you letting me know, even though I won't need to get someone to fill in for you for months yet."

"I thought it only fair to tell you now. So far I feel fine, so that's good."

"That's very good," he said, smiling at her. "Lara, you don't need to answer if you don't want to, but I really know nothing about your private life. Do you have family here who will be with you?"

She gazed at him with a solemn look that was so unlike her, he was startled. She shook her head. "I have friends. I don't have relatives. My mom died of leukemia when I was eighteen. I had an older sister who died of acute leukemia when she was seven. My dad walked out when I was a little kid. I don't remember him or know him. There are no relatives."

Marc was shocked, but tried to hide his surprise. "I'm so sorry. I didn't know that. I know you have friends and a lot of them here in this office. People like you."

He couldn't stop thinking of her being so alone. He had never known anyone who had no living relatives. He was so locked into his relationships with his family, he couldn't imagine her solitary situation. She needed his help so much more than he had thought and it made him feel better to think that he could be a huge help to her and her baby. If this had been his wife, he would hope someone would have helped her.

He could set up a trust for Lara's baby. He could let the baby have his name. If they married now, most people would assume he was the father, which would be fine with him because it would help her.

"I have wonderful friends here. This is a great office and a great place to work," she said, giving him a radiant smile. Idly, he wondered how many single guys in his office had tried to date her.

"You have a master's degree. When you came to work here, you told me you wanted to work to save enough money to go to medical school. Is that still on your agenda?" he asked.

"Oh, yes. My pregnancy is a setback, but I still intend to pursue my dreams. I want to go into medical research someday. With my mother's illness I saw that there is still so much to be discovered about such diseases. If I can do anything to help in that field, I want to, for my mother's memory. Doctors just couldn't do anything to save her, but medical science makes new discoveries constantly. I want to help people. If I don't get into medical school, I can do something else to help others."

"That's commendable. I hope you get to carry out your plans," he said, thinking he should be able to help her meet some of her financial needs for her education.

"It will take me a little longer to earn and save the money to go back to school, but I intend to do so. If I can get accepted into medical school, I definitely plan to go. If not, I'll become a chemist."

"That's tough without family members to help and to babysit."

"I'll manage," she replied with a lift of her chin.

"I'm sure you will," he said, and meant it. It hadn't taken long to recognize her drive and ambition after she came to work for him. He'd seen it in himself and his mother all his life.

"If you don't feel well, I want you to stay home. If you're already here and don't feel well, please don't keep working. Take off and tell me if you need help getting home or anything."

She smiled again. "Thanks. That's nice but I'll be all right. I've been fine so far. Not even morning sickness."

"That's good. I assume you have a doctor."

"Oh, yes, I have a doctor who came with lots of recommendations from friends." She smiled at him. "Well…I guess there's nothing more to say but thank you for being so cooperative and helpful. I'll let you know when I tell anyone else in the office and this is no longer a secret. It can't be a secret for long," she said, forcing a smile. Then she stood up, and as she did, his gaze swept over her and he liked what he saw. Her white blouse revealed full curves and a tiny waist.

There were moments—like this one—when he forgot her secretarial status and their business relationship, but he always caught himself before he said or did anything to indicate he saw her as an attractive woman instead of his very competent secretary. He caught himself again now, going to open the door for her.

"Take care of yourself and, again, if you need anything or don't feel well, don't hesitate to tell me," he repeated. She turned to face him and suddenly he was aware of how close they stood. His gaze shifted to her full lips and he felt a tightening deep inside. For just a flash, he saw a flicker of her lashes and her cheeks became a deeper pink.

"Thanks, Marc. You're always understanding," she said softly and hurried out, crossing the room to her desk, which had everything in its proper place and ready for the next morning. She opened a drawer, retrieved her purse and turned to smile at him again. "I'll see you in the morning."

"Sure," he said, still watching her as she walked away.

He turned, walked back to his desk and sat, seeing the glass door to the outer office close behind her.

It always surprised him when he noticed her, because he still mourned his wife and he didn't pay attention to women the way he had before his marriage. Even though in the past few months he had started taking women friends out, he would never be serious about any of them. In fact, he wasn't even interested in any of them.

He thought about Lara.

And the more he thought about her, the more he knew she was the perfect "wife." He hadn't gotten over Kathy and wasn't ready for any kind of relationship, but Lara wouldn't expect one. She wouldn't want to fall in love any more than he wanted to, because she had other plans for her future. And while he stood to gain from this crazy marriage of convenience, so would she. She'd reap the reward of the help he could give her and her baby—not only in a trust he'd set up for the child but in giving the baby his name.

No doubt about it, Lara was the right person to ask.

Well, maybe there was one doubt…

For an instant he thought of the moments when he'd had to bank an electrifying awareness of her as an appealing woman. Could he push aside that attraction? He had to, because Lara and he would both get what they wanted from the marriage. He'd get the ranch and she'd get the financial and maybe emotional support she needed for this pregnancy. Then, when they dissolved the marriage, they'd go their separate ways and both be happy about it and much better off because of the marriage of convenience.

Meanwhile, he knew he could live with her and still

continue their business relationship. After all, they didn't need to go to bed with each other. He hadn't gotten over the loss of his wife, and she had just broken an engagement.

No matter how he looked at it, marriage to Lara would benefit both of them, as well as his family. It would benefit Lara's baby, too. And some part of him wanted that. Somehow, helping the baby pleased him a lot and made him feel closer to the little baby of his own that he had lost.

He looked up Lara's number, picked up his phone and called to invite her to dinner.

By half past six Wednesday evening, Lara was ready and waiting. She had dressed just as conservatively as she did at the office, in a black, long-sleeved dress with a high round neckline and straight skirt. But as she took a final glance at herself in the mirror, she noticed the dress was shorter and dressier than anything she'd worn to the office. She told herself it was the perfect compromise for a dinner date with her boss. She couldn't imagine why he had asked her out.

When he'd called last night he hadn't made it sound as if this was social. At the same time, it wasn't business related or he would have told her. She had accepted his dinner invitation knowing she'd find out the reason soon enough.

She tried to ignore the flutters in her belly when she thought of dining with her boss. Marc was handsome, charming, capable, a strong, sexy man—something she tried to avoid thinking about most of the time. She had heard all the office talk—how his pregnant wife of three months had died in a plane crash and he still mourned her and had no interest in any other woman.

She suspected he was smart enough to avoid getting sexually or emotionally involved with anyone at work.

She was attracted to him and had been from the first moment she met him, but she'd resisted with all her being because at first there was no future in it and later she became engaged. His heart was locked away, and even if it wasn't, she had plans for her life. Plans that did not call for her to get romantically involved with her boss, no matter how good-looking he was. Still, what was the harm in admitting that the man was handsome and had sex appeal? Bushels of it. In fact, sometimes she found it difficult to keep remote, professional and cool around him. Nevertheless, she did.

Thinking about him, she sighed. Surely Marc wasn't taking her out tonight to let her go. He wouldn't do that. As for his motives, she'd know in a matter of minutes.

She took one last look in the mirror. Her hair was looped and pinned up on her head, just the way she wore it at work today. Her makeup was light but flawless, optimally highlighting her blue eyes and high cheekbones. As she gazed into the mirror, her mind must have started playing tricks on her, because she suddenly saw Marc's image beside her. His thick, black, unruly hair, slightly tanned skin, the shadow of stubble on his jaw and his thickly lashed dark brown eyes. He stood next to her, over six feet tall, broad shouldered and strong, and he reached out to touch her and—

Her thoughts were interrupted by the sound of a car door closing. In seconds her doorbell rang. She took a deep breath and hurried to answer it. She swung it open to face her boss and her heart lurched.

Dressed in a navy suit and red tie that she had seen before, he looked handsome. She smiled, but felt odd flutters and she assumed it was because it seemed so much like a date. She banished that thought and looked up at him. "Do you want to come in?"

"Thanks, but we have reservations shortly, and I think we better go."

"I'm more than happy to go have dinner with you, Marc, but I'm a little puzzled as to why we're doing this. I don't feel as if it's a social event."

He smiled at her. "Smart woman. I have something I want to talk to you about and I want to be away from the office and away from interruptions."

"Ahhh," she said, nodding. While that clarified their dinner engagement slightly, she still had questions. She suspected his "something" concerned work because his office manner hadn't changed from what it had been all day. "I'll get my purse," she said, stepping back into her entryway briefly before joining him.

She closed her door and heard the lock click into place. As she walked beside him to the car, she was acutely conscious of how close he was and how tall he was. She had far more physical awareness of him now that they were out of the routine office setting, but his demeanor was the same. He didn't take her arm as they walked to the car. He didn't touch her in any way. So why couldn't she stop the prickly awareness that plagued her?

She told herself to pretend she was in the office, that it was just lunch together on a weekday. That didn't work.

He held the car door and she slid into the seat. She watched him walk around the car, the wind blowing unruly locks of his curly hair. What did he have to talk to her about here that he couldn't discuss at the office?

Her curiosity mushroomed when they went to a town club where he was a member. Inside, they were taken to a private room.

"Now I am curious about tonight," she said as she sat across from him.

He merely nodded. "Let's get our drinks and order dinner before we talk. I don't want any interruptions. But I will tell you this is personal and involves my grandfather."

Startled, she couldn't imagine what could concern her and involve his very ill grandfather. "There's no guessing why I'm here having dinner with you if it involves Mr. Ruiz. That lets out anything regarding the office."

"Not altogether," Marc said. "I have a proposition I want you to consider."

Her curiosity reached a fevered peak but she reined in her questions when the waiter came to ask their drink preferences. Marc ordered sparkling water for her and a martini for himself.

She sat quietly until finally they had ordered dinner and been served their drinks. He raised his glass in a toast.

"Here's to the best secretary I've ever worked with and, hopefully, to a mutually bright future together."

She touched her glass to his and sipped, watching him and waiting as he set his martini on the table. Her curiosity increased because, whatever he was about to discuss, it involved both of their futures.

He folded his hands on the table and cleared his throat. "I'll cut to the chase now. My grandfather is very ill with pancreatic cancer and doctors have given him three months to live."

"I'm sorry," she said, hearing the pain in Marc's voice even though he seemed in control of his emotions.

"I'm close to him. My dad died when I was twelve and my grandfather has always been there for me. I've spent a lot of time with my grandparents on their ranch. I love that life and I love that ranch. It's beautiful." He smiled at her. "At least, it is to me."

"I'm sorry, Marc, that your grandfather's health isn't good," she said, still unable to see how any of this involved her.

"Thanks. My grandparents love that ranch. They've worked it all their lives."

He paused when the waitstaff came in with their dinners—a thick steak for Marc and Alaskan salmon for her. When they were alone again, she had a bite of salmon and closed her eyes. "Mmm, this is delicious."

"Yes, it is," he said, his voice deeper than usual. She opened her eyes to see him watching her. Heat flashed through her and she was aware of the intense way he looked at her. His dark brown eyes hid his feelings.

"Go ahead with your story," she said, suddenly tingling with awareness. She knew whatever he was going to ask her, it had nothing to do with the office. Not with the look she had just received from him.

He took a deep breath and nodded. "Now that my grandfather is ill, he's worried about my grandmother. She wants to stay on the ranch and live out her life there, but—this is where I come in—she can't run it or deal with it herself. And this is where you come in." He paused and nodded at her plate. "Maybe you should enjoy a few more bites of dinner before I continue."

She shook her head. "My curiosity will overcome me." She wondered if he was thinking about trying to hire her as a companion for his grandmother. "What on earth is it, that I won't be able to eat after you tell me?"

"I think I'm going to shock you. Frankly, I'm still reeling in shock myself," he said, forcing a smile at her. "My grandfather wants me to move to the ranch and I have to agree to stay at least one year. That way I'll be there to see that my grandmother is all right."

"You're leaving the company for a year?" Lara asked. "Or will it be longer?" Was she losing her boss permanently? She felt a pang at the thought and immediately thought of his vice presidents, wondering whom she would work for.

"It'll only be a year. I know my grandpa and how he thinks. He thinks if I live out there a year, I'll never want to leave."

"I can understand what he wants, but is that what you want to do?"

"He's given me an offer—actually, it's more an ultimatum. I live there a year and I inherit the ranch, also one third of the mineral rights and one third of the producing wells on the ranch. My mother will also inherit a third, the same as I will, and the remainder of the estate will go to my grandmother."

"I see." She put down her fork and wiped her lips on her napkin. "You wanted to tell me that I'll have a new boss."

"Oh, no. I'm not through. I love my grandfather too much to refuse to do what he wants. Even if I didn't feel that way, this offer is too big to turn down. And I love that ranch. As I said, I love Grandpa and I want his last days to be happy. I want to do what he wants and make him happy."

"That's wonderful, Marc. I can understand. I loved my mother, and at the last, I did everything I could to make her happy. I'll miss working for you," she said, hoping she didn't sound too depressed, but she would miss him terribly. She liked working for him. He was a fair, considerate boss and a handsome, appealing man, so it was nice to be around him.

"There's more, Lara, but I'm trying to wait until you've had enough of your dinner that you won't go home hungry."

She picked up her fork again, to placate him, and smiled up at him. "I'm eating, okay? But you've told me your news—that you're leaving."

"I haven't reached the part that includes you," he reminded her.

Startled, she stared at him as curiosity gripped her. Maybe he wanted a secretary on the ranch. Was that it?

"Lara, I've only told you part of my grandfather's demands. There's another part. Besides living on the ranch for a year, I'm to marry this month."

He reached across the table to take her hand, which was something so unlike him that she nearly gasped. For a few seconds, she couldn't speak. She could only stare at him.

"Don't say anything until I'm through. You're surprised, just as I was."

While she heard his words, she was still focused on his hand wrapped around hers. His hand was warm, his grip light, yet the instant they touched she tingled from head to toe. Somehow, she felt the touch of his hand had changed their relationship in a subtle way. She was certainly more aware of him as a man. And that awareness made it impossible to respond.

"I need a wife for a marriage of convenience, possibly for one year, possibly much shorter," he continued. "In order to inherit, I have to marry this month and live on the ranch for one year. That is what my grandfather has in his will. I want a wife as long as my grandfather is alive, which doctors have only given him a few months. I want his last days happy. After he is gone, I will stay on the ranch that full year, but there is nothing in his will about how long I have to stay married. When he is gone, I will end the marriage—that's a promise," he said. "I want to see if I can make a deal with you. Make you my wife."

# Two

Stunned, she stared at him, looking into unfathomable brown eyes that hid his feelings so well. Marry Marc and then dissolve it? She couldn't imagine doing such a thing. Those dark eyes so intently focused on her took her breath away. Marry Marc. Without love. A marriage for convenience. Her heart raced at the thought.

"Marc, that's very flattering, but I can't do that," she said, her pulse pounding. *Marry* Marc? For a moment she felt light-headed. She couldn't agree to what he was proposing.

"Wait a minute. Just listen to the whole thing. What's in this for me, and more importantly, what's in this for you. Please, just listen."

"I am," she said. Breathless, still in such shock, she could only stare at him, trying to hear and process what he was saying.

"You haven't heard my part of this bargain. I stand to get big financial gains if I do what my grandfather wants. And I'll inherit his ranch—a fine, working ranch. But, Lara, I intend for this deal to benefit the woman I marry, also."

She gazed into eyes so dark they were almost black and knew that, whatever the outcome, she would remember this moment and what he had just said to her for the rest of her life. She had a feeling that her life might be about to change in a manner she had never envisioned. If she married him. She couldn't imagine that happening.

"You and I are compatible," he said. "We're able to be together and we know we can work together. I want to help you in your endeavors and help you take care of your baby. I want to give you and your baby a great start in your new life. I want to give your baby security and legitimacy—my name. If you'll marry me in this marriage of convenience, I'll draw up the papers and give you two hundred thousand dollars when we marry and two hundred thousand when we divorce. After my grandfather is gone, I want us both free."

"That's staggering, Marc," she whispered, so stunned by his offer that she could only stare at him. "That's almost half a million dollars," she whispered. "I can go to school and I won't have to work in the office."

"That's right. As much as I hate to lose you as a secretary, I need you more in this."

"But you go out and have women friends. Why are you asking me? We haven't even dated."

"This isn't a marriage made from a romance. It's a marriage of convenience and my grandfather just required that I live on the ranch for one year. When my

grandfather is gone, I want to return to my single status—and I will," Marc said, giving her a direct look
that spoke volumes about his determination to do just
that. "The women I take to parties and concerts and
shows—I don't think any of them would go into a marriage with the agreement that it would be over, maybe
in several months."

"I can see that," she said without thinking, and his
lips curved in a faint smile.

"You, on the other hand, have an agenda. You plan
on medical school and you'll have a baby. I think you'll
be willing to walk away from this when we divorce."

"Will we…will we live as man and wife?" she asked.
"Including sex?"

"If that's your preference, yes, we can. If it's not—
and since this marriage is definitely temporary—I think
we can manage. We did well working together for the
past year. This should be even easier because we won't
see each other on a daily basis the way we have at the
office. I still love and miss my wife. I'm not interested
in a relationship."

"I just broke an engagement and I'm not interested
in one, either," she said, her cheeks turning pink.

"Then that settles that question. We'll continue in a
friendly manner the way we did at the office. This way,
we won't have emotional complications," he said, smiling at her, and she smiled in return. "It's not something
that can't be changed if we decide we want to change
it," he added, and she nodded.

"Marc, I have to admit I'm stunned. I can't believe
what you're offering."

"Think about it, Lara. You're alone now, but you
won't be if you take this offer. I can help you so you can

take care of yourself and your baby, get that education you want so you can save some lives or help others in some way. You'll be helping my mother and me get this inheritance. It's mutually beneficial and I hope changes your life for the better."

"Of course it will," she answered. She stared at him and he gazed back in silence. Could she live under the same roof with him without falling into bed with him? Could she live with him and not get emotionally involved? He was a sexy, desirable man. And she knew he could do far more damage to her heart than she'd experienced this past year, and that had been terrible.

"Lara, I'm sure people at the office have talked to you about my wife. You've seen her picture on my desk. She was pregnant with our baby when she was killed in a plane crash after we had been married three months. We had been married three months, four days, fourteen hours to be exact." He looked away, and when he talked, his voice was flat.

"I'm sorry, Marc, for your loss."

"I loved her," he said quietly, and Lara wondered if he had forgotten her presence and was caught in memories. She sat quietly as he drew a deep breath.

"Enough of that, except to say, I will not make this marriage permanent, nor will it become personal. I still love Kathy and miss her with all my being. I know I need to get over my loss, but that hasn't happened and I want to be up front and honest with you."

"I understand. My broken engagement hurt me and left me not trusting my judgment in men. I get it. But I also know you well, since we've worked closely together for the past year."

"I want to help you, especially since you don't have

any family," he said. "In addition to what I've offered, there are some other things."

"There's more?" she asked in surprise.

"Oh, yes. In addition to giving your child my name, I'll set up a two-hundred-thousand-dollar trust fund for your baby."

"Whoever agrees to this marriage will become wealthy. You're willing to give me a fortune and my child your name?" she repeated, knowing she had to accept his offer.

"Yes, I am, because of what I'll inherit from my grandfather. It'll make his last days happier ones, and it will change my mother's life for the better. And I hope it will change yours, as well."

"That's incredibly generous."

"I'll be on the ranch, but when the year is up, I'll have someone else run the ranch and have a companion and help for my grandmother, and I'll return to Dallas and the corporate world. I'll retire later to the ranch."

Still in shock, she sat quietly, her head spinning. "Marc, I can't even absorb this. My life will change totally."

"Yes, it will." His hand tightened around hers. "Lara, I want the ranch and my grandfather's inheritance, and I need this marriage. And I don't want him to be unhappy in his last days. I love him," Marc said gruffly, and impulsively, she squeezed his hand.

"I'm sorry. It hurts to lose someone you love. I know," she said quietly.

She started to pull her hand away, but he held it. "You have soft hands," he said quietly.

She realized they had been circumspect at the office, never even touching. But now his hand on hers was electrifying. For a moment she forgot his proposition, her dinner, everything else except his hand holding hers.

His gaze met hers. "We've worked together well. We can do this. Your engagement is broken. You have your plans for your future. We can help each other."

Her insides trembled again. She was intensely aware of him, yet still trying to grasp the amount of money that could be hers if she accepted his offer. The temptation was great to accept instantly, yet years of caution and self-control caused her to remain silent.

"I'm surprised I didn't faint. I have to think about this."

"How many times in your life have you fainted?"

"None," she answered, startled by his question until she saw his smile.

"I didn't think so. Look, Lara, I know it's a shock. I've been in shock to find out I have to marry this month. I want you to think this over."

"I've worked with you for almost a year now and I've seen you in a lot of different situations. You're one of the good guys, Marc. I feel I can trust you." She diverted her gaze a moment, then looked back into his eyes, deeply and sincerely. "Since I feel that way, with the offer you've made, I can't possibly turn it down. Yes, Marc, I'll marry you in a marriage of convenience that we know will end."

"I'll still give you a little time to think about this and back out if you want. I hope you don't back out, but I don't want a quick decision when this is a life changer. You don't know what I'm like away from the office. We should go out together a few times before we're locked into this."

He released her hand and she wondered if he had

given the contact any thought. "All good ideas, Marc." Her mind reeled with questions. "Your grandmother has a house there, right? Or will she live in the same house with us? Oh, my heavens! *With us*—that sounds so impossible," she said breathlessly while she gazed into his eyes. *I'm going to marry Marc. I'm going to be his wife.* The thoughts swirled and she could feel her face flush. "I can't imagine any of this."

"See why I wanted you to eat some of your dinner?" he asked. "You haven't eaten a bite since I told you why I asked you out."

"You were right. My appetite is gone. The dinner is delicious, but my head is spinning and my stomach is churning." She grasped his hand again. His hand was warm and solid, and her reaction to the physical contact was just as electrifying as before. She was conscious that his fingers closed gently around hers.

"Damn, your hand is cold as ice," he said and clutched it between both of his.

"I'm in shock and nervous and excited. This is something I never dreamed would happen. I'm excited, scared, flattered—countless reactions that keep shifting and changing with each breath I take. Right now, the money is dazzling, but I know I have to look beyond the money. The prospect of us being married— that's shocking and something I've never considered."

He leaned closer across the table. "I understand some of your feelings. That's exactly why I said you should take some time to think about your answer," he said, brushing loose strands of her hair away from her face. His touch was feathery, except it was Marc and she was acutely aware of him. He gazed at her intently and his steady look took her breath away. What were these intense reactions she was having to him? She didn't have those at the office. But at the office, she had never had to consider marriage to him, even if it wasn't forever, wasn't out of love and wasn't even real.

"I'll do that if you want, but the offer you just made to me—I don't have to think about what I want to do. You'll solve so many of my problems for me," she said, leaning closer to him and lowering her voice. "I'll say goodbye to you when we divorce, so I can go on with my dream to become a doctor and to go into medical research."

They both leaned over the table, till mere inches separated them. She searched his gaze, yet his eyes revealed nothing of what was truly going on in his head.

He looked intently at her and then his gaze lowered to her mouth.

She tingled all over and drew a deep breath. She could practically feel his lips on hers as he looked at her mouth. Without thinking she ran her tongue over her lower lip, realized what she was doing and closed her mouth, looking up to meet his knowing gaze. When she felt the heat in her cheeks, she knew she had blushed.

"Our boss-and-secretary relationship just went up in smoke," she whispered, and he nodded.

"Absolutely."

For a moment he was silent, staring at her lips, then just like a rogue wind, the moment was swept away. Slowly he sat back and she followed suit, feeling bereft after his near kiss.

"You were the best secretary I could've wished for," he said finally. "But that's gone for good. I need you more for this marriage of convenience because that's a role almost impossible to fill."

"You just changed my life forever, for the better. You've given me and my baby opportunities in life."

"We'll get to know each other," he said in a husky voice. Then, as if he'd suddenly thought of a pressing question, he asked, "When is your baby due?"

"Next April."

"If we plan to stay together for a year, I'll be there for those early months when I can help while you get settled into motherhood."

She smiled at him.

"If we marry, even if it is just a bargain marriage, we'll be thrown into close, constant contact—although it's a big house. Just remember, Lara, I won't change my mind. This marriage will never turn into something permanent, which I know you don't want, anyway."

"No, I don't. I know from the start that it's a business deal and it's temporary. I can deal with that."

"I'm sure you can," he remarked dryly. "I just wanted you to clearly understand my feelings. I don't want you hurt by this or having a broken heart. I feel as if my heart turned to stone when I lost my wife. You don't even have to stay on the ranch all the time. I'd like you around some of the time while my grandfather is alive. I just want him happy."

"I know. Losing someone you love hurts badly," she answered. "Remember, I lost my mother and I had an engagement shattered and it hurt. I don't want to go through that again, so I'll be careful."

"If you accept, and you sound as if you plan to accept, I don't care what kind of wedding we have. I'll leave that up to you. Whatever you want is fine. I can pay for it. It just has to be soon. I mean, like next week or the week after at the latest. I don't want any last-minute thing. With Grandpa's health the way it is, the sooner our wedding, the better."

"*The sooner the better.* Oh, my. My head is spinning. I can't believe all this. One thing. I'm enrolled in a night class this semester. The doctor said it's fine. The class ends in December."

"Lara, you said you don't have any relatives. Who's closest to you? Who will you tell about this?"

"There's my friend Melanie, and Patsy from work, and some friends in my neighborhood, including an older couple next door who think they're substitute grandparents. Mr. and Mrs. Vickers."

"We really don't have long to pull a wedding together. I want you to think everything over tonight and give me an answer tomorrow. You're saying yes now, but I want you to be sure," he said.

"I am so sure, Marc," she said. "I promise you, I'm ready to accept your offer. And I will get out of the marriage, just as surely as you want to."

"You don't want to sleep on it?"

Aware she was changing her future, her life, her baby's life, she shook her head. "My answer to your proposal is yes."

"Then I'll have my lawyer draw up an agreement and a prenup. If you back out, you forfeit everything except one hundred dollars that will be a token."

"Fine," she said. They sat gazing at each other, and her heartbeat quickened as she looked into his eyes. His hand covered hers again.

"We're getting married," he whispered. "We're not in love, but we can get to know each other a little better and let the friendship grow. We've always gotten along and worked well together as boss and secretary. And now we have decisions to make as a couple—wedding decisions, decisions about when you quit your job, when we announce our engagement, a lot of things. Can you go to dinner tomorrow night?" He smiled suddenly. "Maybe then I won't send you into shock and you'll get to eat your meal."

"Yes, I can."

He nodded at her plate. "Want your dinner now?"

She shook her head. "I can't eat a bite. I'm too excited. Actually, I'd like to take a walk. By now the weather outside should have cooled some and I feel like I need to move around."

"Let's go. They'll put dinner on my tab. We don't need to wait."

He stood and held her chair as she rose. When she turned, she faced him and they were only inches apart. Her pulse jumped and she felt riveted, unable to move at all.

*Our boss-and-secretary relationship just went up in smoke.*

She remembered her words from a moment ago and realized how true they really were. Going forward, their relationship would be different. *Very different*, she thought, barely able to catch her breath. She had always tried to keep her distance and squelch any physical reaction she had to him. She had always avoided physical contact. Now they would be husband and wife. Even though it was in name only, nothing would ever be the same.

Shocking her almost as much as his proposal was a sudden, intense awareness of him, far beyond anything she had ever felt before. His eyes narrowed the barest fraction, but she noticed, and she felt as if sparks flew between them. A sizzling attraction made her want to lean toward him, to touch him. Her lips tingled and her gaze lowered to his mouth as she wondered what it would be like to kiss him.

How could their coming change invoke this hot attraction so swiftly?

She needed to get back her detached business personality and keep a wall between them. That's what both of them wanted. This would not be a marriage made in love and she needed to guard her heart all the time because he clearly would not fall in love and she didn't want to fall in love—or fall into his bed, either.

With an effort she stepped away from him.

He took her arm and they left the club, turning on the sidewalk in downtown Dallas. How long would it be before she would get accustomed to him touching her? She had a prickly awareness of how close he was when he took her arm to cross the street. People were still out, but she was conscious of no one and nothing except him. His height as he walked beside her, his hand grazing hers as they strolled. Was she stepping into a situation where she would have a bigger heartbreak than ever? When she'd ended her engagement, she had been the one who wanted out of the relationship. This time, Marc would end the relationship, so she needed to be careful to protect her heart and stay out of his bed.

"I don't know much about your private life," she said. "If I'm going to marry you, I think you better tell me, at least briefly."

"Sure. I was born in Downly, Texas."

She smiled. "You don't have to start that far back."

With a flash of even, white teeth, he grinned. "My

mom's family all came from Mexico because of relatives in Downly. Are you familiar with Downly?"

"I've heard of it, but I've never been there."

"Mom and her family got jobs there and their citizenship. My mom got a job as a maid for a wealthy family. Actually, it was Dirkson Callahan."

Startled, she looked up at him. "Oh, my. You're about to buy some of his wells in South Dakota. You told me at the office that it was routine business. I know you're close friends with his son, Gabe Callahan, but will buying the wells be something more personal?"

"You've already moved into the fiancée mode. You wouldn't have asked me that at the office," he said, sounding amused again.

"Are you going to be one of those men who's got everything bottled up and keeps a lot to yourself? Maybe I should learn the parameters here."

He laughed and put his arm around her to squeeze her shoulder as they walked. "I'm teasing you. Gabe always thought Dirkson was an uncaring dad. He didn't keep up with his boys or share in their lives. None of them were happy with him. I talked to Gabe about it before I did anything, and he said it wouldn't mean anything to his dad or any of them if I bought those wells and to go ahead. So I am. And you can ask whatever you want."

"Oh, really?" she said, stopping to put her hand on her hip, unable to resist flirting with him.

"Oh, yeah," he answered in a husky voice, his eyes twinkling, and her pulse jumped. "What very private thing would you like to know?"

She caught her lower lip with her teeth as she thought for a few seconds. "Am I ever going to get breakfast in bed?"

"If you're in our bed, you will," he answered.

"You are quick. I'll remember that."

"So will I," he said in a deeper voice. They looked at each other and both laughed.

When they did, he hugged her lightly again. "I'm liking this deal better by the minute."

"Don't get excited. You're accustomed to me being your secretary and doing whatever you ask. That isn't necessarily going to happen when I become your wife."

He leaned closer, tilting her chin up with his forefinger and gazing at her. "Then I'll just have to butter you up so I get my way."

She smiled when he did and they turned to continue walking. "Does your mom still work for him?" Lara asked.

"No. She quit to open a small tamale stand and tiny café—I mean, really small. This was before I was born, so I know little about it. My mom met my dad and I think it must have been love at first sight. They were married three weeks after they met and they loved each other deeply. He was a good dad, too. He had immigrated to the US earlier, gotten his citizenship and had a job. He worked in construction. He really wasn't a strong man and shouldn't have been doing that."

"You don't take after him there," she said without thinking about it.

"I didn't know I'd exhibited any great stamina in the office," Marc said, sounding amused and looking down at her.

"You carry things around sometimes. I've seen you do things. I'm observant," she said, aware her cheeks were suddenly hot.

"Oh, yeah?" He touched her arm as he stepped in

front of her again. "Maybe I should ask what else you know about me from observation."

She thought a moment. "You send roses to women you've been out with, and if it's someone a little more special, you send a big mixed bouquet. Right?"

"Damn. I must be as predictable as hell. How did you figure that out?" He stared at her.

"That's a guess. The mixed bouquet has roses. The lady who gets the mixed bouquet gets roses plus other flowers."

"Well, you're right." He nodded and they continued walking.

"Go on about your family," she urged him. "I don't know anything about them."

"When my family moved to Texas, they didn't have money, but they were successful. Mom's little café grew and when my dad's health began to fail, as long as he could, he helped in the café. By that time, my grandfather was doing better and he put some money into her café. Then my dad's health got worse and he had heart problems. I had wonderful parents and wonderful grandparents and I'm sorry you lost your family so early in life. It hurt to lose my dad and it's going to hurt like hell to lose Grandpa."

She grasped Marc's hand and squeezed lightly, releasing him swiftly and trying to ignore the inevitable tingles. "I know, Marc. I was so close to my mother."

"When I lost my dad, I got closer to my grandfather on Mom's side. He was the father figure in my life after Dad was gone."

"You had a lot of family."

"My mom's dad worked for a successful rancher and moved up to become foreman. On that side of the family I come from people who are driven and work hard. My mom put work first in her life always. So did Grandpa. Sometimes I think they both worked too much. The man who owned the ranch didn't have children. When the rancher's wife died, he willed the ranch to my grandfather and four years later, when the rancher died, Grandpa inherited it. I was seven years old then and already loved to visit my grandparents. It's a great ranch."

She noticed his voice changed and she wondered how much he liked ranching versus working in Dallas in an office.

That question and others would have to wait. She was getting tired of walking and her feet were killing her in her heels. She looked at her surroundings. "I'm not familiar with where we are now and we've walked quite a way."

He swung her around and they headed back as she laughed. "Oooh, I get what I want the minute I ask. I'm going to like my new role."

He stopped and faced her. Surprised, she looked up at him as wind caught locks of his dark, curly hair.

"I'm beginning to look forward to our deal. And we better get on with it. So, we're on for dinner tomorrow night?"

"Yes, thank you. We need to make wedding plans if you want to move so fast."

He stepped beside her again and they continued walking. "Think of the secretaries in the office. Is there anyone who'd be a good replacement? If we can find someone who's already working there, it'll be easier for you to train them before you leave."

"You have two who should be perfect. They're quiet

about their work and I don't think most people realize how much they get done. Let me think about that tonight before I give you names. But you should know you've got good employees."

"That's what I like to hear."

By the time they walked back to his car and drove to her house, the sun was setting in the western sky. When they walked up onto her porch, Marc stepped between her and the door. Surprised, she looked up at him, suddenly feeling caught in the depths of his brown eyes.

"Definitely, I've made a good choice here," he said in husky tones that gave her a tingle.

"And I know I made a good decision in accepting your offer. You've solved so many problems in my life. My world will change, thanks to you. The thing we need to remember is you have plans and I have plans. I've had my goals since the first six months of my mom's illness. I don't intend to give them up. I got engaged and we thought we could work it out, but we didn't plan on a baby. This baby is part of me and my mom and my family, and I'm not giving it up. Now I'll be free to get my education. I feel I owe that to my mom."

"That's one reason you were such a good choice. You have an agenda. You won't want to stay married. Even if we get along great, you'll want to go to med school and I won't want a wife who is wrapped up in school and becoming a doctor. Besides, you know, Lara, that I still love my wife and I'm not over that loss."

"I understand that. You know you have to let go, but part of you can't ever let go when it's someone you love," she said solemnly.

He nodded. "How about seven tomorrow night?"

"Excellent. Tonight I'll have my own little celebration all by myself. Tomorrow night we'll make wedding plans."

"Are you taking charge of my life?" he asked, looking amused.

"I wouldn't dream of it. You're capable of taking care of yourself."

"I'm glad to hear you think so," he said, smiling at her.

"I'm going in and celebrate."

"Save some celebration for tomorrow night. When I leave here, I'll go see my mom. I want to tell her and my grandfather about you. My grandfather's days are really limited. He's a sick old man."

Marc caught her lightly beneath her chin, making her heart flutter. "You're absolutely sure, Lara? You can take tonight to think—"

She stifled his words with a finger to his lips. "I'm absolutely sure I want to marry you on a temporary basis."

He smiled and she pulled her hand away. "Good. You've made me happy, and you've solved a big dilemma for me. I want to keep Grandpa happy in his last days. I don't want him to worry about his family."

"That's good, Marc. You're a good guy."

"Maybe not quite so good," he said as he shook his head. "I am going to inherit a lot if I do what he wants."

"You could get along without all that. You love the ranch because of your grandfather."

"You keep seeing that halo over my head," he said.

"There are moments it's there. Moments," she said, smiling at him.

He laughed. "That's what I thought from my very practical secretary. You don't really see me as such a saint."

"With what you're going to do for me, oh, yes, I do see a halo. Now, I think you should let me say good-night and go inside."

"Of course," he said, stepping away. "I'll see you tomorrow, and tomorrow night I'll take you to dinner and we'll plan our wedding."

"I can't believe it."

"Start believing. I'm really happy, Lara, and I hope you are, too."

She smiled as she watched him walk toward his car. Only when he pulled away did she go inside.

When she shut the door behind her, she finally let go. Shouting for joy, she spun around her entryway and stopped in front of a mirror that had belonged to her mother. She looked at herself. "Mrs. Marc Medina. Hello, Mrs. Marc Medina," she said, feeling tingles each time she said her future name. She was going to marry him. She would have enough money for her future, for her education, for her baby. More than enough money. She'd even be able to pay some of her mother's medical bills. Marc was being incredibly generous. He was a multi-millionaire, but he must be inheriting a lot to be so generous. She waved her arms in the air and spun around again.

"Mrs. Marc Medina," she repeated, looking at herself again. This time, though, her exuberance was tempered. She told herself she needed to guard her heart well, because Marc would stick with his plan and end their marriage. She knew he was strong-willed and she would be deluding herself if she thought he would fall in love and want to stay married. That wasn't what she wanted, anyway. She wanted to be a doctor and to pursue a career in medical research.

Meanwhile, Lara intended to enjoy Marc, have a good time with him and keep her heart absolutely locked away. She turned to face the mirror again. "Can you do that when he is handsome, fun, and oh, so sexy?"

Yes, she could keep from going to bed with him. She'd known him a year and hadn't slept with him, hadn't fallen in love with him. She didn't want emotional hang-ups tangling up her life now that she could do so many things she'd planned on doing. She had to resist his appeal.

"After this marriage I have plans for my future and Marc Medina is no part of them. And Marc has plans for his future and I'm not part of his plans," she told her reflection in the mirror. "Remember that. I have plans for my future and I can't wait to start."

She rushed to her closet to plan what she would wear to work.

It was past 2:00 a.m. when she fell asleep, and her dreams all included Marc Medina.

To her relief, the next day at work she was too busy to think about her new life or her dinner plans, and she barely saw Marc until after four when he postponed their talk and told her he would pick her up shortly before seven.

After work she rushed home to shower, change clothes and take down her hair, aware it was the first time that she'd have her hair down with him and be dressed in a flirty, flattering outfit. Was he even a fraction as excited as she? She suspected he merely viewed their dinner the same way he would one of his business dinners where he was about to close a deal.

She, on the other hand, could barely contain her excitement or stop thinking about the fantastic fortune he would give her. But along with her excitement came a constant nagging worry that she should guard her heart or risk getting badly hurt. She had to stay out of his bed, because sex would mean nothing to him except physical satisfaction. She had to be on constant guard against seduction that would be briefly satisfying and then could bring down all sorts of problems for her.

She needed to keep a wall between them, she reminded herself. Eventually, they would part and he would never look back. By then if she had her baby, she'd better have her life in order.

As she laid out clothes to wear, she looked at herself in the mirror, studying her stomach, which was still flat. She wasn't far along in her pregnancy and she was tall and slender. Most people would think this baby was Marc's and he was agreeable to that. Why was he being so generous with her? Was it because of the loss of his own baby and his wife? She knew he was relieved to find someone who would be happy to part when he ended their marriage—she could understand that one and how she was probably the only woman he knew who would walk away with a smile. And she'd better maintain that distance from him so she would be able to leave without any kind of hurt. She had worked for him for a year and she could say goodbye and be okay right now. She wanted to feel the same way when they ended their marriage.

When her doorbell rang, she took a deep breath, picked up her purse and went to answer. Her new husband-to-be and her new life stood waiting on the other side of her closed door.

# Three

While he waited for Lara to come to the door, Marc looked at the neat flowerbeds bordering the porch of the small house where Lara lived. He wondered how much they would see each other once they wed. She could settle on the ranch because he knew that's what his grandfather wanted. Other than that, he didn't care what she did to get ready for her baby and to go back to school when their marriage ended.

The door swung open and he turned, momentarily startled. "Lara?" His gaze swept over her and his pulse jumped unexpectedly. His eyes narrowed as he stared at her. "You worked until your regular closing time, so you had just an hour to get ready."

"That's right," she said, looking at him with wide, curious blue eyes.

"You look gorgeous."

She smiled. "Thank you. Come in and see where I live."

He walked into her place, not because he was interested in seeing where she lived. He merely wanted to look at her longer.

"You let your hair down. I never see you like this."

"No, this isn't how I want to look at the office. I stick to business there, as you know. We get things done, and that's what I want. Tonight's a little different and it's not an office event. It's a celebration, so I dressed for the occasion."

"Did you ever," he said. "You look absolutely wonderful. I'm happy all over again that I asked you and you accepted." His gaze swept over her again. Her thick, long dark brown hair was brushed back from her face, caught and pinned on the sides of her head to fall freely with the ends in big, loose curls. He had the ridiculous impulse to tangle his fingers in the inviting mass.

"Come in and look around." She turned and he followed her, his gaze slipping over her much more slowly, drifting down to her tiny waist. She had a slight, sexy sway to her hips as she walked. She wore a sleeveless black dress that ended above her knees. It was formfitting, beautiful and seductive with her figure. And she did have a figure, something she hadn't shown to this extent before.

And he had never seen as much of her legs before. Now he discovered her legs were long, so long and shapely that he couldn't stop admiring them. But this new discovery was disturbing. He didn't want to find her highly appealing. He wanted the kind of impersonal relationship they'd had all year at the office. His heart was still locked away, numb after losing Kathy, and he didn't want involvement with Lara, a night in bed with her because of lust and then all kinds of emotional complications. He wanted to stay out of her bed and keep this marriage in name only. But he'd just discovered that was going to be more difficult than he had imagined. He tried to reassure himself by thinking about their past year working closely together. There had never been even one second of flirting, much less anything more.

As he glanced again at her legs, he didn't feel reassured.

Her home was filled with furniture that looked as if she had inherited it from her mother—a big comfortable-looking wooden rocking chair plus two wingback chairs in deep blue upholstery and a matching sofa. He gave his surroundings a cursory glance and returned to looking at her.

"You have a nice place."

She smiled at him as she picked up her purse. "It's plain and small, but adequate for me."

"If you're ready, shall we go?"

"I'm ready," she said, and she locked up as she left.

He couldn't keep from looking at her. "You've never looked like this at the office."

"I think the way I look at the office is more conducive to a business atmosphere and I don't care to draw undo attention to myself."

"I think all that might have worked to my advantage," he said, wondering if this was going to be the purely businesslike arrangement he had anticipated.

He held the door for her, and when she slid into the seat, he glimpsed her gorgeous long legs as her dress slipped high above her knees before she pulled it down slightly.

As he closed the door and walked around the car, he was hot, intensely aware of her and wanting to get another long look at her. And that's when he had his answer. He would never see his secretary quite the same way as he had before this evening. Not after he'd had a glimpse of the good-looking woman she actually was.

At the restaurant they sat in a secluded corner. He ordered a glass of milk for her and white wine for himself, and she laughed when he held up his wine glass. "To a fabulous, brief marriage that will reward us both," he said.

Her eyes sparkled and her full lips curved in a tempting smile as their glasses clinked slightly.

"A glass of milk doesn't have quite the ring that two wine glasses do when touched in a toast," she observed.

"No, it doesn't." They both drank and he set down his glass. "Let's order and then we can talk about a wedding."

After they had given their orders, he reached across to take her soft hand into his. To his amazement he felt sparks from the slight touch. Since when did he feel any electrifying reaction from merely touching a woman's hand—particularly his secretary, whom he saw every day? As he released her hand, he wondered how much she was going to become involved in his life in this brief, fake marriage of convenience.

He hadn't expected he would notice her much more at the ranch than he had at the office, but he had miscalculated where his quiet secretary was concerned. He should have paid closer attention, but he was still pleased with his choice. She would be perfect in so many ways, mainly in moving on when the year was up. Plus, she needed someone and he could help her and her baby. He knew she was locked into that education and career, and neither hell nor high water nor anything he did would change it. He was completely familiar with a woman driven to accomplish something.

"Now, what kind of wedding would you like to have?" he asked. "Remember, it has to be this month."

"I think, given the circumstances that you and I are not in love," she said quietly, her big, blue eyes making his heart race, "I think we should have a small wedding. I'm not far along in my pregnancy and if we have a small wedding this month, by the time I have to announce that I'm pregnant, people will think it's your baby that I'm carrying. Are you all right with that?"

"Yes, I am. That was part of this deal. I told you that your baby can have my name."

"Marc, you're really generous," she said, her eyes shining.

"Just remember, I'm gaining, too."

"Is a small wedding all right with you? Because you have all sorts of people you probably are obligated to ask. I have no idea about your relatives except what you've recently told me."

"My close relatives will be there—my mom, my grandmother. My closest friends, Gabe Callahan and his wife. I'll ask Gabe to be my best man. After the ceremony, we'll have a big reception and invite our friends, everyone we want."

"Since I don't have relatives and you do, if you'd like, we could just have a small wedding at the hospital— then your grandfather could be present. If he's able, we could have it in his room or just outside his room."

"You're willing to do that?" Marc asked, surprised and pleased.

"Yes, because it doesn't matter to me, and I can marry in a week, if you want."

His pulse jumped because he didn't expect this much cooperation from anyone, even her. It was enough that she'd accepted his proposal. "That's fantastic, Lara. The sooner we marry, the sooner the clock starts ticking on the year I have to stay on the ranch. Also, something could happen to my grandfather at any point and I would like for him to know that I married and did what he wanted."

"That's good. We need to get the license."

"I'll take care of that," he said, guessing she was moving back into secretary-boss mode. They paused when the waiter set green salads in front of them, and once they were alone, they continued discussing the wedding.

"We should be able to marry Saturday, if you can, or even Friday," he said, and she nodded.

"Either one is fine. I'd prefer to avoid missing the class I'm enrolled in. I go to Denton to school on Wednesday nights, so Friday or Saturday won't be an interference."

"When we move to the ranch, you'll have a hell of a drive."

"It's only once a week until December. I'll do it," she said, and he knew she would. He gazed at her. She was perfect for this temporary marriage of convenience. She would walk away as easily as he would. For a real marriage, though, she was the type of woman he vowed he would never marry—a driven woman who put business first even though her motives were to help others and work toward a cure for illness. She would work long hours—just like his mother always had. He didn't need her for the real thing, though, so this would work beautifully.

"I expected a lot from this job, but never marriage to the boss. Wow," she said, laughing, her eyes sparkling.

"I'll have my accountant contact you and set up an appointment. You need to open an account where we can deposit funds on a regular basis, so you'll have money available. Before we part tonight, I'll give you a check for the wedding, your dress, that sort of thing."

She laughed again. "I cannot believe this is happening to me."

"It's real and it'll get more real when you're Mrs. Marc Medina."

"Mrs. Marc Medina," she repeated, shaking her head. "Absolutely impossible."

"It's possible and it's happening, and we'll both benefit," he said.

When she turned those wide blue eyes on him, his pulse jumped. Still, he knew if they could resist going to bed together and manage to keep this relationship just like it was tonight—no desire or flirting or wanting each other—then when it came time, parting would be easy. But he suddenly had a feeling it wasn't going to be as easy as he anticipated. His reaction to her had changed, and it shocked him how much restraint he was having to use around her. How could she cause the sexy reactions he was having?

He tamped down those tingles of awareness and focused on the business at hand.

"I didn't talk to my mom or grandfather last night," he said. "I wanted to wait until dinner tonight and see if you had second thoughts. You do understand that when the year is up, we'll divorce, right? I'll have a contract drawn up. I don't want you to have any illusions about staying married."

"I understand and I won't. I'm marrying to pay for my baby and my education, not for romance," she said and then blushed. "Sorry, that sounded very crass."

"No, it didn't. It sounded very honest. So am I. We have the same motives and goals so we understand each other and we'll walk away and never look back."

"I'm thrilled," she said, smiling at him, and his insides clutched. In an instant she could make him hot and wanting her. Where was this physical attraction coming from? That had not happened in the office and she wasn't causing it deliberately now. Was he getting in deeper than he had intended? He brushed that question aside as impossible.

"I've been totally alone and on my own for so long. This is going to be a different world, even a marriage of convenience that is only temporary."

"I guess that's why you're very independent."

"I didn't know it showed," she said.

"A little. It's not bad to be independent," he said.

He thought about how much time they'd be spending together over the coming year. The ranch house was big. Would they naturally drift together or would they gradually drift apart and barely see each other? He hadn't put many stipulations in his proposal, nor could he, really. But in his mind he knew what he had to do. Keep his distance.

He kept telling himself that all through dinner, whenever the urge to take her hand threatened him.

Dinner was pleasant, despite the undercurrent of tension. They talked about the wedding and life on the ranch. Finally, he took her home, walking her to her door.

"Want to come in?" she asked, smiling at him.

He shook his head. There was only one thing he wanted.

He put a hand on the door and leaned down till his mouth was a breath from hers.

He was about to kiss her.

She backed up quickly, resisting the urge to place her hands on his chest and push him away. She didn't need the physical contact.

"We agreed to avoid sex in this union. We might as well stick with that tonight," she said, feeling he was on the verge of changing their relationship. "We both have to remember this marriage of convenience is headed for a divorce in one year. Let's pass on kisses."

He looked amused as he nodded. "That's the smart thing to do." He took a step back. "I'll talk to my family and get back with you about when you can meet them." He looked down into her eyes. "Lara, you're right in that we'll both be better off to leave kisses out of this. You and I want to walk away someday and it'll be a lot easier if we keep this relationship somewhat like what we've had this past year."

"I agree. Now, you may have certain expectations, since I've been your secretary and at your beck and call every work day for almost a year. I think we need to establish right now that that's over."

"Are you going all independent woman on me?"

"I might be. After all, this isn't a boss-secretary relationship we're entering into. We'll have adjustments to make. You'll have adjustments to make, I'm sure, because I won't be your secretary any longer," she said. "What's far more standard now, if I'm your wife, is for me to start giving you some orders."

His smile grew. "Have you ever been hiding yourself. You're a whole different woman," he said, his gaze drifting over her.

"This is a brand-new situation. We're just getting started in our new relationship, and of course, there will be adjustments, but I will not be at your beck and call as I have been."

He looked amused as she leaned closer and patted his arm. "Whatever we say and do, when the time is up, the marriage is over. You want that and I want that and we both should keep that goal in sight."

"You have an agenda that evidently you don't think can include marriage and a husband."

"I think it'll work better without a husband. Mostly, I know you don't want to stay married, either."

"You're right. That's almost enough right there to make me fall in love with you—you have an agenda you'll stick by, a bargain we made that you'll keep, and I can trust you completely to do as you promised. I can't say that about any other woman I know. Don't think you aren't greatly appreciated."

"I can be even more appreciated," she said in a sultry voice, flirting with him. Instantly, she stepped back. "Oh, Marc. I take that last remark back. That's a line I don't want to cross. Let's keep this relationship as much like it has been as possible."

"I agree, Lara. That's the sensible thing to do and it'll be best for both of us in the long run. I have to tell you, though, I'm appreciating you more by the second right now," he said.

"Then I'll just say goodnight," she said. "It was a fun evening and we're moving along."

"This is going to be good for both of us. You'll see. I'm happy with it," he said, meaning what he was saying. "I'll see you tomorrow. It was a fun evening, Lara."

"I had a wonderful time."

"I feel very fortunate to have you for my secretary and to have the wits to propose to you. You're perfect for this and you won't fritter away a lot of the money on clothes and jewelry. And you've agreed that we'll avoid sex, which we easily did this past year."

"I should hope I wouldn't have sex with my boss. As for clothes and jewelry, there is enough money coming that I can get some new duds if I want them," she teased, and he smiled again. Impulsively, he hugged her.

"Wait, let me get a picture to show Mom. I want to tell her about you before I take you to meet her." He held out his phone and took Lara's picture. He then stepped beside her, slipping his arm around her waist to take a picture of the two of them.

"There," he said, showing the pictures to her.

"Will she approve of me?"

"Of course. If I've proposed to you, she'll trust my judgment. We're close. We've always been a close family. I was close with my dad."

"Do you look like your dad?"

He laughed. "Not at all. He was much shorter and had straight black hair. He had brown eyes, too. That's about the only similarity. I look a little like my mom, but she's short. I don't know where I get this height. My grandfathers aren't tall."

"I'm glad you're close with your family. I look forward to meeting your mother. Tell your mom you didn't get me pregnant. She'll think this is your baby and her first grandchild. I don't want her to be upset when the marriage is over in the fall."

"I'll tell her the whole deal. But I'm warning you now. My mom will get attached to your baby. She miscarried several times and she loves babies. No matter what we tell her, she'll treat this baby like her first grandchild for sure."

"She'll always be welcome to come see us. I'll be in the area."

"We don't have to worry about that now. I'll see you tomorrow."

She stepped back and her eyes were wide as she gazed at him. "Dinner was delicious. I had a fun, interesting time and I'll see you tomorrow evening. Thank you for dinner."

"We're off to the best possible start," he said.

"As long as we aren't stirring up trouble."

"No. You have your eye on your agenda and my heart is locked away."

Her expression changed and she looked solemn. "That's right, Marc. I'll see you tomorrow." She opened her door and stepped inside. "Good night," she said.

"Night, Lara." He turned and walked down the steps and headed to his car. In minutes his taillights disappeared around the corner.

It was early in the evening and Marc drove from Dallas to Downly where his mother still lived and had her successful restaurant that drew people from Dallas daily in spite of the distance.

He turned into the house his mother had built when he was in college. By then, the money problems had vanished and her restaurant was a success; his grandfather was a help and Marc was on a scholarship. The one-story house was set back on a landscaped lawn with flowers still blooming in the warm Texas fall.

He had called her and when he circled the white stucco house to the back, she stood in the doorway waiting for him.

Pilar Medina was short with thick black hair and brown eyes, and he loved her and appreciated all she had done for him as he grew up. He hurried to the house, and as soon as he stepped inside, he hugged her and kissed her cheek.

"Come in. Have a drink. We can sit and talk and you can tell me what you're doing."

"How's Grandpa today?"

"He had an easier day and the nurses are so good to him."

"Good. I'll have a beer and I'll get it. What can I get for you?"

She waved her hand. "Nothing, thank you. I'll just listen."

He smiled, knowing she would do more than just listen.

Out of habit, they sat at the kitchen table and she placed a bowl of pretzels in front of him. She sat and gazed expectantly at Marc.

"I want to do what Grandpa wants. I'll marry this month."

"Marc, I don't know about this pushing you into a

marriage. He keeps telling me to stop worrying. He says he knows what he's doing and he says he knows his grandson and what's best for you."

Marc had to laugh as he shook his head. "Sometimes I don't think he realizes I'm a grown man now."

She smiled and patted Marc's hand. "He loves you with all his heart. He's been a good father to me and a good grandfather to you. And he stepped in when we lost your father."

"What Grandpa doesn't know is that when the year is over, I'll end the marriage. I'll have papers drawn up that the woman I will marry will sign, agreeing to my terms."

Pilar rubbed her forehead. "Marc, I still worry. This marriage of convenience—Grandpa should not be forcing you into that."

"I want to make him happy. I want to do what he wants and I want his last days to be happy, without worries about me and you and, above all, about Grandma and the ranch. He wants me there to run the ranch and he knows I'll see to it that she's taken care of and can live in their house where she wants to stay."

"You're a good son and a good grandson, but this worries me."

"Stop worrying. I've already worked it out. I've proposed to someone, Mom."

"Aye, aye, aye. Who is she?"

"The perfect person. She's Lara Seymour, my secretary." He pulled out his phone. "Here's her picture. She has a master's degree and wants to go to medical school. She has no family. The dad walked out years ago. Her sister died when she was young and her mother died just a few years ago and it's because of her mother she wants to study medicine so she can go into medical research to work toward finding cures. I've made her a good offer, enough money to cover her expenses for her education."

"Ah, Marc, I worry about this and I cannot talk your grandfather out of it. He is determined. He tells me he knows what he is doing. How can he know what he is doing when he interferes in your life and he's a sick old man in a hospital bed?"

"Leave him alone. He won't change his mind and I don't want him worrying."

Pilar wiped her eyes. "I worry. I worry about Grandpa and Grandma. I worry about you. I know you love them and are good to them. You're good to me, too."

He smiled. "I love all of you, Mom. Stop worrying. Let me do the worrying," he said gently, hugging her lightly and kissing her temple. "You're worrying for nothing. Lara is going to be perfect for this, and besides, it's a temporary situation."

"Once she legally becomes your wife, she may not want to leave."

"This one will. Lara has been a great secretary. I know she'll cooperate completely." He told her how she'd been engaged and how she'd broken the engagement. "She hasn't told anyone at the office except me, but she's pregnant with his child."

His mother frowned at him and her face paled. "No," she said softly. "Ahh, Marc."

"It's all right. The money I'm giving her will take care of her and her baby. She can afford a nanny. I'll set up a trust so her baby's education will be paid for. I told her this baby will have my name and that's fine with me."

"Marc, this little baby—you won't be able to dissolve this marriage. You're going to love that child."

"This is not a permanent marriage. It's a marriage of convenience and it will end."

"It may end and it may not end. You might fall in love."

"I won't. I promise I won't. I've worked closely with her for a year now and there's nothing between us except I respect her and want to help her. She's a fine person, but we won't fall in love. She has her life planned out. Don't worry," he said, wishing his mother didn't even have to know the details of the arrangement. She looked shaken and unhappy, even more worried than before.

"Oh, Marc," she said, grasping his hand and gazing at him intently.

"Please, don't worry," he said, surprised by how badly she was taking this because she knew the demands on him that her father had made. "Mom, you know how much you wanted the restaurant to succeed. Well, Lara is like that about becoming a doctor. That's all she really wants for herself and her baby. She will leave me when the year is up and she won't change her mind. She's as driven as you are. Her fiancé wanted her to get an abortion, so she broke the engagement. This baby will give her a family."

Pilar's eyes filled with tears that she hastily brushed away. "Marc, I knew this day might come and I finally think it has. You are marrying and it's different from when you married Kathy. I thought about talking to you then, but you were so in love, so happy. I didn't want to do anything to worry you. You are older now and are marrying again. You think it won't last and it probably won't, but I think it is time for you to know some things that I've never told you."

He smiled. "We have dark family secrets? Tell me. I'm sure there's nothing disastrous."

Surprising him, she didn't smile. She caught his hand and held it. "Your father loved you with all his heart and he was a good father to you."

"The best. I loved him, too. He was a very good dad. And I have a very good mom and very good grandparents. Now, what's worrying you?"

"There is something I haven't ever told you. There is a secret I've never shared with you. Now you're marrying this woman and she's having a baby. It isn't your baby, but it is a reminder that you don't know what your future will be. I think I need to tell you some things."

Startled, he gazed at her, unable to imagine what dark secret his mother could possibly have hidden from him all these years. They had always been a close family and he was at a loss because this was so unlike his mother.

She wiped her eyes. "I was so young when we moved here. So young, so inexperienced. I worked for Gabe's family. I never dreamed you would be best friends."

"We were the same age, went to the same schools growing up and played high school football together. Seemed the natural thing to me."

"I'm glad. I cleaned house for the Callahans and lived in the maid's quarters on the top floor of the mansion. I was only fifteen when I started and my second year there Mrs. Callahan was pregnant with Gabe. By that time my father had gotten a job with the rancher and he and my mother lived on the ranch, so I was on my own. I left the Callahans and got a little place in Downly and started selling my tamales. Then I met your father. We were married the first month we met. He was twenty-two and I loved him with all my heart." To his amazement, his mother covered her eyes with a handkerchief and cried quietly. He knew she was remembering his dad and reached out to squeeze her arm lightly in a sympathetic gesture.

She faced him. "I'm sorry for things I did, but I can't be sorry that I have you. You know how I love you."

"Of course I do. And I love you. What's worrying you, Mom? It can't be that bad."

"Marc, understand that I was very young and on my own. Your father came along and loved me and it was true love for both of us. You are going to marry, and while it is a marriage of convenience, it will change your life. You don't know what tomorrow will bring. I think you need to know what I'm going to tell you. Very few people know the truth because of the time element."

"Mom, just tell me what you're trying to say," he said, smiling at her.

She grasped his hand tightly and her hands were icy. Worry filled her dark eyes and he couldn't imagine what could be so terrible that she was this upset.

"Your bride-to-be—there are some parallels to my life."

"How so?" he asked, staring at her and wondering what she was getting at.

"Marc, I worked for Dirkson Callahan." She closed her eyes and her voice was soft. "I got pregnant with Dirkson Callahan's baby," she whispered.

Stunned, Marc felt as if he had been punched in the gut. He stared at his mother. There was only one reason she was telling him this. Without thinking, he jumped out of his chair and backed up.

"Dad wasn't my blood father," Marc said.

She shook her head. "I married him so soon afterwards, everyone thought he was. I didn't even tell your grandparents. Grandma and Grandpa to this day don't know the truth. Your dad knew the truth and he truly loved me. We loved each other and he was so good to me. Everyone thought I was pregnant by him. There was never any suspicion or breath of scandal."

"I'm Dirkson Callahan's son," Marc whispered. He shook his head as if realizing where he was and that he was standing. He sat down again. "That's why you quit working for the Callahans. Gabe and I are the same age—Dirkson got you pregnant the same time his wife was pregnant," Marc said without realizing he had spoken the words aloud. He didn't want to think about Dirkson Callahan being his father. "He was a lousy dad for Gabe. For all of his sons. He didn't speak to or recognize Blake Callahan, his illegitimate firstborn. And he's my father," he said, stunned by the revelation. "Gabe and I are half brothers. No wonder we get along."

She sobbed. "I'm sorry, son. But you need to know. I always knew the day would come when I'd have to tell you the truth."

"Dirkson Callahan knows he's my father, doesn't he?"

"Yes, of course. He gave me money to leave and I agreed to never reveal the truth to anyone, including you. He wouldn't give me the money unless I did and

I signed a paper to that effect. I told your dad before I married him, and he said he would be your real father."

"He was. John Medina was my true father in every way except biologically. He was a wonderful father and I loved him and respected him." Marc couldn't stop the next statement. "I think Gabe should know."

"If he does, then word will get out and Dirkson will know I finally broke my promise," she said, looking stricken again and wringing her hands. "He gave me money to start my tamale business on the condition I never tell anyone the truth, including you. He's a powerful man, Marc."

"So am I, Mom. Trust me, I don't want to claim him as my father. I promise you that."

"Will you share this with your future bride?"

"No. I'm not sharing this with anyone. Not even Gabe. I don't want to hurt you. And I don't want to hurt Gabe and his brothers—although I think they're immune to being hurt by their dad any longer."

His mother reached out for his hand. "Your Lara. You and she are in the same situation I faced. You will claim another man's child as your own. How could this happen to you? Grandpa should not have made such demands on you."

"He's doing what he thinks is best for me and for Grandma. He's sick and he's old and I don't think he's thinking clearly on this—wanting me to marry this month."

"I know, I know," she said, while tears spilled down her cheeks.

He put his arm around her and hugged her. "Stop worrying. Dad was my dad. So I have some Callahan blood—I can live with that. I didn't have Dirkson in my life. I had a wonderful dad and John Medina is my real father as far as I'm concerned. And he was a great dad and deeply loved. End of story. This is now our shared secret and that's that. When I tell someone—if I ever do—I'll let you know. A part of me feels Gabe should know, but it might not ever happen. It really won't matter. We're already best friends. Otherwise, there's no one now who needs to know."

"I know you'll do what you think is best. Marc, that paper I signed—if I ever let the truth be known, I have to pay Dirkson back the money he gave me."

"Mom, I can pay back every penny and never miss it. I know it wasn't a gigantic sum because you started your tamale business with nothing except a cart. Oh, damn. That's why you worked so hard. You were trying to earn enough to take care of yourself and me. You had a tiny little hut. I've seen the pictures. Oh, Mom, I'm proud of you. You did so well. Don't worry one minute about paying Dirkson Callahan back. I'll take care of him, if necessary." Then the realization sank in and he nearly spat out the words. "Damn, I'm a Callahan."

His mother shook her head. "By blood only. Remember that. You're a wonderful son and, like your real father and your grandfather, you're a fine man. They raised you. Think of it like a blood transfusion."

He laughed and shook his head. "I don't think I can quite see it that way."

"I knew the day would come when I would have to tell you."

"You've told me and that's that. Now stop worrying about it. It's still a secret and I love you and Dad as much as I did when I came through the door an hour ago. I'll always think of John Medina as my dad. I barely know Dirkson Callahan."

She smiled at him and patted his cheek. "You're a precious boy."

He grinned. "I love you, Mom. Now, we better get back to the wedding discussion. It's coming up soon. I want to bring Lara by to meet you."

"Let's all have dinner at the restaurant. I'll get Grandma there, and we'll take a plate to your grandfather."

"You know he can't eat tamales and chili. Or he isn't supposed to. I'll take Lara by to meet him, too. I think you're going to like her."

"If you do, I will," she said, smiling at him.

"I have to get going now. I want to go by the hospital and tell Grandpa, if I can get in to see him and he's awake. Otherwise, I'll go in the morning on the way to work."

She followed him to the door and he turned to hug her. "I love you. You're the best mom in the whole world."

She laughed as she hugged him in return. "And you are the best son," she said. "I love you so much."

He smiled at her and left, but as he drove, he couldn't stop thinking about his mother's secret. Dirkson Callahan was his biological father. He felt like Gabe should know. But what would it hurt if he never knew? He and Gabe would be the same friends either way. And there was no reason to share the news with Lara. She was temporary in his life and it wasn't his child she was carrying. For now, the secret was going no farther than his mother's kitchen.

He was thankful his mother had never told him until

now. That he had grown up thinking the father he loved was truly his dad. And he was, as far as Marc was concerned. Blood was the only tie he had to Dirkson Callahan. He'd be happy to have Gabe for a half brother, but he already had him for best friend, so that was good enough.

He thought about Dirkson giving all his attention and efforts to business. Marc had a workaholic blood father on one side and a workaholic mother on the other. He could understand why his mother put work first when he was young. She was only sixteen when he was born. Along with his dad, she was trying to make a living. Growing up, he'd wanted her to be homeroom mother or to come to more of his ball games, but she'd been so busy.

Sometimes he had felt neglected, but looking back now, he realized that he had seen his mother's devotion to her work through the eyes of a child. He never thought about how young she was. Fortunately, John Medina came into their lives. Though he'd never made the income that Grandpa or Mom did, he'd shared the load and made his mother happy.

His mother still worked long hours each day when she didn't need to work at all. She was a micromanager, too. He'd always promised himself he'd never get that way or marry someone who was.

He was marrying Lara. She was as driven as his mother, but now he was grateful she had him to help her so she wouldn't have to worry constantly about money or care for her baby alone.

He thought back to the evening he'd spent with her. He'd had a good time discovering her sense of humor and quick wit. If they continued the same kind of relationship they had at the office, he was confident he made an excellent choice for his temporary wife.

Had he?

Or had he brought a heap of trouble on himself by getting tied up with a woman he found attractive?

# Four

A week later, on Saturday morning, Lara had butterflies in her stomach. This was her wedding day. A marriage of convenience wedding day. A temporary marriage that was a business deal, actually.

Whatever she called it, this morning she was marrying Marc Medina. She still hadn't met his grandfather because he hadn't been well enough to have company, but she had met Marc's sweet mother, who looked amazingly young. She'd learned Marc had been born when his mother was sixteen.

Wedding traditions had gone out the window and Marc was picking her up. They were going to marry in his grandfather's hospital room—a very unromantic place and definitely not a beautiful one, but hopefully, it would please his grandfather and Marc was doing what he could for the man.

When the doorbell rang, her racing pulse jumped again. Her groom waited at the door. She still couldn't believe this was happening. Not in her wildest dreams a year ago would she have been able to guess what she'd be doing on this date. She glanced down at her tailored pale-pink silk dress. It was conservative, with long sleeves and a skirt that fell to midcalf. She wore matching high-heeled pumps.

She opened the door and her breath caught as she smiled at Marc. In a charcoal suit, white shirt and red tie, he looked handsome, successful and self-assured. And so appealing. She tried to ignore that last thought.

He smiled, stepping into her house and closing the door behind him. "You look beautiful," he said, his gaze sweeping over her again.

"Thank you."

"I'm ready to go."

The sun was bright on the cool, brisk September morning. He took her arm and they left to get into his black sports car. She was aware of Marc's every touch, of a constant buzzing excitement when she was with him, a continual warning to keep that reserve between them she'd always had at the office. He was more relaxed with her now and she was going to have to keep up her guard. There was no love in this marriage and she needed to always remember that.

"I'm a little nervous about meeting your grandparents," she told him when they parked at the hospital.

"So far this has been a good day for my grandfather, and up until five minutes ago, it was clear to go see him. Hopefully it will still be that way when we get upstairs. I'm sorry you couldn't meet them before today."

"Me, too." She put a trembling hand to her belly. "I have butterflies in my stomach."

"You shouldn't," he said quietly. "My grandfather will be happy today. Mom will be Mom, looking at you to see if you're suitable to marry her son."

Lara smiled and he took her arm as they walked down the hospital corridor.

Marc had had a dinner party the night before for the small group of relatives and friends who could attend. Most of them were at the hospital now, gathered in the waiting room on his grandfather's floor.

When they reached the lounge, Lara moved around the room with Marc, greeting Gabe Callahan, who would be best man, and Gabe's new wife, Meg. Lara's single attendant was her friend Patsy Wilson, who'd be stepping into Lara's vacated job.

Lara smiled politely as she greeted Marc's mother, who hugged her lightly.

"You look beautiful." She took Lara's hand. "I pray you and Marc find happiness."

"Thank you. My life will be easier because of your son."

"Family, the heart—these are what's important in life. Keep each other happy when you're together. That's what I tell Marc."

"Thank you," Lara said, smiling at his mother. "He has such a nice family."

"Lara, I'm sorry your mother isn't here to see you today," Pilar said.

"Thank you. I wish she was here," Lara said, thinking it was nice of Marc's mother to make such a comment.

Minutes later, when the minister arrived, Marc

quietly got the group into their places in his grandfather's room. He took Lara to his grandfather's bedside. "Grandpa, this is my bride, Lara Seymour. I've told you about her."

"I'm happy to meet you," she said, as she looked at the small, frail, white-haired man whose bony hands lay on his chest. When he gazed at her, she felt as if he was alert and very aware of what was happening.

"Grandpa," Marc said, leaning down. "Do you want us to get married here in your room or would you rather sleep and have us go to the visitor's lounge?"

"You marry here where I can see you," he whispered hoarsely.

With Marc directing, everyone lined up and someone started music playing softly on a phone. The wedding was as surreal to her as everything else about Marc's proposal had been.

Lara glanced up at Marc and saw a muscle flex in his jaw. He seemed highly fond of his grandfather, so this might be a tough event, because it made it painfully obvious how frail the old man was.

Everything was in hushed tones, yet she was aware of Marc's grandmother holding her husband's hand and his eyes focused on Marc as Marc repeated his vows. Marc slipped a gorgeous diamond band on Lara's finger and then, finally, she heard the minister say, "You may kiss the bride."

Marc turned her to face him and she looked into his inscrutable brown eyes. She had no idea what he thought, except this was what he wanted.

He brushed her lips lightly with a fleeting, tender kiss, the faintest caress of his warm lips on hers, a feathery touch, yet she tingled to her toes. For a moment she thought this marriage might not be as easy to manage as they'd both anticipated. She had a definite physical reaction to him. Now that they'd be living together, it might be far more difficult to avoid a physical relationship than she had thought.

As soon as the ceremony was over, Marc walked up to his grandfather, who smiled and took Marc's hand in his shaky grip. "The ranch is yours. Take good care of Grandma. You're a good boy. Be happy, Marc, and may you and Lara have a long and joyous union," he whispered, closing his eyes.

Marc leaned down to kiss his grandfather's cheek, and when he turned to Lara, she saw that he battled tears. She thought of her own loss and could understand. She stepped close to take Marc's other hand and squeeze lightly to reassure him. He smiled at her, and for a moment she felt a closeness with him she hadn't ever felt before. To anyone watching, the gesture would seem a natural one between husband and wife. To her, it was a reminder that she needed to keep her distance. That this marriage would be brief and never hold love.

In the lounge, the others congratulated them and Marc's mother hugged her.

"Welcome to our family," she said, and Lara felt a mixed rush of gratitude for Pilar's easy acceptance while she knew it was only temporary. For an instant she felt a stabbing pang, a fleeting wish that this ceremony was real and she was becoming part of this family that seemed so filled with love for one another.

Would she ever find that for herself? She and her mother had been each other's only family for so long, and now Lara didn't even have her. She thought of the tiny baby she carried and looked at Marc as someone said something to him that made him laugh. She wished this baby was his. Another silly wish that couldn't possibly be.

Marc's mother hugged her again. "Be kind to Marc," she whispered for Lara's ears only. "He's a good man."

"I will be," Lara said. She couldn't help but find the comment odd, because from what she could see, Marc didn't need anything from anyone. He seemed as self-sufficient and self-confident as a human could be.

She looked over at him as he talked to Gabe Callahan. The two men were almost the same height, and they shared the same dark hair, though Marc's was far curlier.

He turned and their gazes met, and she felt as if sparks danced between them. Once again she heard that voice inside her head telling her to guard her heart with all her being. In spite of all this and how nice he had been to her, she knew absolutely, when the time came, he would dissolve this marriage and walk away without ever looking back. She knew his iron will, and there was no way Marc was going to fall in love so she'd better not, either, unless she wanted another big hurt and loss.

He walked up to her, interrupting her thoughts. "Hey, Mrs. Medina, let's move this party to the country club where we can cut loose and have a blast."

"Sounds good to me," she said and hurried out with him as he waved his hand in the air for the others to follow.

To her surprise, Marc had hired someone to plan the reception. She'd figured he would turn that over to her, but she had to admit it was fun to walk into the big ballroom and be surprised by the flowers and the food.

Before long they was seated at a round table with

the Callahan brothers. Marc sat on her right and Gabe's wife Meg was on her left. The woman's dark brown eyes sparkled as she gushed, "I love weddings, and you make a beautiful bride."

"Thank you," Lara answered. "Your husband is Marc's best friend, so I'm glad we'll be friends."

"Me too," Meg replied. "Those two guys know how to have fun. I've known both of them all my life, it seems. The Callahans are a great bunch except for their dad, but he's out of the picture most of the time."

Blake Callahan and his wife Sierra were also at the table. Meg pointed them out. "Sometime you'll get to meet the kids. There's Sierra and Blake's little girl, Emily, and of course Cade has adopted their niece, Amelia."

Lara had heard the story. The brother between Gabe and Cade—Nate, Amelia's daddy—was killed in a car crash along with Lydia, his wife. Because Cade had agreed to be guardian if anything happened, he had taken in Amelia. Since then he and Erin had adopted the child.

Meg laughed. "Come to think of it, we all seem to have girls in this family of men."

As if on cue, Cade Callahan joined them, along with his wife. Erin greeted Lara warmly. "Now you get to be friends with the entire Callahan clan. And we're glad to have you. We needed another woman in this group," she said, smiling at Lara.

"Everyone has made me feel so welcome," Lara said, aware of Marc's arm still across her shoulders.

"To a beautiful bride and a lucky groom," Blake said, his blue eyes twinkling. He held up his glass of champagne in a toast. "May you have a long and happy marriage." They all touched glasses and everyone sipped their champagne except Lara, who only smiled as she set her glass on the table.

As the Callahans talked to each other, she looked around the table. "You have nice friends," she said to Marc.

"I think so." He reached out and took her hand. "And now I think I should dance with my wife."

Three hours later people were still dancing and singing. She had to admit she'd had fun with Marc, who had shed his suit coat to dance all night. He caught her hand when the number ended.

"We've had pictures, cut the cake, danced with those we should. I'd say let's slip out and head to the ranch."

"I'm ready when you are," she said, her pulse jumping at the idea of leaving with him and starting life as Mrs. Marc Medina, even though love wasn't part of the deal. Now they would be living together in the ranch house and she would have to be on alert constantly. She hoped she could get back that very business-like atmosphere she'd had with him at the office, because she could not end up in his bed.

"You go one direction around the room and I'll go the other," Marc whispered to her. "Otherwise we'll just draw a crowd. I'll meet you outside that last door. Go down the hall and turn right."

"Got it. See you soon," she said.

As she spoke to others and drifted toward a door, she glanced over the room one more time. She'd had a fun, touching, beautiful wedding with loads of friends, yet it really was a meaningless event. She wondered why Marc had had the big blowout for a marriage of convenience that would end after twelve months. Maybe it made the event seem more real for his family. His mother certainly seemed happy.

Lara finally stepped out of the ballroom into the quiet hall. At the moment it was empty, and she hurried to the end where Marc had told her to turn right. Before she could, a hand stretched out and snagged hers, and Marc pulled her around the corner.

"Let's get out of here," he said, taking her hand and hurrying to the stairs. In minutes they slid into his waiting car.

"There's a big decorated limo waiting out front and a few people already hanging around it, I suppose to see us come out and leave. Sorry to disappoint them, but this is easier."

He pulled out onto the street. "Well, so far, so good. We did it. We got married in front of my grandparents and my mother. Thanks again, Lara. You're the perfect choice and it all went well. My grandfather was a happy man."

"Marc, he's so frail. I'm sorry because I know how much you love him."

"I do, but I've made him happy in his last days and he's made me happy, and we'll manage living on the ranch this year."

They drove to a private airport where Marc had a plane waiting and shortly they were airborne, buckled into seats in a luxurious lounge. "I stocked champagne for me and lemonade for you. We can sit back and relax. The rest of the day will be peace and quiet, which I'm ready for."

"So now I get to see this ranch I've been hearing about," she said, thinking more about being there with

Marc. He stretched out his long legs. Locks of black hair curled on his forehead.

"Know much about ranching?"

"Absolutely zero. I'm a city person. I don't even know anything about small towns like Downly."

"Since you're pregnant and you've never ridden, you'll have to stay away from the horses and the barns."

"Believe me, you don't have to tell me twice," she said, and they both smiled.

How was she going to resist him? This wasn't like the office, which was so businesslike and fast paced. Outside of work, Marc was far more laid-back and re-laxed. As she thought about it, he reached up to remove his tie and unbutton his collar.

"That feels better. Got anything you want to undo or take off?" he asked.

"No, I don't." She laughed, but her insides jumped at his innuendo. She scrambled to change the subject. "Once we're on the ranch, am I going to be isolated un-less I get back to Dallas?"

"Not at all. You'll have me there," he said, leaning close to touch her hand, a casual touch like he'd done several times today. But as with the ones that came be-fore it, the contact caused a sizzling response up her spine. The prospect of guarding her heart seemed more difficult each time she was with him. But she had to re-sist him, because they each had plans for their futures and none of those plans included the other. If she told him to stop being so friendly, she thought he would laugh it off and pay no attention. Those slight contacts with him didn't have the same effect on him. She was sure of it.

"At the ranch we can think of some way to pass the time," he told her.

"I've already enrolled in some online courses to keep up with my chemistry," she said. "I'm going for a doctorate in chemistry in case I don't get into medical school."

"Chemistry." He leaned forward, placing his hands on the arms of her chair. "I can show you some chemistry we can study right now in this plane," he said in a husky voice.

"You're flirting with me," she said. "We weren't going to do that. I thought this was going to be mostly a business arrangement."

"Relax a little. We might as well have some fun. Sure, I'm flirting with you. You're a beautiful woman and you're my wife now." His eyes were filled with devilment that made her laugh in spite of knowing that the more she encouraged him, the deeper she might sink into flirting and kissing and seduction—all of which she wanted to avoid as long as possible.

"Don't get too appealing and fun," she warned. "You don't want me falling in love with you and vice versa. We agreed about that."

"Once I get to working and go back to Dallas to take care of business along the way, you'll hardly see me," he said. "For now, this is our wedding day and we might as well party a little." He leaned closer, hemming her in.

"That was a really chaste kiss in the wedding ceremony," he said in a low voice. "We might try again and have a little more excitement today."

Sitting like this, she was skirting trouble and breaking her own rules before they even got to the ranch. She put up a hand between them.

"You know full well that we agreed to avoid a sexual relationship. Kissing might lead there," she said. "I don't want to fall in love with you—or even in bed with you. We agreed on that one."

"But you'll hurt my feelings," he said, smiling at her.

"No, I won't," she answered. Before she could utter another word he closed the last bit of distance and covered her mouth with his. His hands slipped off the arms of her seat to wrap around her and pull her closer.

The minute his mouth covered hers, her heart thudded and she couldn't resist his kiss. She wrapped her arms around his neck and clung to him. When their tongues met, a flame of passion sparked deep within her.

Desire—white hot, too long banked—ignited, and she kissed him in return. His hand slipped down over her breast and even though he caressed her through her clothing, his touches were fiery and made her want to be pressed against him even as she knew she shouldn't. Holding him, kissing him, letting him stroke her was taking them straight to disaster. Common sense cautioned her to stop, but her desire was stronger. Marc was incredibly sexy, more than any other man she had known—a discovery she wished she hadn't made—and she couldn't stop kissing him.

She moaned softly and wound her fingers in the short hair at the back of his neck.

She felt his fingers twist loose the buttons on her dress and then drift lightly across her bare breast, and she gasped with pleasure. In minutes he had the front of her dress open, and his fingers pushed away her lacy bra, caressing her lightly. She closed her eyes as she kissed him while sensations rocked her. She was unaware of what he was doing until he lifted her to his lap.

She opened her eyes. "You've put me in danger. We're flying and I should stay buckled into my seat."

"I'm holding you and I won't let go."

"You can't hold me as tightly as a seatbelt," she whispered between kisses.

"Yes, I can, and this is a smooth, safe ride and you're safe in my arms."

"I'm not safe from falling in love with you," she whispered.

She gasped with pleasure as he caressed her breasts with feathery strokes that made her tingle. With an effort she opened her eyes and wiggled out of his arms.

He looked at her intently. "I want you, Lara."

"That wasn't necessarily going to be part of the deal."

"Whatever we both want and whatever works out is part of the deal. I don't have to be in a rush, but Lara, you can't tell me you didn't like that just now or that you didn't like it when we kissed."

"You know I did," she said, feeling a blush heat her face. "But that doesn't make it the smart thing to do."

He smiled and moved his hands so she could go back to her own seat and buckle up again. She looked up to find him watching her intently. "What?"

"You're a beautiful woman. This has been a good plan and a good day. I did the best I could for my grandparents. My grandfather was happy and that makes me happy. He's been good to me all my life and I want to be good to him. You're perfect for this and I'm thankful you accepted the deal."

"Marc, I've benefitted maybe more than anyone. But

I think we need to try to keep to our original agreement and avoid sex."

"I'm sure that's the smart thing to do." He nodded, then added, "Relax, Lara. A few kisses are fun and it's not like we'll fall in love because of them. You know I haven't really desired any woman since my wife. You're pretty safe from a heavy relationship."

She didn't want seduction and she wasn't flying to the ranch to go to bed with him. He had been clear that was not part of the deal and for a minute she wondered if he had changed his mind, but evidently not. She took his advice and relaxed.

"Did you tell your mother I'm pregnant?"

"Yes. You told me I could. Believe me, it will end with her. She doesn't gossip."

"It won't be a secret much longer, anyway. Hopefully long enough that a lot of people think this is your baby. That is the nicest thing of all that you offered."

"We're coming in over the ranch. Come here, I want you to see this. I'll buckle you in with me." She laughed as she sat on his lap and he buckled them both in. He slipped his arm around her waist. "This is beautiful country. Look down there at that river."

She looked at lush greenery with the silvery ribbon of sparkling, splashing clear water running through it, spilling over rocks and tumbling between banks.

"This is a beautiful cattle ranch and I love every inch of it," he said, his voice deepening.

"You may not want to go back to Dallas and the corporate world after a year here."

"No, I'll want to go back. I like business and making money. I like both worlds, but now, while I'm young, I want the corporate life and the competition. Later, I can take the peace and quiet out here, the hard, physical work that has a whole different set of rewards."

She moved back to her seat and buckled up again. "I can see that same view out my window," she remarked.

"Yeah, I know. It was more fun to have you sit in my lap and show it to you and know exactly what you were seeing at the time. We'll be landing at the ranch in a few minutes."

"I'm excited." Then a crazy thought hit her out of the blue. "I didn't bring my recipe books."

"That's good, because I have a cook. You won't have to cook or clean. Someone else will do that. For the first week, while we settle in, the cook won't be there, but there'll be enough frozen and ready meals that we'll just have to heat up. And I can grill burgers and steaks, whatever we want."

"In that case, I may enroll in one more course," she said, sitting back for the rest of the flight.

As soon as they landed, they were picked up in a limo, and in a short time she saw a sprawling, one-story house with a porch running the length of the front. "Marc, it's a beautiful house."

"I agree. It was built by the man who owned the ranch before Grandpa, but Grandpa added to it and changed it, so it's his house now. Actually, with this wedding, I'll inherit the house and it'll be mine. That's hard to realize in some ways. In other ways, I've always felt as if this was my family home."

She felt a bubbling excitement as she climbed the porch steps and started to go inside. Marc caught her wrist. "Hey, wait. Let's do this right," he said and dropped the suitcases he carried. He scooped her up into his arms and unlocked the door, carrying her over the threshold.

With her arms wrapped around his neck, she laughed. "This isn't a real marriage."

"It's all you and I have today, and today it is real. For you it's the first, so let's make it as good as we can."

"I told you you're a nice guy," she said, looking into his eyes. She saw the flicker in the depth of his brown eyes and knew when the moment changed. She felt the hot flash of desire and wanted to be pressed against his hard strength. She wanted to be kissed.

His arms tightened to pull her closer and he bent his head. When his mouth covered hers, she tightened her arms around his neck and kissed him back, spinning off into one of his hot, passionate kisses that set her ablaze. The world narrowed down to Marc and she forgot everything else. His kiss deepened, and her insides knotted. Desire made her hot and aching for him. She clung tightly to him, barely aware when he let her slide down against him and then pulled her up tightly. Her heart pounded and desire shook her while she continued to kiss him. Without noticing what she was doing, she wound her fingers in his hair at the back of his head. Her moan of pleasure was a soft sound barely heard above the pounding of her heart.

This kiss was sexy, demanding her response. She didn't want it to ever end and she clung to him, kissing him in return, wanting more, losing all sense of time and place. Finally, he raised his head slightly and she gazed up into his dark eyes that seemed to consume her. Stunned, she was on fire with wanting him. She ran her hands across his shoulders while she fought the temptation to kiss him again. She gasped for breath as she looked at his mouth only inches from hers.

"That got out of hand," she whispered. "We were not going to do this. We can't start out this way, Marc. This isn't going to work if we kiss."

He stared at her as if seeing her for the first time. "I think you're right," he said, and his voice sounded gruff. He still had that penetrating stare that made her wonder what he was thinking, but she didn't want to ask.

"We can forget that ever happened."

"Not in my lifetime," he said gruffly, and she was startled by the harsh note in his voice.

"Just try," she said. "This is a beautiful house." She looked around, groping for something to get both their thoughts off kisses.

She walked away from him, gazing at her surroundings and trying to focus on anything besides Marc. Her heart still pounded and she had to fight to keep from turning around and walking back into his arms.

"Marc, this is like a set in a movie." She stood in the entryway of what looked like a luxurious mansion. Dark wood paneling covered the walls of the wide hallway that divided and ran in three directions. Overhead a huge crystal chandelier sparkled in the light from the front windows and open door. Gilt-framed oils of Western scenes hung on the walls, while potted palms and other massive greenery lined the walls between settees and groupings of tables and wing chairs.

"I never thought about where you live or what it's like," she said aloud without thinking as she stared at the opulence surrounding her. "For the ranch I pictured something like an ordinary house or a large, rustic cabin. This is a palace."

"It's Grandpa's ranch home. At least, it was for a while. When they got older, he and Grandma moved into the guest house. They had it enlarged and renovated first, and they've built on to it through the years. Remember, this home belonged to a rancher before my grandfather, and that man never had children. They said he entertained a lot."

"This looks as if it belongs in the city and not out on a ranch."

"This part is a bit formal, I admit, but the great room where we do most of the living, plus the kitchen and informal dining area are casual and comfy. You'll get a full tour later, but right now let's get you to a bedroom. Most of the staff is off this week, but—"

Her laugh cut him off. "The staff? What am I going to be doing here for a year, other than my own plans of studying and going to my classes?"

"Enjoy life. Enjoy the ranch. My grandmother sewed a lot," he said, grinning. "I had a lot of pajamas as a kid because I was the only grandchild. C'mon. I'll show you my bedroom. Bedrooms are off to the left."

"Well, I don't sew. Thank goodness I'm enrolled in courses and can get some things done." Carrying her purse and laptop, she walked beside him and still was more aware of Marc close beside her than of her surroundings. This was her home as long as she was married to Marc. It was palatial, and she couldn't imagine anyone coming inside in muddy boots and walking through the place.

She thought about being here alone when he was out on the ranch or back in Dallas.

"When you're gone, this will be like being alone in an empty hotel."

He smiled. "No, it won't, but you can go into Dallas with me when I go, if you want. You don't have to stay out here every minute. We're married, Lara. You're not working for me and required to remain on the ranch," he said with amusement.

"I'll remember that," she said.

"I'll show you where I told them to put your things. If you don't like it, you can move. We have plenty of rooms. Today is a lazy day, hanging out here, because my grandfather will get a report about our arrival. After that, he probably won't even inquire because he's gotten what he wanted."

"Suppose I went back to Dallas and stayed. Would he know?"

"Yes, he would, but he wouldn't ask. I think he expects things to work out the way he wants. Mainly, I'm sure he thinks when I get back to work on the ranch, I won't want to leave. I *will* want to leave, though. This isn't the life I want right now. It'll be quiet for you to study, so you should get a lot done, and when you need to get to Dallas for your doctor visits, I'll get you there. One of our cowboys, Randall, is also a driver for my grandparents. If you want to have a chauffeur to Dallas, he'll be available."

"I'll remember," she replied as they headed down the hall.

He paused in front of the door to a sitting room. "This is your suite. But first I want to show you mine." He pointed to an open door at the end of the hall. "If you like your room you'll be next to mine." He led her from the hall into a big, comfortable sitting room with a large flat-screen TV mounted on a wall, a desk, shelves with books and pictures, and a big fireplace.

He took her hand and walked through the sitting room into a huge bedroom with a king-size bed, another desk and more walls of bookshelves. Another flat-screen television filled one wall. The moment his hand closed over hers, he drew her attention away from her surroundings. Her pulse began to race at his nearness and touch. She kept telling herself that after the first few days, they would probably go their separate ways and life would be easier. Now she prayed that was true.

Marc turned to her. "You were great today, Lara. My mom really liked you and, of course, my grand-parents did." He reached around her and picked up a small, shiny red sack from his desk. "This is for you. Something from me to you that isn't part of a bargain."

# Five

Surprised, she looked up at him. "You've given me the world. You don't need to do another thing."

"It's a token of my thanks for not only accepting this deal and marrying me in what is really a marriage of convenience, but also for being nice to my family. That made today better for my grandparents. It made them happy and it made my mom happy. I know she hopes we'll stay together. Mom wants me married." He paused a second. "Anyway," he said, "this is just a thank-you." He handed her the sack.

"Marc, I stand to gain so much from this. You didn't need to get anything for me. I'm thrilled that you asked me and thrilled to do this."

"Open your present."

She smiled at him and opened the sack, taking out a long, black box. She opened it and gasped at the round diamond pendant on a gold filigree necklace with tiny diamonds scattered on the gold. "This is beautiful. It's lovely," she said, touched that he would get it for her. "I'll treasure it all my life."

"Turn around and I'll put it on you," he said. He removed it from the box and she held up her hair as he fastened the necklace.

She was aware of his warm fingers brushing her nape. She turned to look at him and felt his eyes pulling her in. She could feel her resistance wavering. Being here alone with him was dangerous. "Don't make me fall in love with you, Marc."

"You won't fall in love with me because I gave you a necklace. And don't worry. You won't see me for days at a time here."

She nodded, wondering whether it would work out that way or not. But she had meant what she said, when she asked him to avoid making her fall in love with him. He was doing too many considerate things. Making too many sexy moves. Instigating too many fun moments. It would be good when he was out on the ranch working and she was studying. She needed to keep as busy as possible and stay away from him.

"Thank you, Lara, for marrying me," he said quietly, and she nodded. Once again she felt a pang that this wasn't a real marriage. Then she told herself that was ridiculous. They weren't in love and this was nothing more than a business arrangement.

"I hope we both find happiness, Marc," she said solemnly, and he nodded.

"Now let's look where you'll be living while you're here," he said. He led her back to her suite. It was elegant, luxurious and comfortable, like his, but here the decor was done in burgundy, pink and white.

"This is beautiful," she said, thinking her entire house would fit into her suite.

"We'll stroll through the place and I'll give you a tour unless you get tired."

"No, I want to know where things are," she said.

He draped his arm across her shoulders and they left to walk down the hall and look at other suites. "There's an entertainment center on this floor," he said, pointing to an open door. "There's another entertainment center in the wing with the gym."

She wondered if he was even aware of his arm around her. She was, but he talked about his friends and about the ranch and didn't seem to notice. Except he had never done anything like that at the office, so she was certain he was aware of what he was doing.

She thought of the gorgeous diamond necklace she wore, something he hadn't needed to do at all. If he kept up gestures like that, she would fall in love with him, for sure. She shook her head as if to banish the thought and then realized he was prattling on about cattle.

Two wings led off the central part of the house. They walked down the central hall and she saw a huge dining room with a table that would easily seat twenty. Too bad they wouldn't be doing much entertaining in the next year. Not when he viewed their marriage as purely a business arrangement.

She reminded herself to do the same. But Marc was too sexy, too appealing, and now that they had kissed, his appeal had compounded and was far stronger than at the office. She needed to stay so busy she couldn't think about him. If she hardly saw him, he wouldn't care at all. She was a means to an end for him and nothing more. He'd have no struggle in trying to resist falling in love. He knew what he wanted and he had that goal in sight and the rest didn't matter.

Now she just needed to do the same. As if it was that easy.

She followed him into the adjoining room. The kitchen was big, with state-of-the-art equipment. It opened onto a great room that ran across the entire back of the house. A huge stone fireplace dominated the room that also held comfortable furniture placed around a large flat-screen television, and a large desk with two computers and four screens. A pool table stood on one side of the room and a gaming table on the other.

"You have everything in here," she said as she walked around. The back wall was all glass and gave a panoramic view of the landscaped backyard, the patio and the swimming pool with a fountain and a waterfall. "It's impossible for me to imagine your frail grandparents living in this big house."

"Well, they did, and they seemed to fill it. I was here a lot. They've gotten frail now, but they weren't when I was growing up. I visited them at the ranch a lot. Grandpa inherited it when I was seven and I spent lots of time with them all the years I was growing up. Still want to see the rest of the place?"

"Yes, it's fascinating."

"Shucks, I thought maybe you liked my company."

"I wasn't going to tell you," she said and they both laughed.

"Bedroom, great room, kitchen—you're good to go, but I'll show you the other wing of the house. It has a big office for me and I do have it set up so I can work from here and keep in touch with the office while we're living here."

"So, you're not completely letting go during this time."

He shook his head. "No, I'm not. I don't want to turn everything over to someone else and let them run my business. I'll manage it from here. If it works out, I'll go to Dallas for a couple of days every other week. That way I won't lose touch. If you want to go with me, you're welcome to join me or you can go in the limo."

"Thanks. I probably will go to Dallas," she said, jumping at the chance to be back in the city. "I need to fix up a room for a nursery and this will give me a chance to shop."

"Are you going to live in the same house when this is over?"

"Sure. I just rent, but it's convenient and I know my neighbors and have friends."

"Lara, I'll bet you're married in no time," he said.

She gave him a puzzled look. "Why would you make that statement?"

"You're a beautiful and smart, very capable woman."

"Thank you. That's nice to hear. But remember, I'll have a new baby in seven more months."

"You're the most unpregnant-looking woman I've known. And it's great you feel so well."

"I think it's my height that keeps my stomach flat," she said, placing her hand on it.

"Whatever it is, you don't look or act pregnant."

"I promise you, I am. You can call my doctor."

"Oh, I believe you. You wouldn't make that up."

"No. Marc, I'm so thrilled to be having a baby. This

wasn't what I planned, but I just feel like I'll finally have a family again."

He smiled at her. "I'm glad. As long as we're married, you've got a big family because you're part of mine."

"Which I love. Your mother is so nice to me."

"That's because she wants me to marry and settle and give her grandkids. She had me when she was sixteen, so she thinks I'm getting really old to be without a family."

Lara had to laugh and he smiled. "Sometimes I wonder if she was in cahoots with Grandpa on this stipulation to get me married, but then I remember that she stood to lose too much for her to be part of it." They came to another room and he opened the door. "Well, here's my gym."

She looked in on the large gym, then another big office and a sitting room.

"Now you've had the grand tour unless you want to see another office, a ballroom and an indoor tennis court."

"I think I'll unpack and put away my things."

"Sure," he said and once more draped his arm across her shoulders as they walked back to the bedrooms and she turned to enter hers.

"Change to jeans and, later, I'll drive you around the ranch."

"I really should study."

"Maybe you really should, but you can put it off until tomorrow when I'm gone. Besides, you'll be happier if you know your way around here."

"Jeans it is," she said, looking at her suitcases and boxes that had already been put in the suite. When he left, she closed the door behind him and turned to change, but she couldn't stop her errant thoughts. Instead of the upcoming tour, all she could think about was kissing him, no matter how hard she tried to avoid it. She picked up her laptop, as if to remind herself that she had chemistry courses to focus on. She hoped they kept her busy because she didn't want time on her hands and she certainly didn't want time to be with Marc. This marriage was for him to get his inheritance and that was all. She had to keep distance between them and concentrate on her own goals.

She changed to jeans and an aqua sweater, and braided her hair, letting it hang down her back.

She left to find Marc so they could go look at the ranch. When she couldn't find him, she sat in the great room that ran across most of the back of the house.

She heard his boot heels on the wood floor and knew he was coming. Then he swept into the room, and once again, she realized she would be challenged far more than she had expected to keep from falling in love with her new husband in this marriage of convenience.

In boots and a Western shirt, Marc looked even more sexy and appealing than in his wedding suit. His big smile just added to his attraction.

"Ready? We'll drive over some of the ranch. Don't worry, I won't begin to show you all of it and you wouldn't want me to."

She walked out beside him, listening to him talk about the ranch and what his grandfather did to change and update it, but she was far more aware of Marc as he drove the pickup and talked. After an hour of looking at herds of cattle, a corral with horses, a field of bales of hay, windmills and water troughs, she was ready to go back to the house.

"I can find my way in here," she said as they walked in the back door, "but I can't find anything out there on the ranch. I would be lost."

"I've grown up looking at landmarks. I feel like I know the land as well as I know the house. Always keep your phone with you. If you get lost, call me and I'll come get you. Now let's stir up some grub."

She laughed. "I don't think you'll even have to stir. We're stocked until next year."

In a short time he cooked burgers. They sat on the patio in the cool and ate and listened to the waterfall and the tumbling water of the fountain.

Finally she stood, picking up her dishes to carry them inside. "It's been an interesting, memorable day. I'm turning in. I should study."

He stood. "I'll go, too. I'm going to Dallas one day this week. You can go along if you want."

"Thanks, but I think I'll pass this time. I have plenty of studying to do."

"Chasing your dream, huh? I picked the right woman for this marriage," he said.

They walked down the hall together, and at her door she stepped away. "Goodnight, Marc. Thank you for the marriage and for my beautiful ring and for my gorgeous necklace. You did way more than we agreed on."

"I did what I wanted to do. You helped me make my grandparents happy. That's important. You made this deal possible and I didn't know one other woman I could ask. I was really in a bind."

She smiled. "Glad to oblige, though I really think you could have found a few takers."

"And worried every day how I would get rid of them later," he said, shaking his head. "You'll be gone in a flash, off to do your own thing."

"Yes, I will. I'm thrilled that you're enabling me to do that." She slipped into her room. "See you in the morning." She closed the door before he reached out to kiss her. He hadn't stopped her and he might not have reached for her if she had stood there longer, but this way was better. She needed to get on track for her own goals.

She sat down on her bed to study, amazed by her new life and the prospects she had for her future and her baby's future. If she had a boy, she wondered if Marc would like for her to name him Marc. He had been so good to her and that was a good, strong name. There wouldn't be a mix-up later because she and her son would be on their own. Lara Medina. That amazed her. And now her baby would have the Medina name, too.

Later, when she lay in the dark, she thought about her baby and Marc and his name. He would let people think this was his baby. That was the most generous of all the nice things he had done for her. He would claim her baby as his. It would give her baby a father—at least while they were together. It would give her baby legitimacy. Somehow, she was reluctant to reveal the true birth father because he didn't even want his child to live. Marc, on the other hand, had made her child's future bright, with enough money to cover his or her education.

Yes, Marc Medina was a good man. And sexy. And downright dangerous…

That was her last thought before she drifted to sleep.

\* \* \*

Marc was seated in the kitchen when she entered the room the next morning. He came to his feet instantly. "You're up early."

"I thought you might be gone," she said, her heart missing a beat as she looked at him. He wore jeans, a navy long-sleeved Western shirt and black boots. He looked incredibly handsome.

"Good morning," he said, his gaze sweeping over her as he walked to her, wrapped his arms around her and kissed her. For one startled moment, she grabbed his shoulders because she felt as if she would fall, but he held her firmly. Then her arms went around him and she kissed him back and forgot to wonder why he kissed her. She was too consumed by the kiss that made her heart race.

When he finally let her go, he smiled down at her. "I thought we should at least kiss this morning. After all, we're newlyweds."

She placed her hand on her hip and looked at him. "I thought we weren't going to have that kind of relationship," she said, her heart still racing. She tingled and was aware of his gaze drifting over her. How was she going to avoid seduction if this was the way he started each day?

Instead of answering her, Marc swept his gaze from her sneakers and jeans up to her sweater. "I have to say, you look damn good in those jeans. You should have worn them to the office."

"Marc, you're not paying attention to anything I just said."

His eyes finally met hers. "You're serious, aren't you?"

"Yes, I'm serious. I don't want end up in bed. We

discussed this and we both agreed to keep it like we had at the office."

"Okay. I can go back to our office hands-off relationship. I was just having some fun. I really didn't mean anything by it and didn't think it would have any kind of lasting effect."

"One kiss now and then might not, but it's still better to keep distance between us and that's what we agreed on. I can't have too big a say in this, I know, because you're the one who made me such a wonderful deal—"

"Stop right there. If you don't want me to kiss you— even just in fun—you got a deal. We worked together for a year without any kind of physical contact and it was mutually beneficial. We'll go right back to that. I can live with that."

"Thanks. I may hate myself in an hour, but I think that's the smart thing to do."

"You let me know if you change your mind. Or if I get carried away and start to kiss you, just remind me again."

She smiled. "Thanks. I'm trying to see to it that I'll happily say goodbye to you at the year's end."

He walked away to pour a cup of coffee and she wondered if she was going to be filled with regret and longing the rest of the day. The solace was knowing that she had done the smart thing and stopped his casual kisses.

He ate breakfast with her, and then he was gone and the house seemed silent. She realized when he was around it wasn't very quiet, which surprised her because his office had usually been a quiet place. Maybe it was partly the sound of the cowboy boots on the hardwood and terrazzo floors. She had the house to herself until he returned, which would probably be sundown. She suspected he was trying to keep his distance as much as she had tried last night.

She spent the day unpacking and got into the first of her courses. Soon she was immersed in studying, a relief, in that it took her mind off Marc most of the time.

She ate early and left him a note that she was studying. She escaped to her suite and closed the door, knowing she was running from spending the evening with him, but that was the sensible thing to do. He'd promised to maintain a professional demeanor around her, but she wasn't one to tempt fate.

They managed to avoid each other for the next two days. He was up and gone before she was out of bed, and at night she ate an early dinner alone and then went to her suite. He had been right in saying there was enough food cooked and ready that they wouldn't have to prepare anything. Without any household demands on her time, she got her course work done quickly and efficiently, which pleased her. She missed seeing Marc because he was fun, but it was better to simply back off and avoid him.

Friday night she was in the kitchen to get dinner when she heard a car. She looked out the window and saw Marc's pickup stop at the gate.

Instantly, she was aware of herself in cutoffs and a blue T-shirt with her hair falling around her face. She shook it back and tried to smooth it down with her hand while her heartbeat raced as she watched Marc get out of his pickup and head for the back door in long, fast strides. She wondered if something had happened.

He opened the door. "Hi, darlin', your husband is home." She had to laugh as he swept into the room with a huge grin on his face. "Get your—" He stopped as his gaze swept her from head to toe, making her tingle.

"My, oh, my, you kept your talents hidden at the office," he said.

She laughed as he looked at her legs. "I don't believe this is appropriate office attire."

"This is one boss it would have pleased," he said.

"I think when you came through the door you were saying for me to get something. Right?"

He finally lifted his gaze and blinked. "Hey, as much as I hate to tell you to cover up a pair of million-dollar legs, get your party jeans. We're going two-stepping. Gabe and Meg are coming, and some guys from the ranch, and we're going to party. I told them we'd meet them in two hours at a honky-tonk in Downly. It's a long drive for us, so that's why the two hours. As soon as you're ready, we'll go."

"Give me a few minutes." Luckily, she'd showered earlier, so all she had to do was change and fix her hair.

"See you here when you're ready. The guys from the ranch are already on their way and they're party animals. Most of them are young and single, but they'll leave the boss's wife alone. And they're a great bunch of guys."

She barely heard him as she ran to change. Twenty minutes later she dashed from her room to find him waiting in the hall. Her heart missed a beat as her gaze ran over him. He wore tight jeans, a black Western shirt, his black Stetson and black boots. Excitement slithered down her spine and she smiled as he straightened up and his gaze ran appreciatively over her.

"You do look great," he said and she smiled.

"Thank you," she said, glancing down at her new

boots, jeans and her red Western shirt. Her hair was loose, hanging on both sides of her face and combed straight, although she knew a slight natural curl would make it wavy before the night was over.

"I'm ready."

"Let's go party," he said, taking her arm and hurrying out to his waiting pickup. In minutes they were on the highway. Darkness had set in and she wondered about the evening.

"There's not a person in the world who will know you're pregnant," he said. "You don't show at all. Are you sure you're expecting?"

She smiled at him. "You can stop asking. I'm sure. I'm pregnant, but I don't feel any different yet and I don't think I look different, either."

"I can't believe the doctor has it right. You really don't look it."

"Time will tell," she said, amused that he doubted her.

"You'll have a good time tonight. This is a fun bunch. I've known Gabe and Meg for years, and the guys I work with know how to cut loose and party."

"I can be your designated driver."

"I did better than that. I got us booked into a hotel for the night. Everybody will be staying." He glanced at her as she stared at him and he grinned. "Don't panic. You'll have your very own private room."

She shook her head. "You surprised me there. Thank you. That was a wise decision to get me my own room."

"I'm really good company."

She laughed. "I have to agree on that one."

"I might be better company in the bedroom than anywhere else, for all you know."

"We're not going to find out tonight," she said, laughing at him. "I think you're ready for a party. Are you sure you haven't already had a sip?"

"Me? No. I've been working. I'm just ready for tonight. And I'm tired of cowboys, cattle, bales of hay and my own company. I want to hear someone with a voice higher than mine and dance with my new bride."

"Well, I can accommodate that," she said, enjoying his company after making sure she hadn't seen him for the past week.

"What do you want to drink tonight? I might as well find out now while we can discuss it."

"Think there's any chance of lemonade? If not, I'll take water. If not water, then maybe apple juice."

"I'm sure I'll find something you'll like and can drink," he said.

By the time they parked in the dusty lot in front of Buster's Beer and Bar-B-Q, the place was packed. Red neon flickered over the parking lot and music floated from the building. Marc took her hand and they entered a big open room with a large dance floor and a stage. Low lights illuminated the inside. Some people played pool near the front. On the dance floor, couples doing the two-step circled the room. Marc waved at someone as he made his way through the crowd. He kept his arm around her waist and held her close against his side. It was easy to put her other arm around his waist, and she thought that would make them look like a happily married couple to anyone who saw them.

She met the men he worked with, greeted Meg and Gabe, and then Marc took her hand to go to the dance floor.

It was fun to get out there with him, to dance and

move around the floor in time to the music. Marc turned her so she danced backward and when he smiled at her, her heart skipped a beat. It was exciting being with him, even just dancing in a big circle and not talking to each other at all.

He was the best-looking guy in the place. She realized he was even more handsome and appealing to her now than he had been in the office. Then again, she knew him better now. She'd been with him when he was teasing her, having fun, just being friendly and kissing her soundly. Her views of him were changing—had already changed from the days she was his secretary. He meant more to her now. And tonight would move them even closer together, make them closer friends, make him more appealing and make her want his kisses. It would be a night of fun and excitement, as well as temptation and worries.

She felt the warnings and was aware she hadn't even spent a full week on the ranch with him yet, but she didn't heed them. Not tonight. Tonight she was just going to have a good time.

As they danced in a big circle, she faced him and he smiled at her. His hat was squarely on his head and he looked like the other cowboys in the room.

She was having a wonderful time and wondered how she would fare by the time they finally parted at her suite door. She suspected some kisses at the end of the evening were inevitable. She just needed to remember to stop with kisses.

His appeal heightened as they danced. He was filled with energy and his enthusiasm was contagious. There was no way to resist his appeal tonight. Marc made her feel as if he cared about her and as if this was the best fun ever. At the moment, it was, and she laughed as she danced with him. Once he pulled her close as he spun her around.

"If you think this is fun, just wait until later," he whispered, causing tingles to tickle her insides. He had always looked handsome and confident in his business suits at the office. Now, dressed like the rancher he was, he was sexy, hot and irresistible. He was filled with vitality and she wanted to stay in his arms.

She had to resist him later, but not now. Now she could dance and laugh with him and work off some of the blazing desire that consumed her.

*Enjoy dancing with him*, she told herself as he spun her around again. *Just don't go to bed with him.*

In one year he would end the marriage as promised and she didn't want a broken heart when he did. She wanted to be able to walk away as easily as he would. To do that, she needed to stay out of his bed.

She had no idea what time it was when Gabe and Meg told everyone good-night and left. "Should we be going?" she asked Marc.

"Do you want to?"

"Not if you don't. Dancing is fun and I haven't done any in a long time," she answered.

"Gabe and Meg are newlyweds. They want to be off to themselves. These guys we're with will party all night."

"I'm not for all night. Just another hour."

"Sounds good to me," he said. "Let's dance." He took her hand and moved to the dance floor to waltz around the room with her. Their feet flew and she loved dancing. As she enjoyed herself, she realized they danced together as if they had been doing so for years. He was

easy to follow and she loved moving to the music, waltz-
ing around the big ballroom and having a wonderful
time in Marc's arms.

Finally, over an hour later, he took her hand and
leaned close. "Ready to go?"

"Yes, I am," she said, standing when he did. They
said goodbyes and waved, and finally left, stepping into
the cool night air. The cars had thinned in the parking
lot, but there was still a crowd. Marc walked with his
arm around her waist and she had hers around him.

"That was so much fun," she said, still thinking
about dancing. "We do well together."

"We're perfect together," he stated, stopping beside
his pickup. "We have about four blocks to the hotel.
We can walk and come back for my pickup tomorrow,
if you want."

"The hotel? I don't think so."

"Wait a minute," he said, laughing. "You can have
your very own room and I'll have mine if that's what
you want."

"It would be, but these are the only clothes I have
with me."

"I covered that, too. I have a few things in my pickup
and you can get through the night if you can wear the
same clothes home in the morning."

Laughing, she shook her head. "I assume you have
stuff in that box in your pickup. Walk to the hotel it is."

"Good." He turned to rummage in the back of his
pickup and handed her a small backpack and got one
for himself. "How's that?"

"It works," she said, glad to walk to their hotel, since
it was a nice night and she could use the fresh air. "I'm
glad you asked me tonight," she said.

"Yeah. We needed an evening out. How're the courses coming?"

"I'm doing way better than I expected, and faster. That's really all I have to do right now."

"I talked to my mom today. My grandpa wants to come home to the ranch. They can't do anything more for him at the hospital, so we can either move him to a skilled nursing facility or to the ranch. He wants to come here and I can get it set up so he can have home health care and be fine. It'll move Grandma home, too, of course, and that would be good for both of them. I know he'd be happier here, so that's what I'm going to do. I just wanted you to know."

"This is his home," she replied with a nod. "Will that change anything as far as we're concerned?"

"Not at all. They'll be in their house and the only time we'll see them is if we go there," he explained. "I'll have someone to take care of Grandma, too. She just needs someone to help her with little things."

"That's good, Marc."

"I'll go see them, but it won't involve you."

"Take me with you sometimes. Your grandfather wanted this marriage, so it should make him happy to see me. He thinks I'm in your life forever."

He smiled down at her. "That's nice, Lara."

"Tonight was fun. I haven't danced like that in a long time."

"I haven't either when I stop and think about it."

"You work hard. You've told me how hard your mom works. Well, you do, too. You know, I think this year will be a break from all the traveling you've had to do. You fly to look at leases, at wells you have, to corporate meetings with companies where you plan to buy land or rights from them. This is a whole different way of life. I'm sure it's hard, physical work, very different from what you've been doing. And now you're home nights."

"I like that corporate world and I don't mind the travel. I'm not that locked into being home nights."

She laughed. "I'm glad we don't have a real marriage, then."

He grinned and hugged her. "If you were in my bed every night, I wouldn't want to leave the ranch. I wouldn't want to leave the bedroom."

"Yes, well, enough about that."

Luckily they reached the hotel then, calling a halt to that line of conversation. It was a new, three-story building, part of a national chain with well-lit, landscaped grounds.

"Our rooms are the penthouse suite."

She laughed. "The penthouse suite on the third floor."

"Actually, there is a small fourth floor and they do call it the penthouse suite. As I said, you have your own room—in our penthouse suite."

"So we share the suite, but I have my own room. I can live with that."

He wiped his brow in an exaggerated gesture. "That was easier than I thought it would be. Maybe I should have tried sharing a room tonight."

"That wouldn't have worked," she told him, wagging a finger.

He laughed. "It was a thought."

She waited while he checked in and then he took her arm and they went to their suite. When she walked inside, he closed the door, shed the backpack, just as she had. He tossed his hat on the sofa and crossed the room to her. She turned around to say something to him and forgot what she intended to say when she looked into his eyes. She couldn't get her breath. She was torn between what she should do, what she wanted to do and what he could coax her into doing. Was she going to blow all her resolutions the first night out with him?

# Six

He slipped his arms around her and pulled her to him as he leaned down. "I've been waiting to do this all evening long," he said and kissed her.

The minute his mouth covered hers, her heart slammed against her ribs and she was breathless. She couldn't say no or step away. They had constantly touched while dancing, constantly been with each other. But this was different. She was in his arms and she wanted his kisses.

She clung to him tightly as he held her close and leaned over her, kissing her hard and making her pulse race.

His hand ran down her back and over her bottom, and she moaned softly. She thrust her hips against him. There was no denying she wanted him now. How was she going to resist his kisses? Did she really want to resist?

One night with her husband—would that be a disaster?

She wound her fingers in his thick hair, feeling the short locks curl around her fingers. When his hand slipped beneath her shirt to caress her breast, she gasped with pleasure.

"Marc," she whispered, knowing she should stop him, yet wanting his hands and his mouth on her. She wanted to hold and kiss him and wanted him to touch and kiss her. Temptation and desire had built all evening, if she was honest. Sure, she'd had fun, an exciting time, and his appeal had increased with each hour of dancing and touching each other and laughing together. When had she had that much fun with a man? Not ever. Marc was more fun than any other man she had known. That thought scared her. She didn't want to find Marc anything more than any other man. He would go out of her life later, so she needed to show some restraint.

He kissed her again and then all thought was gone. She was consumed by him. Marc's passionate kisses shut the world away and all she could think about was holding him and kissing him. He ran his thumb lightly over her nipple, tightening it into a taut peak. She loved the feel of it, but it wasn't enough for him, because in seconds he tugged her blouse out of her jeans and twisted free the buttons, opening her blouse while never removing his lips from hers. Each caress, each touch built her need, until longing had her trembling.

Moaning softly, she slid her hands across his broad shoulders. She could feel his erection pressing against her. She knew she should stop. She had promised herself she would use restraint and do what she could to avoid seduction. She hadn't been here a week yet, and she was in his arms, letting him fondle her breast. This wasn't the way to guard against heartbreak. The warning was dim, a whisper to her conscience, and she ignored it momentarily. She wanted just a few minutes more in his arms. All evening she had wanted his kiss, wanted to be in his arms. She couldn't stop this yet.

She leaned away to pull his shirt free of his jeans, just as he had done her blouse. In minutes she had his shirt unbuttoned and she ran her hand over his bare chest while they continued to kiss. His hard muscles did not surprise her because she knew he went to the gym every lunch hour he was in the office. Her fingers tangled in the fine curls before they slid to his flat belly and lower. Her foray was stopped when he pushed aside her bra and leaned down to take her nipple into his mouth, his tongue stroking her, hot and wet, a torment that made her want more.

She gasped with pleasure while she clutched his shoulders. Her eyes were closed and she was captured by sensation, captivated by his mouth and his hands moving so lightly on her, yet setting her ablaze with longing.

"Marc," she whispered. She knew she should stop, knew every kiss, every touch was bringing trouble, heading her toward seduction.

He shoved her blouse off her shoulders and unfastened her bra, pushing it aside so he could cup her breasts and kiss her. "You're beautiful," he whispered. "So beautiful." His hungry gaze made her tremble and want his hands and mouth all over her.

She gasped when he bent to pick her up and carry her to a bedroom.

When he set her on her feet, she caught his arms

to steady herself. Then she looked up at him. "You're going too fast for me."

"We're married, Lara," he whispered. "And I want you."

"It's still too fast, Marc. We're married in a marriage of convenience. There isn't a shred of love and that's a gigantic difference for me. This is pure sex without any love. I need to slow down. We talked about each of us wanting to avoid falling in love. Well, I'm sure you're impervious and could sleep all year with me and still walk away at the end of the year. But going to bed and making love with someone is emotional for me. I can't do that all year and then walk away. I'll be in love," she said, emphasizing *in love* and hoped that would cool him. "We've kissed and we've had a fun evening. Let's call it a night."

He stroked locks of hair away from her face, and she saw the battle play out in his eyes, desire at war with common sense. Then, finally, he brushed a kiss on her cheek and let her go. "Okay. It's a deal," he said. "It still was the best evening I've had in a long, long time."

She smiled at him. "That's the best possible thing you could say. I'm so glad. It was a fantastic evening for me and I had a wonderful time, you sexy man. I couldn't wait to come back and kiss you. You're very exciting, my convenient husband."

"Damn, you send a mixed message."

"You got my message and I appreciate your cooperation. I hope we get to do that again sometime. Just go a little slower so I can deal with my emotions. I'm trying to stop myself from crawling into your bed and wanting to stay. That would mean getting hurt badly when we part."

He nodded his understanding, but he didn't move
away. He stood watching her as she pulled her blouse
back into place and blushed as she fastened the middle button.

"That'll do for now," she said, picked up her backpack and walked with him across the hall into another
large bedroom. While he switched on the lights, she
dropped her things on a chair.

"Here you are. I hope you sleep well." She turned to
look at him and once again was caught in thickly lashed
eyes that conveyed so much desire, she was riveted. All
she could think about was kissing him again.

"Aw, hell," he whispered as he grabbed her and
kissed her passionately. Finally, he released her and
stepped back. She opened her eyes to find him watching her.

"Marc—"

He put a finger to her lips to silence her. "It was a
good night and we'll do it again. And sometime, maybe
sooner than you think, you won't tell me to go away. But
for now, good night." After a few steps he turned back.
"If you want anything, or if you want me, just call."

She laughed and shook her head. "Thank you. Don't
lay awake waiting for my call," she said.


He grinned and left, closing the door behind him.
As he walked away, he wiped sweat off his brow. She
made him hot enough to melt. He was surprised by the
fun he'd had with her tonight and for the last hour they
were there, all he could think about was coming back
and kissing her and making love to her. But that wasn't
going to happen. Not tonight. But it wouldn't be long,

because she couldn't resist kissing him. Meanwhile, he
feared he'd get little sleep this night.

He'd had a fun evening—far more than he had expected. When he decided to go to the bar, he'd known
the guys would be fun. He hadn't expected much from
his city-bred secretary, but he'd thought she might like
to get out. How she had surprised him. She could dance
and she was exciting, bouncing with eagerness, her big,
blue eyes sparkling. He'd wanted to take her back to the
hotel, to his bed, make love, hold and kiss her all night
long. And the realization shocked him.

He had been numb to women since he lost Kathy.
Well, Lara was bringing him out of mourning. He hadn't
wanted to dance, to kiss, to take anyone out since he
had lost his wife—his real wife, whom he loved with
all his heart. He felt as if he had been wrapped in grief
for the past fourteen months, but tonight he'd been
able to shake off some of the numbness. And he knew
Kathy would want him to. She wouldn't want him to go
through life dulled by pain and grieving for his losses.
She had been filled with a love of life and she would
want him to live again. It was just surprising that it was
Lara who had vanquished some of that terrible numbness in his life.

Still, he wasn't ready to fall in love. He couldn't,
wouldn't. And he didn't want Lara to fall in love, either.
He didn't want to hurt her when they parted.

*I'm trying to stop myself from crawling into bed and
wanting to stay.*

He recalled her words.

They had kissed more tonight than he had expected
she would let him. At the same time, he also knew that
wasn't what she really wanted. She was guarding her

heart and she had requested no sex—and he had agreed. He couldn't go back on his promise. He needed to resist temptation and keep this relationship in the friend zone. Could he be a good guy and an honorable man, and keep his word?

Wednesday night Lara drove to Denton to go to class—an hour and a half each way. Despite the distance, Marc was sure she wouldn't miss one class. She'd be a good doctor, that was certain. She was smart, determined, caring.

He missed her tonight. Alone in the house, he grabbed a beer and went outside to the balcony off his suite. He lay back on a chaise, looking at the stars and thinking.

There was much about Lara that reminded him of his mother. Her drive and determination, for example. And he appreciated it, because, like his mother, she had gone above and beyond for him, too, starting with suggesting they marry in his grandfather's hospital room. Very few women would have done that and Marc would always be grateful to her.

And she'd bowled over his mother, too.

He thought of Pilar Medina and was grateful for her sacrifices, as well. Now that he knew Dirkson Callahan was his blood father, he could understand her struggling against terrible odds to make a success of her tiny business when she lost her job with the Callahans.

Dirkson Callahan—his father.

Marc took a long pull on the beer. He couldn't believe that Dirkson was his biological father. He was a selfish man who seemed to love no one and nothing except himself, money and power.

Marc thought of his mother being pregnant, fifteen, on her own until she met his dad, no money, nothing. She didn't want to tell her parents. She hadn't wanted to rely on them because they were struggling to make a home and a life for themselves here. She'd met his real dad, the dad Marc loved and the dad who loved him. With John Medina they were a family with strong ties, and Dirkson Callahan was no part of it.

Marc took another swallow of beer, the bitter taste in his mouth not from the brew but from the mere thought of that horrible man.

He stared into the darkness. There was no reason to tell Lara, but a part of him wanted to share the news that still had him in knots. But he wouldn't. When this marriage ended, they would go their separate ways and he wouldn't see her again. And that wasn't his baby she carried.

He thought of his own child, who had been cruelly taken from him. His mom had said he wouldn't be able to walk away from Lara's baby when it was born. Was that true? For a few months he would be that baby's father. Would the child capture his heart?

And what about its mother?

He couldn't stop thinking about how he wanted Lara in his bed. How much would that complicate his life? How much would it make him want her as part of his life longer than this one year they had planned? He couldn't imagine falling in love, not when he wasn't truly over losing his wife. Would it make for a stronger tie to Lara when her baby came? That gave him pause. He needed to back off and stick to his original plan to avoid sex with her, but nights like tonight—with nothing to do but think about her—made him want her in spite of common sense and the upheaval she could cause in his life.

He finished the beer and closed his eyes on his disturbing thoughts. It was two in the morning when he woke in the darkness and moved inside, flopped on the bed and went back to sleep.

When he woke again, it was daylight. Frowning, he looked at the clock and jumped out of bed. He had overslept. Something he never did. He rushed to shower and soon was in jeans and a flannel shirt and ready for the day. As he walked down the hall, tempting smells of hot coffee and bacon frying assailed him. He rushed into the kitchen.

Lara spun around. She wore a blue cotton robe that was open and thin blue cotton pajamas beneath the robe. Her hair tumbled over her shoulders and fell freely around her face. She looked as if she had been awake only a short time.

"Good morning," he said, crossing to her, drawn as if by a magnet. Last night's warning to be cautious in getting involved with her vanished like smoke on the wind.

Her cheeks turned pink and she put down a spatula to pull her robe together. "Good morning. I figured you were long gone."

"I overslept," he said. He slipped his arm around her waist and pulled her close. She was soft and the thin cotton robe and pajamas were almost nonexistent. As her soft curves pressed against him, her eyes flew wide. "Marc, I'm not dressed."

"Yeah, I noticed and I like it. You look gorgeous," he said and kissed away her answer. For one startled second, she was still, and then her arms went around his neck and she kissed him in return.

He was hard instantly. He wanted her. He wanted to slip her out of the robe and pajamas and carry her back to bed. Instead, he stood there kissing her, relishing her softness, her warmth, her kiss that was setting him on fire.

"Marc." She finally moved out of his embrace. Her cheeks were pink and her mouth red from their kiss. "Breakfast is burning," she said, turning to grab the spatula and turn the strips of bacon. "Now look." She poked the scorched bacon.

"I'm looking," he said, his gaze roaming over her.

She put down the spatula and tied her robe. He laughed and walked away to pour himself some coffee. "I'm leaving, but I've been having breakfast by myself at the wrong time of the morning. I'll have to change that."

"And I'll have to dress for breakfast."

"Don't be ridiculous. We're married." He walked up to her to put his finger beneath her chin and tilt her face up. "Sooner or later we'll consummate this union."

"You don't know that."

"Oh, yes, I do," he said, looking into her wide blue eyes and seeing a blush turn her cheeks rosy. "You know it, too. And you want it, too. Gives us both something to look forward to. We miscalculated when we agreed on no sex. We didn't know about the attraction that would spring to life between us. We know it isn't a serious one and it isn't going to last. You still have your agenda and I have mine. But you do like to kiss and so do I."

"You don't know that we'll succumb to passion. We might and we might not," she said in a haughty tone that made him grin.

"We definitely will and you know it or you wouldn't

be blushing. Want me to prove it to you right now?" he asked, walking toward her.

"No, I don't," she answered quickly, moving out of his reach.

"I think I just did," he said, laughing. "I'll see you tonight, darlin'."

Smiling, he left, but his thoughts stayed on the moment when he held her in his arms. The flimsy cotton robe and pajamas might as well have been nonexistent. She had been warm and soft. That image would be with him for the day. He couldn't resist pursuing her and she liked it when he did.

He realized he was already looking forward to being with her tonight. That was something new in his life, which, little by little, she seemed to be changing for the better. He hadn't expected to even be aware of her once they were on the ranch and each doing their own thing. Had he ever been wrong. He couldn't shake her out of his thoughts now, and that startled him. She was turning his life upside down in her own quiet way.

It occurred to him that he might miss her later, when she was gone. He shook his head as if to chase away that thought. She was a tiny, brief part of his life. He wouldn't miss her. He would go back to life the way it had been before he had brought her to the ranch. After all, that was the deal they'd made. And Marc Medina was a master of the deal.

Lara had showered and dressed in jeans and a blue knit shirt. Her hair was in one long, thick braid. She was sitting and studying when she heard a pickup, and in minutes a door slammed.

"Hi, sweetie. Your lover's home."

She had to laugh at his corny greeting. "I'm in here, in the great room."

He came through the door seeming to bring sizzling energy just by walking into the room. He had dust on his face. He had already shed his hat and jacket and wore mud-spattered jeans, muddy boots and a long-sleeved blue shirt that had some smudges of dirt and a tear.

"You look like you fell out of the pickup."

He crossed the room to her and pulled her up. "Well, you look beautiful and absolutely irresistible," he said, wrapping her in his arms and kissing away her protest until she responded in kind.

He finally released her slightly to look at her. He smelled like hay and his tousled hair fell on his forehead. He had a dark shadow of stubble on his jaw.

"Well, now I'm dusty, too," she said. "I can't get used to this marriage thing. We're sort of half-married. You kiss like it's the real thing, but then we turn around and it definitely isn't the real thing."

"It is the real thing. We had a real ceremony and we are very legally wed."

"For a little while and there's not one shred of love in this deal. And it's better that way, so back off, cowboy, before you get us both in deep trouble."

"You are really killing the fun," he said.

"Maybe so, but you'll thank me when you get to thinking about it."

She sat back down. "What about your grandfather? Did they bring him to the ranch today?"

"Change of plans. He's coming tomorrow morning, instead. At ten o'clock. That's why you didn't hear from me or see me today. I was getting their place ready."

"I'll go with you in the morning if you'd like. I can say hello to your grandmother."

"That's another thing I like about you," he said, suddenly sounding as if he meant what he said. "You're considerate."

"I understand the importance of family and losing family. I went through it with my mother, don't forget. You try to be as kind and loving as you can while you have them."

He hugged her. "There are a lot of facets to you."

"That's a new one," she said, laughing and wiggling away from him. "You did manage to kill all the cleanliness from my shower." She brushed dirt off her blouse.

"It just makes you a little earthy and sexy."

"Somehow I find cleanliness sexy."

"I'll remember that." He waggled his eyebrows at her, then tossed an envelope on the table near her. "The wedding pictures were in the mail today," he said.

She dropped everything and rushed over to pick up the envelope.

"I love pictures. I want to see. Want to come look with me?"

"Oh, sure," he said, too quickly and eagerly.

She regarded him shrewdly. "Why do I suspect your motives for looking at pictures with me?"

He grinned and she knew she was right. She shook her head as she sat on the sofa and he sat close beside her, putting his arm around her shoulders. "I can't wait to see them," he said.

"Maybe we should do this after you shower."

"I'm already here against you and seated on the sofa. I can't do more damage here, so let's look."

"I can't argue with that logic," she said and pulled out a few glossy pictures.

"You watch your hands," she said, smiling at him, and he smiled in return. Her heart beat faster because she was certain he would kiss her again soon. She shouldn't want him to, and she shouldn't let him. If she could just keep her wits about her when she was near him.

She turned back to look at the pictures. She emptied the envelope of a thick stack of prints and began to go through them. She paused to study one.

"Marc, you and Gabe look exactly alike here. Your eyes are dark brown and his are blue, but the two of you could be brothers instead of friends."

"People have told us that before," he said casually.

"Surely you can see the resemblance."

"I suppose."

"I'm sure you've met his father."

"Oh, yeah. Dirkson paid no attention to his sons. They might as well not have existed as far as he was concerned, from what Gabe always told me."

"Well, Gabe looks nothing like Dirkson Callahan. I don't think you'd know Gabe is related to him if he didn't have that Callahan name."

"That would probably suit Gabe just fine. None of the Callahan boys like him. That would be a hell of a note—none of your sons liking you, but it's his own fault. They wanted to be a family and he disappointed them and hurt them time and again."

"That's sad. He can't make it up now."

"No, those years are gone. I'll bet each one of the brothers is a fantastic dad to make up for the way Dirkson was. They never want to be like him."

She shuffled through the prints then held one up. "Ah, here's a fun picture. This one I want," she said, holding out a picture of her dancing with Marc at the reception.

"You can have all of them."

"You're going to forget me and this marriage when I'm gone," she said, laughing. "Thank you. I'll be happy to keep these pictures."

Startling her, he picked her up and placed her on his lap. "I'm not going to forget you." His arm wrapped around her waist as he pulled her close and kissed her.

She wrapped her arms around him and clung to him as she kissed him in return.

"I'm not going to forget you or this marriage. I think you're seeing to that hour by hour. That night when we went dancing, I had the best time I've had since Kathy passed away. That's unique, Lara. I'm not going to forget that."

He gazed at her solemnly as he talked and she realized he wasn't teasing. Her heart beat faster. That was awesome and made her feel better, but it scared her, too.

"I don't want to make this marriage permanent, Marc, because you never would. Don't mess up my future plans."

"We won't. We just had a good time together, and that's great because it means you're getting me out of that terrible grief I've been sunk into since I lost her. Thanks for that."

"I'm glad, Marc. There's a time to move on from being steeped in grief." As she gazed at him, she had the feeling that there had been a subtle shift in their relationship—that she had more influence on him now than she had had previously. She wasn't happy with the discovery. She didn't want to get too close to him or become too important to him. He wouldn't change when they ended this marriage and he definitely would end it. She needed to always remember that. This was a temporary situation.

She got out of his lap and warmed up the casserole she'd taken out of the freezer that morning. They ate together, and after dinner she stayed in the great room instead of fleeing to her suite. She sat with her laptop, doing her studies, while Marc sat at the desk going over the ranch books and bringing them up to date.

She finally stood as the grandfather clock chimed out in the hallway. "It's ten o'clock and I'm turning in."

Instantly Marc stood. "I will, too."

"I meant alone in my own room," she said, smiling at him.

He smiled back at her. "I tried." He shrugged. "I'll still head to my room. Now, if you ever get lonesome or change your mind—"

"I know. I'm welcome in your bed."

"Any time you want to be there. I just don't want you to forget me."

She had to laugh. "I'll try not to," she remarked. "So, what time will we go see your grandfather tomorrow?" she asked, carrying the envelope with the wedding pictures.

"Probably about eleven. If you change your mind, you don't have to go. That's not part of your duties."

"I want to. He's old and frail and he wanted this marriage badly, so I think it would make him happy to think that I'm part of the family."

"That's very nice."

"Really, it's the least I can do," she said as they

walked down the hall. At the door to her room, she turned to him. "Good night, Marc. I'll see you at breakfast in the morning."

"I hope you do. Wear the same pajamas and robe. I like them."

She shook her head at him. He really was incorrigible.

He stepped close to embrace her, ending her protest when his mouth covered hers. He pushed her back against the wall and she clung to him, returning his kiss. She couldn't say she was sorry to be trapped there. In fact, when he released her, she felt disappointed. Her breathing was as ragged as his.

"Some night you'll invite me in."

"We talked about that. I don't plan on it."

"Some night you'll invite me in," he repeated, running his forefinger down her cheek and making her heart beat faster.

She shook her head and stepped into her suite, closing the door. "Not if I have good sense, I won't," she whispered to herself, but her answer was for him. "I don't want to long for you in my bed every night and that would happen if we started sleeping together." She just prayed she wasn't already getting too attached to him.

# Seven

The next morning Marc was in the great room waiting for Lara, looking out at his patio, pool and, beyond the fence, the endless vistas of the ranch. His grandfather was coming home today. Marc felt certain the old man was hanging on to see the land once more and to take his last breath on the ranch he loved.

Marc realized that life was short and that family was what was important. He thought about Lara and how she had already changed his life for the better. He hoped he had changed hers for the better, too, and enabled her to do what she wanted when they parted.

She was his wife—so far, in name only. One minute he intended to change that and the next minute he thought that if he did, he might make everything worse for both of them. He didn't want that to happen. He wanted her, but common sense warned him to stick to their original plan so no one got hurt when they parted ways. And they would part; he knew that for certain.

He heard her high heels on the hardwood floor and he stood as she swept into the room. His heart thudded. She wore a cheerful, bright-red dress with a straight skirt that ended just above her knees. She had on red high-heeled pumps and her hair was scooped up on either side of her head and pinned to fall freely in the back.

"You look gorgeous." He crossed the room to her, drawn without conscious thought. "I just can't resist, Mrs. Medina," he said, reminding her of her marital status as he wrapped his arms around her, leaned over her and kissed her.

Her eyes flew wide and then closed, and she wrapped her arms around his neck, pressed against him and kissed him in return, making his heart pound. She could be instantly responsive, and when she was, it set him on fire. He wanted her with all his being. He'd spent a restless night, tossing and turning, dreaming about her, waking and being unable to go back to sleep for a long time, arguing with himself about pursuing her.

"If we didn't have to go see my grandparents," he said, raising his head, "I would carry you off to bed."

She opened her eyes and had a dazed look that made his pulse jump another notch. "We have to go," she stated, but there wasn't any conviction in her voice. Her mouth was red from his kiss and desire filled her blue eyes.

He pulled her up to whisper in her ear. "One day I'm going to make love to you for hours and you'll want me to."

She froze in his arms and he wasn't sure what her reaction would be. Finally, she turned her head slightly and looked into his eyes. Her emotions were unreadable. She didn't pull away. Instead, she cupped his cheek in her hand and softly said, "We both know that's not the sensible thing to do. We need to get back on a safe track until we say goodbye. Goodbye is still in our lives, Marc. Now, I think we were going somewhere," she said, smoothing her dress and shaking her head to get her hair to fall back in place.

He wanted her with all his being. He was amazed by the effect she had on him. She was changing his life, hour by hour, day by day, bringing him back to life. "Marrying you was the smartest thing I ever did."

She smiled, her blue eyes getting a twinkle. "Is that so? I'm very flattered. Then I have to say, we have a good bargain."

"Yes, we do." And he needed to remember the terms of that bargain.

"Let's get going. My grandpa awaits." He put his hand on the small of her back as he ushered her out of the great room. "You know, my grandpa does like beautiful women. You'll make him happy today."

"I hope so. Your grandmother, too. Will your mom be here?"

"No, because she knows I'll handle it and she'll be at the restaurant, making sure everything is running smoothly there the way it has each day it's been open for the last thirty years." Then he paused. "At least, as far as I know, she won't be there. She surprises me sometimes."

He took his pickup, aware it was one of the few times he'd been in the truck in a suit and tie.

They arrived before his grandfather, but within ten minutes an entourage came up the road with the ambulance in the lead. Marc and Lara went out to meet the car carrying his grandmother, and Marc took her arm to help her into the guest house. Lara walked along with them, with a nurse on the other side of his grandmother.

Medics brought his grandfather in and took him to the room that Marc had made sure was ready.

Finally, Marc and Lara went to see him. Marc brushed a kiss on his grandfather's forehead and came back to stand by Lara, who greeted his grandfather.

His grandfather smiled. "You look beautiful, Lara," he said in a raspy voice.

"Thank you," she said, smiling at him. "We're glad you're home."

He nodded and folded his hands.

Marc told him about the ranch, and while he talked, he stood beside her with his arm around her waist. She was sure they looked like happily married newlyweds.

They didn't stay a long time, once they'd finished talking to his grandfather and made sure his grandmother was settled in and needed nothing. Then they said their goodbyes.

"He's happy and it was nice of you to come. He told me I married a beautiful woman," Marc said as they got into the pickup. He smiled at Lara. "He's right."

"Thank you. But I'm not sure he can see very well."

"He can see well enough. Your red dress is perfect. That would cheer up a skeleton."

"I hope I don't have to do that," she said, laughing at him.

"Hey, the guys are going out again tonight. Want to join them?"

"Sure. That was a fun evening last time."

"I hoped you'd say that. Seven tonight, then?"

"Seven it is."

When they got back to Marc's house he went inside to change to go to work.

He didn't see Lara again before he left, but tonight they would go dancing and he would be with her all evening. He had plans for afterward, too. He had already gotten a hotel room so they would not have to worry about driving back to the ranch.

Lara had more fun than she'd had the first time. This time, some of the guys politely asked her to dance. She suspected they did so to be nice to the boss's new wife, but she accepted their offers nonetheless. The evening was fun, but it was Marc who took her breath away. Tonight, his navy Western shirt was open at the throat. He had a hand-tooled leather belt with a big silver belt buckle that she suspected he'd won in a rodeo. He was charming and exciting, and when they drove to the hotel, her heart raced because she knew they would kiss.

She was supposed to be guarding her heart, so what was she doing going dancing with him and kissing him?

She had the perfect answer to that nagging voice inside her head. She wasn't in love with him and she hadn't gone to bed with him. As long as she could honestly say she wasn't in love, she would be okay. There'd be no heartbreak in her future.

When they walked up to her room, he took her key and opened her door. She entered and turned to say something to him but forgot her words when she looked up at him. His brown eyes held so much desire, she felt weak in the knees.

"You're gorgeous, Lara. I want you," he whispered as he wrapped his arms around her and pulled her against him for a heated kiss.

Kissing him in return, their tongues stroking, stirring sensations that made her moan with pleasure, she held him tightly. His waist was narrow and she could feel his hard arousal pressing against her through his thick jeans. She wanted him, too. She wanted his kisses, his hands on her, his mouth on her.

His arms tightened around her as he kissed her. In minutes he had her red blouse unbuttoned and pushed open. He unfastened her bra and cupped her breasts in his warm hands. As his thumbs circled each taut point, he stepped back to look at her.

"You're beautiful," he whispered. "I want to make love to you all night."

"Marc, you know where that will lead."

"We're married. I'm your husband. You're already pregnant. You want my hands and mouth on you just as badly as I want to kiss and make love to you. You're gorgeous, Lara, and I've wanted you all evening," he said, repeating the arguments he had given her before. He drew her to him to kiss away any protest she had.

He was right about everything. She ached for his hands and mouth on her. Would once be so terrible? Could she go to bed with him and still say no the next time? One time didn't have to mean she would fall in love with him. Far from it.

His kiss was making it difficult to think about the consequences and the reasons she didn't want to make love. They seemed not as threatening when she was in his arms and his kisses were driving all thoughts into oblivion. She could do this and go back to life like it was. One night with him wouldn't change her life. She could say no later after this one time.

One by one, her protests crumbled.

His black hair fell in ringlets on his forehead and he had the dark shadow of stubble on his jaw. He was handsome and exciting, a man who always knew what he wanted and went after it. And he usually got it.

She was his wife and she wanted his loving, his kisses and caresses. He was fabulous in every way, exciting, handsome, sexy, fun and capable. Tonight she wanted to make love with him, to be a real wife to him. For one night. Tomorrow she would go back to a sensible restraint. One night would not change everything, she repeated to herself.

He kissed her again, passionately, his tongue stroking hers, touching the corners of her mouth, making her shake with need. His hands roamed over her, unfastening her belt and pulling it free. She barely noticed, but soon she leaned away to undo his big buckle and then unfasten his jeans and push them away. He stepped back to yank off his boots and shed his clothes, watching her as she did the same, and in minutes he'd peeled away the last of her clothes.

"You're beautiful," he said hoarsely, picking her up and carrying her into the bedroom where he yanked the covers off the bed and set her on her feet. After one long glance at her nakedness that had her skin burning, he pulled her into his embrace and kissed her again.

Her heart pounded with excitement and desire. His masculine body was perfection. She ran her hands across his broad, muscled shoulders, his hard, bulging biceps. His stomach was flat, a washboard of muscle. His manhood was thick and hard and ready to love her.

He showered kisses on first one breast and then the other, slowly circling each nipple with his warm, wet tongue, making her gasp with pleasure as her fingers tangled in his hair.

"I want to kiss you from your head to your toes," he whispered. His breath was hot on her flesh as his tongue traced circles on each breast and then moved lower over her belly and down farther. His hands played over her thighs and stroked slowly between them.

She reached between them to caress his thick rod, running her fingers over him, and then she stepped back, knelt and let her tongue stroke him. Boldly, she took him in her mouth to excite him as he had her.

He groaned, his hands tangling in her hair again as he gasped. But she did not stop.

Suddenly he reached beneath her arms to lift her up so that they faced each other. The desire that burned in his expression was so potent it made her tremble.

"You can't imagine how much I want you. You're beautiful. Every inch of you," he whispered. He picked her up and laid her on the bed, then knelt to kiss her ankle, working his way slowly up her legs. His lips blazed the trail with hot, wet kisses and his hands followed the path as they caressed every inch he'd kissed.

She moaned with need. As he moved higher, caressing her inner thighs, running his tongue over her smooth skin, she spread her legs and his fingers explored and rubbed between her thighs.

She gasped, moving her hips as he stroked her, as tension built and she sought release. She cried out, arching beneath his hands and then his mouth and tongue were on her, hot and wet and driving her wild. When she couldn't take any more of the delicious onslaught, she sat up and clutched his shoulders.

He looked up into her eyes and longing tore at her.

She pulled him up, his body flush with hers, and kissed him. She locked her arms around him, holding him tightly while she poured herself into her kiss.

Each stroke, each kiss made her want him more. She couldn't touch him enough, feverishly running her hands over his marvelous male body that was all hard muscle. "You're wasting yourself in that office. This body was meant for ranch work," she whispered, trailing kisses over his flat stomach as she caressed him.

He pulled her up again to gaze at her in another long, hot, probing look and then he kissed her, a kiss she knew she would remember forever. It was a kiss that made her feel he wanted her and he cared about her. And she kissed him back, just as passionately.

He laid her back on the bed and then moved above her to continue showering kisses from her head to her toes, as he pushed her down gently whenever she attempted to kiss him or to sit up.

He turned her over and his hands drifted over her back, down over her bottom, tickling and stroking her, moving between her legs again and then pulling her up on her knees to move over her, his hands on her breasts as he trailed his tongue on her nape.

With a cry she rolled over and pulled him down on top of her.

"Love me, Marc. I want you inside me. I want us together for this night. Tonight we're husband and wife."

"I know it, Lara. Don't rush. Let's take our time. I want to start over. I want you to want me so badly, you can't possibly wait."

"I already do."

"Not like I want you to. Shh, just wait," he whispered, showering kisses on her again, taking first one breast and then the other into his mouth, kissing her all over again.

He kissed her from head to toe and then she returned the favor. His hands were still everywhere on her, tickling, stroking, teasing and loving her.

Finally she grasped his shoulders. "Now. I want you now," she said, looking intently at him.

He moved between her legs as she watched him. Her heart raced, she wanted him so badly. She ran her hands over his muscled thighs, feeling the short, crisp, curly hairs against her palms.

He lowered his weight, entering her gradually. With a muffled cry as he kissed her, she wrapped her long legs around him and ran her hands over his back and hard buttocks.

He filled her, thick and hot, making her arch beneath him and cry out for him. "Love me." She gasped as she arched her hips against him, higher and higher, wanting more.

He held back, drawing out their loving while she writhed beneath him, wanting him more by the second. Each thrust was torment and ecstasy.

Her eyes were closed tightly as she clung to him, holding him with one arm while her other hand ran over his hard body.

He began to move his hips, thrusting and withdrawing, repeating it as she moved with him until, finally, he lost control and began to pump hard and fast.

With a cry she moved with him, arching her hips higher, tightening her legs around him as she moved wildly and her head thrashed back and forth.

"Marc, I want you," she cried.

They built to a crisis and finally spilled over a brink

that was shattering. Lights exploded behind her closed eyes and she rocked hard and fast with him while rapture enveloped her.

Groaning, Marc held her tightly, thrusting hard and reaching his climax.

They slowed gradually, gasping for breath until they were finally still. Marc rolled to his side, keeping her with him as he caught locks of her hair and pushed them away from her face. He placed his hand at her throat and she knew he could feel her racing pulse.

"See what you do to me?" she whispered.

"My pulse is just as fast," he said. "We do that to each other." He showered light kisses on her ear, her throat, her cheek. "You're marvelous, Lara. This has been a fabulous night. I want you to stay right here in my bed, in my arms, all night long," he said as she wound her arms around him and held him.

"It was good, Marc," she said, kissing him lightly, her fingers wandering over his smooth back. She wanted to hold him all night.

"I want you to stay with me tonight. Don't go," he repeated.

"I'm not moving. I'm not going anywhere out of your arms," she whispered. Ecstasy, euphoria, happiness filled her, and for a moment in time, she felt wanted and loved. She held him in her arms and wished she never had to let go. She knew that was impossible, but for a few more minutes, this was paradise.

She had no idea how late it was when she woke in his arms. Needing a bathroom break, she slipped out from beside his sleeping body.

When she returned to the bed, he stirred. "Don't go."

She didn't bother correcting him. Instead, she burrowed against him. "That suits me."

While he kissed her throat, she clung to him, twisting her fingers in his chest hair.

"I don't want to let you go," he whispered as he tightened his arms around her.

"But you will let me go," she said quietly, wondering how much their relationship had changed tonight and how significant making love would be in their lives.

"Shh. No tomorrows. Tonight you're in my arms, in my bed, and I want you to stay."

"And tonight, that's fine with me," she said. Their legs were intertwined and she felt as close as she could get to him. "We've been good together, Marc."

"I think so. I think asking you to marry me was one of the best things I've ever done. You're perfect and you've made my grandparents and my mom happy. And all that family happiness—and some of my own—is going to make our breakup hurt a little. My mom isn't going to like it when we break up. I'm going to hurt her and I don't want to do that."

"I suppose that's unavoidable since you couldn't find someone you really loved and wanted forever."

"Not in one month," he remarked.

She didn't say anything about how she would feel when Marc divorced her and the marriage of convenience was over.

As he held her close, they stopped talking and lay together, holding each other and caressing each other. She knew when the moment changed and he wanted to make love again.

In seconds, his arms tightened around her and he leaned down to kiss her. She slipped her arms around his neck and kissed him in return. She didn't think it was possible, but in no time he had her wanting him as much as she had earlier in the evening. They made love again, taking even longer than the time before.

Midmorning she stirred and looked around to find him propped on his hand looking at her. He smiled at her. "That was a fantastic night."

"And long over. I think we better shower and go home. Are all those guys here who work for you?"

"I have no idea where they are. I haven't stepped out of this bed since the sun came over the horizon, but I imagine they're long gone. But not to worry. They know we're newlyweds."

"That's a little embarrassing. Your car is still here."

"We're married. What's wrong with us staying in for a while?"

She laughed. "I don't feel very married."

He caught her hand and held up her ring finger. "I'd say that's very married."

"Yes, you're right when you put it that way," she agreed when she looked at the diamonds glittering on her finger. She sat up, pulling the sheet to her chin, aware of him with the sheet over his hips, his skin looking darker than ever against the white sheets.

"I'm going to shower and dress. We should go home. I have an assignment that's due Monday that I need to work on."

"Do you really?" he asked, pulling her down against his chest. He was warm, and his intense look made her heart miss beats. "I have a better idea. You come here, and in a few minutes we'll both go shower. In the meantime, I want a morning kiss," he said, shifting and turning on his side, pulling her closer and kissing her.

The minute his mouth touched hers, she forgot her protest. His arms tightened around her and she wrapped her arms around him, clinging to him, pressing against him, feeling the chest hairs against her bare breasts. She wanted him again, was ready to make love. She didn't want to get out of bed and have the idyll end.

Last night she had felt really married, desired by him, loved by him, a part of his life. They'd had fun all evening, and then making love locked them into intimacy, shifted their relationship to something much more important, much deeper for her. It was an illusion that she didn't want to end yet. Their marriage was real, but not based on love and it would not last. She had had her moment with him. Now she needed to step away before she made herself far more vulnerable to hurt. She had to say no to him after this. If she lived as his wife the rest of the time with him, the divorce would hurt terribly. It would break her heart.

This was a fling and it would end—right after this.

He kissed her, his tongue going deep, stroking her mouth, stirring and arousing her until she moaned softly and ran her hands over him, moving her hips against him.

He shifted, throwing aside the sheet to uncover both of them, getting on his knees and moving between her legs. She gazed into his eyes and saw desire blazing in their depths. He wanted her and he was ready to love again.

She wrapped her legs around him as he entered her slowly, making her gasp with pleasure as she arched beneath him and clung to him tightly. He withdrew, only to enter her again and again, filling her deeper each time until she went over the edge. She cried out, clutching his butt, pulling him to her as she thrashed beneath him and he began to pump faster.

She held him tightly while she climaxed, hearing his moan and knowing he reached a climax also.

Finally they were still, locked together, holding each other while she opened her eyes to look at him.

"Now I can't move."

"Good. I don't want you to move anyway. I want you here in my arms. You know I can get this room for the day."

She laughed. "Don't you dare. We need to get back to the ranch. I have things to do."

"You don't have anything nearly as important as making me happy," he said, and she laughed.

"That's a hoot. There might be a thing or two that comes before you and your well-being."

"Be careful or you'll hurt my feelings," he teased. He rose up on his arm to look down at her. "See, we can have a good time together in bed. We can have a really good time together naked in bed. Move into my suite when we get back to the ranch."

"Marc, this has been fantastic, but I can't move in with you knowing that this will end and that we don't love each other. I don't want a broken heart. I don't want a temporary relationship and you don't want a permanent marriage—which I understand. This is a business arrangement with papers. It's a contract marriage of convenience. I can't move in with you and I can't sleep with you anymore. We did and it was wonderful. But we have to stop now while I can still say goodbye."

"Think about it, Lara. You know you enjoy my company."

She shook her head. "I don't think you're listening to me."

"We're married. Why can't we live together?"

"You know there's no love in this marriage. That is an enormous difference in everything we do with each other."

"True, but we aren't going to fall in love."

"If I start sleeping in your bed with you, it'll be a possibility for me, and you'll still want a divorce."

"But you won't fall in love. You have all that cool control you exhibit all the time. You'll be in charge of your feelings and just because you're in my bed, you won't necessarily be any wilder about me than you are now."

"That I would seriously doubt."

He hugged her and smiled at her, combing long strands of her hair away from her face with his fingers. "All joking aside, you've got me beyond that terrible grief. I'm so amazed because I've lived with that since I lost Kathy and I had sort of accepted it as a way of life. What's funny—you didn't consciously try to do that. It just happened. I've come back to life. It's fun to be with you and it's relaxed. You haven't tried to make me fall in love with you. Far from it," he added and she smiled.

"We went into this marriage knowing we would not fall in love with each other and we would divorce later this year. That makes a difference in how we deal with each other. And moving in with you definitely won't work."

"I don't know that it made such a damn big difference last night."

"Maybe not. Last night was an exception," she said. "I think it would make it more painful to divorce if we're together a lot and living and sleeping together and making love. That doesn't seem the way to stay on track for a divorce. I have plans for my future and I don't want to be in upheaval and turmoil because of a heartbreak." She shook her head. "Besides, you think I'm driven and I put work first and you don't like that. You didn't like it with your mother. Frankly, I think you're just as driven. I think that would cause all kinds of trouble between us. I think—"

He stopped her rant with a finger to her lips. "Don't take life so seriously, Lara."

She pushed his finger away. "I have to. I'm having a baby, Marc, remember?" She had to think of her child in addition to her own future. "And I don't hear you denying it. I doubt if you like my determination to become a doctor."

Her secretarial work had been fine with him, but to devote herself to a demanding career that took extra hours of work, he had made it clear many times before that he didn't like that. And she didn't want an emotional entanglement with another man who didn't agree with her life choices.

"I didn't say I didn't like it."

She pressed him. "Do you want to be married to someone going to medical school? To a doctor?"

He ran a hand through his dark curls. "It's beside the point because we're not staying together forever. If you want an answer, no, I wouldn't want my wife to be a doctor. I've had that all my life with my mother tied to her work. You're blowing this out of proportion. I just asked you to move in with me."

"If I did, we would have this conversation down the road." She sat up, feeling the chill that came with leaving his arms. "Sorry, Marc, I'm not moving in with you."

She drew in a deep breath and looked down at him. "We're just not compatible. Look how we're arguing now. Right after we've made love all night. No, moving in with you will just cause more problems and interfere in our futures." Her voice echoed the dejection she felt. "Marc, there is no love in this, don't you see? You're not in love with me and I'm not in love with you. And we're getting divorced eventually. You're still planning on a divorce, aren't you?"

"Yes, I am." He paused and his gaze deepened, his eyes roving over every inch of her face, as if to memorize her. "I've got your answer—you're not moving in. So why, after all that, do I still want to kiss you?" He pulled her down to him, but she placed her hands against his chest.

"Are you paying attention at all? We should be putting distance between us instead of staying in bed and kissing."

"Why don't you forget that divorce for ten minutes?"

He looked at her mouth and against every shred of good judgment she felt her insides tighten. He brushed her lips with his, lightly, yet her heart surged. Every part of her knew this was wrong, but she couldn't stop it, the desire she felt when his mouth settled on hers. His tongue stroked hers and, as if of their own volition, her arms wrapped around him and she kissed him back. With one kiss she forgot their conversation and all her arguments.

It was midafternoon when they finally packed and returned to the ranch. As they entered the house, tempting smells of a pot roast filled the air.

"Ah, come meet my cook," he said, putting their

things by the door. He took her arm as they walked to the kitchen.

"Penelope, I'm home and I want you to meet my new wife."

A short woman with curly red hair turned and smiled. She wore a blue cotton apron that covered her from her neck to her ankles. Her blue eyes filled with curiosity.

"Penelope, this is Lara Medina. Lara, meet Penelope Wendell."

Lara offered her hand. "I'm glad to meet you. It smells wonderful in this kitchen."

Penelope's smile widened as they shook hands. "Pot roast for supper tonight. It will be ready about six."

"That's great," Marc said. "We'll eat about seven, so just leave it and we can get it on the table." He turned to Lara. "Penelope has been with us for fifteen years. She worked for my grandparents first. She's been with me the past four years. She works in Dallas or here on the ranch."

"I'm anxious to taste that pot roast," Lara said. They talked briefly and then left to take their things upstairs.

As they walked down the hall, she asked him, "Why do you want to return to the corporate world? Why don't you stay on the ranch? You seem way happier and more relaxed since you've been here. The problems you have here don't seem to get you down as much as the ones at the Dallas office."

"I like making money in the corporate world. I like the challenges. Maybe I am happier here. I hadn't really thought about it. I didn't have you in my bed before, so maybe that's making me happy."

She shook her head at him. "Marc—"

But he quickly changed the subject. "This afternoon I'm going to see my grandparents."

"I'll go if you think they'd like to see me."

"I think they would. As far as they're concerned, you're part of the family now. A pretty lady is sure to cheer up my grandfather. You know, in her day my grandmother was a beauty. At least, she looked quite pretty in her pictures."

Lara smiled at him. "Let me get cleaned up. I don't want to go like this."

"Want to shower together?"

She laughed as she shook her head. "I don't think we would ever get there if we shower together first."

"Meet you here in…what? An hour? Half an hour?"

"Half an hour," she said and walked with him to their rooms, leaving him to go into her suite and close the door.

When they returned from their visit, she knew he would bring up moving in with him again before the evening was over. Had her decision changed since this morning in Downly? She'd better make up her mind once and for all and stick with it. Vacillating wasn't helping anyone. "No" was the safe and smart thing to tell him. Did she want to risk her heart for sex with Marc or did she want to play it safe as she had promised herself she would do?

No pressure. Only her future was at stake.

# Eight

Marc laughed as he went to his room. He was having fun with Lara, but he was serious when he urged her to move in with him. He wanted her in his bed, in his arms at night. He wanted to hold her and make love and have her with him. He had surprised himself when he blurted out the invitation to move in with him.

He hadn't given it thought ahead of time—something so unlike himself that he had been shocked. She was changing him, changing his life. He had a feeling she wasn't trying to do so, it was just happening with her around.

He also had a feeling that he was a small part of her life, not the focus, which was something that usually didn't happen to him with his women friends. Lara had plans for her life, goals. She was more interested in adding *Doctor* to her name than *Mrs*. And he'd best remember that, he reminded himself. Despite his physical attraction to her, she was not the woman for him with her drive to tie her life to her work.

But the sex…

The sex he'd had with Lara had been the best he'd ever experienced. Another shocker. She was intensely responsive and she had an enthusiasm for lovemaking that made everything more exciting and sexy.

He realized he better change his train of thought because he had to get ready to go see his grandparents, and thinking about sex with Lara wasn't the way to do it.

In twenty minutes, dressed in gray slacks and a charcoal sport coat, he went down to the great room to wait for Lara. He stood when he heard her heels and she swept into the room, taking his breath away.

"Oh, you do know how to dress for my grandparents," he said, looking at her bright blue dress. The neckline was high, which would please his grandmother. The hemline was high, too, which would please his grandpa. She wore the necklace he had given her, and high-heeled blue pumps, and her hair fell freely around her face.

"You look stunning," he said quietly.

"Thank you. You look very nice yourself."

He pulled on the cuffs of his white dress shirt, the gold cufflinks catching glints of sunlight. Then he took her arm and led her down the hall. "They're looking forward to seeing us. I talked to Grandma. She repeated how glad they are to be home. She thanked me for getting them home."

"I'm glad, Marc. Does it worry you that our marriage won't be permanent like he wants?"

"No, because he shouldn't tell me to get a wife and

get married in one month. He wasn't himself and he wasn't thinking it through. I know he always thinks he knows what's best for me, but I'm a grown man and I can make my own choices. Anyway, you and I have worked things out, and we'll be happy and he's happy. And, once again, this is nice of you to come with me to see them."

"Oh, sure. That's a small thing."

"Maybe, but I just want you to know I appreciate it."

He held the door as she stepped into his pickup, and he couldn't help but glance down at her endless legs.

When they arrived at his grandparents' place, they greeted his grandmother first. When Marc held her shoulders lightly and kissed her cheek, she felt so frail, it made his heart lurch.

"Would Grandpa like to see both of us or just me?"

"Both of you, of course," his grandmother answered. "Come with me and we'll say hello. He'll want to see your beautiful bride," she said, smiling at Lara who smiled in return.

"Thank you, Mrs. Ruiz."

After greeting the nurse on duty, they stepped into a room with the sound of a monitor beeping, keeping track of Marc's grandfather's vital signs.

"Hi, Grandpa," Marc said, taking Lara's arm and moving to the bed.

"Marc and his bride are here to see you, Papa," Grandma said, and he waved his hand.

"Get a chair."

"I have a chair. Lara, would you like to sit here?" Marc asked.

She said hello to his grandfather and sat in the chair near the bed. Marc stood behind her.

"How are you feeling today?" Marc asked him.

His grandfather looked at Lara. "Do you love my grandson?"

"I married him, sir," she said.

Marc wondered what his grandfather was up to. There were moments he could be quite shrewd and Marc wondered if he had guessed that Marc wasn't in love with Lara.

"I hear you have no family at all."

"Not until I married your grandson. Now Marc's family is my family. Isn't that right?"

His grandfather smiled at her. "You're part of our family and we welcome you."

"Thank you," she answered.

Marc placed his hand on her shoulder, wondering if his grandfather's questions disturbed her.

"Let me see the rings Marc gave you."

She stood and held out her hand, and his grandfather took it in his, rubbing his thumb across her fingers.

"Soft hands," he said. "Very beautiful hands. Beautiful diamonds that mean he loves you very much."

Rico released her. "I hope you and my grandson will always love each other. You took a vow to do that."

"Yes, sir, we did," she replied, sitting in her chair again and crossing her legs, a motion that caught his grandfather's glance.

"You're a beautiful woman, and you and Marc should have beautiful children. Marc was a beautiful child."

"I'll bet he was," she said, laughing. "And thank you for the compliment."

Grandpa smiled at her and Marc shook his head realizing she was not intimidated in the least by his grandfather and his questions.

"Today must be a better day," Marc said, and his grandmother nodded.

"It is a better day and he has rallied some, they tell us."

"Good. Maybe it's from being home."

They talked for another fifteen minutes and then Marc stood and said goodbye. In a short time they were back in the pickup for the drive home.

"I don't know what some of Grandpa's questions were about, especially that remark that we vowed to love each other."

"He may have guessed what you're doing—a marriage of convenience."

"I'm glad he didn't intimidate you. I think he was trying to."

She smiled. "I thought he was adorable. And I feel like part of your family, Marc, even though common sense tells me that I'm certainly not. They've been so welcoming and I guess I just want a family."

Marc sensed her mood change and lightened the tone. "Grandpa—adorable?"

Lara laughed and he loved the sight of her smile. Loved that he made her smile. "I'm glad you went with me," Marc said, and meant it.

"I'm glad I did, too."

He parked at the back of the house under the carport and they entered the great room. The minute he closed the door behind her, he reached out, caught her hand and pulled her into his arms.

"I can't wait one minute longer."

She placed her fingers on his lips, stopping his kiss. "Marc, you'll only make parting much more difficult."

"Stop worrying about tomorrow. You'll go to school

and get the career you want. Hell and high water won't stop you."

"I've told you, Marc, it's a tribute to my mom. I want to help people like her—through medicine, through research, whatever works out. It's for my mother and makes me feel part of her is with me."

He nodded. "That's admirable. You're really dedicated to it."

"Yes, I am," she admitted. She smiled at him. "I don't think you get it, but you work just as hard."

"It doesn't seem the same to me."

"That's because you're not really looking at yourself."

"I'll guarantee you, you're more interesting." He pulled her closer, till she was flush against him. "In the meantime, you look gorgeous and it's been way too long since I held you and kissed you." His mouth took hers and he kissed away any answer she might have had.

The kiss was worth waiting for.

But as he was about to make his next move, Lara stepped back.

"I think we need to catch our breath. I'll put dinner on. I can't wait to try that pot roast."

"I'll get a beer and get you a lemonade, and then we can sit and talk while it heats up. How's that sound?"

"Like another good deal," she said. "I'll see you in a few minutes. I'm going to go change first." She left him to enter her suite and close the door. As she changed, she thought about moving in with him as he wanted her to do. She had wanted to say yes—oh, how she had wanted to—but wisdom said no. She needed to keep enough distance from him that she didn't make this marriage seem real to herself. He'd never fall in love with her and she couldn't risk her heart by falling in love with him.

On the other hand, if she moved in with him, he might not ever want her to move out.

She laughed at herself and shook her head. How many women had slept with men because each one convinced herself that she was the woman he would want forever and ask to stay? The world was filled with women who'd had that foolish thought and she didn't want to become a statistic.

She went downstairs and they had dinner out on the patio. Afterward they talked for hours, until darkness fell. And before she knew what was happening, Marc rose from his chair and picked her up to carry her to his big bedroom.

During the night she stirred and turned to look at him, holding her close against his side as he slept. Was she already falling in love with him?

If she was, there wasn't any way to stop it. He wanted her in his bed at night and she wanted to be there. Her gaze ran over him and her pulse quickened. How long would he have that effect on her? She suspected it would be for as long as she knew him.

She realized now that no matter what she did, the divorce was going to hurt. On the other hand, she would move on with her life and now her financial worries were gone, thanks to Marc.

She shifted slowly, trying to avoid disturbing him, and propped her head on her hand to look at him. He excited her. He was incredibly handsome and sexy, more so now than he had been before their marriage. Or was she just in love and dazzled by him?

She wanted to run her hand over Marc's chest, but

he was a light sleeper and she was afraid her touch would wake him.

"Like what you see?" he drawled, startling her.

She looked at him. His eyes were still closed.

"How did you know I was looking at you? Your eyes are closed."

"Magic. Besides, I know you find me fascinating," he said and grinned. He pulled her down onto his chest and kissed her, ending their conversation.

Later, she lay in his arms, pressed against him.

"Lara, I feel I can trust you and I want to share something with you that's worrying me. You have a sensible view of the world and I want your take on something. But what I tell you has to end with you."

"Sure. It sounds serious."

"It is serious. Because you're pregnant and it's not my baby, when I told my mom, she got very upset."

Lara sat up to look down at him. "Oh, Marc. She doesn't want me married to you."

"Don't be ridiculous. Mom loves you and loves that I'm married to you. You're already really a part of my family and I want your opinion on a family thing that I'm worried about. Just listen."

They both sat up and she turned to face him. Her eyes had adjusted to the dim light of the one small table lamp that was on in the room. His eyes, she saw, were dark and somber as he related what his mother told him.

"Oh, Marc. Dirkson Callahan is your blood father," she said. "I am so sorry, but thank heavens he wasn't part of your life. Have you told Gabe?"

"No. Besides Mom and Dirkson, you and I are the only other people to know. Gabe is already my best friend so I don't think I should tell him. This is what worries me, because I want to do what's best for Gabe. What do you think?"

She looked away, thinking it over. She glanced back to see him watching her. "Thank you for confiding in me," she said. "That makes me feel very close to you. Maybe even important to you."

"You are important to me and you're trustworthy and you're levelheaded. I value your opinion."

She lapsed into silence while she thought about what he had told her. "You said Blake is a half brother."

"Yes, he is. He was good friends with Cade. Dirkson never acknowledged Blake until after he was married and even then, Blake called Dirkson. Cade drew Blake into the family circle of brothers. Cade isn't quite as close as I am with Gabe. In a way, I feel like leaving them alone. We're all close anyway."

She sat thinking about it. "Well, you told me because you want my opinion, so I'm going to give it to you. I have no family, so family seems the most important thing there is for anyone. You and Gabe are blood brothers. I think you should tell him and let him decide if he wants to keep it to himself."

Marc clamped his lips together. "Well, I wanted your opinion. I'll still think about it, but you've got a strong point for telling him. I'll tell you, as far as I'm concerned, my real dad is John Medina. He was a wonderful dad and I loved him, and I hate claiming Dirkson, even to tell Gabe."

"I understand. You'll make the best choice, I'm sure."

"Enough about that. I think now we should talk about what makes me happy in bed."

She laughed and kissed his throat. "I'm beginning to find out. Actually, you're rather easy to please."

"Am I ever," he said, pulling her in for a kiss.

For the next two weeks she slept in his room at night. Marc wondered if he would ever tire of her. He couldn't imagine that happening. One night, as he held her in his arms after making love, he toyed with her hair. "I've never brought a woman to the ranch until you. I mean, someone I was going out with. I'm not talking about Mom."

Lara turned on her side to look at him. "Really? I'm flattered, I guess. Unless you didn't bring them because you seldom came yourself."

"Oh, no. I've been here plenty. I haven't taken anyone home with me in Dallas, either. I go with them so I can leave."

"That makes sense and sounds like you."

"Well, I thought you might find that fact flattering, that I brought you home with me."

"Not exactly, because you married me. You had to take me with you. We really have a business deal between us."

He laughed. "I guess you can look at it that way."

"You had no choice." She ran her fingers along his jaw and when the moonlight caught the glitter of diamonds on her hand, she grew pensive. Finally she said, "How long have your grandparents been married?"

"A thousand years," he answered. "Actually, how's sixty-three?"

"Impossible. I can't remotely imagine."

He nodded. "A long time." He pulled long locks of her hair through his fingers and let them fall. He loved the feel of her silky strands and loved when she wore it down for him. "I've been thinking about us. Lara, let's just separate for a while instead of divorcing, and see how that works and if we want to go ahead with the divorce."

She shook her head. "No. When it's over, it's over and we'll each go on with our lives."

"I have a feeling that I'm not very important to you," he said.

"You're incredibly important, but I know you're not going to want to stay together."

"I want to stay together now. I don't want to get out of this bed today. Maybe this week," he said, rolling over on top of her and letting his kiss keep her right where he wanted her.

That morning, when she stirred Marc had already gone. Lara slipped out of bed and went to her suite to shower and dress. She moved routinely, her thoughts on her husband. She was falling in love with him and every night she spent in his bed made that love just a bit stronger.

She had to end it before she was so in love with him it would hurt forever. He was everything wonderful—handsome, intelligent, sexy, caring, fun, strong and filled with energy and enthusiasm for life. She had intended to guard her heart, and then she had turned around and fallen into his arms and into his bed, and now she was in love with him.

He didn't want a lasting marriage and she had to follow her plans, ones that he really didn't like. She had to get off the ranch, get her life together. Marc wouldn't change. And neither would she.

She knew he didn't approve of the time she put in to become a doctor. But she'd never give up her goal because it was so tied to her love for her mother. She couldn't shake the feeling that she'd failed her mother when she hadn't been able to stop the disease that killed her. Mark didn't get how important her career was to her, yet his career was essential to him. He thought she was a workaholic like his mother, but ironically he was one himself, but he didn't recognize that.

She needed to go back to Dallas for a while and get some space between them before she was hopelessly in love with him. And she prayed that hadn't already happened.

A few days later Lara was pouring over a book when the phone rang. It was Marc's landline and only his mother and grandparents used it. She answered and thought someone had the wrong number because the noise was garbled. She started to hang up and then realized someone was crying. There were scrambling noises, words she couldn't catch, but then someone spoke clearly. "Is Marc Medina there?"

"No. Have you tried his cell phone?"

"Yes, and he didn't answer. This is the nurse and we need to get in touch with him."

"I'll text him right now and get him to call you," Lara said, replacing the phone. She grabbed her cell phone to send Marc a text. She couldn't shake the chill that overcame her, afraid that something had happened to his grandfather.

In minutes Marc called her. "I'm on my way home. My grandpa died this morning. I'll come home and get you, and we'll go over there to see Grandma. Mom's on her way, too. You don't have to go, Lara, if you don't—"

She interrupted him. "Marc, I'm getting ready now. I'll be ready when you get here. I'm so sorry. Is there anything I can do for you?"

"No. See you soon."

Then he was off the phone and she quickly went to change, pulling on a tailored black dress and putting her hair up in a bun at the back of her head the way she used to wear it to the office.

She heard his pickup and heard him running to the door. He swept inside and she ran to him. "I'm sorry, Marc."

"Thanks. I want to get over there as soon as I can and I hope I can get there before Mom does. Someone is driving her out here. I'll be ready in ten minutes."

"Can I do anything?"

He just shook his head as he left the room.

They spent the next couple of days with relatives and getting ready for the service. It was a whirlwind of activity leading up to what was a solemn funeral.

When they walked into Marc's darkened house after the burial, he switched on the lights. She crossed the great room to him and slid her arms around his waist. "There's nothing else I can tell you, Marc, except that I'm sorry for your loss. I know how much you loved him."

He placed his head against hers and stood in her embrace. "Thank you," he whispered, and from the sound of his voice she realized he was finally giving in to his grief.

After a few minutes he raised his head while he still held her. "Thanks for going with me and for all your help through this."

"Of course. I'm glad I got to know him."

Marc released her and wiped his eyes. He walked over to the window and looked out at the lighted pool. "I think he hung on to get home to the ranch and to see me married. You're probably right. He probably guessed we just had a marriage of convenience. He seemed happy enough, though. You impressed him. He liked you." As he talked, Marc shed his coat and tie, and partially unbuttoned his shirt while he kicked off his shoes.

"We didn't have much time with each other, but I hope he liked me. I liked him."

"I promise he liked you. I think he wanted you to stay in the family."

"That's nice, Marc. Well, now you'll have your ranch and your inheritance. And your mom will, too. Will she retire?"

"Put yourself in her place. Would you retire?"

She smiled. "Be glad she's active."

"Neither you nor my mom know how to let go and enjoy life."

"I have to do what I have to do. I know we will divorce."

His gaze was stormy and she shivered, suddenly feeling as if the marriage was already disintegrating. "You'll have your divorce and you can go to med school, but tonight I want to say goodbye." He crossed the room to pick her up, carrying her to a bedroom while he kissed her, a demanding, possessive kiss that made her heart race. He stood her on her feet, peeling away her black dress as he kissed her and then flinging aside his shirt and belt. He stepped back to look at her.

"You take my breath away. You're so beautiful—every inch of you. I want you. I don't want you to go, but I know you're going to school no matter what and we're going to have to say goodbye. Tonight I need you. I want your kisses and I want to touch and kiss you."

Her heart thudded and desire overrode all her other feelings. It had been an emotional day and tomorrow might even be more emotional because, any time now, she knew they would part. She wanted to give Marc a night that would make him remember her. And she wanted to take memories with her when she said goodbye. She loved him and she knew he wasn't in love with her. Tonight he was hurting and angry she was going, but she couldn't stay. There had never been words of love from him. She wrapped her arms around his neck and kissed him, pouring her feelings into her kiss, wanting to drive away both his demons and hers.

He made a sound deep in his throat and his right hand tangled in her hair while he cupped her breast with his other hand, his thumb circling lightly, slowly around her nipple, making her moan with desire and pleasure.

Running her tongue over his male nipples, first one and then the other, she wanted to heighten his pleasure. He gasped and his hand was still tangled in her hair while he caressed her breast in feathery strokes that made her tremble with longing for more. As she ran her tongue over him, she slowly slid down until she took his thick rod in her hand, stroking him with her tongue, taking him in her mouth. She felt him shudder and gasp while she slipped one hand between his legs to caress him. He grew even larger with every touch.

He moaned and reached beneath her arms to pull her to her feet. She gazed into his dark eyes, which blazed with so much desire she couldn't get her breath.

"Marc," she whispered while wrapping her arms

around him and kissing him. Her heart pounded so violently she wondered if he felt it as he held her pressed against him. His strength, his maleness, his caresses and kisses all drove her wild. She loved him, but she wasn't going to tell him when he didn't love her in return.

She put one leg up around him and he slipped his hand beneath her thigh to pick her up and lay her on the bed. He moved between her legs, caressing her with his fingers before using his mouth. He drew his hot, wet tongue over her, taking his time. Her hips arched beneath his touch.

"Marc, I want you," she whispered.

He stretched on the bed beside her and easily lifted her on top of him. She sat astride him as he caressed her breasts.

Closing her eyes, she gasped with pleasure. For a moment she was still, relishing his hands on her body, his caresses that heightened desire. Finally, she leaned down to kiss him while he held her hips and moved her over him, his thick manhood easing inside her slowly. Crying out with need and pleasure, she tossed her head, her hair swinging over her shoulder as she rode him and he held her.

Her eyes flew open while he toyed with her breasts and then both of them were moving, faster and faster, as he pumped inside her. Need for release, for all of him, hot and wet, consumed her. The spiral increased until she cried out as she went over the brink. Seconds later, he reached his climax, shuddering and thrusting fast and hard, driving her to another climax. Finally she fell on top of him, turning her head to look at him as she shifted her hips and moved so they were no longer one.

When she did, he wrapped his arms around her, holding her close.

"You can't know what a gift you just gave me," he whispered, leaning closer to brush a light kiss on her forehead. "You've demolished me, but you drove away the demons for a little. You're a fantastic woman, Lara," he whispered.

"I wanted to make you forget your hurt for just a little while. And I wanted to make sure you'll remember me."

"I couldn't possibly forget you. Tonight you took me to another place, and our loving held the pain at bay."

"I'm glad," she whispered.

Silence came and in the quiet her thoughts were in turmoil. She had to face the truth. She had fallen in love with him and there was no future for them except divorce. Their last kiss was her kiss goodbye.

Hours later, after Marc had gone to sleep, she lay awake in the dark, thinking about the changes that would be coming. They'd go ahead now with the divorce and she would move back to Dallas. There she'd keep taking chemistry courses that would count toward a doctorate in chemistry in case she didn't get into med school. When her baby was six months or a year, she would see about going to school, but at this point, she felt she needed to give her attention to her baby.

Tears stung her eyes because she loved Marc with her whole heart. She had never been in love to this extent before. Breaking her engagement to Leonard Crane had been relatively easy because she hadn't been that deeply in love, and when he wanted to have an abortion, she'd known he wasn't the man for her. But Marc had really captured her heart. Until she left the ranch, she was going to have a difficult time keeping her true feelings hidden from him, but she had to. Nothing good could come from him knowing how deeply in love with him she was.

She hurt all over at the thought of telling him goodbye. But there wasn't any reason for her to stay on the ranch now. He had said he wanted to be there when she had her baby, but she couldn't live months with him or into more than a year and then say goodbye. That would be far more devastating than now and this was terrible. She had to face him and tell him she was leaving.

At breakfast the next morning, she got to the kitchen early so she could catch him. Shortly after, he came in. He usually brought an energy and vitality into the room, but this morning he wore a slight frown.

She wasted no time but went straight into the speech she'd prepared in the wee hours of the morning. "I wanted to talk to you. I know you have a lot of legal things to do to settle your grandfather's estate, but this is important. We're still headed toward divorce, but there's no reason now for me to stay on the ranch. Whether we divorce now or not, I'm going back home to Dallas, Marc."

His frown deepened and he gazed at her in silence for a moment. "I suppose I should have known that's what you'd want to do. When do you want to go?"

She hurt inside, a tight knot in her throat, and she battled tears. He didn't even try to stop her or say he wanted her to stay a while longer. She might have been able to compromise if there was love and acceptance, but he'd simply asked when she wanted to go. That hurt, but it shouldn't have surprised her. He was letting her go as he'd always said he would.

"I'll get your things moved, so don't worry about that. Just pack and leave them. You can take the limo to Dallas. I'll get your car loaded and one of my guys can drive your car. That'll be easier for you."

"I'm ready," she managed to say. "I don't really have that much here at the ranch."

He crossed the room to her and placed his hands on her shoulders. "I know you have to go. I'd like to be around when your baby is born, but life may change a lot by then."

She nodded, because she couldn't speak. Tears had blocked her throat.

"I'll miss you, Lara."

She looked up into his stormy dark-brown eyes and wondered what he was really feeling. Would he just miss her in bed? She had to get away from him before she started crying and couldn't stop.

"I'll miss you, too," she choked out. She brushed past him and hurried to her suite, leaving him standing there. He was letting her go, just as he had told her he would from the very first.

Even in her suite she fought back her tears. She wouldn't cry until she could get away from the ranch.

His words hurt because he didn't sound as if breaking up their marriage disturbed him. And why would it? She was the one who had lost her heart—just what she didn't want to do.

It was noon before the limo and her car were packed and ready. She stood looking at herself in the mirror in her suite. She wore her red dress and let her hair fall around her face. She wondered when she would see him again—in divorce court?

Leaving him hurt her more than she had dreamed

possible, but she straightened her shoulders, drew in a breath and walked out of her room.

Marc sat on the back porch by the portico, waiting for her. When she stepped out, he came to his feet. The limo was ready and Randall, one of his ranch hands, waited by the passenger door with his back to them.

She turned to Marc. "I'll see you in Dallas."

"Yeah, I'll call you. We're not saying goodbye yet. I'll see you in the city and I'll take you to dinner soon." He walked closer. "We don't have to rush this divorce, Lara. I still want to be there when you have your baby. Mom will want to be there, too. She'll help you with your baby if you'll let her."

"You know that's wonderful for me. I'd like for both of you to be with me," she said, surprised that was still what he wanted to do.

"I want to stay in your life when you have your baby."

"Sure, Marc," she said, doubting if he would continue to feel that way next spring.

"We'll see each other and stay in touch," he said.

She nodded. She couldn't talk because she would start crying. "Bye, Marc," she said. She couldn't kiss him either. She merely turned and rushed for the limo, hurrying around to climb inside while Randall closed the door behind her. She didn't look back as they drove away. She turned in the seat so Randall wouldn't see her face and finally she let the tears come. Marc had let her go and her heart was breaking.

As the limo disappeared down the drive, Marc watched her go. She was unhappy and he wasn't happy, either, but he figured a lot of his sorrow was caused by the loss of his grandfather. He hated to see Lara go out of his life, but they had planned this from the beginning. He'd always intended to let her go, so why—he pulled up short as he corrected his thought. He never even *had* her to let her go.

He told himself that, given time, he'd settle back into the life he had before this crazy marriage of convenience, but right now, he wasn't happy. Lara had brought him joy and happiness. He hadn't stopped to think about the changes she had made in his life. Truthfully, he didn't want her to go, but there wasn't a choice. She wouldn't change and he didn't want to change. From the beginning they had planned this split. That's why she had been the perfect selection for his wife.

He walked back to his office, but he couldn't work. When he looked out the window all he saw was Lara in his arms, smiling and gazing up at him. "Dammit," he said aloud and stood impatiently. Maybe he just needed a few hours, a few days, and then he'd go back into his routine and go on with his life. He better, because she didn't have room in her plans for him. Right now, he hated to admit that he hurt. It shocked him, but he expected the pain of separation to go away.

# Nine

Lara tried to keep busy, seeing her doctor, making appointments to talk to a counselor at the university about a doctorate. She still thought it would be best to put off starting medical school until her baby was six months or a year old. She needed a nursery in her house and needed to decide if she wanted to stay in the house she was in now.

She missed Marc every day, but she missed him at night even more. Her nights were empty, lonely, and it was difficult to sleep without him by her side. She knew that wasn't good for her or the baby.

She had another month to go on the courses she was currently enrolled in and then she would have papers to write. She wanted to keep so busy she didn't think about Marc, but that hadn't happened. She thought about him constantly.

After being in her life each day and night, he was

suddenly gone out of it and she was having a difficult adjustment even though she was constantly busy.
Even if he had asked her to give up her career, which
he hadn't, could she? Absolutely not, because it was too
important to her. She might compromise, but she still
wanted to help people. Besides, Marc didn't love her
enough to ask. He didn't love her at all.

Soon he would be back, working at the office in
Dallas. Would she see him when he was in town? She
doubted it. They had gone their separate ways, yet her
heart had gone with him. She had known from the first
that she should guard her heart, but how could she guard
her heart against a man who excited her more than anyone else ever had? Who was sexier than any other man?
Who was more fun and considerate and a thousand
other things that she loved about him?

She couldn't. She hadn't. She'd fallen for him, hard.

And the worst part was that she knew she'd love him
the rest of her life.

Marc spent the next week working at the ranch, going
to see his grandmother. Only one day did he drive into
Dallas and go by the office, but he was too aware that
Lara was in Dallas.

He missed her in his bed at night. He missed her
other times, missed her company, but nights were hell
now and there was no quick, easy way to forget her.

He tried to forget her, but that was absolutely impossible. When his mother asked about her, he didn't
tell his mother that Lara had moved back to Dallas and
out of his life.

He hadn't started proceedings for the divorce. He

had a great reluctance to do that and kept putting it off without really thinking about what he was doing.

One day he drove to Downly to see his mother at the restaurant at about ten in the morning because it would be quiet at that time. She was in her office and smiled when he entered.

"I'm glad you came to see me. I've been thinking about you and about Grandma. How's she doing?"

"She's doing okay. Her companion that I hired to stay with her said she's handling losing Grandpa quite well. I helped her go through his things and we got that all sorted out."

Pilar wiped her eyes. "I miss him, but he wasn't going to get well. He was so happy that you married. He told me."

Marc felt a streak of guilt that Lara had already gone out of his life. "It made me happy, too, Mom. Lara liked him and he liked her. She told me she thought he was adorable, and I'm quoting her," he said, and his mother laughed.

"Adorable? Grandpa?" She laughed again. "I never thought of him that way. When he was young, he was always a force to be reckoned with. You're very much like him."

"Don't tell me that. I hope to heaven I never tell a grandson that he has to marry in a month."

She smiled. "He knew what he was doing. It worked out, didn't it? She's sweet and friendly, and you're happy and she seems happy. Actually, Marc, you've seemed much happier since your wedding. I think marriage is very good for you. Maybe it's being on the ranch, too."

"Lara told me that. She said I was happier than when I worked in town. I hadn't really thought about it," he said, thinking again that perhaps having Lara in his bed at night had been the real reason for his lightheartedness.

His mother grasped his hand. "You picked well, Marc. She's a wonderful young woman. Before you married, you told me that this was a marriage of convenience and she understood that. I hope you and Lara are not separating. I am so happy you're married and you'll be a father to her baby just as your dad was a father to you."

Marc felt another stab of guilt and wondered how he would ever break the news to his mother that he and Lara were divorcing now.

"Actually, Mom, Lara is very much like you. She's driven to go to medical school, if she's accepted, and become a doctor. If she doesn't get in medical school, she'll get a doctorate in chemistry. She wants to work in medical research because of losing her mother at such a young age. She feels that's a tribute to her Mom and it will help others. That's what drives her, just like you were driven to get this restaurant going."

"Marc, I had to do that because I had a baby and we needed to eat and have a roof over our heads. Your dad worked hard, but his health wasn't good."

"I know, Mom, but you went way beyond what you had to do. I used to want you at everything I did, my ball games, my programs at school, and I felt neglected when you missed something."

"Oh, Marc."

"I realize now that you came to most everything. You didn't miss the important events. And now I can understand why you worked like you did. Actually, Lara says

I work hard. If I do, I got it from you. You were there for me always when it really mattered."

"I'm sorry I couldn't have been there one hundred percent of the time. I did the best I could."

"Which was wonderful." He smiled at her. "You still work hard."

"Now it's different, Marc. It keeps me busy. I still miss your dad and I need to keep busy."

"Lara is the same way you are. Her work is going to be her life, but then, my work is my life."

"Well, she has a noble goal—helping others, trying to find a medical cure and doing it for her mother. For so many reasons, I'm glad you married her. Her life will be good and so will yours. And so will mine with a grandchild." She squeezed his hand. "Marc, I can't wait. Grandpa was so happy about your marriage. You did the right thing."

Guilt swamped him. Even more, pain overtook him. The pain from realizing that he'd let Lara walk out of his life. For a moment it crossed his mind that he would be better off if he could get her back into it.

He thought about what his mother had said. Maybe she was right and he was looking at Lara's dedication to her career in the wrong way. He'd never thought about her noble motives. Till now.

He looked up at his mother. "You're a wonderful mom and I love you. And right now I better move along."

"Tell Lara hello."

"Sure, Mom. You take care of yourself," he said, kissing her cheek. He wasn't going to tell her yet about the divorce. He was in no hurry to get it and evidently Lara wasn't, either.

When he got into his car, he sat staring into the distance and seeing only Lara, remembering waking with her in his arms. How long would it take to forget her? *Maybe a lifetime* was the first answer that popped into mind. He grimaced and then realized he was still sitting in his car in front of his mother's restaurant. He started the car and drove away. It was a wonder she hadn't come out to see why he was still there.

Too many times during the day he was lost in thought about Lara. In her quiet way, she had wiggled into his life, and memories of her were everywhere at the ranch. He thought about spending the next week in Dallas at the office because it would get his mind off her. She didn't work there anymore. Whatever memories he had of her there were good memories of her as his secretary, quiet, in the background and not in his arms or in his bed. Maybe if he worked in the office, he could shake Lara the woman out of his thoughts.

He drove to the office and spent the day trying to catch up and get back into things there. To his dismay, too many times during the day he would realize he had stopped working and was lost in thought about Lara. Twice he got out his phone and looked at her number, wanting to call her and hear her voice.

Why was he missing her more instead of less, the longer she was gone?

He stood and went to the window to gaze out over the city of Dallas. She was out there somewhere, going to class or going to the doctor or at home studying. He pulled up his phone again and stared at it. What would it hurt to ask her to dinner? That was a simple thing. He was in town and he could catch up on what she was doing and how she was. What was the harm in sharing dinner?

He called her but she didn't answer. Was she out on a date? That thought made him unhappy and he knew that was ridiculous. He was going to divorce her. Of course she would go out with other men. But he didn't like that idea, no matter how he rationalized it.

Finding no peace at the office, he drove home to his Dallas mansion. But he didn't want to stay in a big empty house. Since when was he unhappy in his own home?

It was a chilly fall night with dark coming earlier now. He left and went to a drive-in and got a burger, taking a bite and then losing his appetite.

He couldn't stop thinking about her, but he had to. Either that or get her back into his life.

Could he live with her career if she was a doctor? Could he live with her work ethic? If it meant getting her back into his life, he could. He had made big mistakes, but that could change. For better or for worse, he was in love with his wife and he was wrong to try to get her to give up her career goals. She had unselfish, wonderful reasons for wanting the training she was trying to get. Far more lofty reasons for her hard work than he had.

He thought about himself and his own career. Was he happier at the ranch, as Lara said? He liked the competition and making deals in the corporate world, but was it worth it if he was uptight and not as happy?

With his inheritance and the money and business he already had, he could get someone to run the office while he settled on the ranch and had a very good life. A good life if Lara was in it.

Why had he let her go? Why hadn't he realized he loved her?

The cattle ranch was a success, plus there was oil on

his land. Could he rethink everything he thought he'd believed so he could have the woman he loved?

And he was in love. No doubt about it.

He groaned out loud and thought there was an old man in heaven chuckling about getting his grandson married off and settled on the ranch.

Now it was up to him. What was he going to do to win her back?


Marc stopped in Downly to see his mother. As he left the restaurant a pickup passed, stopped and backed up. Gabe Callahan got out of his truck and came striding toward him.

"Hey, buddy. What goes? You look like a man on a mission," Marc said, noting his friend's tight look and hooded eyes.

"I just saw you so I thought I'd stop. I ought to slug you."

"What the hell have I done? This sounds serious."

"When Meg is bothered about something, everyone is bothered about something."

"What are you talking about?"

"She told me that you and Lara have separated."

"I don't see that that's really much of your business."

"It's not, except it makes me angry. Lara's pregnant with your baby and you've left her." Gabe looked away and clenched his fists. "You know who that reminds me of, don't you?"

For the first time, Marc realized everyone would think exactly like Gabe—that he had left Lara when she was carrying his baby. And he wasn't going to deny it because of the promises he'd made to her.

"Don't even say it," Marc replied. "I know Lara didn't send you over here to get us back together."

"She didn't send me over here at all. I just wanted to tell you that I think that's rotten. And I'm going now. I've said what I wanted to say." He turned on his heel, but Marc stopped him.

"I know you mean well. And I intend to get us back together. I might have to do a little groveling."

"I should hope you would," Gabe said. "Look, I know I poked my nose in your business." He took a deep breath. "Just don't you dare be the damn dad I had."

"Under the circumstances, I can't get angry with you for that one. It was a mutual parting that we knew was coming, but I should have thought that one through." Marc ran a hand through his hair, struck hard by so many conflicting emotions. He didn't know how to navigate these waters, had never had to before. But in this moment he knew one thing he had to do.

He looked up at Gabe. "I want to tell you something. I've been over this with Lara to get her advice. She said to tell you. I wasn't going to, but Lara said family is the most important thing of all. My mom was supposed to never tell anyone this and she didn't—at least, not until after I married Lara and Mom found out Lara is pregnant."

"What in the hell are you talking about?"

"My mom was fifteen when she went to work for your family and lived in the house. She had me when she was sixteen."

"Yeah, the year my mother was pregnant with me. What—"

"Figure it out, Gabe." He knew his friend would connect the dots. He gave him time to put it all together. Their same ages, how much they looked alike.

He saw the moment it dawned on Gabe.

"That bastard father of mine," he spat out. "I'll be damned. We're half brothers."

"As far as I'm concerned, Gabe, you can forget you ever learned the truth. You don't need to claim me as kin. My dad was John Medina. He was a wonderful dad and the only dad I want to acknowledge. Frankly, I'd just as soon bury this bit of information. We're grown men and we're best friends. That's good enough. But you have a right to know. Lara thought so."

"I'll think about it, and if I ever tell my family, I'll let you know. I may not even tell Meg. If you can live without all the Callahans knowing, I think I may just leave it that way."

"I'd be happy if you would. I don't like having to claim any relationship with your father."

"Yeah, I understand, and I appreciate you telling me. You're not missing much in the family doings. If you feel you need a big family because Lara doesn't have anyone, let me know and we'll get you into the family circle." He kicked his boot into the dust on the road. "Oh, hell. This is what I get for butting into your affairs. I'm going home." Gabe started walking back to his truck, then he suddenly stopped and turned around. "Don't ever be like him, Marc. You're a better man than that."

"Well, I wasn't for a while there, but I'm going to try to change that. Thanks, Gabe. You are a brother."

As Gabe drove away, Marc called Lara but she didn't answer again. He was just going to go camp on her doorstep because he wanted to straighten things out.

Actually, he better apologize to her and see if she would take him back. He was so in love with her. How could he have been so blind and let her go?

He turned around to head to her house in Dallas. He was tempted to just go get her and take her home with him, but he was certain she would have her own ideas.

He banished the thought that floated at the edges of his mind. What if she wouldn't even let him back in her life?

# Ten

As Lara walked through her living room, she saw a familiar car turn into her drive. Her heartbeat quickened, speeding again when she watched Marc come bounding up the drive, crossing her porch. Wearing jeans, a thick brown sweater, his boots and a black hat, he looked sexy, strong and so appealing. She rushed to open the door, but before she could speak, he swung her up into his arms and kissed her.

She wrapped her arms around him and held him, closing her eyes when his arms went around her. "I'm glad you're here."

He set her on her feet. "I have some big-time apologizing to do."

Perplexed, she stared at him. "Apologizing for what?" she asked, her heart beating even faster as surprise rocked her. "What are you doing here?"

He took her hands in his.

"First of all, I love you with all my heart."

His words took her breath away. "I've dreamed of hearing that from you, but we have—"

He put his finger lightly on her lips. "Listen to me. I love you and I apologize for being so damn bullheaded. You want to go to med school, I can support you. I hope I get to see you sometimes, but you're my wife and I want to keep right on being your husband."

"I can't believe what I'm hearing," she whispered, wondering what had happened in his life to cause such a change. Her heart raced. "You love me and you can accept it if I go to med school?"

"Yes, and if that doesn't work out, you'll get some kind of doctorate." He nodded at her and smiled. "I think that's fantastic. At least, I think it is if it keeps you in my life. Lara, I have been in hell without you. You brought me back into the world and then I let you slip away. Well, I guess I ran you off. I'm sorry. I've been such a fool. Will you forgive me and take me back?"

Her heart raced and she couldn't keep from laughing for joy. "Oh, Marc, of course I'll take you back. How can I not? You'll support my ambition and be a daddy to my baby."

"From now on, darlin', this is *our* baby. Okay?"

"I love you, Marc Medina. With all my heart."

"And I love you. After the baby comes, if we can work things out with your schedule, I'd like to move to the ranch permanently. I got to thinking about what you said and I am happier at the ranch. Would you like to live there?"

"Yes, if it's with you."

"With me and with our baby. I'll do anything I can

to help you get into med school, to get the classes you need. You can go to your classes in the limo. Whatever it takes. I am so sorry I was so blind. I was about my mom. I was about you. Please forgive me."

"I love you and accept all apologies. I don't want to give it up, but what I've planned is to postpone going to school when the baby comes. I might take six months or I might take a year." She laughed. "We'll work it out. I'm not in a hurry, Marc."

"That's the best news possible, darlin'. I'll support whatever you want to do."

She laughed again. "I'll hold you to that one."

"I love you, Lara," he said solemnly. "I missed you and I never want to go through that agony again. I was incredibly wrong. I should never have let you go out of my life and I never will again. I've been in hell since you left, and this time I'm not letting you go."

"You won't have to. You have my love completely and you've had it for some time now." Her brows rose and she winked at him. "You're a little dense about love."

He grinned. "Maybe, but not about sex. Let me show you my talents."

He kissed her then, and she felt it all the way to her toes. And she felt his love, too.

Smiling, she looked up at him. "Am I dreaming? I can't believe this is happening."

"Believe it, darlin'."

"You know, little towns need doctors, too. I could live on the ranch and probably work in some small town out near Downly."

"Whatever makes you happy and keeps you married to me."

"I'll be married to you forever," she said. "Oh, how I love you." She laughed before she stood on tiptoe to kiss him. She paused to look up at him.

"Marc, I think your grandpa knew what he was doing."

Marc shook his head. "He probably did. He probably figured I'd find someone I'd love, and when I started living on the ranch, I wouldn't want to leave it. He was a crafty fellow and managed to get his way a lot."

"I'm glad I got to know him, even that little bit."

"By the way, I told Gabe about my bloodline. He wants to bury that bit of info, which is just fine with me. I'm happy with his friendship. Actually, I'm friends with all the Callahan brothers and that's good enough."

"I'm so happy," she said. She clung tightly to him, joyous and looking forward to the future. She leaned away and flashed her hand at him. Her diamond ring sparkled. "See, I'm still wearing my wedding band and I'm still married to you. I wasn't going to take that off until that divorce was final."

"It will never be final. You're mine forever, sweetie. I love you more than I can tell you."

He kissed her then, pulling her tightly to him and leaning over her. She clung to him while happiness made her tremble. She would have Marc in her life, her new little baby, and someday, she would be able to work somewhere to help sick people feel better as a tribute to her mother.

She leaned away and placed her hand on his cheek.

"I want to spend a lifetime showing you how much I love you."

"Sounds like a good deal to me. Come here, my sweet wife."

She smiled at him. Then she closed her eyes as he kissed her.

He framed her face with his hands. "I love you, Lara. From now on I'll spend every minute of my life trying to make you happy."

She hugged him. "You've made me so happy already." She leaned back and looked into his eyes. "A couple of years from now, I want to be pregnant with *your* baby. I love you, Marc. I love you now and forever."

She stood on tiptoe to kiss him as he wrapped his arms around her and held her tightly. Joy filled her and she knew the biggest fortune she had was his love that she would treasure all her life. A life filled with his love and their children.

\* \* \* \* \*

*If you liked this story of love beneath the Texan skies, pick up these other* CALLAHAN'S CLAN *novels from USA TODAY bestselling author Sara Orwig!*

EXPECTING THE RANCHER'S CHILD
THE RANCHER'S NANNY BARGAIN
THE RANCHER'S CINDERELLA BRIDE

*And don't miss her other great Western romances!*
*TEXAS-SIZED TEMPTATION*
*THE TEXAN'S FORBIDDEN FIANCÉE*
*Available now from Mills & Boon Desire!*

# MILLS & BOON®

## *Desire*™

**PASSIONATE AND DRAMATIC LOVE STORIES**

---

## sneak peek at next month's titles...

### In stores from 10th August 2017:

**A Family for the Billionaire** – Dani Wade *and*
**Little Secrets: The Baby Merger** – Yvonne Lindsay

**Taking Home the Tycoon** – Catherine Mann
*and* **The Heir Affair** – Cat Schield

**Convenient Cinderella Bride** – Joss Wood
*and* **Expecting the Rancher's Baby?** – Kristi Gold

---

*Just can't wait?*
Buy our books online before they hit the shops!
**www.millsandboon.co.uk**

**Also available as eBooks.**

# MILLS & BOON®

## Why shop at millsandboon.co.uk?

Each year, thousands of romance readers
find their perfect read at millsandboon.co.uk.
That's because we're passionate about
bringing you the very best romantic fiction.
Here are some of the advantages of
shopping at www.millsandboon.co.uk:

* **Get new books first**—you'll be able to buy
  your favourite books one month before they
  hit the shops

* **Get exclusive discounts**—you'll also be
  able to buy our specially created monthly
  collections, with up to 50% off the RRP

* **Find your favourite authors**—latest news,
  interviews  and new releases for all your
  favourite authors and series on our website,
  plus ideas for what to try next

* **Join in**—once you've bought your favourite
  books, don't forget to register with us to rate,
  review and join in the discussions

Visit **www.millsandboon.co.uk**
for all this and more today!